2040
American Exodus

Also by Douglas Fain

The Phantom's Song

2040
American Exodus

Douglas Fain

Bergen Peak Publishing, Evergreen, Colorado

This book is fiction; the premise, however, might be more real than we would like to imagine. All events, locations, and characters were created from the author's imagination. Any resemblance to actual people (living or dead), events, or locations is strictly coincidental.

To the men and women who paid the ultimate price for the freedoms that many take for granted today.

Acknowledgements

I would like to thank my editor, Denny Dressman, for his expertise in helping me put this book together. It was a pleasure working with such a professional. His skill and advice were critical in the development of this book. I send a salute to the artist, Lorna Clubb. Her art and her recommendations are appreciated and evident for all to see. Finally, to my wife, Mary Jo, my friend, Tom Calandra, and Shirley Weaver, thanks for your encouragement as I struggled through the process of writing a story I feel to be very important.

"Those who would give up essential liberty to purchase a little temporary safety deserve neither liberty nor safety."
Benjamin Franklin

As the nuclear submarine moved silently through the dark waters of the Mediterranean, the captain leaned against his desk and re-read the message he had received just five minutes before. Chaim's legs buckled as he struggled to comprehend it; he still could not believe the words. Slowly he sank into the worn chair beside the small desk. His heart said the message could not be correct, but his mind knew the codes checked out and therefore the message must be true. Once again he compared the security codes with the ones from his safe; they were consistent. He read the message again for the third time, carefully analyzing each word in case he had overlooked something.

At 1014 hours on September 14, 2016, an Iranian nuclear bomb struck Tel Aviv; a second struck Haifa. Execute: Special Order X-1003 immediately.

Beads of sweat gathered on his forehead and ran across the deeply furrowed face, joining the single tear that had escaped his right eye. He breathed deeply and steeled himself for the next vision that lurked in the recesses of his mind. Rebecca and little Daniel were gone; the wife and son who gave him purpose and joy were lost forever. His mind moved slowly toward the question he feared most. What was it like when the blast reached them? Did she call his name? Did she even realize what had happened? There were two nuclear bombs—probably dirty bombs set to explode several thousand feet above the ground to cause maximum nuclear fallout. He knew what that would do to such a small country.

1

There would be few survivors. How would he tell his men? How could he face them and still maintain control over his own emotions? But he was their captain; he was their leader. They needed him now.

Chaim wiped his face with a soiled handkerchief and stuck his head out of the small door to his room. "Call the entire crew together—everyone! Now!"

* * *

As the captain stared blankly into the darkness of his small room, the spirit of his wife moved behind him and silently watched the desolate man.

How could this happen, she thought? How could she be standing beside her husband in this dark vessel when only a moment earlier she had been rocking her child in her living room in Tel Aviv? And why does he look so sad as he leans over the small table with the map on it? The child in her arms was as light as a feather and looked so much like the tired man before her. Chaim was staring at the map, but he did not see it. His eyes were glazed, and tears blinded his vision. She called his name and reached to touch his shoulder, but neither of them heard her voice or felt her touch. She jerked her hand back and stared at it in disbelief. A long low moan came from his throat as he wiped his face and re-read the message he held with shaking hands. Chaim raised his eyes for a moment and stared off into space without seeing. He knew the message was real; it had all the proper codes. He also knew it would change his world forever.

Rebecca moved closer to him and spoke again—this time with fear in her voice. What did all of this mean? How, how could a person travel so quickly into such a desolate place? What was happening? Was it possible that the love between a man and a woman could draw them together like this?

Chaim grimaced in pain and anguish. She was gone, gone forever. And his Daniel; he was gone, too. How could he live with this knowledge? How could he live with this pain?

Rebecca watched his face. He was not aware of her presence. But why, she wondered? Could he not see her? She spoke again into the silence; then she screamed. He did not move; he did not hear; he only stood with his head down. A single tear rolled down his cheek and fell from his face. She reached instinctively and caught the tear before it splashed onto the map. She pulled it to her and looked into the prism of light sparkling back at her. It was then that she felt the pull that was drawing her away. It was a powerful sensation.

Something inside her cried out in defiance. She could not leave the man she loved in such pain—but the strange source that drew her was more powerful and so peaceful. She looked down at the sleeping child in her arms and smiled, then she looked back at her husband as she relaxed and submitted to the peace. She was smiling as she disappeared from the dark room and the sad man looking at the map. She raised her hand and looked briefly at the small droplet of water. The prism of light flashed a rainbow of colors into her eyes; she reached for him once more; and then she was gone.

*   *   *

The captain felt a sudden touch on his shoulder. When he turned, it was one of the sailors. As he moved, a prism of light flashed somewhere in the darkness of the room, and Chaim felt the anguish flowing from his body. There was a growing peace in his heart. Where had that come from? Was it his training? His discipline? Or was he simply accepting the reality that faced him the rest of his life—however long that might be.

"Captain, the men are assembled."

"I'll be right there." He brushed at the map to erase the tear that had escaped, but the tear was gone. He turned, confused for a moment, then stood as tall as he could and walked out to his crew. "Is everyone here?"

As the young sailors crowded together, a sense of shock hung in the heavy air of the submarine. Perhaps the rumors of the past ten minutes were true. But they couldn't be. The radio mate must have been wrong. Perhaps it was a military exercise. It had to be. As the last members of the crew crowded into the cramped space, one of the junior officers spoke. "Captain, is it true?"

Chaim watched their eyes. He feared their reactions, but they had served together far too long to lie to them now. Inhaling deeply, he stood as tall as he could, and spoke very slowly, very deliberately. "At 1014 hours this morning, Tel Aviv was struck by a nuclear missile from Iran; another struck Haifa. They were most likely *dirty* bombs; we can assume that Israel was destroyed." The captain fought to maintain his own control and fixed his eyes on one young man before him. He watched the young eyes widen with shock; then the bottom lip began to quiver slightly as the sailor fought to control his emotions before his captain and his shipmates. Several others began to curse, while others cried openly. The captain slammed his fist on one of the small tables at his side. "Stop! Stop your weeping!" There was anger in his voice as he shouted at his crew. "There will be time for that later—after we finish our mission. Does everyone understand that?"

"Yes Sir." The entire crew mumbled in response.

"Now, put aside your thoughts of this day and concentrate fully on your jobs. We will not fail our nation; we will not fail the innocent blood of our people. Our enemies will know the price of their treachery!" He paused and watched the young men's faces. "We have spent years training for this day, a day we prayed would never come. Well, it is here. This is the measure of our will, the measure of our determination, the measure of Israel's response! We will not fail our brothers and our families; we will not fail Israel." He paused and then stood erect before his men. "We weep tomorrow—today we fight!" There was a shout from the back of the group. Others joined in, and the crew pulled itself to its full measure and screamed for revenge. "Now get to your battle stations. Let's show the cowards in Tehran that Israel still fights. As long as there is one lone Star of David worn by one lone Israeli, this fight continues. Today they may cheer in Damascus, in Riyadh, in Tehran, and Cairo, but their celebrations will be short!" As the men rushed to their stations, the captain turned to his second in command. "Dekel, contact the American sub we are evading; tell them we have national tasking and will be ending the joint exercise."

"Yes captain. Do you think they might be a problem? Will they be aware of what we are doing?" There was neither joy nor fear in his voice, only a quiet resignation to a situation he did not desire or understand.

"It will take their government time to receive the notification and react. They will be in a state of shock for a while. Then they will start to assess the situation and make decisions. That should give us enough time to disappear. Turn to a heading of 240 degrees and tell the crew to run silent. After twenty minutes turn right to a heading of….no, turn *left* to a heading of 170 degrees. This time it is no exercise. We must evade the American sub."

"Why? They are our allies."

"We can't take a risk that the American President will support us. He has not been our friend in the past. The risk is simply too great; our mission is too important."

"Aye, Sir. 240 degrees then 170."

"And Dekel, monitor the American sub's position. If they follow us, let me know." He stood looking at the floor for a moment then added. "And start the launch checklist. Tell the men I want to beat our best time by five minutes. We've got to finish the checklist, stabilize, and launch before the Americans can find us. I don't know how much lead time we will have, so we must proceed carefully, but quickly." As Dekel departed Chaim turned and walked slowly into his small room and closed the door, something he seldom did. When he was alone, he hung his head and cried. How could there be a world without his family? After a few moments he raised his head, wiped his eyes, and washed his face in the small sink. He was focused on one thing; he had to slip away from the American sub and avenge his nation. He wasn't sure how long it would take the American government to assess the situation and make a decision, and he didn't want to commence launch operations with the American sub so close to his position. There was still a chance they might try to stop him. He wasn't sure how much time he had, but twenty minutes should be enough, he told himself.

* * *

5

Twenty-eight minutes after the Israeli sub had ended the exercise, Captain Donald Thompson in an American Los Angeles Class nuclear-powered, fast-attack submarine read the orders he had just received by coded satellite communication and shook his head in utter shock. He understood the words, but not the message. He read them again to ensure it said what he had read just moments before. For four days his crew had been shadowing the Israeli sub across the Mediterranean on a routine exercise. The Los Angeles Class attack subs had been around almost half a century, and less than forty remained in service. Though his boat was old, his crew was the best. They had silently located the sub, then they had shadowed it as it moved silently through the warm waters of the Mediterranean. This had started as a routine training exercise; now it had become much more than a simple test of skills. Thompson removed his ball cap and wiped the sweat from his forehead. It was decision time. The Israeli sub had disappeared immediately after breaking off the exercise. They had obviously received notification of the Iranian nuclear strike earlier than he. As usual, the U.S. government wheels turned slowly. Now he had to find his prey again, because he had just received orders to sink it. He understood the mission; but he also knew the Israeli sub was not his enemy. There had to be some mistake. He checked the code validation again. It was good.

Lieutenant Commander Francis Perez watched his captain with interest. "Captain, do we have confirmation of a nuclear strike on Israel?"

"Yes. It appears the Iranian leaders were as crazy as our intelligence suggested."

"How bad was it, sir?"

"The strike was against Tel Aviv and Haifa; I think it is realistic to assume that Israel is gone. I suspect that Gaza and Jordan were affected as well."

"Damn!" There was both anger and shock in the young man's voice. He looked at the official orders in the captain's hand. "What are we going to do, sir?"

Thompson looked at the orders a third time then back to Perez. "We've been ordered to sink the Israeli sub." His voice was low and controlled.

6

Perez's eyes widened in shock. "What? Sink the Israeli sub? There must be some mistake!"

"The codes check out. We have verifiable orders."

Like all men who wore the submariner's patch, Perez was a professional warrior. He had been trained all of his career to follow orders, but these were orders he found difficult to comprehend. They had to be wrong. "These orders can't be right." There was disgust and incredulity in the junior officer's voice; he paused before continuing. "Are we really going to do that?"

Twenty-seven years of Naval service had not prepared Thompson to answer that question. He was an Annapolis graduate with an outstanding career. Honor and integrity were burned into his very soul, and now he was being ordered to violate everything he believed in. He didn't understand the orders he had received, but he knew he would execute them to the best of his ability. Was this simply a decision to stop the carnage before it escalated even further? Was this a decision to save the oil rich region? Or was it a decision to buy time for negotiations? Someone with far more information had made that decision; his assignment was to follow orders, whether he liked them or not—whether he agreed with his Commander-in-Chief or not. He looked at the sonar scope; the Israeli sub had vanished, and now he knew why.

*   *   *

Dekel spoke quietly to his captain. "If the American politicians had courage, this would never have happened. Their lack of will allowed today to occur. When they were strong, we were safe. When they became weak and indecisive, we became a target."

Chaim looked at Dekel with deep lines on his face. "I probably know the captain of that sub. He probably wishes he could help us, but, like us, he is controlled by politicians. And the American President is not a friend of Israel."

"But the American military are our friends!"

"This is not a decision the military will make; the politicians will decide our fate. They deserted their own military just as surely as they deserted us. They took their weapons, their resources, their dignity—everything except their honor." The older man threw the papers in his hand onto the small desk at this side. "And as honorable professionals, they will follow the orders of lesser men who control them." Chaim rubbed his forehead vigorously. "But the very men who might order us destroyed will delay long enough in their arrogance to allow us to complete our mission anyway." Chaim looked away briefly and studied the sonar scope beside him. There was no indication of the American boat in his vicinity. "Our own American Jewish brothers helped elect the men who then abandoned us. I wonder what they are thinking today as they sit in their comfortable New York apartments and sip their morning coffee. Damn their arrogance! Damn their selfishness and their stupidity!" He stopped and visibly got control of himself. "We can discuss this tomorrow, if there is a tomorrow. Right now we have only one thing left to do, we launch our missiles, then we surrender to the Americans."

"Surrender?" There was shock in the younger officer's voice.

"Where would we go, Dekel? We have no home to return to."

*   *   *

Thompson and the American crew were scrambling. They knew the original direction of the Israeli sub had been southwest, but it could have turned in any direction after that. It had over half an hour head start and he needed to find it fast. He had turned southwest and was proceeding at full speed. The captain walked back and forth and talked to his crew. "Anything out there?" His voice was measured and low.

"Nothing, Sir."

"Turn right to a heading of 250 degrees. He turned right three times in a row. In fact, he always turns right. And keep listening. We found them before; we can find them again."

"I just got a sound."

"Where is it?"

"Is somewhere far behind us. Oh shit! They're flooding tubes." After a few seconds. "I can hear pressure equalization."

8

Perez looked at Thompson. "Does that mean what I think?"

"They are preparing to launch their missiles." Thompson's voice was no longer low. "Where are they?"

"I hear a hatch opening." Thompson walked quickly to the sailor's side. In slow cadence the sailor began counting. "One, two, three, four, five, six, seven, eight—eight missiles have launched. Wait! Nine, ten, eleven, twelve."

Another sailor called to the officers. "Sir, I have a message from the Israeli crew. They are surrendering. They will surface and surrender to us."

*   *   *

The Israeli sub was on the surface when an Iranian destroyer raced toward it from the northeast. It was traveling at a high rate of speed, leaving a large white wake through the clear blue waters. Commander Thompson was studying the Israeli sub when the destroyer suddenly showed up on the console next to him. He looked at both targets for only a second. He could see the smoke from the destroyer's guns as they fired toward the Israeli sub. "Prepare two torpedoes!" He looked at the sailor standing beside him, then at Perez. "Sink the destroyer!"

"Ready to fire."

"Fire one!" A few seconds later. "Fire Two!" The two torpedoes raced through the Mediterranean and caught the Iranian ship off guard. They had seen the first sub break the surface, but they had not seen the second that was following it. Both weapons hit the destroyer and enveloped it in a huge ball of fire. The captain watched the Iranian ship sinking into the sea; finally, he turned to his second-in-command who was smiling. "Good work men!"

"Good decision, Sir."

"I had no choice; we were under attack from an Iranian destroyer." The captain was grinning.

"That's right, Sir; we had no choice at all. Let the log show we were defending ourselves from an Iranian ship—that was firing in our direction."

"Mr. Perez, prepare to surface to take on our Israeli friends. Also, send an urgent message back to command headquarters to the effect that we captured the Israeli sub, but that we could not get to them before they launched their missiles."

* * *

On board the Israeli sub, Chaim watched the Iranian destroyer sinking into the sea. "I'll be damned, Dekel. In my haste I completely missed that destroyer, but the Americans sank it." Chaim walked back into his small room and retrieved a picture of his lost family. He looked at it for several moments then put it into his pocket. "Tell the men to come on deck. We may be close enough to see the result of our mission. But unlike our barbaric enemy, we will not be celebrating the result. May God help us all."

At 1408 local time, September 14, 2016, the Israeli nuclear sub launched its entire arsenal of nuclear missiles. In the Middle East every major city from Tehran to Cairo was filled with people dancing in the streets, celebrating their great victory over Israel when the missiles rained down upon them. After centuries of warfare, the Middle East conflict was finally resolved in a ball of fire that reached into the gates of hell.

* * *

As the stunned Israeli sailors sat in the cramped American sub, they stared quietly at the floor, each lost in his own thoughts of the momentous and frightening events. Their world would never be the same, their lives changed forever. Above them the world was also changing very rapidly. The actions they had set in motion would leave much of the world in chaos. Entire cities were destroyed, countless people were killed, and a way of life had vanished. The horror of nuclear power was now evident to the terrified world and would lead to cries to abandon such weapons. The fabric of humanity had been irreversibly torn, and the world would rise together to seek answers to prevent such catastrophes in the future. Fear would dominate international relations for years, and the United

Nations would be called upon to rise above its mediocrity and act responsibly as a world organ for peace. Politicians the world over would find ways to use this disaster to enhance their own power and further their political goals. Citizens would demand their governments provide safety at all cost, and inept governments would find support from frightened citizens who would incrementally sell their precious freedoms for promises of safety and survival. And in that exchange, free people the world over would become little more than the children they insisted they were trying to protect. People would be pulled into a giant politically correct mold that regurgitated citizens of similar thoughts and values.

There would be some who would stand apart, independently defiant people of strong values and a passion for individual freedom. They would be ostracized and cast out by robotic citizens who would not accept their moral strength. Eventually they would be destroyed or incarcerated as enemies of the state, while very quietly a small, unseen group would mold the very thought processes of an entire generation mired in inertia. And in doing so, they would gain unquestionable power over the masses, while those they enslaved praised them for their beneficent wisdom.

Liberty would die a slow but inevitable death, and only a few patriots would stand at the graveside to mourn its passing.

Chapter 1

June 10, 2017
Denver, Colorado

The smell of fear soaked through the woman's tattered dress and filled the small room as she sat trembling, frozen in place as she watched the apartment door. She was oblivious to the sound of dripping water from the leaky faucet in the cluttered kitchen and the dark stains on her tattered dress under her arms. The building was old and dark, and the naked light bulbs hanging in the hallway did little to remove the feeling of neglect that permeated both it and the people who lived there. She looked down at her hands and tried to calm them, but, they, like her, were captives of the moment. She heard a sound, and her pulse quickened. Tears brimmed her swollen eyes and raced down her stained cheeks. The door opened slowly, and a boy peeked inside. "Mark, what are you doing here? I told you to stay at Maria's house."

"I'm hungry, Mama. I didn't get my sandwich."

She ran forward and wrapped the boy in her arms. "The fixin's are in the kitchen. Quick, get it and go."

The boy had just turned into the kitchen when the door slammed open. A very large man stood there, swaying from side to side. He was dressed in soiled work clothes that smelled of whiskey and sweat. He was obviously very drunk. As his eyes adjusted to the darkness in the dingy apartment, he staggered forward, following his wife into their bedroom. As he stumbled after her he began cursing and shouting at the frightened woman. He grabbed her and threw her to the floor. Behind him the boy raced to the living room and dived behind the large brown

12

couch adjacent to the entry. The boy crawled quickly behind the worn furniture and covered his ears so that he might not hear his mother pleading with the man who stood over her. But the shrill screams of the woman penetrated his ears and his mind, and finally his heart.

He was eleven years old, and he knew that he could not block the screams; he could not erase the knowledge of what was happening. He was afraid to intervene; he feared the drunken man screaming obscenities in the night; but he also began to realize in his boy's mind that if he did nothing he would regret it for the rest of his life. As he lay there struggling with the decision he faced, he covered his ears as tightly as he could and tried to focus on a brown spider that scurried under the couch. It moved quickly across the scarred floor, then stopped abruptly, frozen in time, like he. Then the cursing and the screams intensified and the spider moved forward a few inches into the dim light in the room. Then it moved back into the darkness. Finally, it raced forward again out into the room, leaving only the dust balls under the couch dancing around as if they were alive. The boy's shoulders began to shake as tears sprang from his eyes. Then his heart overcame the fear, and he sat up. With determination he pushed the couch away from the wall and tentatively crawled from his hiding place. He could listen to the shouting no longer. The screams gave way to the voices in his small mind, and he rose slowly in the dim room. Standing as tall as he could, he walked, trembling, into his parents' bedroom. His mother was cowering in the far corner, screaming at the man who was lashing at her with both of his fists.

Mark took a deep breath and stepped forward. He was a frightened child, so afraid, but he knew he had to do something. He had listened to his mother's screams so many times. He had seen her bruised face and the fear in her eyes, and he had wept. He knew he could not watch this happen again. The voice that came from the small boy was filled with fear, but it was the best he could muster. He raised his head and shouted toward the back of the father he loved but also hated. "Stop! Stop! Dad, stop!"

The man did not appear to even hear the small boy behind him. Instead, he swung at his wife again, missing and hitting the wall beside her head. The pain shocked him and only angered him more. Herman

Sagan was lost in a reality in which he could not cope; the collapsing economy had betrayed him, as it had so many other men. It had robbed him of his work, his income, and mostly, his self-respect. And like so many others he had finally turned in desperation to drink. What the economy had done to Herman was only accentuated by the whiskey he poured into his stomach each evening. The economy had killed his future; but the whiskey was killing his present.

As the staggering man became even more enraged he grabbed his wife by her hair and drug her from the protection of the corner. He was just raising his fist to strike her when the glass vase flew through the air and struck him in the middle of his back. "Dad, stop! Please Dad, don't hit Mom!" The man turned slowly and glared at the boy. There was confusion in his eyes for only a moment, then he started toward the child. Mark was more frightened than he had ever been. He watched the man stumbling toward him for only a split second then turned to run.

A foot race between an eleven-year-old boy and a drunken forty-year-old man is a fairly even match, but Mark had a ten-foot head start. He was out the door of the small apartment in a flash, his father right behind him. The apartment was in an old brick building built fifty years earlier. It had no elevator, only the dark stairs that climbed the center of the building. The boy exited the apartment and headed toward the three flights of stairs. His drunken father ran awkwardly down the narrow hallway, cursing loudly after his son. The boy navigated the sharp turn to the stairs easily; the drunken man did not. As Herman Sagan stumbled he grabbed for the bannister, but it only changed his trajectory slightly. In an instant he plunged over the bannister and fell three stories to the floor below. The curses stopped in mid-air. Then there was the thudding crash of flesh on concrete. In that moment silence returned.

*　　*　　*

The policeman stood and watched helplessly as the woman cradled her son on the dark stairs. Over and over the small woman whispered into his hair as she hugged him close to her thin shoulders. "It's going to be okay, Mark. It's okay. It was not your fault." The child's face was one of total fear and shock. His small body shook visibly, and he could not stop crying. The officer finally walked over and put his hand on the woman's shoulder. She also appeared to be in shock, but she continued to rock back and forth, holding the crying boy. The policeman understood; he had seen the bruises on her forehead and the blood that had been smeared around her mouth. He had also talked to the neighbors.

The woman finally rose and walked to her husband's body. As she knelt beside the dead man one could almost see the fear draining from her body. She was shaking as she reached her apron and tried to wipe her mouth. Then she touched the dead man's face and wept gently. She used the stained apron to wipe blood from his forehead as she spoke quietly, to no one. "You were not a bad man, Herman. You just drank too much." As her sobs intensified, the policeman put his right hand on her shoulder and patted her gently. Officer Harpe was a large, burley man. He was as tough as they came and had little patience with the common criminals he dealt with each day. But his life had changed three years ago when he had suffered a personal loss of his own. His tragedy was not of drunken anger, but leukemia. The child he had lost was never beaten, but loved with all his heart. Sadly, that was not enough to save her life. Luke Harpe had not known for some time if he could survive that loss, but a kind pastor and a loving congregation had made the difference he needed. Out of his grief and pain he had found a new patience and a growing compassion for the defenseless people he encountered so often in his work.

"It's going to be okay. Come with me, both of you."

"What will I do? I have nothing. I have a son, and we are alone."

"You're going to be okay. I know someone who can help. It's going to be okay. I promise." He looked directly into her eyes and spoke very slowly. "I promise." As he lifted her to her feet, two men arrived with a gurney for the body. "I'll take care of your husband. You need not worry about that. I'll take care of him."

The traumatized boy was sitting on the second step of the worn staircase. He sat stiffly and was no longer crying. He simply stared out into a reality that had changed so drastically in such a short space of time. The policeman motioned to the boy. "Come on, son. It's time to go back upstairs." The boy sat there staring into the fading light that seeped through the opened door. He said nothing, and he did not move. The giant of a man looked at him for several moments then reached down and scooped him up in his arms. "What is your name, son?" The boy remained silent but just looked at the man who was carrying him up the stairs. He was a tall boy for eleven, but very thin. When the officer entered the apartment he understood why. He took the boy to his room and deposited him on his bed. He then helped the woman to the small table in the kitchen and put a pot of water on the stove. Then he did what he had planned and confirmed what he had suspected. He found very little food in the cupboards.

"Do you have other children?"

"No, only Mark."

"Have you and the boy eaten?"

"Mark had something."

"What?"

"A peanut butter sandwich."

"And you?" She said nothing. "Stay here; I'll be back." Thirty minutes later the large man returned with two bags of food.

Neither the boy or his mother ate much. The boy had not spoken since the accident. After the boy was in bed, the officer sat in the small living room and tried to talk to the woman. She looked tired and confused. She would listen to his questions intently then suddenly burst into tears. Over and over she would look at the kind man and ask, "What will I do? What will I do?"

"Mrs. Sagan, do you or your husband have any family? Is there anyone I can contact for you?"

"No, there is no one. I'm alone."

"No, Mrs. Sagan, you're not alone. Someone will be here tomorrow. You are not alone." He rose and put his hand on her shoulder. She was a small woman, and very thin. "You and your son will be taken care of. You have a family you don't even know yet. They will be here tomorrow. Just trust me."

* * *

16

The morning sun was still low on the horizon when the stranger started up the stairs. He carried a large cardboard box that was obviously heavy because he stopped at the second floor landing and placed it on the stairs to rest a few moments. The neighbors all knew where he was going. He obviously was someone trying to help the new widow on the third floor. They had all heard the story of the accident on the stairs. Several of them would have liked to help, but, like her, they also were destitute. Their hearts were good, but it is hard to be generous when your own cupboards are bare.

Ken Wilson mounted the final set of stairs, placed the box beside the door with a large fifteen printed on it, and knocked gently. He was breathing deeply as he muttered to himself — "Today I am Your hands." Ken was a thin man with dark, receding hair. He had a kind face and a warm smile. The woman who opened the scarred door had dark circles under her eyes. Like the door, she appeared old and worn. She looked totally defeated and appeared on the verge of tears. "Hello, I'm Pastor Wilson; Officer Harpe called me last night." She looked at the kind-faced man and stepped back as he reached for the large box. "I brought a few things."

"Thank you, pastor, but my husband and I didn't go to church."

"That's not required. I just know you need some help, and that's why I'm here." He looked into her swollen eyes. "I'm sorry for your loss and your pain." Wilson walked into the small room and sat the box on a bare table in the kitchen. Without asking he walked quickly through the apartment and stuck his head into each of the rooms. "Where is your son?"

"I don't know. He was gone when I got up this morning."

"How old is he, and what is his name?"

"Mark is eleven."

"Where does he play?"

"Mostly in the vacant lot down the street, by the bodega."

"I've brought food and milk for your breakfast. There's coffee in that bag if you like. I'll be back soon." He turned and walked quickly from the room.

The minister walked through the neighborhood of old worn buildings. Now eyesores, these had once been nice apartments. Three years earlier the government had instituted rent controls. Since then there had been little incentive to maintain the buildings and certainly none to build new ones. So the poor had cheaper rents, but available housing had almost totally disappeared. What had been a good intention had failed from lack of foresight. Wilson stepped over strewn trash on the sidewalk but smiled broadly; the buildings and the neighborhood might be decrepit, but the day was glorious. *Humans have the propensity to screw thing up quite badly, but God could always be depended upon to provide beauty, even in a squalid neighborhood like this one*, he thought. Ken Wilson squinted into the glaring sunshine that brightened even this area of town and stepped quickly over an inebriated man sleeping beside a broken window. A few minutes later he spotted the boy in the distance, sitting under an old tree, his elbows on his knees and his head cradled in his hands. He was staring off into the distance. Wilson walked over and sat down beside the boy but said nothing. After several minutes the boy turned and looked at the man carefully. Neither said a word. The minister pulled a package from his coat pocket and unwrapped two bagels. They were smeared with peanut butter and jelly. He said nothing but simply began eating one of them. He pushed the other over to the boy and continued to munch on his. The boy looked at the stranger for a moment then at the bagel. He looked away, but his hand moved slowly toward the bagel. Finally the boy picked it up and looked again at the stranger. A kind face nodded back, and the boy began eating. Together they ate in silence until the food was gone. The boy licked his fingers then rubbed his mouth. "Who are you?"

"I'm Ken Wilson. And I'm guessing you must be Mark." The boy said nothing. "I'm sorry about your dad. That was a terrible accident."

"It wasn't an accident. It was my fault."

"Did you want to kill your dad?"

"No." It was a very small voice. Wilson had to lean close to hear the child.

"Then it wasn't your fault. It was an accident." He said it with finality. "Did you love your dad?"

18

"Sometimes."

"He loved you. Did you know that?"

"He did?"

"Sure. But sometimes he drank too much. That confused him. When he was well he loved you very much. When he drank he didn't know what he was doing, but that wasn't the real dad. The real dad loved you very much."

"Are you sure?"

"Absolutely."

"Are you a policeman like Mr. Harpe?"

"Nope, I'm a pastor."

"What's pastor?"

"Someone who knows a lot about boys and their dads. Someone you can depend on; you know, like family."

"We don't have any family. "

"You do now, son. You do now." Little did the pastor know how prophetic his words would be, for as they sat in the grass eating their bagels, Vera Sagan lay dying on the floor of her dark apartment. The repeated beatings had done irreparable damage to her frail body, and she collapsed, suddenly. She finally found the peace that had evaded her most of her life.

Chapter 2

July 3, 2017
Washington, DC

Alec Woodward sat quietly in the corner of the congressional office and read a comic book while his father filled his expensive calf skin briefcase with stacks of papers and reports. Alec was excited because his father had promised to take him to his favorite restaurant for spaghetti. Spaghetti was one of the few things, other than comic books, that could keep the eleven-year-old's attention for very long. His father's office was almost square with a door centered opposite the littered desk. Two large windows flanked the desk but were shuttered to prevent the afternoon sun from filling the dark room. The musky smell of scotch whiskey permeated the entire environment. It was a man's office, comfortably so.

When the door swung open and two men rushed into the room, Alec paid little heed to them until the taller of the two began shouting in a very angry voice. He was facing Alec's father and did not notice the boy in the corner. "Woodward, just what the hell are you doing? I guess you didn't think we would read the papers maybe." The man threw a newspaper folded in thirds across the desk. The representative from Illinois did not even look at it. He just stood and watched the man until his venom was all poured out. It took the man several minutes of cursing and shouting before he was finally quiet.

"Are you through?"

"Am I through? I'm just getting started! We practically financed your last campaign all by ourselves, then you pull a stunt like this. What the hell were you thinking?"

"When you think you can get control of yourself I'll tell you what I was thinking. And when I do, it will all make sense."

"Make sense? You betrayed us; you betrayed the union that worked damned hard to get you elected."

"Wrong!"

"Wrong? You stand there and tell me I'm wrong? What the hell is this?" He pounded his fist on the article lying on the congressman's desk.

George Woodward smiled as he leaned across the desk. George was a good two inches shorter than the man he was facing, but he was powerfully built; his very presence demanded attention. He had been a first-string center on the Harvard football team and had beaten larger men to win that position. "You!" He pointed to the union driver who had escorted the official into the office. "Take a hike. Now!" The confused underling looked at the union boss for direction. After a moment the taller man in the expensive suit nodded toward the door and the driver turned and left.

"Good show Frank. That even looked real to me."

"What the hell are you talking about?" The official's face was red, his ample jowls shaking with rage.

"That," the congressman pointed to the article, "is how you are going to become the next president of the AFL/CIO."

"What?" It was said in a normal voice. The anger was gone.

"We both know that McKinney is going to lose the next election. He's stepped in it too many times. The rank and file aren't happy. We both know that. If he runs and loses, you're back to doing plumbing on some construction site. Have you thought about that? No more drivers and limos. No more quarter million in salaries. Just fixing some old lady's toilet for ten bucks an hour. Is that what you want? Are you willing to back McKinney with that in the balance? Are you willing to take that risk?"

The angry man's shoulders drooped as if he were suddenly very, very tired. He walked slowly to one of the easy chairs facing the desk. He slid into the red leather chair and looked up at the smiling congressman behind the desk. "So what you got in mind?"

21

"Look, we both like McKinney. He's a great guy, but he got careless. When he paid off those goons to rig the election in Chicago he didn't even check to see who they were. Who knew they were FBI agents? Certainly he didn't! Damn that was stupid. They got him cold; he's done. He's definitely going to lose the election, and he damn well might go to jail."

"You think he could get indicted?"

Woodward sat back down in his black leather chair and tented his fingers as he leaned his elbows on his desk. "We both know the President would normally stop that, but some idiots in the press put it on the evening news. Now the President has no way to cover for him; the best he can do is soften the sentence if he gets convicted. It's out in the open. So, when the press caught me in the hall, what do I do? I know it's too late for McKinney, but not for you—or me. The corporate world now thinks I'm a straight guy, looking to clean up the process. I speak up with a loud voice about vice of any kind, and suddenly I'm on TV and the public is listening. I'm the new poster boy for union ethics. I even got some contributions flowing in from some high level corporate executives. But you and I know this all leaves a big vacuum at the top, one that needs to be filled. And who do we know who has the respect of the rank and file and also the knowledge to run the largest union in the country?" The union official was leaning forward attentively, listening to every word. "You, Frank!" He waited while the man nodded affirmatively. "We both hate what has happened to McKinney, but there is nothing we can do for him now. You know that; I know that; he knows that. He stepped in his own shit. A man has to be more careful than that. All we can do now is pick up the pieces. We damned sure don't want some son-of-a-bitch like Franklin stepping in to take over, do we?"

"Hell no. Franklin is an idiot."

"One more thing we agree on."

For the first time Woodward glanced to see his son attentively listening to every word between the two men. Inwardly Alec's father smiled, but he continued as if the boy were not even in the room. "I'm going to be on two major news shows tomorrow morning. The entire nation will be watching. Do you want to know what I'm going to do?"

22

"What?"

"I'm going to talk about this terrible event, and I'm going to quietly begin two campaigns, me for senate and you for president of the AFL/CIO." He watched the man's face carefully. "And fifty million people are going to be watching."

The man smiled for the first time. "You know, Woodward, we always did work good together."

"Yes we do. We work together very well, indeed. And, we also always win."

In the corner the boy watched carefully, his young mind slowly beginning to sort out what he had just witnessed. He did not understand all of the details of the discussion, but he did recognize the skill his father had exhibited in dealing with the other man. He seemed to understand the man, what drove him, and what he really wanted. That gave his father power, and when he was also able to provide what the man wanted, his father was in control. And that was what young Alec was slowly beginning to comprehend in his youthful mind; if you understand people and what they really want, the ability to give that to them, or at least make them think you can, can easily be converted to control over what they do. The union executive rose, shook his father's hand, and walked from the room with a smile on his face. When he had gone, George Woodward looked over at his son and smiled.

"What was that all about, dad?"

"Politics son, just politics."

Chapter 3

October 2, 2018
Denver, Colorado

Pastor Ken Wilson walked into the principal's office and sat across from the lady behind the large desk. Her straight hair was pulled back severely around her oval head. The desk was surprisingly clean. It contained only two items: a handwritten report, which he surmised was about his adopted son, and a single ball point pen. "Mr. Wilson, I asked you here to discuss your son. He is your son, isn't he? It seems Mark struck another student today. We don't allow that kind of action at our school."

"Yes, I adopted him after his parents died. And I certainly understand your position on fighting in school; physical violence is seldom acceptable."

"Did you just say *seldom* acceptable? Physical violence is *never* acceptable." The large woman stared at the thin man seated before her.

"Do you know what caused the boys to fight?" Ken was not intimidated by the principal's words or her demeaning approach.

"I know your son struck another boy in school. That is all I need to know."

"Then you don't know what caused Mark to hit the other boy? Was he, perhaps, defending himself or another child?"

"As I said, striking another in school is not permissible in any situation. It brings an automatic three-day suspension from school. We have a zero-tolerance policy regarding fighting."

"I see. You really don't seem to know many of the details regarding this incident and don't seem to feel the need to learn them. But don't worry, I'll talk to Mark." Ken rose and turned for the door.

"I hope you will set a good example for your son."

Ken stopped abruptly and turned to face the woman seated behind the clean desk. "Mrs. Watson, I happen to be a pastor; I try to set an example for everyone." As he walked into the hallway, he heard her mumbling something about evangelical Christians. He just smiled and said a short prayer for her and especially for the kids in her school. Mark was seated outside the principal's office on a long bench. Three other boys also sat there. All of them looked guilty of something. Ken smiled and motioned for his son to follow him. "Come on Mark. Let's take a walk." The two left the school and walked for several minutes in silence.

"I'm sorry I got in trouble."

"That's all right. Are you hungry?"

Mark's face brightened. "Sure."

"Me, too. Let's get a burger and maybe a shake to share."

"Are you mad at me?"

"Should I be?"

"Maybe. I hit Jason."

"What did Jason do to make you that angry?"

"I wasn't angry. I was just tired of watching him pick on William."

"Is William small?"

"No, but he's really shy. He's afraid of Jason. I told Jason to leave him alone, but he just kept punching William every time he passed by."

Wilson stopped walking and looked straight into the boy's face. "I'm proud of you, son. You did the right thing."

"I did?"

"Yes. There are times when you must stand your ground for yourself or others against mean people. That takes courage and a lot of discernment."

"What's discernment?"

"That is when you decide what is right and what you should do. It is about judgment." He watched the boy's face for understanding then continued. "Generally there are consequences for doing the right thing.

25

Sometimes you get into trouble for having the courage to stand for what is right."

"Consequences like getting expelled from class for three days?"

"That's right. But there are also rewards as well."

"Rewards?" Mark thought for a moment. "I know, like a burger and a shake."

"That's right. So let's go find that reward. I'm hungry."

Chapter 4

January 14, 2024
Washington, DC

Senator George Thomas Woodward placed the phone in its cradle and turned to his family. His wife and their three children were watching TV and paid little attention to George. Unlike his staff and the rest of the nation, to his family he was just "dad." He walked into the dim family room and stood before them. "Alec, I need to talk to you in my study."

"Can we do it later, dad, we're in the middle of this movie."

"No son. We will do it now." With that the senator turned and walked from the room toward his office. Alec reluctantly climbed to his feet and followed his father into the ornate office with wooden paneling that covered the twelve-foot walls. George took a crystal bottle from his credenza and poured a scotch for himself while motioning for his son to take a seat opposite his desk. "Son, we need to talk about your college. Do you know what you want to study? Are you still intent on politics?"

"I think so dad. I really don't think medicine or engineering will work for me, so law and politics might be a good choice."

"Well, I guess that narrows it to Yale or Harvard. It's hard to beat Harvard for a law degree."

"I was thinking about Georgetown. They have the best foreign service school in the country, and it's right in Washington D.C., the heart of all politics."

"That is not a bad idea. Georgetown is a fine school. They even have a good basketball team." He smiled, knowing his son's disdain for sports. At five feet eight inches tall Alec was, to use the vernacular of the day, "vertically challenged." He hated all sports, especially basketball.

"Right dad!" The derision in his voice was quite evident. "But I've been thinking about it, and I think Georgetown would be my best choice."

"I agree. I'll take care of it son. I think you'll do well there." George turned to his desk and jotted a note on a small pad beside his computer. "By the way, did you send your applications as I told you to?"

"Georgetown, Harvard, and Stanford."

"Great. I like Washington. Seems most politicians are mediocre lawyers who didn't do so well in court, so a degree in foreign service might set you apart." He smiled at his son. "Have you thought of the direction you want to take? Running for office is a tough road, but government service can be very rewarding. I think you might like that approach."

"I looked at law school, but frankly I think a degree in foreign service studies might give me an edge in the area I wish to work. Foreign service could lead to Secretary of State or some job like that. That sounds interesting."

The senator looked at his son and remembered the long road he, himself, had taken to become a senator. It had been fraught with countless opportunities to fail: all the lies told to those he represented, the surprising compromises he had to make regarding everything he had believed in when he first entered the arena. Was Alec tough enough to do that? Did he have the stomach for the arena and the competition? He considered his son briefly and concluded he did not. "You know, son, foreign service sounds like an interesting and rewarding career for you."

"Thanks, dad. Now can I return to the movie I was watching."

"Sure, son."

As Alec walked down the hallway, he breathed a sigh of relief. It had been easier than he expected. He had been afraid that his dad would insist on law school. He knew law school was not something he could excel at. It was a tough and highly competitive arena with so many bright young applicants. He was not at all sure he wanted that. But civil service in foreign affairs, now that was something he could find interesting.

Alec felt a twinge of remorse; he knew what his father had been thinking. It was a gift he had developed and was refining. He understood people; he studied how they thought; he understood what drove them. Watching his father, he had concluded that if you know a man's mind, you can control his life. It was a powerful tool, one he would continue to develop, for his own purposes. Yes, Georgetown would do quite nicely. It would be a stepping-stone to a career that could be redirected at a moment's notice. Alec knew he would never succeed in the arena of congressional politics. But he also knew if he could find the right person, he could do the very next thing, help that person rise as high as he or she could go, while Alec learned to exercise some degree of power over what they wanted and what they did. They would be the puppet, and he would pull the strings.

He smiled; he had a plan. Now he just had to find the right star to guide across the skies of Washington, and perhaps the entire nation.

Chapter 5

May 20, 2024
Denver, Colorado

The young man tossed the official letter onto the kitchen table and walked to the refrigerator to find a snack. Ken Wilson placed his Bible on the coffee table before him and watched Mark with interest. "Aren't you going to open it? It's from Georgetown."

"You know there's no chance I could ever get into Georgetown."

"Why not? You graduated top in your class. And no one could match your SAT scores. You almost maxed them."

Mark turned and smiled at the man who had become his second father. "No man could have a finer father to teach him about life and what is important in this world, but he could have a richer one." They both laughed at that remark.

"Well, if the measure that matters is richness in money, I'm afraid you are right, you got the short end of that stick."

Mark was building a sandwich and paused only long enough to stare out the window toward another glorious Colorado sunset. It was a mixture of golden orange and the bluest sky he had ever seen. "Unfortunately, getting into Georgetown depends on more mundane things like money instead of what is truly important, so there is very little chance of my getting into that school. And, then there is also the fact that I am a male and white. Male, poor, and white; three strikes and you're out." He smiled at Ken.

"Don't you believe in miracles? Didn't I teach you about that?" The older man stood and began pacing around the small room. Mark knew

Ken's mind was working on something important he wanted to say. How many times had he watched him do that? How many times had he been blessed with the words that would eventually follow? "Son, during your life you will face many situations when you are uncertain or perhaps even afraid. Those are special moments. They are moments when you can be very close to the God who loves you and watches over you. Be free in those moments. Let your heart and your mind soar with confidence and unending joy. Pray for guidance, then fly into the moment; banish fear and uncertainty; act with the decisiveness of faith that you are never alone in anything you attempt. When you need it, you will be strengthened with a power greater than you can know, and you will taste life as never before. In that moment you will truly live."

"Well, I'm guessing a miracle is about the only way I could get into Georgetown, or most any good school for that matter."

Wilson walked into the kitchen, picked up the letter, and pushed it closer to the young man. "Where is that faith I've been teaching you about?"

"Right now I have more faith in a baseball scholarship; that at least has a chance." In a matter of minutes the sandwich was devoured and Mark was rechecking the refrigerator."

"You know, for a skinny kid you sure eat a lot."

"I'll never make it in baseball if I don't put on another 25 pounds at least."

The pastor pushed the letter closer. "Read this, maybe you won't need to try for a sports scholarship."

"Right. Even if I were accepted, how would we find enough money for a school like Georgetown. Did you forget that they are Jesuits? They understand money better than most bankers." Mark laughed at his own joke as he reached for the letter. "Okay. I have a good set of values. I can handle disappointment. Better still, I'll practice your advice." He closed his eyes tightly for a moment then, smiling, he opened the letter with the same knife he had used to make his sandwich, leaving mayonnaise on the envelope. He scanned it quickly, his eyes growing larger with each line. "My gosh, I've got a scholarship—to Georgetown's pre-med program!"

Wilson walked over and wrapped the boy in his arms. "I just knew it! I just knew it! I told you; You have a guardian angel!"

"Well, dad, you always say that God works in mysterious ways, but this is amazing."

Wilson took the letter from his son's hand and scanned it quickly. Then he re-read it very slowly. "Pre-med! He did it!"

"He?"

"Well, God of course."

"He?" Mark looked intently at Wilson. "He, dad?"

"Well, I did put in a good word with Terry Williams, a friend who teaches there now and then. We were friends from childhood. I just told him you needed a fair shot, in spite of the fact that you lived with a poor pastor and just happened to be a white male." He looked at Mark for a moment before finishing. "A fair shot; that was all I asked. You earned this on your own, son. I just asked Terry to make sure you at least got considered."

"Thanks, dad. I don't know what to say."

"You don't need to say anything to anyone. Just go and show them what a good choice they made." He watched Mark's smile growing wider. "But a prayer of thanksgiving would certainly be appropriate."

"I'm going to Georgetown!"

"Yes you are, son. Yes you are, and when you finish pre-med at Georgetown you can get into any Medical program in the country." Ken looked straight into Mark's eyes and spoke very quietly. "Now tell me, son. Do you feel that freedom I talked about? Can you feel your very spirit soar with joy?"

Chapter 6

May 29, 2024
Denver, Colorado

Marion Wilson watched with quiet satisfaction as Mark and her husband walked slowly through the men's department in the clothing store. She and Ken had been married 19 years, and she had seldom seen him so excited to buy clothes, even though they were for someone else. Getting ready for college was quite an affair. She looked at the two men she loved more than life itself, the pastor who had spent his life serving others and the young man they had rescued and who had become their son. She and Ken had wanted a large family, but God had other ideas. It had been a very difficult pill for her to swallow; she had wanted so desperately to have children. Had it not been for Ken, she might have succumbed to her deep depression. How could the God they both served deprive her of something so basic, something she desired so strongly? How often had Ken counseled young women caught in an unwanted pregnancy? How many times had he helped convince fragile minds of the finality of an abortion? Marion had envied them their ability to carry another human in their bodies. What a blessing above all others, a gift that had not been bestowed upon her. Still, Mark had come into their lives and had done much to fill that emptiness in her heart.

Mark had been such a gift to them, and, she supposed, they had been a Godsend to him. But Marion worried about Mark leaving for college. How would Ken handle that change? The two of them were closer than any natural parent and child she had ever seen. Mark was so bright, but life had started so wrong. He came to them with little trust and demons that frightened him in the night. It had taken time, but slowly Ken had built bridges between the two. Over the years those bridges had become granite pillars that would sustain his adopted son, regardless of what life offered. Those same pillars lifted the pastor's heart into the sunlight and gave him great joy in his life.

Mark's young mind was always questioning and often challenging. But he had his equal in Ken Wilson. Ken was a pastor first, but he also had a very broad education that allowed him to guide the boy he took to be his son. Marion had watched as Ken let Mark win in the constant chess games they played. Then she watched as her husband struggled to win even a few of the later contests. Ken taught Mark to seek knowledge of every type. They read and discussed a wide array of topics into the evenings as the young boy grew. But mostly he taught Mark the secrets of the heart. Mark was skeptical at first, but the pastor's persistence won in the end. Mark developed an amazing mind, but also a beautiful soul, and Ken Wilson could take a lot of the credit for both.

"Marion, what do you think about this sport coat?"

"I think it looks expensive. Are you two keeping to your budget?"

Wilson frowned at his wife. "Marion, Mark is going to Georgetown. He mustn't look homeless."

"You're right honey. Get that sport coat and a couple pairs of matching pants. But leave a little for spending money. You never know. He might even meet a girl at college." Mark's face turned slightly red at the comment.

"Are you kidding? He's going to be so busy studying he won't have time for girls."

"Let's see, how did that work for you, Honey?" She smiled at her husband. Now his own face turned a bit red.

Later that evening, when the dishes were finished, Wilson walked into the room with his hands behind his back. He looked at his wife and son and smiled. "One more thing for the newest student at Georgetown." He swung his hands around and produced a laptop computer. "It's not new, but it's good. One of my flock donated it for your studies."

Mark took the computer and studied it carefully. He looked at it for several minutes before speaking. "Thanks, dad; I really didn't expect this.

My own laptop. I'll write a thank you note if you just tell me to whom it should be addressed."

"It may need a little work to get it up to peak performance. But if there's anyone who can do that, it's you." He watched as the young man opened the machine and began scrolling through the programs.

"This is going to be great."

Ken smiled. "No, that is just a machine. Greatness depends on what you do with it."

Chapter 7

May 31, 2024
Phoenix, Arizona

Mackenzie Selms read her acceptance letter from Georgetown and danced up and down like a small child. "Mom, Dad, I made it. I'm going to Georgetown."

Her father took the letter and reviewed it carefully. "Yes you did. You made it into one of the finest schools in the country. Hell, one of the finest in the world! I'm proud of you, BooBoo." Tom Selms stood and watched his daughter. She was a tall young woman and also beautiful. He glanced over at the older version of the same beauty and smiled at his wife. How alike they were, smart, beautiful, driven — and he loved them dearly.

Marlene Selms watched as her daughter ran to her room to call her friends, then she too read the letter carefully. "No scholarship was mentioned."

"She made it in. That alone is a major feat today."

"I had hoped she would get at least some financial assistance."

Tom Selms looked at this wife and smiled. "No way, honey. I have a job, a very good job. Airline pilots are in the upper middle class. Scholarships go to minorities and the poor. I'm just glad Mackenzie made it into the program. Frankly, I had my doubts."

"You had doubts? About Mac?"

"Look, people like us don't get priority in this world. I have a good job. That means good pay, but not rich. Rich people's kids go to Georgetown; poor people's kids go to Georgetown. Working people's kids go to junior colleges or state schools—or none at all." He smiled a broad smile. "But if they have a daughter who worked her butt off and graduated with honors and also played first string on both the soccer team and the softball team—then she has a shot."

"And if we had a son?"

"He'd most likely be on his way to some junior college." Tom took the letter from his wife's hand. "That is the way the world works today. But we don't have a son. We have a beautiful, smart, talented daughter— just like her mom." Tom Selms placed the letter on the corner of his desk and looked at it a long time. "I wish I could have gone to college. It would have been so much fun. But at least now she has a chance."

"You have done rather well in this life, Tom." His wife walked over and put her arms around him. She pulled his head down and kissed him affectionately. "You have worked hard, and you've taken very good care of us. When you decided to go to pilot training instead of the university, it was a very good decision. You know that."

"Yes, I guess you are right. Still, sometimes I wonder about what it must have been like to be 20 years old and in a great university."

"Well, our daughter is going to find out." Marlene kissed her husband again. "Thanks to all of your hard work, our daughter is going to Georgetown University. And somehow we will find a way to pay for it."

"Yes we will, but honey, this is not going to be easy. After the nuclear war in the Middle East, things have not been the same. Airline flights are down over 30%, and the constant pay cuts have been difficult. There was a time when airline pilots were highly paid, but that was years ago."

"We can sacrifice for Mackenzie; she worked very hard for this chance, and I want her to have it."

"There will be a lot of kids there who didn't work so hard and who pay very little or nothing for this opportunity." There was a touch of anger in Tom's voice.

"Yes, but think of the difficult time they will have keeping up with our daughter."

The pilot smiled as he re-read the letter. "You're right about that!"

Chapter 8

October 24, 2025
Georgetown University, Washington, D.C.

Alec Woodward stood at the window and watched her walk across campus toward Healy Hall. Georgetown University was busy with students and faculty rushing to class and various meetings. It was the oldest Catholic and Jesuit university in the country, established in 1789 by John Carroll. It was also one of the finest examples of the 450-year-old legacy of Jesuit education, a legacy begun by Saint Ignatius who led his followers to develop both the heart and the mind of mankind. As a result of that reputation more than 20,000 prospective students applied to Georgetown each year, but fewer than 3,500 undergraduates were admitted. But Alec was not concerned about the weather or the school's acceptance rate, he was enthralled with a beautiful young woman crossing the campus.

It was late October of the second year of college, and the day was cold and overcast. A downpour threatened at any moment. The young woman Alec was watching, like everyone else, was walking quickly to avoid the unpredictable weather. Alec noted everything about her; he had watched her on several occasions around campus. She was taller than he by over an inch. She walked with a grace that few women ever mastered, and her blue eyes sparkled when she was excited or angry. Her name was Mackenzie Selms, and she wore little make-up but was always strikingly beautiful. He wondered what she must look like when she first woke in the morning. That was something he wanted to know more than anything else. He had called her a week earlier about getting together for a small party with his family. She had said no; she had an exam the following day. She was always concerned about her grades. Alec's eyes opened wide when he heard her explanation. He now knew something she wanted very badly. She was obsessed with her grades. He didn't know why, but he knew she was. He smiled and filed that information in its proper place in his mind. Now that he understood her he only needed a plan, and he was very good at planning.

*   *   *

Alec selected his newest sweater and slipped it over a white shirt. He pulled the collar out and arranged it over the maroon fabric carefully as he walked into the bathroom in the crowded dorm. The dorms were loud and rowdy; he would have much preferred the privacy of a single room, but his father had insisted that the friendships he would make might be the most important thing he could garner in college. Alec knew his dad was right, so he relented and moved into the men's dorm, determined to surround himself with the best and brightest that Georgetown had to offer. Besides, it would provide him with an excellent opportunity to practice his skills at analyzing people and determining what motivated them and what could be used to influence their behavior.

Alec combed his dark hair straight back and stood for several seconds checking the remaining two pimples on his forehead. The doctor's prescriptions were working; his face was almost clear. Tonight would be a special evening; he had finally arranged a date with the beautiful co-ed he had been watching since his sophomore year began just two months earlier. Mackenzie Selms was absolutely gorgeous and obviously quite smart. He had bought her coffee twice in the student lounge, and they had talked. He was very interested in her — no, he was obsessed with her. However, she appeared to have little interest in him. That can change, he thought. That can change. All he needed was time to get to know her better, time to understand what she valued in life, what she wanted. When he determined that, he would know how to win her. The only person he had met who was as complex as Mackenzie was his new roommate, a tall guy named Mark Sagan. There was something in

39

both of them that eluded his perception. Perhaps if he got the two of them together, perhaps then he might get a glimpse into their psyches. He thought about that a minute and determined it might just be the solution he was seeking. He walked back into the room. "Hey Mark, are you going to the dance tonight?"

"I hadn't planned to."

"C'mon, the entire sophomore class will be there—except you. Besides, I can introduce you to my date. She's a doll. Maybe she has a friend. I assume you're interested in girls."

Mark looked up from the large stack of books on his desk. He considered the last remark. "Yes, I do like girls, but I have a paper due on Monday." Mark was looking at Alec's new sweater. "Nice sweater."

"Look, I really want you to meet Mackenzie. We're going down to M-street for pizza. Come along; I'm buying. Besides, you need a break."

* * *

Their conversation ranged from school to the dire state of the economy. Mackenzie brought up the topic of literature and how she wished she had more time to read something other than textbooks. Mark agreed that when he finished school, he wanted at least a year to do nothing but read all of the good books he had missed. At present he only had time to read one or two books a week. Mackenzie looked at him in amazement. "Really? You read a book or two a week? Plus your schoolwork?"

Alec interrupted the conversation in an effort to change the topic. "He reads about a thousand pages a minute. He can go through a history book in less than half an hour."

Mark grinned. "Well, I'm not really that fast."

"I watched you read 1776 in less than an hour. I know; I timed you."

"Yes, but that's a novel. They go very quickly."

The young woman studied the pre-med student carefully. Without thinking she blurted out. "I'll bet you are on scholarship." Mark nodded, but said nothing. "I could have guessed. Did you get a full ride?" Mark looked down but still said nothing. She realized she had embarrassed him. "Hey, that's something to be proud of. You actually earned this education. Good for you."

"I guess." Mark finished his Coke.

"Most people here had this opportunity handed to them. I intend to prove that I am worthy of this. You've already done that." She looked directly into Mark's eyes and reached and touched his arm.

Alec made a mental note of all that had just transpired. He also had had enough of the conversation and reached across the table with a pitcher of beer.

Mark spoke quickly. "No thanks."

"You don't drink beer? You're a college student; therefore, you drink beer."

"Not tonight, thanks." Mark took the pitcher, pouring the remaining beer into Alec's and Mackenzie's glasses. "Did you notice the time. We need to get started. It's a long walk to the dance."

"Walk? I have a car." Alec pulled a set of keys from his pocket and rattled them before his classmates. It's a sports version, so you'll have to sit sideways in the back, Mark. But it's a short ride."

Mackenzie looked at Alec with surprise. "You have a car? How do you get gas rations?"

Alec sat quietly for a moment, his mind working in high gear. "It really isn't my car; it belongs to a friend. He let me borrow it for the evening."

Mark finished the last piece of pizza as the three rose to leave. "Where are you going to park tonight. It will be impossible."

"I have a plan."

"A plan for parking?" Mackenzie stood for a moment, admiring the BMW.

As they slid into the car, Alec pulled a handicap placard from under his seat.

Mark looked at it and immediately protested. "Wait a minute, Alec, you're not handicapped; what if a person arrives who needs it, and there is no place to park."

"The good thing about universities is that everyone is young and the handicapped sites seldom get used. So tonight we will ensure that at least one handicapped parking place is not wasted."

Mackenzie squeezed into the front seat and combed her auburn hair with her fingers. "You don't worry about getting caught?"

"A twenty-five-dollar parking ticket is not on my priority list of things to worry about; besides, it's not my car."

Mark reached into his pocket and felt nothing but change there. "It would be for me. I'd be washing dishes in the student lounge for a week to pay for that."

Mackenzie turned to look at Mark. "Ah, the poor student, struggling to get through college."

Alec watched with frustration as his date flirted with his roommate. He stepped on the gas and sped away toward the university. Two blocks later he was pulled over on M Street by a cop who had been cruising the area. "License, registration, and proof of insurance please."

"Did you check my tag carefully, officer?"

"Should I?"

"That might be a good idea."

The officer walked to the rear of the car and flashed his light on the tag. He returned and handed the paperwork to Alec. "Thank you, Mr. Woodward. Please drive carefully." In a moment he was gone, and the three were back on the road.

"What just happened?" Mackenzie had turned and was looking at Alec.

"I wasn't really going all that fast. It was just a warning."

"Alec's dad is a Senator. A U.S. Senator. There is a sticker on his tag."

"Oh." She considered this new information for a moment. "You didn't tell me that, and you also said it was a friend's car." Alec said nothing but continued driving toward the dance. She smiled and lightly punched his shoulder. "You're embarrassed because you're rich." Then she turned toward Mark. "And you're embarrassed because you're poor." Alec's eyes widened as she spoke. "I guess it isn't easy being either rich or poor. I guess I'm lucky to be in the middle."

Mark smiled. Mackenzie didn't pull any punches. He liked that.

Chapter 9

February 5, 2026
Georgetown University, Washington, D.C.

"Did you go down and sign up, Mark?"

"I went to the selective service last week; did you?" The five young men were sitting inside McShain lounge in McCarthy Hall, which, along with Kennedy and Reynolds Halls, formed the complex of upperclassmen residence halls. Ostensibly they were preparing for a group assignment in one of their classes. Alec joined them and pulled a chair from a nearby table.

"Well, what is new in the medical field today? Found a cure for hemorrhoids yet?" Alec rose and turned toward the service area. "Anyone want a beer?"

"Sounds great."

Alec returned with a pitcher of beer and a stack of glasses on a tray. He also had a Coke for Mark. "What is the reason for all this seriousness. We are supposed to be having fun, remember."

"We're talking about the draft. Speaking of hemorrhoids, Afghanistan just doesn't want to leave the seventh century. Have you registered yet? The new law only gave us three weeks to comply."

Alec looked at the group for a moment. "Sure, it's been taken care of."

"Like your dad fixed it for you?" The young black man said it without malice. "Must be nice."

"Nobody fixed anything. That's not what I meant."

"Of course not. We all know everyone has an equal shot at being called up. Right?"

Another in the group spoke up forcefully. There was a tinge of anger in his voice. "Look, all wars are fought by kids from poor or middle class families. Everyone knows that. You rich guys get a pass, and we fight the wars. That's the way it works."

"Really, how do you know so much?"

"My grandpa died in Vietnam and my dad died in Afghanistan the last time we tried to clean up that sewer." He looked directly into Alec's eyes. "Tell me, did your dad ever serve in a war?" Alec said nothing. "I guessed not."

Alec got up slowly, replaced his chair at the nearby table and left. Mark looked at the group. "Hey, it isn't his fault that his father is a senator."

"And it's not my fault that my father was killed when I was two years old."

Mark rose, finished his soda and walked out into the misty afternoon to find his roommate. He caught Alec about half a block away. "Sorry about that. They didn't mean any harm. I think they are just a bit stressed about exams. This med school is a bitch."

"I don't fit in, do I? I just can't be one of the guys."

"Is that what you really want, to be one of the guys?"

"Yeah, sometimes I want that more than anything else." He stopped walking and turned to Mark. "You fit in. How do you do it?"

"I don't really know, Alec. I'm just me."

"It's damned hard to fit in when you are from a wealthy family. Sometimes I wish my dad were a plumber."

"A plumber? Then you'd really be rich!" That broke the tension and they turned right and headed toward the dorm.

"By the way, Mark, I need some help with some math on a paper I'm preparing for one of my classes. Think you'd have a few minutes tonight?"

"Not a problem. But in return you'll have to get Mackenzie to introduce me to her roommate."

45

Alec smiled. "That's a deal. Shall I make a reservation at my dad's club?"

"No, just pizza down on M Street and then a movie Friday night."

"How about Saturday?"

"I'm working at the hospital Saturday till 9:00 pm"

"Then the two best looking guys at Georgetown will take the two prettiest girls at Georgetown to pizza and a movie on Friday. How lucky they are."

*　*　*

Mark reread the last paragraph in Alec's paper then looked up, puzzled. He finally picked up the entire paper and began reading again from the beginning. As he finished each page he dropped it on the floor. Alec watched him with concern on his face. "What are you doing, Mark?"

"I was working on your projections and had to recheck something in your paper. I've got the math solved, but I have questions about your general thesis. Do you really believe this? Really?"

"What's wrong with it?"

"Alec, this is preposterous. Marx, Lenin, or Mao might have approved, but we know a lot better than this now. This is almost communist propaganda. Tell me you don't believe this drivel. Besides, what will your professor say?"

"Hey, this paper will guarantee me an A in this course. My professor is about as far left as you can get. He'll love this."

"Is that what he's teaching you?"

"That is exactly what she's teaching. Listen, you have to give them what they want."

"Doesn't that bother you?"

"Mark, you guys in med school might not have to deal with this, but in the poly-sci department, this is the gospel they want to see."

"Good thing I'm in pre-med."

"Yeah, you'd probably flunk out of our program pretty fast."

"If this is what they want, you are absolutely right. Somehow I find this hard to read, much less to write."

"Look Mark, this is the way the country is going. Like it or not, America is quickly becoming a socialist country. We've a lot of folks out there who need to be led by the nose. They're dumb as a stone, and someone has to take control—that is the government's role, to tend to the herd."

"I don't share your enthusiasm for socialism or the poor state of America's citizens."

"Watch what they vote for. Then you'll know I'm right." Alec began picking up the various pages of his paper. "Remember that guy back in Obama's administration who got caught saying that most Americans were so dumb that it was really easy to mislead them and take care of them at the same time? Well, he was right."

"Do you think the move toward socialism has really helped most people? Seems to me that folks are getting worse off every year. Unemployment is up, and those who work can barely make ends meet." Mark placed the remaining stack of paper on Alec's bed. "We're still accumulating debt at an alarming rate, and the country is basically bankrupt already. Sorry, but I just don't see it."

"Socialism will work; we just need some really smart folks running things. The idiots we have now are not smart enough for the job. They're corrupt to the core as well."

Mark sat back in his chair and studied his roommate for several minutes. "Alec, I am not an expert at politics and things like that, but one thing seems rather certain. An economy has two major jobs, producing goods and services then distributing them to the population. Seems we spend a lot of time trying to be "fair" about the distribution side, but we seem to miss the production area. We worry too much about who gets what size slice of the pie and not nearly enough about how to produce a bigger pie for everyone. Then there's the incentives thing. How do we get the most productive among us to work even harder to produce even more? Right now with the exorbitant tax rates on our top producers, we seem to be sending a message that working hard is not encouraged."

"You're right about the top rates being high. But where else would we get the money to pay for all the things the public needs, like roads and national defense?"

"Roads and national defense are a snap. It's the social welfare programs that absorb most of the national budget."

"But aren't people more important than roads?" Alec's voice was rising.

"Have you noticed that the more welfare you hand out the more you need? What will you do when everyone is on welfare and no one is working? What will you do then?"

"The greedy will always work."

"But what if you dampen their incentives to work, and they all work just a bit less every year. Look at our economy now. It is slowly sliding downhill. Fewer and fewer are working, and those who do take home less and less. How will we encourage personal excellence in that scenario?"

"The government will do it, Mark. The government will do it."

"The government has been running things since about 2010, and the only growth we see is in unemployment numbers, welfare recipients, crime rates, and public debt."

"Who cares about those things. We want fairness. As a religious guy, I'd think you'd embrace that."

"I do want the best for people, but somehow having more people on welfare and surviving on food stamps doesn't seem *fair* to me. Whatever happened to individual excellence and personal freedom?"

"People decided to give all that up after Iran attacked Israel and the Israelis wiped out the entire Middle East. That frightened people; that changed everything. It changed the way they thought. After that it was easy to get them to believe the government was the answer to everything. In fact, they were already well along on that road when the nukes started flying. They were willing to trade those freedoms for security and a government check."

"Didn't anyone ever figure out that it was our government that okayed the Iranian nuclear program? That was a major achievement in the Obama legacy. Do you really think people are safer now? The price we've paid for that shadow security is very high, and I don't think it is a very good bargain."

"What we think is unimportant. What counts is what we can get the population to believe, and they've okayed the price with their votes. Now most Americans are becoming more and more dependent on the government for survival. And that's the plan, Mark. That's the plan."

Chapter 10

February 11, 2026
Georgetown University, Washington, D.C.

Alec walked into the dorm room and threw his books onto his bed. He was obviously upset. He walked over to Mark's desk and stood silently until Mark looked up. "Did you do it?"

"Did I do what?" Mark pushed his text book aside and turned to face his roommate.

"Report the test."

"What test? What are you talking about?"

"The test questions for macroeconomics."

Mark studied Alec's face for several moments. "What did you do, Alec?"

"Somebody reported that the questions had been compromised."

"Did you get a copy of the exam?" Mark's voice was accusing.

"Well, let's just say I had a chance to see the exam. I knew Mac was worried about it, and you know how she is about her grades. I just saw it as insurance for the Dean's List."

"You stole a copy of the exam?" Mark was incredulous.

"I didn't steal anything. I just *secured* a copy." Alec looked at the floor. "Besides it's a dumb class."

"I'm guessing Mackenzie didn't look at it."

"No, she didn't."

"Then what's the problem? You aren't in that class this session."

"No, but five of the guys are."

"You gave them a copy of the exam?"

"I thought it would help me fit in better. You know the guys don't like me."

"So now they owe you, right?"

"Someone must have told the professor. He changed the exam, and they didn't do very well."

"Are you aware that you could be thrown out of Georgetown for a stunt like that?"

"I'm not going to be expelled from school; I just want to know how the professor found out." He looked back into Mark's eyes. "You didn't do it?"

"If I had known what you were planning I would have talked you out of that stupid idea." Mark turned back to his notes. "I can't believe you pulled a stunt like that."

"Hey, what's the big deal. All I did was get a stupid exam in a stupid class. What's wrong with that?"

"What's wrong with you studying like everyone else? Why should others work for their grades while you cheat?"

Alec turned disgustedly to leave but stopped abruptly. "Wait, you knew that Mac would refuse the exam. How did you know that?"

"Mackenzie?" Mark turned back to his roommate. "You really don't understand her do you? Did you really think she would cheat for a grade?"

"Seems like she is always obsessing about grades. I was just trying to help her, that's all."

"Dammit Alec, for such a smart guy, you can be downright stupid now and then. It isn't about the grades with Mackenzie. It's about knowing she did her best and that she's competent. The grades are simply a shadow of that measurement. If she got an A by cheating she would feel like a complete failure. She has a lot of pride in her accomplishments. There is none in a stolen grade." Mark shook his head. "I can't believe you couldn't see that. It's really quite obvious."

Alec stood silent for a long time. "I see. I never looked at it that way. I guess I really did misjudge her." He walked over and punched Mark's shoulder gently. "Thanks, I'll remember that."

51

"Have you ever thought that the professor might have simply decided it was time to change the test?"

"I suppose that could have occurred."

"Maybe you should address that with the guys. I'm guessing they are not very happy right now."

"No, they aren't."

"For your sake, I hope they don't decide to contest their grades."

"You think you could help me out with the guys on this one?"

"I'm afraid this one is yours. I frankly don't know what I would say that would be of any help. I guess you just tell them the truth, that you screwed up and you're sorry."

"That doesn't sound encouraging."

"No, it doesn't." Mark returned to his book. "I hope you learned something out of all this."

"Yeah, if you're going to pull a fast one, be smarter about it."

"You get an F in ethics, my friend."

* * *

Mark was hurrying across the campus when a hand was placed on his arm. He stopped to look into Mackenzie's face. "Hi, handsome; got time for a Coke?"

"Of course. I'll race you to the student lounge. It's starting to rain." The two raced through the first drops of rain as dark clouds gathered above. They arrived at the lounge laughing and winded. "You know you should be on the track team. You're fast."

"I had a little brother to chase when I was growing up, and he actually is on a track team." Mark went for sodas, and Mackenzie selected a small secluded table in the rear of the room. "Thanks for the Coke." Mark nodded as he watched her face. After several minutes of light conversation, Mackenzie looked straight into Mark's face. "I guess Alec is a bit upset about the economics test."

"That was a pretty dumb thing to do. He could get thrown out of school for a stunt like that."

"Did he tell you he offered me a copy?"

"He did, but I knew you wouldn't take it."

"You did?"

"Of course; you would never want a grade you didn't earn. For you it's about earning the grade; that's what's important. The grade itself is little more than proof of your competency. You're smart; stealing a grade would only demean that competency. How you feel about yourself is far more important than some grade in a file somewhere."

She looked at him in silence for several minutes. Finally, she smiled nervously. "You're right. You really know me quite well." Mark nodded. He, too, was smiling a bit nervously.

Mackenzie decided she didn't need to ask the question she had come to pose. Mark certainly understood her, but she was fairly sure she understood him as well. She had her answer. She was now convinced that Alec had lied. Mark would never have stolen the test for him. She was as sure of that as anything she knew in her life. "You are a good man, Mark Sagan." She reached across the table and kissed him on the cheek. As he looked up in complete surprise, she rose and walked out into the rain.

Chapter 11

March 8, 2026
Washington, D.C.

Senator Woodward looked at his son without speaking for several minutes. "Look son, I don't like the idea of your going to Afghanistan. We've already lost a lot of good men over there. Why do you want to be a part of that mess?" Woodward leaned back in his expensive leather chair and eyed his son across a large cluttered desk.

"It's a stupid war for sure, dad, but I need to go. A lot of guys at school have been giving me a hard time about being a senator's son and getting special privileges."

"So what? When did their opinions about anything make a difference to us?"

"You're right, dad. I really don't give a damn what they think. But it did give me pause to consider what it might mean later in my life. While I really don't want to run for public office like you did, I still want to be in the political arena, and being a military veteran might make a big difference down the road. It doesn't hurt being a veteran if you're involved in politics."

"Are you willing to risk your life in some God-forsaken hole in Afghanistan?"

"Who said anything about risking my life? I don't intend to go to the front lines. There must be tons of jobs there in the Green Zone that are relatively safe."

The senator leaned back in his chair and smiled. "Damn, I think you do have a calling in politics. I like the way you think." He walked over to the small cupboard under his window and pulled a bottle of whiskey from the bottom shelf. "I think we should have a drink to your future."

"I figure you probably know some generals you could speak to. Just make sure they don't know I had anything to do with your request. You know, a dad concerned about his son. That sort of thing."

George Woodward poured the whiskey into two glasses. He dropped a couple ice cubes into each and turned to his son. "You know, son, I'm really proud of you. You've thought through this very well, and your solution is quite good. It just so happens that I know the Army Vice Chief of Staff. I was the one who pushed his recommendation for his first star. He knows he can always count on me, and I know I can count on him as well. You just might want to bone up on logistics. Who knows, that might be your new job in Afghanistan."

The two men clinked their glasses and celebrated the new plan. Alec wondered if Mackenzie would find him attractive in a uniform.

Chapter 12

March 16, 2026
Georgetown University, Washington, D.C.

Alec was explaining his decision to join the Army and volunteer for Afghanistan when he stopped in mid-sentence. He was acutely aware that Mackenzie was not listening to him at all but rather was busily trying to explain something to Mark. Alec watched the two for several minutes in complete silence. They were oblivious to his presence, and that realization was both shocking and embarrassing to him. How could he have made such a mistake? He was the one who was so good at reading other people. How had he missed the growing friendship between his roommate and the girl he was enamored with? He was watching her face when she finally turned to examine the sudden silence. When their eyes met, she blushed. She was embarrassed. "I'm sorry Alec, we were discussing one of the problems on the mid-term in Business Finance class. What were you saying?"

Alec looked into her beautiful eyes and felt a bit of his self-control slipping away. With great effort he struggled to regain some semblance of control. "Not important; I'll explain it to you later. Right now I just want some pizza. I see you two already finished this one."

"Well, I had a little. I think Mark ate most of it." She glanced back at the taller man. "If you order another, you'd better guard it carefully or he might get that as well."

"Wait a minute! I told you there was a consulting cost for my assistance on that problem." Mark poured more beer into Mackenzie's glass.

The three sat and talked and laughed and enjoyed the evening. Finally, Alec decided it was time to escape his roommate and suggested a movie. Mackenzie agreed and immediately turned to Mark. "Want to join us, Mark?" It was at that moment that Alec realized he had a problem. He was getting ready to leave for Afghanistan, and Mark would be left with Mackenzie.

* * *

Alec waited until his dad walked down the hall to his home office before joining him. "Dad, I submitted my paperwork to the Army today. I sent it to the officer you suggested."

"Good. I talked to General Logan. He said he'll have his adjutant take care of it. He'll let me know the details in a day or so. I told him they should hold off until the end of the semester, but that's only a few months away."

"Thanks, dad. One other thing. I'd really like to have one of my friends along when I deploy. You know, Mark Sagan, my roommate. Perhaps he could be assigned to my unit." Alec paused a moment before continuing. "But not as an officer."

The senator looked up suddenly and searched his son's face. There was obviously something there that he did not yet understand, but he would check into that later. After a moment he responded. "That can be arranged. We do have a selective draft ongoing now. And this time we are including university students—to keep it fair. I'm sure I can make that happen. You did volunteer for the Army, didn't you? Not the Navy or Air Force?"

"Right."

"Good, that will be better politically."

"Thanks dad; this might be important in the future."

"It might, son. And I'll help you with your political future. You just be damn careful over there in Afghanistan."

"I plan to do that. Besides, by the time I complete my training we may well be out of that war."

"Don't kid yourself. We've been in and out of that cesspit for years. I doubt it will end anytime soon. The only way we'll ever win that war is to kill every living soul over there, and while that might be tempting, it would not be good for one's political career."

"Well, I just need it to keep up long enough to get it on my resume. Then they can do whatever they wish with it."

"Just don't get any ideas of being a hero. That isn't necessary."

"Don't worry, that's not in my plans."

"Good. Now, have you told your mother yet?"

"No, that is the one thing I haven't figured out thus far."

"Good luck with that. And don't look to me for help there. I still haven't figured that woman out after all these years."

"Maybe we can do this and make you the good guy."

"What do you mean?"

"What if you told mom that I had volunteered as a patriot and that you couldn't talk me out of it. But you did the next best thing; you made sure I would not get in harm's way. You can tell her one of your friends is ensuring I'll get a desk job in the Green Zone where it's safe. Mom will think you are taking care of your son. I'll even act angry that you did it."

"Damn, son. You really are going to be a great politician."

"That's the plan. A great politician, just like my dad." Both men were smiling as they finished their drinks.

Chapter 13

June 9, 2027
Afghanistan

The eight new recruits stood in a loose formation in the hot Afghan afternoon, waiting for their new commander. The temperature was that of an oven, and all of them were wet with perspiration. There were ten of them; three were from Georgetown University and had been drafted during the summer prior to their senior year. They were not happy about being drafted; they were even less happy about being in Afghanistan. Mark Sagan had two stripes; the others only one. "Okay Mark, if we have to wait only fifteen minutes for a full professor, how long do we have to wait for a second lieutenant?"

"Till Hell freezes over. Academia and the army are about as far apart as you can get." The bantering stopped abruptly when Lieutenant Woodward walked out and stood before the assembled men. "Good afternoon men. I'm Lieutenant Woodward; I'm the C.O. of company B, Third Regiment, Transportation Division. Welcome to Afghanistan."

"Well I'll be damned. It's Alec."

"That's Lieutenant Woodward, soldier." There was a sudden silence in the ranks. "Drop off your gear at the barracks and proceed to the mess hall. We'll have a short orientation meeting at base ops at 1500 hours. I'll see you then." He watched as the men started to gather their gear. "Corporal Sagan, come with me please." Mark followed Alec as they started off toward base operations. "How are you doing Mark? Damn, it seems like months since I saw you last."

"It was months. How have you been? Looks like you are fitting into the military quite well."

"You too. I see you got a promotion to corporal."

"The good looking guys always get picked first." They walked into a small office with Woodward's name over the door. "How did you make lieutenant? We haven't graduated yet? That's not normal. I thought a college degree was necessary to be an officer."

"I got a commission through the National Guard unit in my state. They just transferred it over into the regular reserves."

"You seem to have this military figured out. Being an officer is a big advantage."

"I've learned a lot about the army over here. Just do your job, keep your head down, and never volunteer for anything."

"Sounds like the same thing they told us in basic training."

"On a serious note, how good are these guys you came over with."

"I only know about half of them, and they're okay. I guess we'll learn more when the shooting starts." Mark looked at Alec carefully. "Have you seen any action yet?"

"No, I just sit in this office all day and schedule logistics. Supplies is the name of the game in this outfit."

"Any idea what they intend to do with us? We don't drive trucks or load ammo. We're infantry. We also have one of the best sniper recruits the army has ever had, so they tell me."

"You guys will escort the caravans of supplies we ship around this sector. If the bad guys attack a convoy, you take them out."

Mark looked at Alec a long while without speaking. "We just take them out? It's that simple?"

"Well, actually you hold them off long enough to get air support or helicopter gunships involved. Helicopters are generally there within twenty minutes and air support is normally available in about half an hour."

"I see."

Alec changed the subject; he was not comfortable with the direction of the conversation. Besides, the real reason for this meeting was not to

60

talk about the war, but more important things. "Have you heard from Mac recently?"

"Only twice. She sent a letter when we were starting basic training to ask how to solve a math problem in one of her courses. Then about a week later she sent another to thank me for the help. Not much news from school. How about you?"

"Not much; she's busy with school. You know how Mac is, work, work, work." Alec lied; he had written her several letters with no replies.

"Yeah, she's driven all right. She'll probably run the world someday. Mostly she's mad at all of us for being here. She's mad at you for volunteering and the government for drafting the rest of us."

"Well, you'd better get over to the mess hall before they close the lunch line. It's good to have you over here. And Mark, while we are friends and all that, this is the army, so just put up with the formality. Out of this office we are Lieutenant and Corporal. In here it's Mark and Alec. You understand how this works."

"Sure, Alec."

"If you need anything, just let me know."

"Thanks. Right now I just need some food and a shower. And a nap would be nice; it's damned hard to sleep on those transports."

Chapter 14

August 17, 2027, 0900 hours
Afghanistan

The first three convoys were uneventful. Then on number four, the first truck in the column hit an IED. The trucks stopped long enough to pull the bodies out of the twisted metal before they continued along their assigned route. The bodies were packed into black plastic body bags and stacked into the last troop truck in the convoy. Two weeks later three vehicles were hit with mortar fire from mountains along the route. For almost half an hour the troops lay in the dirt firing at an enemy that was largely unseen. Finally, a fighter aircraft flew in and dropped three CBU-52 cluster bombs over the enemy positions. With a small puff of smoke the canisters opened 2500 feet above the mountain side and each dropped 220 small bomblets on the enemy positions. The bomblets fell, spinning, toward the earth. When they hit, they bounced about three feet into the air and exploded, filling the mountainside with deadly shrapnel. Immediately all firing stopped. Three body bags were loaded into the troop truck, the wounded were flown out in helicopters, and the trucks resumed their route, leaving enemy bodies scattered along the side of the mountain.

Two months into his tour, Mark was promoted to staff sergeant when one of the men rotated back to the states. Each day he did his job, wrote letters back to his family, and read every good book he could get his hands on. He was lying in his bunk reading *The Phantom's Song* one morning when one of the men called his name. "Hey Sagan, the lieutenant wants you in Ops ASAP."

"Got it." Five minutes later he was standing in the operations area while a captain explained an urgent assignment to several lieutenants. The captain was young, but his face was hardened by several tours of combat in this same region. He had a scar that extended from just below his left eye to his ear. It gave him immediate credibility.

"Our mission is to get badly needed supplies and ammunition to a Marine unit in contact with the enemy. We will send two decoy convoys to draw fire and identify any ambushes along the way. If contact is made we will have gunships and fighter-bombers standing by for support. This will clear the way for the actual supply convoy which will be thirty minutes behind the two decoys. Companies A and C will depart at 1100 hours and proceed along highway A01 toward Delaram. Company A will turn west at Delaram toward Farah. Company C will continue along A01 toward Adraskan. All of your supply trucks and your troop carriers will be filled with combat troops. The truck beds will be covered to conceal the size of our force."

The captain made several gestures toward a large map mounted on the wall as he spoke. He turned to Alec. "Then Lt. Woodward will lead Company B with two troop transports and three supply trucks along the same route as Company A; you will depart at 1130 hours and rendezvous with Company A five clicks west of Farah. Both A and B will then proceed thirty-five kilometers beyond Farah and meet with the marine outfit you are supplying." The captain marked the large map in red. "Use care in the area; the marines have been engaged for several days. If all goes well, our plan is to entice the enemy into attacking one of the first two convoys. When they do, we'll take them out, clearing the way for Company B to resupply the marines. Any questions?"

Alec raised his hand. "When you said I would lead Company B, did you mean on the actual trip up the mountain? Or will it just be my team?"

"Lieutenant, we need every man we can get on this assignment. You are their leader; I need you in charge up there."

"But what about tomorrow's schedule?"

"Fuck tomorrow's schedule. If this shipment doesn't get through, a lot of guys won't have a tomorrow." The captain looked around the room again. "I'll be with Lieutenant Mavor's unit, Company A, I'll be in touch

63

with each convoy by radio." He paused for a moment. "Any questions? If not, move out and get ready. Watch the time. It's essential we all stay on plan."

When Alec looked over at Mark, his face was quite pale.

Chapter 15

August 17, 2027, 0500 hours
Afghanistan

When the five trucks lumbered out of the American zone and started northwest along A01, the sun was just rising on the distant horizon. For most of the trip the land was relatively flat, but about 80 miles from the intersection to Farah, they began to climb into very steep mountains. It was the perfect place for an ambush. Alec sat in the cab of the lead truck, the first troop transport, while the soldiers sat in back on benches along the sides of the truck bed. There were also two large supply trucks followed by the remaining two troop transports. A large canvas cover that could be thrown aside easily if needed was deployed over the rear of each troop vehicle. The road was hot and dusty as the trucks lumbered along. In all, there were eight drivers, two mechanics, and 31 soldiers in the small convoy. The men in the rear were growing more nervous because they could not see out of the truck very well. The window between the cab and the rear truck bed had been removed to facilitate communications. Mark had positioned himself beside that window to relay orders and also to allow some visibility forward.

One of the men peered from under the canvas to check the terrain. "Damn, there's about a thousand places to hide a company or a regiment out there. We're sitting ducks if they decide to attack."

"Why didn't they bring along a couple of tanks. That would be helpful."

"Screw the tanks. They are too slow and not much help in the mountains. I'd prefer a flight of fighters loaded with CBUs or Gatling guns."

"A flight of Blackhawks would also be nice."

"Damn, what about a battleship? Or a carrier? I think you guys have imagined about everything else." The speaker was a new recruit, fresh over from basic training.

"Yeah, Joe's right. Give me a battleship—one with wheels on it. No, make that tracks. Now that is what you call a real tank!"

The banter relieved the tension among the troops. Finally, Mark spoke. "Jamal, lift that canvas and let me know what you see on the right side of the truck. Is it as steep as the left side?"

After a quick peek the corporal answered. "No, not as steep. Not much in the way of cover either. I'm guessing if we get hit it will be from the left."

"Keep checking that every few minutes and let me know if it changes. Also, watch for any pack animals or vehicles of any kind in the distance. These guys typically drive to within a mile or so of any attack and then walk the rest of the way. So vehicles are a sure sign of problems." He stuck his head through the opened window into the cab of the truck. "Lieutenant Woodward, did anyone do a flyby to check for troops or perhaps enemy vehicles along the way?"

One of the troops opposite Sagan spoke up loudly. "Why don't our generals think of things like that?"

Another replied sarcastically. "We haven't had a real general in a long time. They're all just politicians today. We could sure use another Patton right now."

"Patton? He would never make it in West Point today. He'd get an F in political correctness class, and they'd flunk him out." There was laughter in the truck. "But if we did have him here, this war would have ended two years ago."

"I called about the fly-by after you mentioned it last night, but the captain didn't return my call."

"Perhaps you could give him another call now. The fighters could do a quick fly-by to see if any trucks are parked along any of the mountain

66

passes. If the Taliban is out there waiting for us, it would be nice to know that in advance. Also, maybe the flyboys could hit them first and soften them up a bit." Alec nodded to Mark and tried his radio. After several crackles he started his transmission. He had barely begun to speak when the first two bullets smashed the window of the truck. The driver grabbed his right shoulder and slammed on the breaks. Immediately the troops began streaming out of the rear of the truck.

"Exit left, exit left. Stay behind the truck. Take up defensive positions. Snipers, get busy." Several rounds passed through the canvas covering, but miraculously no one was hit. Mark quickly crawled under the front of the truck and surveyed the ridge to their left. He could see several enemy moving among the rocks. "Appears to be only small arms. I don't see any heavy machine guns on the hill. He turned back to the troops huddled behind the truck. "Check for enemy soldiers below the large outcropping of rock at ten o'clock. Return fire! Return fire!"

Mark crawled from under the truck and looked back at the rest of the convoy behind them. The drivers had abandoned their vehicles and were already returning fire from several large rock formations just east of the road. The troops in the last truck were moving across the road to move south of the enemy and engage them from two directions. The new recruit was huddled in a ditch along the road. Mark jumped into the ditch and grabbed the young man. "Look, dammit, those guys up there are for real. Get your rifle and start shooting back. This is no damn video game; this is for real. Start shooting. The enemy is up there." Two rounds struck the side of the ditch and sent gravel flying around them. "Shoot, dammit! Kill them before they kill us!"

Mark checked to see that most of the men from the second truck were already across the road and climbing up the side of the ridge south of the main enemy force. That is when he saw two enemy soldiers moving along the top of the ridge headed south to maintain their advantage over the American troops. They were walking in the clear, confident the distance was too great for them to be a target. Mark sprinted toward the second troop transport. "Donnie! Donnie! Get those two on the top of the ridge." A young and rather heavy soldier shaded his eyes with his left hand and studied the ridge for a brief moment. Then he fell to a prone position and aimed his rifle in that direction. He peered through a very large scope for a moment then fired once, and the first enemy dropped immediately. Within two seconds he fired again, and the second Taliban crumbled into the rocks.

"Great work, Donnie! Great shooting!" Mark watched one of the enemy climbing down a steep embankment about 70 yards away. He rested his rifle on the hood of the first supply truck and fired one shot. The man fell headfirst down the mountain. Mark watched him briefly. When the man stood again, Mark fired a second round into his chest. He fell backward and did not move. As the bullets ricocheted around the vehicles stranded on the road, Mark ran back toward the lead truck, looking for Alec. He found him curled inside the small ditch along the right side of the road. "Alec, are you hit?" Alec looked up but said nothing. "Get on that radio and call for support. Get some air support in here fast." Bullets slammed into the truck immediately in front of them and made the canvas covering dance from the impacts. A soldier to their right ran toward them then fell forward. He grabbed his chest for a moment then rolled over in a pool of blood. Several rounds whistled by Mark's head and he jumped into the ditch for cover.

Three enemy soldiers were running down the road toward the first of the trucks. Two of them had grenade launchers. Mark swung his rifle toward them and began firing without aiming. He watched the rounds kicking up dirt as they moved toward the enemy. Finally, they began hitting the location of the enemy soldiers. Several others of B Company spotted the attack and joined in the defense. One of the Taliban got off a rocket-propelled grenade. It veered off to the west and exploded fifteen yards beyond the convoy. Mark swung back toward the ditch. "Alec, get on that radio!" Alec just looked up, stunned. Mark grabbed his commander and looked at him momentarily, then he slapped Alec as hard as he could. The blow sent Alec backward into the side of the ditch. When he looked up, there was shock and anger in his eyes. "Good, now get on that radio, dammit. Get some help. Now!"

Chapter 16

August 17, 2027, 1123 hours
Afghanistan

When Alec reached for his radio, Mark climbed from the ditch and began running back toward the rear of the convoy. "Keep firing, Reynolds, keep firing!" When he got no response, he rolled the soldier over. There was a large red stain on the right side of his neck. Mark looked at him for a moment and grabbed his rifle. "Donnie, can you get to the other side of the road and provide cover fire for our guys on the hill? Set up in that ditch over there. It looks to be plenty deep for cover."

"Got it, Sarge." The young sniper grabbed his rifle and started to run across the road. He had just reached the middle of the road when he took a hit on his left thigh and fell face forward into the dust. Mark grabbed one of his men and pointed toward a large boulder on the side of the mountain. "There, see that boulder? Start shooting to the right of that. Kill that son-of-a-bitch! Give me cover while I get Donnie out of that road."

"You go out there, and you're a dead man."

"We can't leave him there; I couldn't live with that for the rest of my life. Shut up and start shooting!" As he crawled to the front of the truck he whispered to himself. "Okay, I'm going out there; You're in charge now." He breathed deeply and with a grimace he stood.

Donnie lay in the middle of the road struggling with consciousness. He could hear the bullets striking the road around him. If only he could get a clear shot at the man who had shot him. Another bullet struck six inches from his head and shook him back into reality. He was a still target in the middle of a road. It was just a matter of time. He had never known fear in battle before, but today he was petrified. He wanted to call out, but he couldn't. No sound came from his mouth as he attempted to call for help. He laid his head down and looked up at the bright sun shining into his eyes, resigned to his fate.

Suddenly the bright rays were blocked by a tall shadow. He felt two hands grab him by the shoulder and the back of his belt. He was aware that he was being dragged across the road as bullets slapped the ground around them. In a moment it was over, and he fell face first into the ditch with someone falling on top of him. "Damn, we made it!" Mark laughed aloud. "We made it!"

"Sarge?"

"Here, use this belt as a tourniquet and prop yourself against this edge of the ditch. I need your rifle taking out those troops on the mountain. You're the best shot I've got. Here's some extra ammo; make them all count."

"Keep the ammo. I load my own shells, and I've got plenty. Just help me get over to the side of this ditch."

"Most of the Taliban are north of that large outcropping up there. They're about 100 to 200 yards out."

"200 yards? Piece of cake!" Donnie peered through his scope for a few seconds and fired a shot. "One down."

Mark watched the young man for a moment. "You've lost a lot of blood, Donnie. Be careful; I'll be back for you as soon as we get this under control." Mark lifted his head for an instant and surveyed the battle. "Looks like we've taken the ridge up there. I'm going to join them and see if we can't get around behind those guys. Unlike you, I'm not much good at this distance."

Donnie fired again. "Two!"

"Be sure to check your six to nine o'clock now and then in case one of them gets through."

Donnie never looked up from his scope but gave Mark a thumbs up. "Three!" As Mark was climbing out of the ditch, Donnie called after him. "Thanks Sarge. I owe you."

Mark sprinted up the side of the hill but stopped when he saw something moving in the scrub brush above him. He ducked behind a small tree and glanced quickly to see two enemy climbing down the hill toward the back of the trucks. He waited until they were twenty yards away and simply rose and shot them both several times. As he began climbing back up the hill, he sensed movement behind him and turned to see one of the Taliban standing with a knife in his hand. There was a dark red stain in the lower part of his abdomen. Mark spun quickly and fired twice. His second shot hit the man in the middle of his chest. He fell backward but struggled back to a kneeling position. He looked up at Mark and spoke unintelligible words. Mark watched as the wounded man raised his hand to throw the knife. He barely got it above his head before collapsing into the dust.

Mark walked over and took the knife from the inert hand. He quickly checked the other enemy as well; he didn't intend on being surprised twice. The second enemy soldier was obviously dead. One of the bullets had struck him in the neck, the other in his chest. He had died quickly. Mark stuck the knife in his belt and resumed his climb up the mountain. He heard his men before he saw them. He called to them and approached carefully. "Good work, you've got the ridge. That gives us a big advantage."

"Yeah, somebody took out those two on the rock up there. Saved our ass!"

"That was Donnie; you can thank him later. Right now let's move down the ridge and catch them in a crossfire. But be careful. I just met two of them climbing down the mountain back there."

Mark surveyed his men. "There's six of us. Jamal, you and Jesse move back about fifty yards and set up a perimeter by that big rock. Make sure no one sneaks around us and tries to climb down the hill like those other two. Matt, you, Carlos, and Jason come with me. Let's give these bastards some of their own medicine. Let's sneak up behind them and do a little ambush of our own." He surveyed the ridge for a moment. "Carlos, you climb over the ridge and make sure we don't get surprised from the west. Willie, you climb down this side about twenty yards and keep an eye out for stragglers. Be careful, and keep us in sight if you can.

71

Let us know if you encounter any troops." Mark moved off toward the north along the ridge line. "Matt, you come with me." They had moved about twenty yards when a rifle fired over the west edge of the ridge. Carlos had already encountered enemy troops moving south along the west side of the ridge. Mark and Matt swung left; the Taliban were focused on Carlos and never saw the two Americans above them until it was too late. The three Americans were continuing north along the ridge when Mark heard the jets. "Oh shit! The Air Force is here already. Retreat! Retreat! The three men started back along the ridge line, but Willie had not responded. Mark pointed toward the large rock formation. "Quick, get over to that rock formation; get Jamal and Jesse and get down to the convoy as quickly as you can. I'll get Jason."

Chapter 17

August 17, 2027, 1203 hours
Afghanistan

Mark found Jason with a Taliban knife still sticking in his right shoulder. An enemy soldier was lying at Jason's feet. The man was dead, but Willie continued to shoot into his body. "Willie, it's Mark. You okay?"

"I'm alright." He looked at Mark and then fired one more round into the dead man.

"That shoulder doesn't look too good. We've got to get out of here. The Air Force is on its way. They probably have CBUs. So we've got to move." Mark pulled the knife from his friend and stuffed the wound with a wad of cloth he tore from the dead Taliban's shirt. As the two men turned and raced along the ridge they could see their team off to their left, climbing down the mountain toward the convoy. Mark looked up and watched the first jet dive toward the ground. He saw the puff of smoke and watched as the jet pulled hard to climb back toward the clouds to the west. The second jet did the same. Instinctively Mark pushed Jason over the ridge to the west. They tumbled down the steep ridge for several minutes, finally coming to rest against a large boulder about half way down the slope. Mark held his side for a moment. "Damn that hurt!" He helped Jason get up. "You okay?"

"Shoulder hurts like hell, but that was good thinking back there. I'm guessing everyone on the other side of this ridge is probably hamburger by now."

"I just hope they didn't get any of our guys." Mark looked around carefully. He saw a trail going down into the opposite valley below them to the west. He also saw several Taliban troops running down toward two old trucks parked near the small stream there. They stopped momentarily and began drinking from the stream. They were shouting excitedly. There are very few things that can excite one's adrenalin like a CBU canister bomb, and they had just witnessed one from a very close proximity. They climbed into the trucks and started driving north along a small road beside the stream. One of the F-16s swooped in from the south and flew up the valley, strafing the two vehicles. Both exploded and crashed along the small road. The plane climbed into the sky and in a moment was gone.

When the two men climbed back down to the road, they heard screams from the ditch where Donnie had been sniping at the enemy. An enemy soldier was lying dead by the side of the road; another jumped to the top of the ditch and had a sword raised above his head. Donnie was screaming with his arms shielding his head. Mark swung his rifle around and began firing. The startled terrorist never knew what hit him. Mark ran toward the ditch and continued firing at the Taliban soldier as he crumpled to the ground. With great effort Donnie climbed to the edge of the embankment and began firing his rifle wildly in all directions. His eyes were wide with fear. Mark dived to the ground and began shouting to the disoriented sniper. When the rifle was empty, Donnie screamed loudly and fell back into the ditch.

Slowly Mark crawled toward the hole. He found the young private lying face down and rolled him over quickly. He was alive. In addition to his original wound, he had a large cut on his face extending from his hairline to his chin. Most importantly, he had lost a lot of blood. Mark shouted across the road to the other troops. "Call for a chopper; Donnie's hit pretty badly. Tell them to expedite. We need them now!" Mark tore the soldier's clothing to find the original wound. It was worse than he had expected. "Damn, get the medic." Matt ran across the road shouting at the troops there. He returned quickly with a kit, but no medic. "The medic's down, too."

"How bad?"

"Arm wound; he'll make it."

Mark tore into the medical kit and began pulling items out and laying them on a shirt he had placed on the ground. "Matt, I'm going to need some help. If we don't get this hemorrhaging stopped, Donnie won't make it. Those choppers can't get here fast enough."

"Do you know what you're doing? We need a doctor."

"Well, I'm the closest thing to that we have right now. And yes, I know what I'm doing." He was already cutting into the wounded soldier's leg.

"Damn!"

"Don't faint on me, Matt. I need you, dammit."

"What do I do?"

"First hand me some of that gauze. Then give me your hand. I need you to put pressure on this blood vessel. Pinch it gently until the bleeding stops…"

Chapter 18

August 17, 2027, 1323 hours
Afghanistan

It had all happened so fast. Mark watched the chopper lift off into the sky and looked at his watch. In two hours the convoy had been attacked; men had died on both sides; and he had saved one of his men. But he also knew the next morning the sun would come up, and the two armies would again start trying to kill each other. Who knows, in twenty or thirty years there would probably be a Starbucks or McDonalds on this site, and no one would know the names of the men who died here today. Most likely they would not even care. But Mark also knew one other thing. Tomorrow when he awoke, and every day thereafter, he would know what he had done today, and he would feel no shame, only pride in doing what he had to do. In the midst of war he had found the peace he needed to save his friend and lead his men. He had lived fearlessly. He smiled to himself. Ken had been right.

For Alec, it would be a far different story.

*   *   *

The men lined up in formation. Two men sat in wheelchairs near the seats designated for dignitaries. Two men were on crutches. The others stood silently at attention while a colonel made a brief speech about the success of their mission and how many American lives had been saved by the bravery of the members of Company B. Company B received a unit citation, and its C.O, Lieutenant Woodward, received a Bronze Star for leading his men in the decisive battle to resupply the besieged marines. Two days later Donnie sat in his hospital bed and wrote a long letter outlining the actual events of the day. The following morning it was deposited with outgoing mail. Shortly thereafter the company commander took it and two others from the stack.

Later that afternoon all three were shredded.

Chapter 19

June 8, 2030
Georgetown University, Washington, D.C.

Mackenzie Selms walked across campus amid the crowds of robed graduates. The day was glorious. It was Spring in Washington, and everything was gilded for the season. She passed several cherry trees in full bloom as she walked quickly through the crowd, searching for her friends. In the distance Mark had already spotted her. He recognized her walk first. She had a certain bounce in her step, and she always seemed in a hurry. He watched her stop momentarily beside an old cherry tree and noted that the color of her dress matched the blossoms so well. His mind noted that it would be a perfect camouflage if needed. Only her auburn hair set her apart from the beautiful pink shades of her dress and the tree. He smiled to himself and wondered how long it would take to fully delete his Army training. Camouflage? Mackenzie? He raised his hand and waved. After a few moments she spotted them.

Mark grabbed three cups of punch and joined Mackenzie and Alec. Neither of the two young men could take their eyes off of the beautiful young employee from National Airlines. Alec spoke first. "I'm so glad you could join us for graduation. It was a little delayed, but it was worth the wait." He looked directly into Mackenzie's eyes. "You are absolutely beautiful today."

She blushed. "I bought this new dress just for the two of you when you returned from Afghanistan." She glanced at both men. "I was so worried today might not come. You were in that terrible war for so long. It must have been awful. But I'm proud of both of you."

Alec smiled briefly. "We were just doing our duty to our country."

Mackenzie smiled and tried to change the tenor of the conversation. "So, gentlemen, what did you two learn from your sojourn into the land of Afghanistan?" Alec suddenly turned very serious. He looked at Mark, and a message passed silently between them. "I guess there are parts of the world that simply are not worth saving. Afghanistan may well be very high on that list."

Mark nodded. "The entire country is not worth one GI's life." He smiled at Alec. "See, we do agree on some things!" The three sat in silence for several minutes. "But enough about the Army; that is the past. What are you doing now in your career, Mackenzie? I understand you are working in the same airline as your dad."

"That's right; I'm working in flight operations at the present. I spent a few months in marketing and sales, but operations is my real love."

Alec looked at his watch and raised his hand. "We've got to run. Dad has a graduation party for all of us this afternoon. It would be a shame to miss our own party!" He motioned toward the parking lot. "I still have my own parking spot as you remember." He walked to the handicapped area and opened the door of a new BMW. Mark shook his head, and Mackenzie just laughed.

Later that afternoon George Woodward raised his glass and waited until the room was silent. "I want to propose a toast. Here's to the past and how it has shaped us. Here's to the future and how we will shape it. And here's to these young people who have reached a turning point in their lives. May their past and their future merge to give them happiness and joy."

Mark raised his glass and joined the celebration. Mackenzie watched him carefully. She had seen him pour water into the empty wine glass. But she understood; Mark had never gotten over the death of his father. He blamed two things for that unfortunate experience, alcohol and himself. He was beginning to forgive an eleven-year-old's efforts to thwart alcohol's grip on his father, but he was not yet ready to do battle with that enemy himself. She looked at Mark carefully. He had changed. He was a bit taller, but he was no longer the skinny kid from college. His shoulders were wider and he was more muscular. He also seemed quieter and more thoughtful. Combat had shown him things that change a man forever. All in all, she liked what she saw.

On the other side of the room, Alec watched Mackenzie's face. Alec had made it a priority in his life to understand other people and what they wanted. It was beginning to become obvious to him what Mackenzie wanted, and it was not something he could give her. Alec also had another intuitive moment. While he was beginning to understand her heart, he suspected she had not yet read its signals. The friendship between her and Mark was growing steadily and was already becoming something more; it was just a matter of time before the two of them recognized what Alec had already seen. He had to find a way to keep the two of them apart. It was a plan that would take some careful strategy.

Chapter 20

June 18, 2030
Echo Lake, Squaw Pass, west of Denver

It was a cold day for June, the kind of day locals tell stories about around evening fires with a glass of sangria in hand. Light snow was still on the ground above seven thousand feet from a spring storm that had passed through three days earlier, and the wind blowing up the mountain carried the few remaining flakes in a horizontal path. Ken Wilson spied his son sitting on the far side of the lake and started in that direction. He was cold, but mostly he was tired. It seemed his energy just couldn't keep up with the changing seasons as it had in the past. He pulled up the collars of his heavy coat and began the walk around the dark lake. The snow made the effort more difficult, but soon he saw Mark wave, and his spirits buoyed him onward. He looked up into the few flakes of snow still falling and muttered to himself — "Today I am Your compassion."

As the two men sat on an old picnic table that surveyed the beautiful landscape, the silence soon became awkward. Mark had been staring out at the beautiful lake and the old log lodge that lay several hundred yards south of their location. The dark evergreen trees were partially covered with a light blanket of snow and rocked slowly back and forth in the wind. He turned to Ken and smiled. "Damn it's cold! I'd forgotten the late snow storms Colorado experiences. Hopefully this is the last one of the season. There's flowers all over Denver, and here we are sitting in snow. Are you warm enough?"

"I'm fine," Wilson lied.

"Me, too." Mark smiled at his father. "I know you've been worried about me, but really, I'm okay." He looked at the older man. "That's why you're here, right? A father's talk with his son recently returned from the war?" Mark was smiling broadly. "Really, I'm okay."

Wilson looked up at the mountains above them and returned the smile. "Of course you are. I'm just being a dad, that's all." Wilson slid off the table and stamped his feet to fend off the cold. "I've never been to war, son. Well, not the kind of war you were in. Sometimes war changes men. Sometimes it damages something inside their minds and their hearts. Sometimes there's a lot of healing to be done."

"You're right. That's what I was doing yesterday. I was visiting a friend who is having some problems after coming home. In fact, that's what I'm doing up here, trying to think how to help him with the demons he's fighting."

"Is he drinking?"

"A lot."

"Well, you know where to start." The two men started walking back toward their cars as a few rays of sun broke through the dark clouds. Ken paused a moment to look Mark directly in the face. "Then you're okay, really."

"Really." Mark paused and looked off at the beautiful mountains. "I'm a bit angry about the way the government handled everything, but that's about what I expected from these clowns. But other than that, I'm fine." He turned and patted his dad on the shoulder.

"Thank God for that. It seems some men don't do well when they return."

"There are also a lot of women returning with their own set of problems." Mark took his dad's arm as they walked on. "It's strange, but some folks really don't deal with combat well when they return, and others do just fine. In my case, I had a great foundation for my life, thanks to you. I guess that helped."

"What about your friend from college? Alec."

"He's okay. I think he got what he wanted out of that war."

"What do you mean, son?"

"Well, most of us were fighting for our country. I think Alec was fighting for Alec."

"I understand; I've known men like that."

"Combat has a way of bringing out the best and the worst in a person. It's where you really meet yourself, the real you. In that moment you get the true measure of the person you are. Actually, it is a good thing to know about yourself."

"And did you like the man you met there?"

"How could I not like him. He was fashioned by a master teacher." Mark took off his scarf and wrapped it around Ken's neck. He looked at him a moment and then exchanged his warm winter hat for Ken's fedora. "Same size. Still fits."

"You should know. You took the measure of the man."

"So I did. So I did."

Chapter 21

June 22, 2036
Chicago, Illinois

"Congratulations, Mr. President. We are there." Alec held a large piece of paper in his hands that contained data from all of the states and most of the precincts in the country. They were seated in a large suite in the Warwick Allerton Hotel in Chicago. The primary campaign had been grueling, but it was almost over, and it would be a resounding success. When the seated president decided not to run again for health reasons, it opened the way for Alec's plan. He had worked hard to be ready for just such an event, and his efforts had paid off. Four Democrats had entered the primary, but victory was already in sight. The vote in California was just a week away and that would finish the race.

"Now Alec, you know it is not complete until the votes are all counted." Santiago Gutierrez knew Alec was right. He would win the Democratic nomination and surely win the presidency in November. He would soon be one of the most powerful men in the world. It had been a difficult and contentious race, but he had walked through that minefield carefully and avoided every problem that could sabotage a presidential hopeful. He knew Alec was the brains behind the planning and execution of that long and arduous trek. He knew he could not have made it this far without Alec, and he also knew he could not govern without that same keen insight into politics and people that Alec possessed. "That said, are you ready to move into the White House as Chief of Staff?"

"Indeed I am. We." Alec caught himself and grinned. "You are going to change America. This is an opportunity few have ever embraced. And we are going to make the best of it." He walked over to the window in the large hotel and looked out at the city. After a moment he turned and placed a pad of paper in front of Gutierrez. Unlike Alec, Gutierrez was tall; he was also thin. His wavy black hair shone in the morning sunlight streaming into the room. Alec looked back out the window. He didn't want anyone to read his face, his thoughts. Gutierrez had been perfect, a man with large ambitions but smaller capabilities. Yet he had been easily manipulated. It had taken Alec less than a year to take a relatively new and unknown senator from obscurity to winning the nomination for the presidency. Luckily, the American people had been easy to manipulate as well. They knew even less about Gutierrez than he knew about being president. Lucky for both, Alec knew a lot about being president, and he would use his new position as presidential Chief of Staff to ensure that the nation was moving in the right direction— his direction. "This is the list of those we are inviting to the inauguration."

Gutierrez studied the list for a few minutes. "I see some names missing."

"Who?"

"Ron Kennedy isn't on the list. Neither is Bill Thurmond."

"Neither of them supported you. We're sending a message. This is a new administration; one that people should not cross."

"Not a bad idea."

"We'll let them think about it for a few months, then we'll reel them in like big fish and win them over to our side. They'll get the message." Alec knew they would have to wait for the power of the presidency, but already he could feel it. It had been a long hard battle, but he had won, and his man would be President of the United States. *His* man, the man he had selected and groomed for the race. He had written every speech; managed every strategy session; selected every advisor and every assistant. Yes, Gutierrez was *his* man; he knew that, and so did Gutierrez. He needed the politician from Illinois for his own ambitions, but the senator from Illinois needed him even more. Gutierrez needed someone who knew how to manage not only a campaign but also the nation.

Chapter 22

July 7, 2036
Washington, D.C.

Mackenzie sat straight in her chair and re-read the reports that had been placed on her desk fifteen minutes earlier. She had eight years with the airline, and her career had been successful. She had earned regular promotions far ahead of her contemporaries, and she had gained the trust of upper management as well as the workers on airport ramps around the system. She reported to the vice president in her division and was widely regarded as his most likely successor. It had required a lot of work and many long hours, and she loved it.

After a third time through the reports she placed them on the side of her desk and leaned back into the leather chair. The last two remaining competitors in the airline business were declaring bankruptcy. They would operate until the end of the following month, then close their doors. She placed a large pad in the center of her desk and drew a line down the center of the top page. On the left she wrote "Positives;" on the right she wrote "Negatives." Quickly she began writing items down the left side: increased load factor (estimate additional passengers); increased availability of fuel; increased availability of trained workers; increased freight revenue (get estimate from freight manager); available aircraft at reasonable prices (purchase best competitor planes); advertising impacts? (talk to marketing department). After several additional items, she turned to the right side: increased union pressures? additional landing fees and other costs from airports? (someone has to pay for the airport facilities); public concerns about the entire airline industry? (talk to marketing);

negative impact to the only airline manufacturer remaining in the U.S. (can we ramp up fast enough? will we need to ramp up?)

Mackenzie sat silently and thought about the last note. If there isn't enough business to maintain three airlines, why isn't there? Will the industry survive at all? The EPA had shut down all fracking in the U.S., and that had driven up airline ticket prices to the point only wealthy people could afford to fly. And with the current tax structure, there were few wealthy people remaining in the country. Mostly only government officials flew anymore. The trains were doing well. They could haul a lot more people for a lot less cost than the airlines. So, the general public had returned to trains as a way of transportation for distance trips. Fracking had been the last hope of the airline industry, and the environmentalists had finished that debate for good. If only another Saudi Arabia could be found—other than the vast untouchable reserves under the U.S. She knew her world was about to change drastically, and as usual, Mackenzie wanted to get out in front of that change as fast as she could. She walked into the office of the Vice President for Operations at National Airlines and handed him a note.

David Thomas was a large man with a long resume of athletic victories. There were large and small trophies all over his office. There were also several pictures on the walls with David and some notable figure in the athletic world standing beside him. Behind his desk was his favorite. David was shaking hands with an earlier Vice President of the United States. Around David's neck were three gold and two silver Olympic awards. "David, did you see this?" She dropped one of the reports on his desk.

He looked at it momentarily. "Nope, it's probably in my stack there." Mackenzie noted that the "In" box was much larger than the "Out" box. Both were filled. "What's it about?"

"United and Delta are calling it quits next month."

The large man sat upright immediately. "I wondered when this would happen."

"We are going to be the only show in town—no, in the country— starting end of next month."

He looked at the beautiful woman standing before him and wondered if she were always so officious. She could be a pain sometime, but she was always a welcomed interruption. "Any suggestions?" He picked up his phone and called for coffee. It was not of good quality, but it beat the tea that most Americans were drinking.

"Here's a list of thirteen experts we need to chat with immediately. There are tremendous implications for us and our airline with this announcement. We need to get out in front of this as soon as possible."

"I agree." He took the list and scanned it quickly. He reached for a very expensive fountain pen and jotted another name at the bottom. "I'm adding Holden at United. Forget Jenkins at Delta; he's probably one of the reasons they are going out of business."

Mackenzie nodded affirmatively. "Think we can get them all together for a one o'clock tomorrow afternoon?"

"Get as many as you can. And you better order dinner. I expect this will be a long meeting." As she walked out, David watched her with interest. He smiled to himself and tried to imagine how such a beautiful woman could also be so smart as well as aggressive. His own wife was a sweet and wonderful woman; she was the mother of their three sons, and he loved her dearly. Still, he did wonder now and then what it might be like to be married to such a strong woman as Mackenzie Selms. He realized some parts of that type of personality would be very difficult for many men to live with. Then again, the positives might be well worth the problems. The large man looked at his reflection in the mirror. He was nearing retirement but still had the physique of a much younger man. Though he could do little other than notice the younger women around him, he was glad that he still wanted to look. His hair might be white, but his imagination was as vivid as ever in his life. David heard steps behind him and turned to see his secretary with two cups of coffee. He took one. "Take Mackenzie's down to her office. I suspect she is going to be working late tonight."

Chapter 23

August 7, 2036
Denver, Colorado

Charles Rael and Ken Wilson were pastors of different denominations in the wide array of protestant churches, but they shared the same dedication and humble faith that set them apart from most men. Though they corresponded frequently, Ken was surprised to see his friend at his door. Charles lived in Texas, and fuel rationing made it extremely difficult to travel in America. "Charles, it's so good to see you. Come in, please." One look at Charles's face prompted the next question. "Is something wrong?" The visitor stood before his friend with a look of desperation on his face. His eyes were dark and sad. He followed Ken into the kitchen of the small house and sat down at the table adjacent to the stove. Wilson poured water into a tea pot and reached for tea bags and sugar. When he sat beside his friend, Rael raised his head to speak.

"Ken, I don't know what to do. It's Jeffery; he's having terrible headaches, and he falls frequently. He's only twenty-eight. Young men don't just fall down."

"Did he see a doctor?"

"They say he needs a specialist, but they won't schedule him for over two months."

"Two months!"

"Yes, you know how this government healthcare system works. I've wondered if my being a pastor had anything to do with it."

"I understand; we're certainly not on their list of allies. That's for sure. Charles, we don't even keep a list of church members anymore.

When the ACLU insisted that our records were open to the public due to our tax status, we burned everything."

"What is it they want? We don't have an exempt tax status anymore. The Democrats did away with that long ago."

"That was just the start. The ACLU and the federal judge in our district have far more sinister plans for us Christians. Who would have ever guessed that we would be persecuted like this in America." Wilson walked over and took the boiling pot off of the stove and poured it over the two tea bags. "Sugar?"

"I know your son studied brain surgery; do you think he could take a look at Jeffery?"

"Of course. Mark is still in residency, but his mentor is the best brain surgeon in this country. If necessary, we can ask for his help as well."

"Thanks, Ken. I know they will be taking a risk. They could get into a lot of trouble if the government finds out they have done medical work outside the government system."

Wilson smiled a very thin smile. "Right, like it's a medical system. It's just another political power grab, and everyone knows it. As long as you support the liberal agenda, you get medical care. If you don't support the regime, you are out of luck. Pretty powerful incentive to play ball by their rules." The two men sat in silence for a few moments. "You know, you are right about keeping this quiet. But we need to get Jeffrey up here as soon as possible."

"Jeff is in the car outside."

"Charles, for heaven's sake. It's hot out there. Go get him; bring him in right now."

When Jeffrey entered the room, seeing his smile was all Ken Wilson needed to realize how serious the situation really was. One side of the young man's face reacted to the sight of his friend. The other did not. He could not have walked into the room without his father's support. "Here, put him in the bedroom on the right."

"Isn't that Mark's room?"

"Don't worry about Mark. Most of his nights are spent at the hospital." Wilson looked at his watch. "He should be home in about an hour. Let me start dinner for us. I have to apologize for my cooking,

Charles. Since Marion's death I've had to do the best I can, but it still isn't great."

"Right now anything would taste good." Rael put his hand on his friend's shoulder. "We all still miss her greatly."

"Thanks Charles. God let me have her for thirty-three years. That was a great gift, but I was not ready to let her go."

"Sometimes I really don't understand God very well, but I still trust him."

After the younger Rael was settled into Mark's bed, the two older men returned to the small kitchen. "I see you drove. How did you ever get enough fuel rations for a trip like this?"

"My congregation, God bless them."

"He already blessed them, Charles; He put you in their lives." He looked back at the tired face of the man seated at his table. "You look tired and Mark will not be here for a while; go lay down on the couch in the den. I'll call you when Mark arrives or when dinner is ready." He pointed into the small room off the hallway. "Go. You're going to need your rest."

*   *   *

Mark walked out of the bedroom and sat down at the table with the two older men. He looked directly into Rael's eyes then put his hand on his arm. "We need to get Jeff in to see Dr. Williams as soon as we can. I'll talk to him tomorrow morning; we may be able to get him in tomorrow evening."

"You can get him into a hospital?"

"Not exactly. We're going to have to do this off the grid. We have a place over on West Colfax. It used to be a clinic for colonoscopies. Now Dr. Williams uses it for urgent surgeries. We're doing a major surgery tomorrow evening, but I think we can get Jeff in for analysis before that."

Ken served four plates and put three on the table. "It's not the Waldorf, but it is the best we have."

"Looks great to me, but I'll take that one to Jeffrey first."

91

"Of course."

When Rael had left, Wilson turned to his son. "How bad is it, son?"

"I'm afraid it's bad; Dr. Williams will look at him tomorrow. My preliminary assessment is a tumor in his brain. If we can get to it and it hasn't spread too far, we may have a chance. But we can't wait. I'm glad Reverend Rael brought him in." The young doctor sipped the hot tea and then reached into his pocket. "Oh yes, look what I got at the hospital today. Coffee!" He held the small plastic bag into the air.

"At least they get a good allotment of decent coffee for doctors."

"Right, so they can work us longer hours." The young man finished his dinner and looked toward the stove. "And for what, about half of what a city councilman gets?" He walked over and looked into the pots. "It's no wonder we are no longer getting the best and brightest in this profession."

"Well, they must have good hearts and want to help others."

"You're right dad, but this profession requires an IQ a little higher than one's age, and I guess I could say the same about engineers. We don't seem to be producing many engineers anymore either."

"Well, at least Jeffery will have a chance with the likes of you and Terry working with him."

"I really don't know how Dr. Williams does it. He works at the hospital for ten hours a day; then he sneaks out to the clinic for another four or five each night."

"He's saved a lot of lives, son. God will bless him for that."

"I hope so. He's a good man, a great surgeon, and the best teacher I've ever known – except you, of course."

Wilson laughed. "He's teaching you about the human brain. I simply tried to teach you about the human heart."

*   *   *

Dr. Terry Williams walked into the small sitting room and sat down. Mark joined him. Both were wearing blue scrubs; both had blood on their clothing. Williams conferred with Mark for several minutes then turned to the two men waiting expectantly for information. "We need to operate

92

immediately. I wish I could wait a week or so, but we cannot." He turned to Mark who nodded agreement. "We have an operation to perform as soon as we leave you. It should take about three hours; as soon as we finish, we'll operate on Jeff."

Rael's eyes were wide and moist. He simply nodded. Finally Ken spoke what was on both of their minds. "Terry, you have had a very long day; will you be okay to perform such an intricate operation at that late hour?"

"I certainly understand your concern, Ken. But Jeff's situation is very serious. I wish we had more time, but we don't. This should have been done weeks ago." He placed his hand on Wilson's shoulder. "Ken, old friend, I'm a doctor; I have ways to keep myself sharp in situations like this, and besides, I have the best backup a brain surgeon could ever have—your son." He rose and motioned to Mark. "Let's go. Sutton's already being prepped."

The two pastors sat silently as nurses and assistants rushed into and out of the small room. Each time they would search the cabinets for some item, smile at the two men then rush out again. Finally, Rael spoke. His voice was weak and far away. "I just feel so helpless."

"No, my friend. You are not helpless. We are the ones who have the *real* power. Will you pray with me?"

The two men bowed their heads and did what they had done so many times in their lives. Only this time it was different. This time the words were not automatic, practiced. Instead these prayers were from the depths of two spirits that had shared a lifetime rejoicing and suffering with their fellow Christians. These prayers were labored, broken, and painful. And in their sorrow and supplication, the two men raised their spirits in rejoicing faith, a faith that had carried them through life, and one that would see them through this trial, regardless of the outcome.

93

Chapter 24

August 20, 2036
Denver, Colorado

Jeffery Rael walked out into the parking lot and stopped abruptly as his eyes adjusted to the bright sunshine. The day was warm, unlike the air-conditioned building he had been in for almost two weeks. He smiled; it felt good. His father held his arm and steadied him. "You okay son?"

"Yes, it has just been awhile since I've seen so much sunlight."

"You've been through a lot, but you're healing well. Dr. Williams says you are going to be as good as new in a month or so."

"I sure hope so."

"He and Dr. Sagan saved your life. God sent them both into our lives just when we needed it most."

The pastor took his son's arm and turned toward the old car waiting for them in the parking lot. That was when he noticed the man in the dark sedan across the street taking their picture.   Mark noticed the man as well and turned his face quickly. "Get Jeff home and to bed. I'll stop by later tonight."

The man in the sedan saw that he had been noticed. He stepped on the gas to leave but found that all four of his tires were flat. He got out to check them, and three young men approached. "Hey man, ain't you Billy Ray?" They crowded around the man at the rear of his car.

"No, my name's Frank."

"Hey dude, don't screw wid me. I know you is Billy Ray Johnson. Right guys? He's the one got my sister pregnant. Ain't you him?"

"I have no idea what you're talking about. My name is not Billy Ray anything. I'm Frank Jones, and I work for the government. See, here's my ID." The frightened man reached into his pocket and withdrew the official ID card that was in his wallet.

One of the men surrounding him took the wallet and the ID card and studied it for a minute then put both in his own pocket. "I'll just keep this and check it out. If I find you been lying to me, you be in a heap of trouble. You understand?" Very suddenly one of the men nodded to the others and they turned and left, calling as they left. "Billy Ray, I know where you live now." The accent stopped immediately. "If we see you around here again, we'll most certainly come looking for you. Understand?"

Breathing heavily, Frank stood and watched them leave. He climbed back into the car to call for help but found his phone missing, along with his camera.

Chapter 25

December 17, 2036
Washington, D.C.

Mackenzie walked out to her car with a large bundle of papers in her right arm. She pulled a small rolling case containing her laptop and other papers with her left hand as she lowered her face for protection from the blowing snow. She was rearranging her load to find her keys when a voice behind her spoke. "Need help?"

She turned to see Alec's smiling face approaching across the parking lot. "Can you take these reports while I find my keys?" She watched as he approached, rather unsteadily. When he got close, it was evident he had been drinking. "Alec, are you all right?"

"I'm fine." He reached for the stack of papers and dropped half of them. "Dammit!" He stood and kicked at the wayward papers, cursing loudly.

"Don't do that; those are important." She looked at him carefully. "Have you been drinking?"

"Hell yes! Last month I got Gutierrez elected president. And you know what? I'm going to be his Chief of Staff."

"Well, that's wonderful, but step back. You're stepping on my files and they are covered with snow."

"Fuck the files. I'm going to be in the White House pretty soon. I'll get you all the files you want." He was slurring his words as he reached back to steady himself against the car.

Mackenzie pushed the intoxicated man backward with one shove. "Good, you can get me more files later. Right now I need these." She was bending to retrieve the files when he lunged and pinned her against her car.

"You need the files, but I need you." He began groping at her breasts and managed to tear her dress.

She was surprised and shoved the drunken man even harder, but he had his arms around her and resisted her efforts. "Stop Alec! What are you doing?"

"What I've wanted to do for a long time."

"Get off me!" Mackenzie freed her right arm and swung her fist at the man groping her. With a punch that would have made a boxer proud, she caught him on the left side of his face and sent him staggering back against another parked car behind them. He slipped and landed flat on his butt in the snow. The blow sobered him immediately. He rose unsteadily and leaned against the car to stabilize himself. When he looked up, his face was one of total embarrassment.

"I'm sorry, Mac. I'm really sorry. I just had too much to drink." His left hand was covering his eye.

"Are you okay?" Mackenzie had surprised herself as much as she had shocked him.

"Yeah, I'll see you later." Alec turned and stumbled off into the darkness while Mackenzie bent to pick up the remaining papers. As she got into her car, she looked carefully into the rear view mirror, then at the sore knuckles on her right hand. There was a small amount of blood, and it hurt a great deal. She quickly wiped it with her handkerchief. There was no cut on her hand, so she assumed the blood was from Alec. She sat there in silence for a couple of minutes, rubbing her hand. Then she burst into laughter. Perhaps she was setting a precedent as the first woman to reject sexual advances from someone in the White House. She might also be the first to clobber the clown who had groped her and torn her new dress. She reached for the steering wheel and the pain was even worse. Better get it checked on the way home she thought. Mark's hospital was not too far away.

*   *   *

Alec ducked his head so that the security detail would not see his swollen face. "Call me a cab and follow that black car pulling out of the parking lot. Make sure she gets home safely, but don't let her see you. And oh yes, let me know if she goes anywhere else." He tapped on the top of the car. "Go! Call me tomorrow."

*   *   *

The next morning Alec was explaining how he had stumbled into a door at his apartment when the leader of his security detail walked into the back of the room and stood silently waiting. Alec finished his story and walked quickly back to the young man in the dark suit. He took the proffered folded paper and tucked it into his pocket. "Thanks Gene." Later, alone in his office, Alec retrieved the message and scanned it quickly. 2013 hours: individual in BMW leaves parking lot of National Airlines. 2047 hours: individual arrives University Hospital. 2138 hours: individual leaves Georgetown Hospital and drives to 4155 Thornton Avenue, Northwind Apartments, Alexandria. 2400 hours: surveillance stops. Alec squinted as if he were in pain as he walked to the shredder and dropped the report into its maw. He returned to his desk and typed Mark Sagan into his address list. There at the bottom of the page he saw what he had been expecting—Georgetown Hospital. Mark was back at school to teach a class for a semester and was working at the hospital. He sat back into his chair and cradled his swollen head with both hands. He was moving into the White House offices, and he should be able to get what he wanted in his life. Damn Mark Sagan.

Chapter 26

January 16, 2037
The White House

After several dozen roses and numerous apologies from Alec, Mackenzie finally agreed to go to the Inauguration Ball at the White House. After all, it was not every day that someone got a direct invitation from the President of the United States.

She stood in front of the floor length mirror and admired the new dress she had bought. It had cost a great deal of money, but the reflection said it was well worth the cost. The chiffon dress had crystal beads embroidered into the bodice and cap sleeves with a portrait neckline. It was fitted to show off her figure and had a slight flair at the hemline. Tendrils from her auburn hair flowed over the black velvet cape as she struggled into the long black gloves. She placed a beautiful crystal clip into her hair that was pulled up on her head. A tiny bit of rouge on her cheeks finished the work of art that would cause a sensation at the dance that night. Mackenzie was a disciplined woman of action. But she was still a woman, and even she was aware of her natural beauty.

When she opened the door, it was not Alec as she had assumed; it was his driver. "Miss Selms?" The uniformed older man stepped back a moment and stared openly. "I'm Howard, Mr. Woodward's chauffer; he asked me to fetch you. He just received an urgent call and is waiting in the car."

Fetch me? Mackenzie smiled in spite of herself. She had already bewitched a man almost twice her age; it would be a fun evening. "Thank you, Howard." She took his arm and walked out into the cold evening to the limo waiting at the curb. When she got into the car Alec was having a lengthy conversation with someone on the phone. He glanced at her and held up a finger to note that he would be finished shortly. He was not. Howard was pulling up to the Walter E. Washington Convention Center when Alec finally finished his conversation. Then he turned to his date for the evening.

"Sorry, that was Senator Baxter from California. She is not terribly bright and is such a bore. I'm sorry it was very difficult to get off the phone." Then he looked at her carefully. His face lit up like a lamp. "Wow! You look beautiful. I'll be the envy of every man here tonight!"

The music was beautiful and the decorations were stunning. The entire band was dressed in white tuxedos, in stark contrast to the politicians attending the black tie affair. The decorations were all in various shades of gold. Waiters filled the room carrying silver trays of champagne and food of all types. Important people mingled with those they wanted to impress, and most wanted more than just a few minutes' conversation with Alec. It was obvious that he was the man of the moment—next to Gutierrez, of course. The President and his Chief of Staff met separately before the gala began and reviewed their plans for the evening. Each had a list in his pocket, key people who needed to be contacted and wooed. It would be a busy evening for both of them. Mackenzie sat with several wives and listened to their complaints that their husbands were never home. She was not certain if the conversations were really complaints or perhaps they were merely bragging that their husbands were so important. Politics seemed to have a way of consuming one's entire family. It was hard to avoid the stain, she concluded.

For the first fifteen minutes she was paraded through the crowd to be studied by the women and admired by the men. She and Alec danced one dance, and then he promptly deposited her at their table and whispered in her ear that he had to "work the room" for a few minutes. After an hour or so, a young captain in his Air Force dress blues walked over and asked if she would like to dance. He was tall and handsome and seemed nice, so she agreed. After several dances he escorted her back to her seat and thanked her for a fun evening. She was just ordering a drink when she saw the Captain stop and talk briefly with Alec on the other side of the room. They smiled as if long friends before Alec returned to their table. Mackenzie frowned. So the Captain was a stand-in. Perhaps there was more to the wives' conversations than she had realized.

When Alec returned, he was excited. He had brokered several political deals that were important to the new administration. Each of the key people had been studied. Everything about their background had been analyzed and listed in special dossiers. His staff had been busy for over a week on this event. He had approached it as a general might approach a major battle—well armed with every piece of information he could attain. He had come prepared, and it had worked.

It was 2:30 a.m. when Howard pulled up in front of her apartment. Alec reached over and kissed her. She savored it carefully and decided that she really felt nothing at all except tired. "Thanks for a beautiful evening, Alec. It was interesting to meet so many people we only see on TV now and then. You are certainly working with some very important people in our country right now."

"You were so beautiful tonight. Most of those important people were thoroughly intrigued by you. I received so many comments on my beautiful date." He looked at her for several moments. "Are you hungry; would you like breakfast? A drink somewhere?"

"Thanks, but no. Actually, I'm exhausted. Right now I just want some sleep." She leaned over and kissed his cheek. "We can talk more tomorrow." She was halfway out the right door before he could exit his side and race to walk her to her door.

Mackenzie hung her new dress carefully in her closet then walked into the bathroom to remove her makeup. She looked at herself in the mirror. She looked tired, but she still looked lovely. Several men and two of the women at the dance had made passes at her. She smiled; everyone except the man who had invited her. Politics; it had a way of consuming people she concluded again. It was also populated by a lot of empty people, and she had met many of them that evening. It all served to reassure her that her decision to focus on her career and remain single was the correct direction to pursue. But if the right man came along, she still had time to reassess. After all, weren't women allowed to change their minds?

Chapter 27

January 20, 2037
Denver, Colorado

Three CEOs from among the largest companies in America walked into the first floor of the high-rise office building in downtown Denver and studied the list of businesses for several minutes. Finally, they proceeded to the elevator that ran between the top five floors of the 27-story building. They got off on the top floor and turned right into a large suite of offices. The sign on the door simply read, "Dalton Enterprises." They all knew it was the headquarters of what had been one of America's most prosperous aerospace companies—a company slowly being strangled by government regulators, the environmental lobby, and their allies in the Environmental Protection Agency. An older woman sat at the reception desk and studied the men carefully. Finally, she rose, took their heavy coats, and escorted them into the office at the end of the hallway. The view was spectacular. From this height, the entire Front Range was on display, and higher mountains were clearly defined farther on the horizon. Both sets of mountains were covered with snow. As they entered the room, five others were already there, drinking coffee and chatting among themselves. They rose to greet the newcomers.

"Is Dalton here?"

"Jake should be here soon. He was delayed at a government hearing this morning."

"He was in a government hearing?" There was surprise in the well-dressed man's voice.

"He's closing his company, and the government demands he turn over his patents and engineering designs. Naturally, he refuses."

"Why do they think they have any rights to his designs and patents?"

"They say the company owes them money in back taxes, and if it closes, then the patents should be submitted to the government as partial payment for the debt. They simply keep raising taxes until the company cannot pay, then they own everything."

"He'll win that, even with our crooked justice system. No way will the government get his designs and patents. We still have some rights!"

"They will if he can't pay the fines and fees they've outlined." The room grew suddenly silent as the receptionist walked back into the room with cups and a fresh pot of coffee. After she left, the group resumed their conversation. "You know, it just doesn't make any sense. Where do they think they will ever get a new airplane if they shut down the last aircraft manufacturer in the country?"

"They will just buy them from China like everything else we need."

"But how will we pay the Chinese?"

"At first we were paying them with debt, then with inflated dollars. But when the Chinese got smart about the rate of inflation in America, they started taking assets instead. At first they took real estate, so the government just increased the taxes on real estate. Then they started buying investments, then entire companies."

"And as the debt grew higher and higher, eventually the interest rates followed, and that killed off the last of the large American companies." The men in the room looked at each other and just shook their heads.

Dalton finally arrived and took the seat at the head of the table. He waved two fingers at the receptionist and she promptly left for more coffee. No one said anything until the coffee had been served. Jake produced a bag of Danish sweets and served his friends. When everyone was settled he rose and walked to a small podium with a computer on top. He switched it on and found the slides he was looking for. "Gentlemen, we are here to discuss the sad state of affairs in this country. We all saw the inevitable results of the last election. I think we all agree that we have a major problem in America, and we need a plan to set things straight. Gutierrez will be another disaster for America—a continuation of the

103

string of failures." He surveyed the group for several moments then continued. "That is why I asked you all to come here today." He clicked a small control unit and the first slide brightened the screen behind him. "These are the major companies that have disappeared in the past three years here in the U.S." He flipped through six slides fairly quickly.

"These are not all of the lost companies, as you know; these are just the major ones I happen to be aware of. As you also are aware, my five corporations will join this list next month. Every time one of these companies dies, thousands of jobs disappear, and within a few months, thousands of new government jobs appear to take up the unemployment slack. But as we also know, government jobs depend upon work in the private sector to pay their salaries. Government is basically a consumer, not a producer. But I guess I am preaching to the choir. On TV last night it was announced that the unemployment rate was 9%. That, of course, is a lie, like so many other things the government is telling us these days. Our own estimates are that the real unemployment rate is closer to 22%, and those who do work are taking home less and less with each paycheck. The liberals are buying votes with taxpayer dollars, and the bucket of money they are pilfering is quickly running dry. I don't know if the government knows that or not, but it is most certainly true. In short, the economic train will soon leave the tracks, and the crash will be disastrous. What the hell are we going to do to save America?"

With that, Jake walked back to his seat and sat down. Those in the room looked at each other for several minutes; finally, a man at the middle of the table spoke.

"Some of us here fought for this country; we have a vested interest in its success. But that isn't going to happen with the shiftless folk we have all over the country now. The problem we face is that the public wants socialism. They aren't educated well enough to know the truth of its constant failures. It seems everyone wants somebody to take care of them, and today that somebody is the federal government."

A balding man across the table spoke up but with a quiet voice. Everyone strained to hear his words. "The problem is they voted for this failure, and we have not been able to convince them that things are headed

104

in the wrong direction. All they want is a government check every month. The liberals also own the press; how can we win against such odds?"

A man with a deep resonant voice spoke from the opposite end of the table. "We built this nation with the blood of patriots; maybe it's time to spill blood in the streets again. Frankly, I'm tired of their whining. Let's round them all up and ship them off to some communist hole where they can live with their own kind."

Ken Wilson stood slowly and the room became suddenly quiet. He obviously had their respect. He studied the room for several minutes before he spoke. "We must find a way without violence. This nation has suffered one civil war; we cannot stand another. There must be a better way."

"There is." The young man to his left stood and addressed the assembly as Ken sat. "I'm Mark, Ken's son, and I've been thinking about this for some time. I figure we are caught in a serious trap. Most of the population lacks the education to understand what they have done to our economy and they care even less what they have done to our basic values. They totally misunderstood the global economy, and they aren't smart enough to figure out what is happening, much less how to solve this problem. And, Bill is right, we are totally outnumbered. Democracy is feeding on itself. So I reckon we have two alternatives: fight to retake our country, or leave and let it collapse on its own accord. A war would be too costly in human lives; none of us wants that."

"I would be willing to fight if necessary." It was spoken from the back of the room and several voices concurred.

There was laughter in the room before Mark continued. "I figure many Americans will never accept our approach until they see just how ridiculous their own way really is. Socialism has never succeeded, never. It won't succeed here either. So, when it finally fails, most of the folks will live through a very defining time in this country, and I suspect the lessons they learn will be quite evident. Who keeps the trains running? Who builds the companies that give them jobs? Who invents the new tools that make their lives easier? Who heals them when they are sick? If we simply leave we take most of the talent, resources, and skills that keep this nation running. Just how long would it last without folks like all of you in this room? So, I propose we simply leave, peacefully, and wait until the implosion takes place. After the collapse of the total economy, I'm guessing they'd be begging us to return and repair the nation." Mark nodded to the group and then sat beside his father

A quiet murmur went through the room; small groups huddled momentarily. Finally, Dalton rose and addressed the group. "Young man, I think you may have the only solution that has a chance of working. However, I think you might possibly be giving far too much credit to the liberal wing of this country. But who knows; there is nothing like a total collapse of one's nation to make one think logically. We don't need to win them all, just enough to take back the government. I, for one, might be willing to give it a try, but I would like to take a week or so and think this through carefully. There may be some risks here we haven't realized. Why don't we all get together in small teams and discuss this proposal further, then we can get together with a slightly larger group in about three weeks."

Ken Wilson rose again. "I have everyone's contact information. I suggest we meet on the third Wednesday of February. That should give us all time to consider the recommendations made here today. I'll find a safe location and will let you know the time of the meeting. I'm guessing it will be in the evening."

Dalton rose. "Listen everyone. You were invited personally to attend this meeting. I know you all, and I trust you all. There must be no discussion of this topic with anyone other than those here today. Do I make myself clear—no one is to know about this. It must be kept in utmost secrecy." He looked into the eyes of each man present. "Is everyone clear about that?" Everyone nodded in unison. "Then our meeting is adjourned. I'll see you all on the eighteenth."

Dalton put his hand on Wilson's arm as the others rose and left. When they were alone he sat back into his chair and motioned for Ken to do the same. "Ken, I'd like to ask you to take the lead in the western region. I don't know a better man for the job, and it will need strong leadership."

The pastor was surprised. "Me? I think you are the man to lead this endeavor. Everyone in this room respects you, Jake. You're the right person for this task."

"Thanks Ken, but I'm going to be taking the national view. Last week the various leaders of our Patriot group asked me to take the overall lead. We have groups spread across America, in every state. Somehow we must coordinate that diverse group and keep everyone in concert with our plans."

"That sounds like a very important, and also a very difficult, job."

"It is, and I'm also the person in the crosshairs of the government bureaucrats right now. They've bugged my home; they follow my every move. I had to have this room electronically swept before we could meet today. We found three surveillance devices just this morning. I'm being watched. But I can handle the Feds as long as I have strong leaders like you running the various regions. You know everyone here respects you. They'll work with you, and they'll know I'm behind you. It's the perfect plan. Who would suspect the pastor of a small church in Colorado to be one of the leaders in our movement."

"Suppose we decided to follow Mark's plan. What could the government do to stop us? We aren't rebelling or fighting them. We would simply be leaving."

Mark looked at the two and injected himself into the conversation. "They could very well try to stop us."

Ken looked at this son. "How?"

"They could take our resources, close air routes, or close shipping lanes…"

Dalton looked at the two men before him and held up his hand. "They could simply take away your passports. This has to be kept secret. It also means if we decide on this plan we have to leave rather quickly. When we start crossing borders, it won't take too long for someone to realize what we are doing. They might even be bright enough to know what that would mean to the country if we all continued to leave together. What is the old saying about the inmates running the asylum?"

Ken walked to the coffee tray and refilled his cup. "I had not thought of that." He savored the strong drink. "Where did you get this great coffee?"

Dalton refreshed his own cup. "There are things I'm willing to do, but drink tea is not one of them. I still have my connections for good coffee." He sipped his drink and continued. "Most liberals couldn't think themselves out of a mousetrap, but they do have some sharp minds as well." Dalton smiled. "Well a few misguided, bright people; a few."

"Do you really think they'd try to stop us?"

"I'm not sure, but I'm also not sure I want to know the answer to that question."

"Jake, I'll give this a go, but I'm going to need your help and guidance along the way."

"Thanks, Ken. We'll make this work, but it won't be easy. The main things now are planning and secrecy. And you'll also need this." He handed the pastor an envelope filled with money.

"I don't need that. Jake, but thanks."

"Oh yes, you will. What we are about to do will not be cheap, whichever approach we choose. And I'd rather give it to you than the government." The aerospace executive smiled at his friend. "I took this money secretly out of my company over the past three years. I gave a similar envelope to each of the leaders of our group. It really isn't for them, however, it is for our grandchildren and every other child who can grow up free somewhere else. I like to think of it as an investment."

Ken's smile vanished quickly. "Do you trust all of the men here today?"

"With my life, but I won't know everyone they will invite to the next session. We'd better have someone checking all names in advance." He looked over at Mark. "Good work, Mark. That was a great idea you had. We'll give it serious consideration."

"What other choice do we have?"

"None that I like thus far, that's for sure." Dalton walked to the window and looked at the mountains. "Damn I've loved this office and this view. I sure hate closing it down."

"You spent a lot of your life building this company, Jake. It's understandable that you regret losing it."

"I'm not losing it, Ken. The government is taking it away from me. Three years ago they started telling me how I could run it, and now they are closing it. It's hard to believe people could be so dumb. They are literally killing this nation bit by bit, and they really don't see it."

"Maybe they don't understand."

"No one could be that dumb!" He turned back to the window. "Except this current government."

Chapter 28

February 4, 2037
Denver, Colorado

West Colfax avenue was mostly dark with only a few cars on the street. It ran east and west through Denver and was named for Vice President Schuyler Colfax who served under President Ulysses Grant from 1869 to 1873. He is known for being only one of two men to serve as both House speaker and vice president. Unfortunately, his political career was ended by charges of corruption in the Credit Mobilier of America Scandal. Nevertheless, a short visit to Denver prompted city officials to name a major thoroughfare after the Vice President. The street, like the politician, has a mixed reputation.

Two bars remained open and several motorcycles were parked in front of each. A half block off the main thoroughfare there was activity in a small industrial building that had several lights on late into the evening. The small tan building was old, and the cheap paint was faded and peeling off the metal siding. Inside, however, was a small and very modern lab and an operating room. A dark van pulled to a stop at the corner of Colfax and Reed avenues, and the lights were immediately extinguished. The driver surveyed the area carefully then walked to the back of the vehicle and opened the two large doors. Six heavily armed FBI agents jumped to the ground and began sprinting toward the tan building. They stopped twenty yards away and squatted behind a four-foot-high concrete wall. The leader of the group spoke quietly to the men then signaled for them to proceed.

Inside the building three men and two women were busily sorting various bottles of liquid and powder onto two of the five large tables in the center of the building. In the background a country and western radio station blared a favorite tune. When the door crashed into the room, everyone stopped and stared at the armed men rushing in with assault weapons and pistols at the ready. "Hands up! Nobody move! FBI!"

One of the workers turned to the leader of the assault and demanded to know what was going on. That earned him a blow to the side of his head that sent him to the floor. A large agent walked over and put his foot on the man's neck while he pointed his weapon at the man's head. "You're under arrest."

"What for? We've done nothing wrong?"

"Making drugs is illegal."

"But these are real drugs. This isn't a pot house."

"If it were a pot house we wouldn't even be here. Pot is legal."

"We're making drugs for doctors—medical drugs."

"You got a government permit to do that?" There was silence from the man on the floor. "I thought so. No one makes drugs without the government's permission. Only the government can produce or distribute drugs. That's the law."

*   *   *

As the handcuffed workers were being taken out of the building, two of the agents brought large boxes and began collecting all of the forms, files, and written material they could find. Computers and hard drives were removed as well. Finally, pictures were taken of all of the pills and bottles of liquid, and then they were thrown on the floor and doused in gasoline.

As he left, one of the agents threw a match into the room. As the van drove off, the entire building erupted in flames.

111

Chapter 29

February 5, 2037
Denver, Colorado

Mark ran through the door and slammed it behind him. He was as angry as Ken had ever seen him. "Mark, what's wrong?"

"Terry Williams got indicted today for practicing medicine in something other than a government facility. He'll most likely lose his medical license, and he may even go to jail."

Ken took his son by the arm and walked him into the kitchen. He immediately put a pot of water on the stove and produced two cups for tea. "When did all this happen, son?"

"Terry walked out of a surgery this morning about ten o'clock and there were several government agents waiting for him. They raided the clinic on West Colfax last night and shut it down for good. Can you imagine; they took Terry Williams into custody and handcuffed him? Terry Williams!" Mark's voice was getting louder and louder. The pastor put his hand on his son's shoulder and calmed him somewhat. A slight smile crossed Mark's face as he continued. "But guess who Terry is scheduled to operate on tomorrow morning at the government hospital? Walter Jenkins! The senator from California has a tumor and needs an operation. That may make those dolts think twice!"

Ken looked at his son for several minutes while Mark calmed down. Finally he spoke in a very quiet voice. "What about you, Mark? Are you involved. Do they know you helped Terry?"

"Terry told them he did it alone. They had pictures of me leaving the clinic, but he told them I was simply bringing him some files he needed. Thus far they've said nothing to me at all. I think they just want to make an example of him."

"That will be one expensive example, especially for Jenkins." Ken poured the tea and stared out the window for several minutes. "Jenkins may well be the key to getting Terry out of this mess, but somehow I don't think the government is going to budge. If they want an example, it appears Terry is it."

"Suppose we do get him freed. So what? Does he then just do what the government folks tell him to do? Do we hide that talent from those who need him?"

"I have a feeling we will have a great place for Terry to practice medicine very soon. Very soon, indeed. We'll just put him in one of the first waves to leave."

Chapter 30

February 18, 2037
Denver Federal Center, west of the City

The two men stood in the cold evening mist and checked their watches. John Evans looked nervously at the government agent he had been directed to brief. "The meeting starts at eight up at Heritage Square, the old abandoned amusement park near Morrison. It should last about two hours, but you should approach about nine o'clock. That will give them time to discuss enough of their plans to incriminate themselves." He looked around to be sure they were not within hearing distance from the various agents packing equipment into a small bus. "If I can, I'll leave before nine. If I can't, take me along as well."

"How many men do you think will be attending this meeting?"

"I'm guessing about thirty, the higher ranking leaders of the group."

"I'll have ten agents with me. We can get most of them. If there are more than thirty, we might miss a few, but that will be okay, we can sweep them up later."

"How will you know who was there if they scatter?"

"Well, I'll have you in custody—for show, of course. And I'll also have the ones we capture tonight."

"They might not cooperate."

"They'll cooperate; trust me, they will cooperate after I have them a few hours." He smiled a devious smile. It made Evans uncomfortable.

Across the small parking lot was a large parking structure that was mostly empty this time of night. Only one car was parked on the second floor, and a rather large man was standing in the shadows of a support column on the third floor. It was dark, and he stayed out of sight. In his hand was a small boom microphone that was capturing the conversation between the agent and the spy. When he had heard enough, he placed the mike into a small briefcase and began walking down the concrete stairs toward his car. Several agents continued loading the bus across the way until their leader called them back into the FBI briefing room located at the Federal Center just west of Denver.

When all of the agents had entered the building, the large man from the parking structure walked quickly across the smaller parking area and stood beside the bus for several minutes, surveying the area carefully. Finally, he lay in the snow beside the vehicle and slid under. When he emerged after several minutes, he stood again and surveyed the area carefully. Assured he was alone, he smoothed the snow with his foot and walked back across the driveway toward the parking structure. A few moments later his car proceeded down the ramp and out into the street. He raised a fake badge for the gate guard and turned north on Kipling Boulevard and then west toward the mountains.

*   *   *

Traffic was fairly heavy on I-70 as the highway began its climb into the mountains west of Denver. The cold mist was changing to snow, and visibility was limited. John Evans already was pulling into the Heritage Square parking area when the bus loaded with government agents climbed the ramp from Kipling and suddenly exploded in a giant fireball as it was just turning into traffic on I-70. By then Evans was greeting his "friends" in the meeting. Several rushed calls had been made to him, but he never received them because the old cellular sites west of Denver were not maintained by the new government agency responsible for telecommunications.

When the two largest telecom carriers finally declared bankruptcy in the face of ever increasing regulations and taxes, the government had taken over, much to the chagrin of the carriers' customers. Cellular service had deteriorated since, as costs increased. The companies had been forced to lay off more than 80,000 competent workers between

115

them. The new government system employed almost forty percent more workers but with far less success. The private sector had hired based on competence; the government hired based on everything else. Race, gender, and political affiliation had much more to do with job placement than whether one really understood telecommunications technology. So costs increased as service plummeted. In time, much of the old system fell into disrepair and was abandoned in all but highly populated centers.

So John Evans' phone sat silent in his coat pocket while he walked into a meeting of the very people he had plotted to betray. The government raid was his escape route, and it had just disappeared.

Chapter 31

February 18, 2037
The mountains west of the Denver

Snowflakes the size of a silver dollar were intensifying across the mountains west of the city. People on their way home from work were escaping the weather, and no one noticed the large number of cars pulling into the old Heritage Square parking lot; it was a little-used road in the foothills. What had once been a park for fun was now deserted, a victim of the continued bad economy. Despite all of the promises, the new socialism had not delivered. Those living on government handouts had not even noticed the dramatic increase in their numbers and the slow reduction in their benefits.

The man standing at the door of the old melodrama playhouse checked each person who entered. Each was known personally by most in the room. There were no strangers. They stomped their feet and shook the snow from their coats as they searched for something warm to drink. At 9:00 pm Ken Wilson walked onto the small stage and quieted the crowd. His erect posture at the podium was that of a man accustomed to speaking to groups. "Can I have everyone's attention!" Immediately everyone turned to the white-haired man on the stage. "I'm glad you came tonight. It may be terrible weather outside, but that might also be advantageous to our purpose." He scanned the room carefully and turned to the man who had allowed each to enter. "Bart, are we all okay?"

"Yes sir! I personally checked everyone."

"Fine, then we can get started."

117

"Wait!" Terry Belinsky walked forward from the back of the room. I'd like to challenge one in our midst!" He turned to face a man standing near the edge of the crowd. Looking directly at the man, he spoke in loud, clear words. "John Evans is not one of us, and I have proof." There was an audible gasp in the room as the accuser walked to the front and handed a piece of paper to the man on the stage.

"Where did you get this?"

"We have a friend in the right place." It was said without emotion. "And if that is not enough, I have more." He produced a small recorder and turned it on. It was a recording of a phone conversation. Two men could be clearly heard discussing the meeting that evening. One of the men assured the other that he would get the group's plans and pass them along tomorrow. The accused man at the edge of the meeting turned and slowly started for the door. Several men grabbed him before he could leave.

"What will we do with him?" Bart had taken control of the agent sent to spy on them.

Wilson thought for only a moment. "Nothing. Let him go."

"But he will report us all."

"What would you do, kill him? We are not like them. Most of us are Christians; we don't condone murder."

The big man smiled. "In this case I wouldn't have a problem with that!" Everyone laughed. They all knew Bart; they knew that in spite of his imposing size, he was more bark than bite.

Several in the room were shoving the accused spy, and he fell to the floor. The white-haired speaker shouted above the crowd. "I said, let him go!" He walked forward and looked directly at the young man. "John, I am very disappointed in you. I knew your father. We were in the Army together; he was a man of honor. If he were alive today, he would be ashamed of his own son." The young man climbed to his feet, looking carefully at the crowd around him. "Now go, but if you ever say one word about who was here, I will announce that you are a spy on our side and that you gave us the names of the other government spies. I know more than 20, so it would be very believable. I doubt your new

118

friends have the same values we do. They would not be so forgiving; I can assure you." He motioned toward the door. "Now go!"

Many in the room were not comfortable about letting the traitor leave, but they would follow their leader. Ken Wilson was a man known and respected by all. After Evans left, the meeting continued. Wilson suddenly looked very tired. He scanned the room and nodded to Mark, reaching the microphone in his direction. Mark talked quietly to his dad then looked out over the crowded room and spoke with authority.

"We have all agreed on several things at our last meeting; let me reiterate. First, a war to take this country back would be far too costly in human lives. America had its first and last civil war; it cannot stand another. Second, our plan is to leave and let the nation founder on its own, and trust me, it will once we all leave. The 65% who depend on the government also depend on us without even realizing it. We are the ones who feed them and pay for everything from their food to their housing. When we leave, this nation will crumble. Third, when it does, we will return and save America. They will most likely welcome us when they don't have enough food and the lights are out. When enough of them finally get smart, I expect they will be glad to have us come back and rebuild this nation. Lastly, we have agreed to do this without violence. Let me repeat, we will leave without violence. We will avoid that at every turn if we can. Only when we are in danger or our families are in danger will we strike back. Otherwise, we avoid all violence. Are we agreed?"

The overwhelming response was concurrence, but the sentiment was not without some disagreement. The dissenters wanted to take the first approach, to take the nation back by force. But they were outnumbered. Reluctantly they agreed to the plan they found less desirable; they understood that success depended on the entire group working together. Individually they would be consumed by the growing federal bureaucracy, just as their assets had been devoured. These were the ones who had been demonized by the liberal press and had lost so much to the government's insatiable greed. Their businesses, their assets, and even some of their homes had been confiscated by a burgeoning government whose appetite could not be satisfied. But when the liberals began

119

attacking their basic core values they crossed a line they did not understand.

Wilson rose and retrieved the microphone. He squinted as he peered across the dimly lit room at some of the best America had to offer. All across the country similar groups were meeting this month, and similar patriotic citizens were decrying the state of the nation. For months a silent network had been built of those who wanted more than the lies and the mediocrity they had witnessed in Washington. These were the men and women who had started companies, built industries, and found answers when others didn't even understand the questions. How long could a nation exist if most of its brainpower left?

Ken said a quick prayer to the God Who had guided his life and began outlining the plan for their departure in his mind. He knew the Patriots would have to leave quickly. If it were drawn out, the government might recognize their plan and intensify efforts to stop them. No, this would have to be like a military strategy, only without the violence. He raised his hands and the room became quiet. "Now, let us begin...."

A man in the back of the room raised his hand and spoke up. "I hear the government is working on a plan to have every citizen injected with a chip that would allow the government to know everything about you. They will know where we are, where we go, everything."

Wilson smiled. "They will give contracts to their political friends for those chips. Then they will have to spend about $30 billion in research to determine if it can even be done. Following that it will take a year or so to negotiate the contracts with China to build them." He raised his hands and laughed. "I suspect the weather will have a far greater influence on when we leave than when this government could complete a plan like they propose. We all will be gone before that day arrives. Remember, this is the same kind of government that could not even build a Web site with $800 million and three years." There was laughter in the room as the meeting continued.

*   *   *

John Evans had run from the room into the dark night, barely noticing the snow that fell around him. When he reached for his cell phone, it was missing. Perhaps he had dropped it when he fell to the floor. Never mind; he would call as soon as he reached home.

Halfway down Interstate 70, his left front tire blew, and the car veered across the median into oncoming traffic. The large semi swerved but could not avoid the speeding car.

Chapter 32

February 19, 2037
Denver, Colorado

Mark Sagan downed the strong tea and the last of his bagel. He hardly noticed either; he was intent on the article he was reading online.

"Ken, did you see this? Not only was John killed last night, but an entire busload of government agents was killed enroute to an assignment west of the city. Guess what that target was! John was leading them to us."

Wilson looked over his shoulder and frowned. "That's a shame. I suppose that explains why John was in such a hurry to get away from the meeting last night." He paused and looked into his tea for a long time. "His father and I were soldiers together. I'm glad Mike is not alive to witness his son's life or death."

"I didn't know you were a soldier." Mark's face was one of surprise.

"The Democrats got rid of the religious exemption from the draft the same time they cancelled our tax status. I was in the Army for two years as a clerk in Fort Benning, Georgia. That's where I first met Mike. We were friends until his death."

Mark held the article up before Wilson. "Did we have anything to do with this?" Mark looked straight into his father's eyes.

Ken Wilson was shocked. "What? You think we might have killed him or those agents? John was killed in an auto accident. Besides, no one left the meeting."

"What about Bart?"

"No way! Bart might be a bit of a hothead, but he wouldn't kill a flea, and how would he do it anyway?" Ken turned to pour more tea. "How do you know it wasn't an accident like the news says? There was lots of snow on the road last night." He tasted the tea and frowned. "I wish we could get some decent coffee these days; I'm getting really tired of this tea."

"If these were just accidents, a coincidence like this changes everything. I'm guessing the liberals think we are in an all-out war with them—a route we chose not to take."

"Like you said, it was a coincidence."

"I don't believe in coincidences."

"So I remember." Wilson was smiling. "Why don't you check it out; then you'll feel better. We aren't out killing the enemy! I'm convinced our side is not doing that." As the pastor spoke, he rubbed the small cross on his lapel. Mark had seen him do that so many times. It was a habit he didn't even realize. It said so much about the man Wilson was. He had been Mark's adopted father and also his best friend for a long time. He had also been his pastor. That is a difficult relationship to manage, but Wilson had done it well.

"Still wearing that cross, I see."

"That's who I am, and even though many in America laugh at us, I will wear this until the day they bury me. America was founded on Judeo-Christian values and was once a Christian nation. This country has changed so much."

"Well, we can blame ourselves for a lot of that. Many of our brethren supported the very politicians who later attacked everything we believed in, or they simply didn't vote at all."

"Well, it was done in good conscience—sometimes."

"Right, but with the same end results." Mark turned to face Wilson. "Do you remember the shock when the Catholics finally realized that the politicians they tacitly backed for years were methodically tearing down everything they stood for? They even supported one candidate for president who had repeatedly voted for partial-birth abortions in the Senate. Can you imagine that? How blind they were."

123

"Obama's administration accelerated that process, but he forgot one of the key rules of life — you don't cross the nuns. While the church hierarchy stayed out of the game or quietly backed the Democrats who supported everything from partial birth abortion to most every value the church despised, the Little Sisters became more and more incensed. That is not a group you want to tangle with."

Wilson smiled broadly as he nodded. "Nestle learned that same lesson years ago; the Democrats were not so smart."

"Really didn't make much difference did it?"

"No, not in the long run. The change was too late in coming. We Christians are now such a minority in this country that we have become a miniscule target on the liberals' radar. Hollywood and the liberal press have significant influence in this country, and they have attacked us at every chance." He frowned and the creases on his forehead deepened. "To them we are now basically irrelevant, the butt of their jokes."

Mark reached over and placed his hand on the pastor's shoulder. "Don't worry, Ken. Just remember Who's *really* in charge." Both men smiled, and Mark walked out into the clear, cold morning.

Chapter 33

February 19, 2037
Denver, Colorado

Mark cursed as he waited outside his father's house. It was dark, and the snow had returned. He was cold, and he was also hungry. "Dad, it's Mark!"

The door opened and a smiling face ushered the snow-covered man into a warm room. "You look frozen. How about some tea? And where are your keys?"

"There were some government folks in the hospital tonight, so I sneaked out in my scrubs. I'm not sure why they were there, but I didn't want to take any chances. How about a sandwich? I'm starving, and anything hot would be great."

Wilson ushered his son into the den where a blazing fire warmed the room. "I'll see what I can find."

"Oh, don't tell me I've got to eat your cooking! Maybe I'm not so hungry after all."

"How about a peanut butter sandwich? It's a specialty of mine!"

Mark smiled. "That sounds great." He was still warming himself by the fire when Ken returned with a cup of tea and the sandwich.

"I figure you checked John's car. What did you find?"

"It was not an accident. It was a small explosive that would take out the left front tire and cause the car to veer across the median into oncoming traffic. Someone had to be following him to know just when to detonate it, so it couldn't have been anyone at the meeting."

"I see." Wilson shook his head. "Any word on the bus with the agents."

"No way I could even get close to it at this time. Those were federal agents, and I'm guessing we will never get the real story there. They have already sanitized the entire area where the explosion occurred. Do you have any contacts who could let us know what happened?"

"I've already made some calls. It was not an accident. It was a very well-made bomb that was most likely planted while the vehicle was in their own garage. I'm told they are quite angry right now. I also understand they are blaming us."

"I was afraid of that." Mark finished his sandwich and took a sip of the hot tea. "Let's go over everything that happened last night."

"Sure, Mark." Slowly and very deliberately the two men reviewed every detail.

"So it appears that no one else knew about John until it was announced?"

"I don't think so. Belinsky reported it and said he had just received the note and the recording."

"He didn't have time to alert you before the meeting?"

Ken stared into the fire for several minutes. "After the meeting he told me that a friend in the government had passed him this information just before he left for the meeting. Seems the "friend" was sympathetic to our cause."

"I'm going to need to talk to Belinsky's friend. Whoever placed that bomb knew exactly what he was doing. Furthermore, he knew ahead of time. Belinsky's friend is the only one who knew about the meeting in sufficient time to prepare a bomb. Or maybe he told someone else."

"I'll talk to Belinsky to arrange a meeting. I'll call him tomorrow."

Mark rubbed his forehead in thought. "No, wait. Let's not do that right now. Someone is aiding our efforts, and I don't want them to know we are aware yet."

"Who could it be?"

"I don't have a clue, but whoever it is seems to know his way around a bomb or two, and furthermore, he has no problem using them."

126

Mark finished his tea while studying his dad carefully. Wilson looked pale. "How are you feeling?"

"Great."

Mark knew Ken was lying. He was protecting Mark, as he had always done. "I heard the government doctors told you it would take over a month to get in for a checkup."

"That's if I would let one of their quacks touch me." Wilson laughed.

"I'll set something up with Dr. Kim; he's a great doc. I took a couple of classes from him at Georgetown. He also doesn't trust the government health program. He's been discreetly taking care of a lot of our people. I'll be glad to have him with us when we leave." Mark looked at his father for a long while. Finally, he spoke. "Do you think it will be Cuba?"

"Thus far that seems the best bet. We got word from the senior leadership last week that they were leaning that way. They've asked for a representative from our group to work on this with them." His lips curled into a slight grin. "They asked for our best, so, of course, I submitted your name."

"Me?"

"That's right. I figured they had enough lawyers and engineers in the group, so I suggested a doctor. They thought it was a great idea."

"Do you think they'll give our folks licenses to practice in Cuba? Could that be a problem?"

"I'll bet they can't wait to get the finest doctors in the world in their country. In fact, the Cuban president is having a new hospital built as we speak. He's ecstatic to have that kind of talent."

"As well he should be."

Mark stood and started for the door. "I'm leading a couple of our best doctors out Saturday morning. Of course, Terry Williams is one of them."

"That's smart. Why would he want to go through the sham of a court trial? Give him my regards. He's a good man."

"And a great surgeon. He taught me all I know; he's probably the finest brain surgeon who ever lived." Mark stopped at the door and turned back to Wilson. "Let's have dinner tomorrow night—a real dinner. I know a really good spot that is off the beaten path, and I even have a half pound of good coffee."

"Sounds good to me. And in the meantime, God bless and be safe."

"I'll let you know what we find." Mark looked at the older man for several minutes. He started to speak, but changed his mind. Finally, he walked out and disappeared into the night.

Chapter 34

April 6, 2037
The White House

Gutierrez looked at his Chief of Staff in utter amazement. "You told Jenkins his doctor was arrested and we could not help him? I'll bet he wasn't happy with that!" Both men were becoming comfortable in the oval office. It was even more impressive than either had imagined.

"Actually I was talking to his aide. Jenkins is too sick to even come to my office." Alec poured another scotch for both of them before continuing. "But you're right; he was not happy."

"Why not just give the doctor a warning? Tell him he'd better get on board? What would that hurt?"

"Your credibility. Besides, this is the opportunity we've been waiting for. Now we can show the country that we are serious about the government's healthcare program. We've had hundreds or maybe even thousands of doctors working secretly behind the system. It's about time we showed them we are serious."

"Yeah, but with a brain surgeon? We don't have many of those left do we?"

"Even more reason to stick to our guns. Now they will all know we mean what we say."

"What about Jenkins?"

"Williams is not the only brain surgeon in America right now. We may be short, but we still have a few left. We'll see that Jenkins gets priority scheduling."

"But Williams may well be the best."

"There is no best or worst in our system. All are equal. And they are equal because we say so."

"So what's to happen with Williams?"

"He'll be tried in a court of law, just like anyone else who gets indicted. If he is found guilty of providing medical care in a non-government facility, he'll go to jail like any other criminal. We also found a medical lab that most likely belongs to Williams. If we can tie that to him, he's really done."

"Isn't that a bit tough for a doctor?"

"When you were elected we told everyone you were tough on crime. Now they will know you mean what you say. You also said you would be fair to everyone. That means a doctor is treated just like anyone else. We don't play favorites—until it is to *our* advantage. You know, like with Hillary. Hillary walked, but the kid who took a picture on a submarine went to jail. Lady Justice really isn't blind after all. *We* are her eyes; *we* decide who gets prosecuted."

"But what about Jenkins? He supported me in the election. I owe him a lot."

"Don't worry, I have another doctor in mind for him. He'll try to help Jenkins, but it will be too late, and when Jenkins dies, the doctor will take the blame. It is all rather simple."

Gutierrez nodded at Alec affirmatively. Finally, he turned to leave. "Keep me advised how this is proceeding."

*   *   *

Dr. Williams smiled at his protégé as Mark met him at the Denver County Jail processing center. "Thanks Mark, I appreciate your help in this, but I have a question: How did you raise so much money? They set my bail really high."

"You have some very important friends out there."

"Anonymous, I assume." He was smiling.

"Of course." Mark was smiling as well. "Friends and colleagues as well."

130

The two men walked out to a car waiting at the curb. "I assume I'm going to need a good lawyer. I hope we have one or two of them on our side."

"We have something even better. We have a permanent "Get out of Jail" card. You're not going to need a lawyer with *this* plan."

Chapter 35

May 6, 2037
Big Bend National Park, Texas/Mexico border

The sun was climbing slowly on the horizon as the two men waded into the muddy water of the Rio Grande River. They were not young and were unaccustomed to the physical exertion required to cross without the benefit of bridge or boat. The slight wind played among the sparse pinons along the river bank; the water was warm and inviting. The dark shadows of night were quickly disappearing as morning stretched across the landscape. They were laughing and joking when they heard the shot. In the time it took their minds to register the sound, the bullet had smashed one man's skull and had splattered them both with blood and brain matter. The shock was overwhelming. George Appleton froze, refusing to acknowledge what had just happened to his friend. His mind said that it simply could not be true. Terry Williams could not be dead. It was not possible. He wiped his cheek and looked at the blood on his hand in disbelief. Then the shocking reality took control of his mind.

Instinctively Appleton reached and pulled his friend from sinking, only to see that the left side of his face and head were missing. He gasped as the ugly realization battered its way into his brain: Terry had been shot, and he was probably next. In terror and panic he released the body and struggled in the water, trying to reach the relative safety of the river bank behind him. He thrashed, crying and cursing, toward the shore. Appleton was overweight and out of shape, but fear and adrenalin forced his body to respond as his legs and arms flailed at the water in his attempt to escape.

High above the two men in the water, Mark Sagan stood watching as daylight crept across the river below. The evening breezes were dissipating, and the morning sun was beginning to heat the earth. But he didn't smell the scent of pinon or see the small cactus blossoms beneath his feet. He was waiting for his two friends and cursing; they were late. They should have made the crossing under cover of darkness. The sound of the shot surprised him, and like Appleton, he froze in disbelief, though only for a moment.

The sound came from just below his perch on the top of the bluff. He leaned forward and spotted two Border Patrol agents just below him. One was holding a rifle and was aiming in the direction of the man struggling toward the river bank. Without thought Mark jumped in the direction of the weapon. Stumbling and clawing his way down the hillside, he flung his body onto the two agents just as the shooter was preparing to fire a second shot. The unexpected assault surprised both, and the rifle fired aimlessly into the sky.

Immediately the two guards turned their attention to their attacker. Mark's training in the Army immediately returned as he took the shooter down with one blow to his neck, but the second man reacted swiftly and kicked him in his side before he could react. A quick blow from a rifle butt ended the attack. The first agent climbed slowly to his feet, looked at the limp figure on the ground and kicked him savagely. Slowly his senses were returning. "Crap! Where's my rifle?" As he spoke, he grabbed it from his colleague and stood quickly, looking back at the river. There was one body floating slowly downstream; the other man was gone. "Damn, the second one got away!" He rubbed his neck briefly. "And who the hell is this guy?"

"Probably one of them."

"He must have been up there on the ridge."

"Doesn't matter, he'll tell us all we want after a night or two in jail." The second agent stood and looked at the body in the water. "What do we do about him?"

"Our orders were to bring them in—dead or alive. I guess we fish him out. Now cuff this guy, and let's get that one before he drifts too far downstream. It'll be easier here where it's not so deep."

133

Mark was shoved painfully into the back of the pickup truck. His body ached all over, and his side felt as if he had been hit by a truck. He was using his medical training to assess his physical condition when the two guards dumped the body of one of his best friends into the truck beside him. Instantly the pain disappeared—replaced with an emotion of both rage and despair. For a moment he struggled to reach his friend, but the handcuffs made movement difficult.

"You bastards, you murdered him! You didn't have to do that!" He was screaming at the two agents.

"Shut up asshole, or I'll just shoot you, too! We can just say you were also escaping."

"Do you have any idea who this man is? Do you know who you just killed?" The raw emotion in his voice shocked the two young men.

"I don't give a shit. He was breaking the law. The border is closed. No one is to leave the U.S. without a permit."

The second agent walked to the back of the truck and looked in. He was obviously upset. Pulling a man out of the water with half his head missing was more than enough to unnerve him. He tried to sound official, but the tremor in his voice gave him away. "If you know so much. Who was he?"

Mark was almost in tears as he screamed at the two young men. "That was Terry Williams. *The* Terry Williams. You killed one of the best brain surgeons in the entire world today. Go home and figure out how you can live with that. Terry was no criminal; he spent his entire life saving others. And you killed him!"

"You're lying, right?" The second agent's face was contorted with doubt and fear. Then he screamed back. "You're lying—right?"

"He has a wife and three children. He's known around the world. He has a wall covered with pictures of people he saved and awards from several countries. And tonight he was shot and killed by two morons wearing uniforms of the United States government. How will you live with that? Or are you just so stupid that it doesn't matter?" His voice ended in a whisper, a moan of despair.

* * *

As the two agents climbed into the truck, a figure moved from behind a small scrub oak and keyed his cell phone. "Two border patrol agents showed up. They killed one of the escapees and took Sagan captive when he tried to help. Shall I rescue him? These two idiots would be easy to take."

There was silence on the line for a moment; then a voice with a heavy Russian accent spoke. "No, that might draw attention to us. Let them go." The man in the shadows listened for further instructions. He knew the man on the other end was not through, even after waiting for 30 seconds. "Next time kill the agents first! What were you thinking?"

"I did not see them until it was too late."

"Follow them. I want to know where they take him."

"Probably it will be Alpine. It's the nearest large town. I'll keep you advised."

* * *

The physical abuse from the agents and the shock of seeing his friend's body had stunned Mark, but his mind was still alert when the car in the distance suddenly pulled onto the road and began following the truck across the barren landscape. As the sun rose slowly, Mark hoisted his body as well as he could and watched as the driver tracked the truck along the dusty road. There were no other roads and few reasons for anyone to be in that particular area this time of year unless they were moving human cargo. If they were, they would not follow the border agents very far. That car, however, was obviously following the truck. The color blended well with the local environment and was difficult to see at a distance. Mark wondered if that were planned or just a coincidence.

Who could it be? He had thought he had seen the silhouette of a man behind him just before he heard the shot. He discounted the possibility of another border agent; another agent would have approached while he was being loaded into the truck. This individual obviously was trying to avoid detection; he was keeping his distance. Mark concluded that this was probably the man he had seen. He watched carefully and waited for a better view of the car or maybe even the man. After ten minutes it was obvious that the tracker understood his job well. He always remained far enough behind to avoid being noticed by the preoccupied pair arguing in the cab. Who could this man in the tan sedan be?

A bump in the road sent Sagan flying across the bed of the truck. He landed on the bloody body of his friend, and suddenly the car in the distance became unimportant.

Chapter 36

May 8, 2037
Alpine, Texas, jail

Alec Woodward walked through the dirty halls of the jail and glanced quickly as he passed the men behind the bars. Unconsciously he brushed the front of his seven-hundred-dollar suit. He didn't want to be in this place, but something from his past compelled him to come. He had to see Mark Sagan, and he had to assess his role in the Patriot cause. After all, they had been friends. He paused momentarily as he walked behind the guard. He had thought in the past tense. Mark "had been" a friend. How odd, he thought, that his subconscious had betrayed the truth in his mind.

"This is it." The old guard unlocked the door and swung it open. The sound of the rusty hinges could be heard throughout the cell block.

Alec straightened his expensive tie and stepped inside. His eyes adjusted slowly and finally focused on Mark, sitting upright on the small bunk against the far wall. "How are you?"

"Terry's dead."

"Dammit, Mark, what were you doing out there?"

"Watching your men kill one of the best brain surgeons in the world." His voice was cold, but after a moment it changed. It became an accusing shout. "Tell me, Alec, how are you going to face his family? What are you going to say to Martha or the boys?"

Alec paced the small room, not looking at his accuser. Finally, he spoke. It was a small quiet voice. "It was his own fault. He was trying to escape. He knew the law." He stopped his pacing and turned to the piercing eyes across the small room. "Why did he do that?"

"Alec, have you considered what you just said?" Mark's voice had regained its composure. It was controlled, but angry. *"He was trying to escape!"* In an instant the composure was lost again, and he was shouting at the man standing above him. "Escape? From his own country? What is this, the Berlin Wall all over again? You've failed! Do you hear me? You've lost!" He was silent for a brief moment, and the composure returned. "When you have to fence people in to keep them, it is over!"

"It is the price we all have to pay until everything settles down. The country comes first; we can't have people deciding what is best for themselves. The government will decide what is best for all—for everyone."

"What? *The price we have to pay?* Terry's life? Is that what you think this is? A price to perpetuate a failed plan, a plan that allows *you* to decide what is best?" Mark stood slowly and looked down into Alec's troubled face. "You killed him. You did it, and now you'll have to live with that."

"Me? *I* killed him?"

Mark's voice was almost a whisper as his eyes glared at the well-dressed government official before him. "Yes, Alec, you! You might as well have pulled the trigger yourself. You ordered his execution."

Neither man spoke for several minutes. Finally, Mark turned and walked to the cell door and stood looking out, talking to the man behind him. "He was a good man—no, a great man. He saved lives his entire career, and in an instant you took his. For what? For an idea that is failing. Dammit, Alec. Socialism has always failed; it always will. When you punish success and reward mediocrity you cannot succeed. Your paradigm is totally flawed, and you proved it again today." Frowning, he turned. "What have we come to? Are we any different than the old Soviet Union? Do we fence people in to control them? You lost today, Alec, and you know it. You lost! Your model is all wrong. Socialism doesn't work. It never has. When you have to shoot surgeons to prove your thesis, you are done. Do you hear? You're done!"

Mark's voice was rising. "What has happened to you?" The composure returned slowly and Mark returned to the bunk. "What have you become?"

"Dammit Mark, how was I to know Terry would try to cross the border?"

"Would it matter, really, if it were someone else? Would that make it right?"

"You know what I mean."

"All I know is that today you killed one of the truly gifted men in the world. We live in a sea of mediocrity and failure, and you killed one of the brightest we had — for your career! Damn you, Alec! Damn your career!"

"Look, I'm doing good things for this country. At last we have some semblance of equality in our society; no more "fat cats" while others work like slaves."

"Right, now we can all starve together—equally!" Mark leaned back against the wall and looked directly into Alec's pale face. "It's crumbling around you, Alec, and worst of all—you know it!"

"Guard!"

"Yes, Mr. Woodward?"

"Open this door." Alec looked back at Mark as he walked from the cell. "I thought you were my friend."

"I was, once, but I don't even know you anymore."

As the two men turned to leave, Mark walked to the barred door and spoke quietly. But it was enough to cause Alec to stop and turn, his face drawn with apprehension. "How will you face Mackenzie when she learns the truth? How will you lie to her? She'll know what you did—and she'll hate you for it."

*　　*　　*

Across from the small jail, a man sat in a dusty tan sedan and keyed his phone. "Woodward's leaving. He was inside 28 minutes."

"Was he alone?"

"Yes."

"I've been thinking; there may be a way to use this incident to expedite the exodus."

"You're right. I've been working on a plan for that already. I'll keep you advised."

"Good work my friend. I'll be in touch later."

The man pulled from the parallel parking spot and accelerated into the deserted road. He was hungry; maybe the quality of the food was better outside the larger cities. Such a shame; America had once been known for its food.

Chapter 37

Evening, May 8, 2037
Alpine, Texas

Billy Joe Dawson had never been much of a success in his short 27 years, but he had done one thing right; he had gotten a government job. The pay was not all that great, but the job was secure, and that was what mattered most in a declining economy. Too many Americans were unemployed and struggling to pay their bills, but he had learned early to save a little along the way. Now he had a steady job, a decent truck to drive (complete with government gas), and the local girls had even begun to notice him in his uniform. He hailed the pretty blond waitress and ordered two more beers, watching her figure carefully as she walked away. She was covered with dark colored tattoos, but that didn't bother Billy Joe at all. Mostly he wondered just how much of her was covered with the ink stains. He had decided to check the answer to that question as soon as he got the chance.

"Billy, do you think that guy was right?" Toby Clark was playing with his beer, drinking it very slowly. The two were sitting at the bar in an old tavern on the outskirts of Alpine. The walls, like the floor, were made of rough planks, and the smell of beer permeated the room. Above the bar and across most of the room neon lights advertised various brands of beer and whiskey. The juke box was playing country music for the working class clientele that gathered there regularly after work.

"What guy you talking about?"

"You know, the one in the truck. You know, about the guy you shot being a famous surgeon and all."

"Screw him! Who cares!" Billy Joe took the two beers, handed one to Toby and slipped the girl an extra dollar. "Keep the change!" She looked at him briefly, then smiled a silly smile and left.

"But what if he was right?"

"So what? We done our job! That's all there is to it. We done what we were told to do."

"Then you don't feel bad about it?"

"Fuck no! Why would I? I have my orders, and I do what the boss says. Besides, this came down from Washington."

Both men resumed their drinking in silence. Toby decided that Billy Joe didn't want to discuss it, so he retreated into his own mind to weigh their actions. He felt badly that the man was killed. Wounding him would have been so much better, but Billy Joe was a better shot than that. He wondered about the dead man's wife and children and hoped his own name would not be in the news report the next day. Mostly he just hoped he would not be in trouble along with Billy Joe. Jobs were so hard to find these days, and welfare payments were barely enough to feed himself, much less his wife and two kids. Toby looked at his beer and suddenly realized that he could not focus very well. The mountains on the label were moving across the bottle at a dizzying pace. Three beers didn't usually phase a young man like him, but today had been very stressful. He placed the beer on the bar and headed for the men's room in the back of the dimly lit building. He didn't want Billy Joe to see him this unsteady. He didn't want to be the butt of more of his buddy's jokes.

As Toby entered the men's room he was vaguely aware of some commotion at the bar behind him, but he was too busy throwing up to look around. When he returned to his place at the bar twenty minutes later, Billy Joe was gone. He frowned, now he would have to put up with Billy's teasing for at least a week. He put a couple of dollars on the bar and left for home, still feeling somewhat dazed.

*   *   *

Billy Joe Dawson was vaguely aware of what was happening to him, but he had absolutely no control over his environment or himself. He looked out onto a very hazy world and would have liked to rub his eyes, but he simply could not raise his own hands. He could hear a man's voice – one side of a phone conversation – but the words made no sense. Then there was laughter and the cell phone snapped shut.

He was aware he was laying on the ground, and that it was dark. There was a slight moon, just enough to allow him to see the tops of trees above him. Then he was picked up into a sitting position. He felt his right arm being moved, and something was being put into his inert hand. It was hard, and it was cold. The adrenalin rushed through his body and stimulated his mind. He wanted to scream, to fight back, but he could not. The drug had rendered him helpless. He tried to utter words, but only unintelligible sounds came from his throat. Now the gun was placed to his temple, his own hand around the handle. He tried to look into the face of the man who controlled him, but he still could not see clearly. He finally uttered one word, "No!" Then there was the explosion.

Chapter 38

May 9, 2037
Alpine, Texas, jail

The young woman stepped quickly from the rental sedan and crossed the dusty street. She was statuesque and moved with the assurance of a woman who knew success and accepted it as a natural part of the world in which she lived. She paused for a moment to assess Alpine. Unlike much of Texas, it was in a hilly area with an elevation of over four thousand feet. Surrounding peaks reached a mile into the cloudless Texas sky. With a population of just over six thousand, it still had the small town feeling; a sign on the sidewalk announced the next meeting of the Busy Bee Quilters. The sun was already blazing overhead, and it was not yet ten o'clock. The streets were deserted with only an inebriated citizen dozing in the shade of a large tree in the small park across the street from the jail. The town looked poor; it had been passed by the development that had changed so many other cities.

She looked quickly at her watch and pulled at the door leading into the sheriff's office. The woman sitting behind the reception desk might have been of the same generation, but that was all the two women had in common. Mackenzie Selms was dressed in an outfit that cost twice what the woman behind the desk earned in a month. The female deputy looked up briefly, examined the beautiful woman before her and grunted something incomprehensible.

"I'm Mackenzie Selms, and I'm here to see Mark Sagan. I understand he was taken into custody two days ago."

"That's right, he made the mistake of attacking two of our border guards."

"I'd like to see him, now!"

"Then just turn around. He's right down the hall." The deputy kept her focus on a stack of paper on the cluttered desk and refused to look back at the woman before her. Mackenzie turned slowly and saw the unshaven man collecting his valuables at a small window in the dark hallway. She said nothing but waited for Mark to look up. He smiled instantly. He stuffed his last belongings into his pockets and walked quickly toward Mackenzie. It was always the same; he felt his heartbeat increase as he watched her walk gracefully toward him. He stood tall and tried to appear composed.

Mackenzie walked toward the one thing in life she had never been able to understand. He was a tall man with broad shoulders. She noticed the hands; they were large and strong—so much like the man before her. Mackenzie had graduated first in every university program she had participated in—until she met Mark. His intellect had shocked her. She had never met such a man before. Yet, today he looked like most any man walking out of a jail cell. He was unshaven and disheveled. There was something on his shirt that appeared to be blood. Then she saw the eyes. The strong, kind eyes she had always known were different. They were more narrow; the wrinkles at the corners were deeper. But it was the intensity that alarmed her. She knew she was looking into absolute anger and rage, not the fear or embarrassment she had expected. Mark was changed, and it frightened her.

"Mackenzie, wow, it's good to see you." He walked forward and took both her hands. He leaned backward slightly to see her better. "You look beautiful."

"And, frankly, you look terrible!" She was smiling as the two turned to walk out into the welcomed sunlight.

"Thanks for posting my bail. I was beginning to think I was going to be a regular in there."

She looked up into his face, the smile gone. "I didn't post your bail. I just arrived."

He looked at her a long moment, but it was apparent that his thoughts were somewhere else. She watched his eyes. So many times before she had watched that same intensity; she knew his mind was moving very quickly, assessing and evaluating something she could not even imagine.

"I'll be right back." Mark turned and walked quickly back into the small office. Five minutes later he emerged.

"It took me a moment, but I guessed you went back to see who bailed you out."

"I thought it might have been Alec. He was here yesterday afternoon."

"He was?" She did not offer that Alec had not mentioned it to her earlier.

"It wasn't him. Must have been my lawyer. But how did he know so soon? I called no one yet." He paused, the mind working again. "The guard said whoever it was just left. Did you happen to see anyone as you arrived?"

"There was a middle-aged man in a baseball cap and slightly graying hair leaving as I pulled up. He got into a tan Nissan and pulled away to the north."

"A tan Nissan? Sounds like my lawyer." He was not convincing. She looked into his eyes; his mind was working again.

"It was in all the papers. It was so tragic. I can't believe they shot Terry."

"Neither can I." He looked off into the distance. "That's probably where my lawyer got the information, from the papers." He knew she did not believe him. "It was so senseless."

"I'm sorry you saw that. It must have been terrible."

"I just wish I could have stopped it. At least George got away."

"George? George Appleton?"

"Yes." Mark turned to ensure that no one was listening to their conversation. "George and Terry were crossing together. Their families got out before the government restrictions were put into place. They were going to join them." Mark looked down at the dirty street and shook his head. "Now I have to tell Amy. I don't know how I will do that."

She reached tentatively and touched his arm. She desperately wanted to hold him, for herself as well as his own comfort. But Mackenzie Selms remembered all too well the last time the two of them had allowed their emotions to control them. It was an evening she would never forget, and one she dreamed of on many lonely nights. "That will be difficult." She motioned toward her car and they turned to cross the street. "Seems the guard who shot Terry committed suicide last night. I guess he couldn't live with what he did."

"He did?" Mark stopped in the middle of the street and turned to look into her face. "How much do you know about all this?"

"I had one of our lawyers check out everything and brief me before I left. He was quite thorough." She handed him a folder with several sheets of paper inside. He scanned them quickly.

"Did the guard leave a note, and was it hand written or from a printer?"

"It was printed, why?" She looked at him in surprise.

"I talked to that guard. He was a dullard. He didn't commit suicide. I'll bet he hasn't touched a computer or typewriter in his entire life."

"Then you think someone murdered him?" She paused in concentration, then resumed. "Why?"

"I don't know. But I'm convinced that he felt nothing for having shot Terry. He could have cared less; I'd more likely believe he was bragging about it over a beer with his idiot friends. No, someone else cared, and enough to have him killed." As he slipped into the car, he continued. "I'll bet the press is having a field day with this—Brain surgeon killed trying to escape the country. Guard commits suicide in state of remorse."

"That's close."

"Can I borrow your cell phone; my battery is dead." He took the phone and dialed quickly. "It's Mark; I'm out. I need all the information you can get on the border guard who shot Terry." He paused to listen. "Yes, I heard. Just get me all you can as soon as possible." He was scanning the report again as he spoke. Suddenly he stopped and reread the details. "I'll be damned!" He was muttering to himself as he listened to the phone and read the report. "Wait. One more thing. See if you can

147

confirm that the guard was left handed." He listened briefly. "Yes, as soon as you can. And thanks."

Mackenzie had been watching Mark carefully. She noted the swollen lip and the blood in his hair. "Are you alright?" He placed the phone into her purse that was sitting between his legs.

"I'm fine." He winced a bit as she touched his head. "What did they do with Terry's body?"

"I think it is being sent to Baltimore, his home."

"That is not his home, not any longer. He was on his way to his new home when they shot him. This is just one more proof that they are wrong. They are wrong Mackenzie, and they are losing."

She hoped his rage would subside. She didn't want to discuss this further. She knew his passion was much greater than hers on this subject. She still held out hope that things would change in America. Mark had given up that hope long ago, but Mackenzie was willing to wait for things to improve, just like the way she ran the operations at National Airlines. She recognized the problems, but she still felt she could change the second most important thing she cared about in life, her airline. She loved his passion, and she marveled at his intellect, but sometimes it just overwhelmed her. The idea of leaving her country was one she still could not accept.

Mark withdrew the phone again. He looked at it as if trying to make a decision. Mackenzie smiled at him. "Go ahead and make your call. I know you don't have a lawyer!"

She turned sharply and pulled into a small gas station. It had one pump and two armed guards. They approached quickly, guns at the ready. Mackenzie climbed from the sedan and fished a small plastic card from her purse. "I have a quota. Here's my card." The older man took the card and walked to a small enclosed office. He swiped the card several times.

"Didn't work."

"Of course it works. It's from National Airlines." She showed her company badge.

"No ma'am, the call didn't work. We haven't been able to get online in a couple of weeks." He looked at the plastic card and then at Mackenzie's ID. "So you are the VP of operations for National?"

"That's right. I am. And I'm in a very big hurry right now."

He looked her up and down, appreciating the beautiful woman standing with her hands on her hips. Quickly he decided she probably was who she said she was. Besides, if he were wrong, little would be said or known. But if he refused the fuel and she was, indeed, who she said she was, he would be in a lot of trouble. And after all, he managed to squeeze about ten percent from every purchase, so why not. "Go right ahead Ms. Mackenzie."

"Thank you." She grabbed the pump handle before the young man standing beside her could. The less she had to do with these two, the better.

Mark frowned as he dialed again. "It's me again. Someone bailed me out, and I don't have a clue who it was. See what you can find out about my mysterious benefactor. Who was he; how did he know I was in jail; and why was he so interested? He may be middle-aged with slightly graying hair. I suspect he was driving a tan rental Nissan, so that may give us a lead as well." He hung up and replaced the phone in Mackenzie's purse.

"Do you think it could have been Alec? I guess he could have sent someone."

"Perhaps, but we didn't part on cordial terms."

She turned momentarily and looked Mark squarely in the face. "You're not blaming him for Terry's death?"

"You don't?"

"He would never do a thing like that."

"Who do you think drafted the new law authorizing the shooting of citizens attempting to leave the country without permission. Alec dreamed this up and pushed it through that group of empty suits we call Congress. Mackenzie, this is the same as East Berlin!"

"That's different. The new law is just to frighten people. Alec said so himself. Terry was his friend as well. I'm sure he feels terrible."

149

"Next time you see Alec, ask him how badly he feels about Terry and how badly he feels that his plan is embarrassing the entire administration."

"I saw him yesterday."

Mark looked at her a long time before speaking. "Really, well tell me, Mackenzie, did he seem upset about Terry's death when you saw him? He seemed more upset over the political fallout when we talked."

She said nothing and pulled onto the road. "He was not as upset as you."

"He didn't see half of Terry's head blown away." Unconsciously his hands went to his face and covered his eyes as if he could erase the vision that was clouding his mind. He sat there, struggling with various emotions. He felt total despair at the loss of his friend; he also felt the closeness of the woman he cherished and desired. His emotions, his intellect, and his heart struggled for control. They were still struggling when she parked in front of a small restaurant.

"Let's get something to eat. I'm sure you must be hungry." She watched as he visibly regained control of the demons racing through his head. She assumed they were visions of Terry floating slowly down the river. She had read the report from her analyst; she could only imagine the reality of it all.

Mark was finishing a rather large, greasy burger when Mackenzie handed him her ringing phone. "I don't recognize that number, so it must be for you—probably your lawyer." She smiled.

"This is Mark." He listened carefully and wrote notes on his napkin. "I thought so. Good work."

"Left handed?" She waited for his answer as he scribbled notes.

"Yes. And your report says he shot himself in the *right* temple— with a nine millimeter pistol. He carried a .38."

"Are you sure?"

Mark pointed to the bloody spot on the side of his head. "I'm sure. He hit me with it." He put the phone back to his ear. "I'm convinced that guard was murdered. Check our people; if anyone did this, I want to know. If someone else did this, someone outside our organization, I need to know who and why. Get back to me as soon as you have anything."

"Mark, what do you mean "our people?" She looked at him carefully as he considered his answer.

"Just a bunch of people who feel we've had enough of this government. We've had enough—no, too much—of the taxes, the control, the rules and regulations. We are watching the nation we love dying right before us, slowly choking on mediocrity and failure. We are tired of being denigrated for success; we are tired of paying for everyone else while the very things we value are being torn down around us. America has changed, and we want it the way it used to be. In 2007 60% of the population paid the nation's bills. In 2014 it was 48%. Last year 26% of us paid 97% of all taxes paid. Over 70% simply went along for the ride. And guess how they voted. I guess the Patriot group is pretty much like the old Tea Party back during the Obama days. Like us, they just had about as much as they could take."

Mark blotted the blood on his scalp with a tissue and continued. "Our economy, our government, our values, and our culture, they have all been destroyed, right along with our Constitution. They rewarded all the wrong things and destroyed achievement along the way. It's like some old politician once said. They are running out of successful people to pay the bills. So, we're leaving. As someone else quipped a long time ago, the inmates are running the asylum. When the government announced that all of us would have chips implanted into our arms, that was just too much. That kind of control and tracking was just more than we could abide. The only alternatives we had left were to fight or leave. Many wanted to fight, but reason prevailed, and we finally agreed to simply leave. I had hoped you would join me—us."

"You would just leave? Can't we change it from within?"

"I'm afraid it's too late. We lost that battle years ago when the Democrats gave all the illegals the right to vote. After that, the numbers were just stacked too heavily against us. Twenty-six percent is simply not enough. We are outvoted."

"Who is *we*?"

"Basically it is most of the twenty-six percent. The dropouts and druggies are staying; the scientists, doctors, business people — most of the brightest and best — are leaving. That's why Alec got the restrictions passed. At first the exodus was a trickle; then it became a stampede. He knows he can't run the nation without us. He needs the brains to keep things going. Yet they denigrate us at every turn. We are hated, ridiculed, and taxed of most everything we produce. We've simply had enough; the load has become too heavy, so we're leaving. It's just like what happened to England in the early 2000s. The socialists took over, and the brainpower left."

"The government is really struggling with so little fuel and resources."

"And whose fault is that? Who restricted the development of our own resources? And as far as the oil from the Middle East, who sat by and did nothing while the Iranians developed their bomb? Obama essentially gave the Iranians permission to build their bombs. Who thought we could simply talk our way out of that mess. Who thought the Iranian government would simply deal with us in an honorable fashion if we gave in to their demands?"

"But it was the Israelis who attacked the Iranian nuclear sites."

"And who told them Iran was still months away from developing the bomb? We led them straight to slaughter. Our intelligence was so poor that we didn't even know they already had two nuclear weapons."

"But who could have guessed that the Iranian government would actually use them." Her voice was suddenly very quiet as she contemplated the destruction of the entire area from Turkey to the southern border of Egypt.

"Well, the people negotiating the deal surely didn't guess that, did they? The folks who negotiated the Iranian nuclear deal were incinerated while in Tel Aviv telling everyone that everything was going to be okay. And we still did nothing." His voice was getting louder. She touched his arm to calm him.

"You're right. It was a big mistake."

"When that Israeli sub surfaced in the Mediterranean and took out every major Muslim city in the entire Middle East, everyone finally woke up. But by then it was too late. People realized that the oil was suddenly under a nuclear waste dump and unavailable for their cars. Seems all the goodwill didn't buy us very much, did it. We elected weak presidents and became a weak nation, and that made all the difference."

Mark closed his eyes for a moment. He suddenly felt very tired. "And things aren't getting any better. Our education system continues to fail most citizens, like our failed healthcare system. The energy shortage hurt us, Mackenzie, but it was the perfect storm of Social Security, federal debt repayment, and the staggering cost of universal healthcare that took America down. Our little sojourn into socialism will end the same as the old Soviet system.

"We didn't learn much there, did we?" He opened his eyes and sat straight. "So we are leaving. We are starting over, and we intend to get it right. We will encourage success, hard work, values we can believe in, a strong defense, capitalism—all those things that made America great in the first place, before truth died and political correctness took over, before the government became a nanny state and bought votes with promises and taxpayer dollars."

She waited until he had calmed himself then spoke very quietly. He had to lean forward to hear her. "Tell me Mark, what were you doing out there when Dr. Williams got shot?"

"Mostly I was getting angrier by the moment that he and George were taking so long. They were supposed to cross under cover of darkness. It's rather hard to shoot something you can't see."

"Then you were part of it, the escape?" He said nothing. "I should have known." Mackenzie finished her coffee and looked straight into his eyes. "Were you also leaving?"

"No." He understood her question and responded quickly. "Not yet. First I have to convince you to come along with me." She rose, threw several bills on the table and turned for the door. "Let's go; we have a plane to catch."

He rose to follow. "I'll take that as a "not yet" response?"

"I've got an airline to run, and you've been ordered to report to D.C. Your residency has been cut short. Seems they need a brain surgeon; they just lost the best they had."

Chapter 39

May 10, 2037
Washington, D.C.

Mackenzie heard the scream and raced from her bed to the small living room in her apartment. Mark was on the couch, his feet hanging over the short frame. He was thrashing in all directions, reliving the horror of seeing his friend shot in the river. When she touched him, he jumped up and grabbed her. For a moment he stood there, wide eyed and frightened. Slowly consciousness returned, and he hung his head. "Sorry."

"That's all right. Are you okay?"

"Yeah, I guess I was having a dream."

"Try nightmare!" She reached and touched his face. For a several moments they just stood there, looking into the others' eyes. Without a word he reached and took her in his arms. She did not resist, even when he kissed her passionately. He started to say something, but she placed her finger on his lips then kissed him back. Together they sank onto the couch and into each other's arms.

Mackenzie knew they would never be able to control the fire they were igniting, but she did not care. She recalled the last time they had crossed that line; she wanted and needed him again. Her ordered world of control melted in that moment of utter joy as she suddenly realized that she had fallen in love with this man. He touched her, and her eyes widened; then she smiled and giggled like a school girl. They rolled off the couch onto the floor in peals of laughter. Then it was quiet. Her eyes met his and told him all the things he wanted to know. Very slowly he pulled her nightgown over her head as he led her into the bedroom. The nightmare's horrors were lost in the darkness of the small room as cries of fear changed to cries of joy and passion.

The vice president of flight operations reached and turned on the small light by the bed where she and Mark were making love. She wanted to see his face; she wanted to witness his joy, and mostly she wanted him to see her joy as well. Love was far too beautiful to savor alone in darkness. She wanted to share it with him.

As the soft light filtered through the room, Mackenzie Selms looked into the eyes of the man above her and smiled. Yes, she thought, this is perfect. Then her own eyes grew very wide as a small cry escaped her lips. She never even heard it; she was lost in the ecstasy that enveloped her. But she did hear the gasp and the low moan from Mark's throat as he collapsed on top of her. She clung to him tightly and smiled into the night. Yes, this was perfect. The disordered world seemed suddenly very far away.

Chapter 40

May 13, 2037
The White House

Alec Woodward walked into the Oval Office with a mug of coffee in his hand. He liked coffee, especially that ordered for the White House. For most other Americans good coffee had become a luxury item, but the White House still had clout. It still had stature to uphold, and good coffee was one of the perks of working at the top of the nation, even a declining nation. Alec stopped and savored the hot drink. It was just as he liked it, steaming and strong.

The president looked up at his friend and smiled. He was busily scanning documents on his desk. "Hello Alec, what's up?"

"I know we're getting bad publicity from the shooting in Texas, but it was necessary. It will also set a precedent and let everyone know we are serious."

The president's smile vanished immediately. "I thought he was a friend of yours."

"I knew him when I was in school. It was regrettable, but it could not be avoided."

"I heard the guard committed suicide."

"I have my doubts. I'm having it investigated. It may have been a publicity stunt by those sneaking across the borders. It damned sure helped their cause. Every news agency in the country is on it now."

"Either way, report it as a murder. Use their tactic against them. Report it was those evading our laws who killed him in retaliation. He was simply doing his job." The president was getting excited. He was

156

not a cautious man, but he was cunning, as his enemies discovered, usually too late. "Was he married? Children?"

"No."

"Damn, that would have been even better. A TV interview of the widow would have been great."

"I've already taken steps to have it reported as a murder. We'll hang it on one of the leaders of the radicals who are leaving."

"Don't focus on the fact that they were leaving. Simply state they were violating Federal law. By the way, are you having any problems with the local police?"

"No, they are cooperating. Your call helped; then I went down and talked to the sheriff. He's on our side."

The president smiled. "What did you promise him?"

"They will probably get a couple new patrol cars and a larger quota of fuel in the next few months. Both are much needed."

"That is probably true everywhere across the land." The President rose and poured himself a cup of coffee, adding both cream and sugar. "Did you visit Sagan while you were there?" The smile was gone.

"I did. I tried to talk some sense into him, but to no avail."

"Have you considered hanging this on him—you know, the ringleader? Maybe he killed the guard."

"I thought about that, but he was in jail at the time. But don't worry, I have plans for him."

"Good, we need to collar all of the ringleaders—make an example of them. We've got to stop people from leaving." He sipped his coffee while watching his Chief of Staff. "And maybe we also need to send a message to those who have already left."

"We did. We confiscated all their properties and whatever was left in their bank accounts. We also assigned all their patents and copyrights to the government. I suspect we may hear about that in the World Court, but what the hell, the World Court is a sham anyway."

"Like an old cat with no claws—a lot of noise and not much else."

"I was thinking of something. What about threatening the Cuban government? If we can intimidate them, perhaps they might decide to be a little less hospitable. Maybe they would throw the Patriots out."

"I thought we already talked to their ambassador about all this."

"We did, and he agreed, but thus far nothing has been done."

"Give them some time. Diplomacy takes time, you know."

"If they don't do something soon, how about sending our carrier down to park off their coast for a while. That might send a message."

"Now Alec, you know I'm against violence."

"No one said we have to bomb them. Just a little intimidation; that's all."

The president paused for a few moments and considered the proposal. "That just might work. It would also look good to have a strong president making tough decisions. We could even say it was to ensure that they didn't take aggressive actions against us. We could fake a document showing how they plan to destabilize southern Florida. Something like that. It would sell to the public. Those new Cuban factories are taking a lot of our union jobs, you know."

"Great idea; I'll have it underway as soon as arrangements and planning can take place. In the meantime, maybe I'll drop a hint to a few of your friends on the Hill—just in case things go wrong—they should be in the loop."

"You mean someone to share the blame."

"Sort of." Now the Chief of Staff was smiling.

"Well, just be careful who knows. It's hard to tell who you can trust these days." The president drained his coffee and placed the cup on his desk.

"I know who to talk to. We're slowly thinning the ranks of those we can't trust. You noticed the support we got on the last budget bill." Woodward didn't bother to mention that some of the people on his hit list had actually left on their own without anyone knowing until it was too late. He was more than willing to take the kudos for their absence in the Congress.

"They are getting in line, aren't they?"

"Yes, they are. We have them; we have the press; we have the people."

158

"We are only losing the malcontents, the selfish, greedy folks who think they are better than the average citizen. Why don't we just let them go?"

Alec looked down at the presidential emblem on the large rug in the oval office. He thought about all of the men and women who had looked at that same floor, the same pictures on the wall. How many of them had struggled to change America? How many of them had just succumbed to the status-quo? World War II, Korea, Vietnam, Iraq. How many conflicts had been planned in this room? And he was sending one lone aircraft carrier out to protect America's interests, one more sign of America's growing weakness. Obama's vision of a weaker, more equal America on the world stage had come to pass, but somehow it seemed limiting right now when he needed that symbol of strength. Equality with the likes of Cuba might not be such a grand achievement after all.

Woodward finished his coffee and turned to leave. He did not want to answer the president. What had happened to the country? It had once been so strong, a leader in the world, but selfishness and greed had enslaved the nation and brought the economy to its knees. The people became weak, like the nation. They lost their will to compete, to excel. Foreign economies grew and challenged the old order while America drowned in debt. The government was the only way. It was there to protect them and lead them to a better life. They had taken over entire segments of the economy, even the healthcare system, but success was taking so long; things were not going as planned. Still, much had been accomplished. There were no longer people living in mansions while others were homeless; there were no longer people driving expensive cars while others walked. No, everyone would share, and if there were those not willing, then they would be forced.

There were those who said the plan had failed and the nation was adrift. But they were wrong; they had to be. The government was the answer, and he would find a way to prove it. But Gross Domestic Product and jobs were down and every measure of welfare was exploding. The people loved their government because it took care of them. The Nanny State had arrived; and it was welcomed by a grateful people, well at least about 60% of the people. If only he could find a way to pay for all of the

159

largess. But even with increasing tax rates, the receipts were dwindling. He must be missing something.

The president's voice brought him back to reality. "Alec, more coffee?"

"Yes, thanks, it's the only decent coffee in town."

"Nothing but the best for our hard-working government officials."

"I'll drink to that!" Alec downed the cup and began pacing the floor.

"What's up Alec? You're pacing again."

Alec stopped walking around the room and stood facing the president. "Did you see the paper today?"

"Why should I read the paper? No one else does." The president smiled at his friend. "Come on, what's bugging you?"

"There was an article that mentioned you attended church on Sunday."

"So?"

"We've discussed this before. You know a large part of our base has a strong bias against religions. We've been working on that for many years. It is a fundamental part of the Left."

"Is it that important? Really?"

"You know the Freedom from Religion crowd and other extreme liberal progressives are especially against Christianity. We've waged that battle for years and our constituency mostly backs us. Those who do are a very loud group. Those who support religion have been pretty much silenced. There may be a few eccentrics out there, but not so many anymore."

"And if I go to Mass it could hurt us?"

"It would just be difficult to explain to our base."

"What if Lydia goes with the children?"

"Not good, but worse if you go as well." Alec looked at the floor for several minutes then raised his eyes to the President's. "I thought you had left the church."

"I haven't been going often. But Lydia is strong in her faith. I mostly do it for her."

160

"Well, it might be a good idea to forego that. Just remember, some of our extremists are watching."

"Seems we have a lot of those these days."

"And they all voted for you."

Chapter 41

Mark walked into the patient's room with two nurses following closely behind. The age of the hospital was reflected in the size of the room. It was larger than its newer counterparts. The floors were worn, but the walls were freshly painted. The man in the bed was a large man in his mid-sixties. His flesh was the color of chalk; he was obviously very ill. The two men studied each other carefully for several minutes before Mark spoke.

"I'm Dr. Sagan. I've just arrived from Denver to take over Dr. Williams' practice."

"What happened to Williams? I thought he was to be my doctor."

"He's dead. Your friends in the government had him executed four days ago. You weren't advised?"

"I haven't been keeping up with the news recently. What happened to him?"

"He was being prosecuted for practicing medicine and helping people get well. He was indicted and ordered to stand trial. When he tried to leave, they shot him."   There was a long silence. "So now you've got me."

"Do I have any say in this? I don't know you."

"It looks like neither of us has a say in this, and while you don't know me, Senator, I know you very well. You are one of the socialists who are killing this nation. You're a disgrace to your office, and frankly I wouldn't give a damn about your sorry ass except for one thing."

The powerful senator looked at the young doctor in amazement. "And what is that?"

"I gave my word to one of the finest men I have ever known that I'd take care of you after he left."

"Williams?"

"Williams. He was a far better man than you will ever dream of being. He saved lives while you guys in Washington destroy everything around you."

The Senator suddenly smiled. "You don't really like me much do you? Maybe I need another doctor."

"That would certainly suit me. But that would be a mistake. There are two men who could save you right now, and one is dead."

"And I'm guessing you think you are number two."

"Actually it was Dr. Williams who decided I was the second chance for your life. Trust me, if he had not asked me, I wouldn't be here today." Mark turned to leave but stopped at the door. He looked at his new patient for several seconds then walked back to his bedside. "Did you know that Williams was developing a drug to cure cancer?"

The senator lowered his head and spoke quietly. "He was trying the new pills on me. He said he was confident but that they had never been tested. I was dying; I was willing to try anything."

The look on Mark's face was one of total surprise. "He didn't tell me you were on the pills already. Were they large red pills?"

"Yes."

"How many have you taken?"

"Three; one each day."

"And how are you feeling?"

"Better, but he told me it would take a couple of weeks to really make a difference."

"That's right, so now you need eleven more doses. How many more pills do you have?"

The senator pulled an orange bottle from beneath his pillow and poured two pills into his hand. "He told me not to talk to anyone about this."

"He was breaking every government regulation there is to try to save you." Mark rubbed his hands together and stared at the floor in thought. Finally, he spoke. "We need nine more of those pills."

"Is that a problem?"

"Last night government agents burned his lab to the ground."

"Why did they do that?"

"Think about it senator; can you imagine how it would look if the world discovered that the government executed the man who had just discovered a cure for cancer? I'm guessing the public would find that very distasteful, to say the least."

"Are you telling me that all that research was lost? My life might depend on that."

"Your life does depend on that."

Jenkins sat upright suddenly. "If Williams is dead and the pills and the plans are gone, I'm a dead man." There was fear in Jenkins eyes. He laid back in the bed and stared at the ceiling.

"No you're not. There is a way."

"How?"

Mark moved closer to the bed and stared into the older eyes for several minutes. It was obvious he was weighing something, deciding something very important. "Senator, if you want to live, I'm your only chance, so we are going to have to trust each other. I'll hold your life in my hands, and you'll hold mine in yours. For once in your life you're going to give your word and keep it. You're going to do what I tell you and keep everything we do secret. Do you think you can do that?"

"I can, Dr. Sagan. I appreciate what you are saying. I'll do everything I can to protect you from the government agents who are doing all of this. Somehow I think I can trust you; you may not totally believe me, but you can also trust me."

"I told Terry that I would take care of you just before he fled. I don't care much for you, but I loved him as a friend and a mentor. I have had few men mean as much to me as he did. I'll never forgive what the government did to him or what all of you have done to this nation. But he asked me to do this, so I will do everything I can to keep you alive. You can count on that."

As Mark walked out of the room, he heard, "Thank you."

Chapter 42

May 22, 2037
Walter Reed Hospital, Washington, D.C.

Mark rushed into the senator's room; he was clearly agitated. Jenkins sat up and watched him carefully. "What's wrong?"

"I'm worried. I was just searched by two agents before I got off the elevator."

"Why would they do that?"

"Did you tell anyone about the drugs?"

"No, Williams made me promise not to."

"I know that Terry didn't have any of the specifics written down about the drug, but he might have had some general notes. They took everything including his computer before burning the building." He looked at Jenkins carefully and began checking his stats. "You seem to be responding to the medicine. How do you feel?"

"A little better. How did the blood tests work out?"

"You're improving. You've a way to go, but you are definitely turning the corner. And you look better too."

"You didn't answer my question. Why would they search you?"

"The only thing I can figure is that they must think I'm bringing something to you. You are the only patient I see on this floor. With Terry gone, they needed someone to take over the brain work in this hospital. I guess they figured someone in Washington needs a brain now and then. So, I was the obvious choice to come here. I worked with Terry more closely than anyone else, so I have the edge in this field. But I also worked with a man who was leaving. I was also there when they killed him. One plus, one negative. I knew they would be watching me, but why only when I come to this floor to see you. Surely they don't think I'd try to kill you or something."

Jenkins looked up suddenly. "Of course. I'm the tie to Dr. Williams' new drug. If I suddenly beat cancer that would be national news. If it were found that I did it from a drug tied to the man they killed, it would be very embarrassing indeed." Jenkins turned and looked out the window for a moment. "They must have found some reference in his notes. The fools, if only they'd realized they had already won. They destroyed the lab and my only chance for life. Damn them."

The young doctor smiled and stared into the eyes of the senator. "Not so fast senator. I don't give up that easy." Mark stuck his finger inside his mouth and fished a small plastic container from beneath his tongue. He opened it and poured out a large red pill.

"Where did you get that?"

"I made it last night. Terry didn't keep his plans on paper or a flash drive. He was afraid the government would take it from him. He stored it another way. He had me memorize it." Mark suddenly looked very serious. "But you must never tell anyone that I know how to do this. Understand?"

"Of course not. You've got my word."

Mark nodded and replied in a mocking voice. "Great, now my life depends on the word of a Democrat politician. I'm a goner for sure." He handed the senator the pill as they both smiled at each other.

The next morning Mark followed a nurse into the senator's room and waited while she took his blood pressure. After she left a man in maintenance overalls walked into the room with a large tool bag. He nodded to Mark and began pulling electronic equipment from a bag. He walked around the room looking at a small instrument while Mark handed a note to the senator. It simply said. "Be quiet. Say nothing." After several minutes the man stopped and held up a finger toward Mark. He then began checking the furniture on the far side of the room. After a moment he motioned for Mark and pointed at a small piece of electronics taped under the chair. Mark gave him a thumbs up and the man repacked his bag and left. Mark pulled a small pad from his pocket and began writing. "Someone entered your room last night. They planted a bug under the chair in the corner. We will leave it there, so be careful what you say." Mark thought for a moment and began scribbling. "This is escalating; we'd better start checking everything they give you—meds, injections, etc.—just to be sure."

The senator took the pad and scribbled on it quickly. "Good idea, one of my nephews spent a couple of years in med school. I'll get him to keep an eye on things around the clock for a while."

Mark answered in kind. "Good idea; have him see me before he comes up. Write his name for me. Also tell him 'buttercup' is the password so I'll know it's him." Mark took both of the sheets they had scribbled on and tore them into small bits. He then flushed them down the toilet.

Chapter 43

May 23, 2037
Walter Reed Hospital, Washington, D.C.

Dr. Sagan felt the hand on his shoulder and turned to see the smiling face of his patient. He was surprised to see him walking the halls of the oncology ward. Mark's greeting was genuine. "Well, senator, you look chipper today."

Jenkins jerked his head toward the hall to indicate he wanted to talk alone. "Let's go down the hall." After they had walked away from the nurses' station, Jenkins continued. "You were right. A nurse came up last night with some pills. I pretended to take them and then gave them to my nephew. They were laced with enough poison to kill a horse."

Mark's eyes widened with surprise. "Damn, I really didn't think they would go that far. Did he get the nurse's name?"

"She doesn't work here. We've checked."

"We've got to get you out of here, immediately. I'll arrange discharge papers with a false doctor's name. Tell your nephew to look for a car at the main entrance at one o'clock. The driver will use "buttercup" and he'll take you to a safe place for now. Don't tell anyone that you are leaving."

Both men turned as the striking young woman walked into the room. Mackenzie smiled at the two and walked over to give Mark a kiss on his cheek. Two minutes later three FBI agents entered the room and grabbed both of Mark's arms. Mark pulled away and faced the three. "What is this all about? Get the hell out of my hospital."

"This isn't your hospital. It belongs to the government." Take him downstairs and strip search him. Check everything, and I mean everything."

"Wait a minute, I haven't done anything wrong. What are you looking for, anyway? These scrubs don't even have pockets."

The senior agent smiled. "Forget the pockets, but search everywhere else." He turned to face Mark. "And if we find any contraband drugs, you'll be playing doctor to a lot of criminals for a very long time."

Mackenzie walked forward and shoved the agent backward with enough power to cause him to trip into a chair in the corner. "Well, if you bastards are going to take him off to prison, I at least expect a last kiss." She walked over and grabbed Mark, giving him a long, passionate kiss. When she finished, she turned to the agents. "And I don't want to hear that either of you tries to kiss him like that. You guys might like other men, but he prefers women."

Jenkins called angrily to the agents. "Donnally, come over here. I know who you are, and as a U.S. Senator, I have a few rights. You release that doctor right now. He's my doctor, and I'll not see him mishandled like this."

The agent looked at Jenkins. "You may be a U.S. Senator, but my orders come from a higher authority than that."

"Just as I thought. Thanks for confirming that, agent. And one other thing. Don't assume that I don't have my own sources in this town. You may be smiling now, but I'm guessing you'll be cleaning the same prison cells you were talking about earlier. Any idea what they do with FBI agents in prison? I doubt they'll bother to kiss you in there."

"Senator, you need to watch your blood pressure, old man. You are in no condition to get so excited. Save your strength. I've been told you don't have a lot of time left." The three men took Mark and walked out of the room.

"Dammit!" Jenkins was furious. He walked over and took the bug from under the chair. He threw it on the floor and stepped on it. "They've got him."

"Why do you think that?"

170

"He has my medicine in a plastic capsule inside his mouth. They've been searching him each day before he comes up to see me, so he's been hiding it inside his mouth. They'll find it with a thorough search; someone wants him really bad—and they also want me dead."

Jenkins watched as Mackenzie eyed him mischievously. "What is so funny?"

She reached inside her own mouth and extracted a small plastic container. "Mark's clean. He gave the pill to me. He could have swallowed it if necessary, but he knows you need this if you're to survive." She unwrapped the red pill and handed it to Jenkins.

"I'll be damned."

"Perhaps, but Mark gave Terry Williams his word that he would get you through this, and he's a man of his word."

Jenkins looked at Mackenzie for several moments, then he spoke. "You're right; he *is* a man of his word. He's damned lucky as well. You love him don't you." Mackenzie smiled immediately. "Look, I may be a politician, but I'm not stupid. One does not get into the senate by being dumb. Well, most don't anyway; I will give you a few that are dumber than rocks, but that is another story for another time. So, he's one lucky young man, and you are one lucky young woman. I guess that's what you call win-win. One could say you both deserve each other. But we may have a problem yet. I wouldn't put it past them to plant some evidence if they need to. Donnally may not be the brightest bulb in the chandelier, but I suspect he thought of the possibility of planted evidence."

"I hope he did. That room where they've been searching Mark is bugged with more cameras and mikes than a Hollywood set. If they pull anything untoward, they'll be on every TV set in America tomorrow."

"You don't think the media is going to help do you? They are our minions; we liberals own them all, except Fox, of course, before we got them shut down. The mainstream media does as the Democrat machine tells them. They are little more than puppets. What was it Limbaugh called them? The "drive-by" media? Journalism died back in the 90s."

"Senator, I suspect they will be as surprised to see those videos on their networks as the people watching. Remember, the Patriots have lots of very smart people on their side."

171

Jenkins sat studying Mackenzie for several minutes before speaking. "Listen, young lady. I am going to make you a promise. Laying here thinking I was going to die very soon gave me the opportunity to think very carefully about a lot of things. I've made a lot of selfish mistakes in my life. I've done a lot I'm not proud of, but that was yesterday. Mark risked everything—including you—to save my life. I promise you today that they will never harm him.

"I'm going to beat this cancer—thanks to Mark and Dr. Williams. I owe them both my life, and I swear to you today that I will fight with all the savvy and skill I have to make sure you and Mark get the future you deserve." Jenkins looked down and continued in barely a whisper. "Williams and Mark saw something in me worth saving; by damn I'm not going to disappoint either of them." Jenkins lay back on his bed. "Now if you'll excuse me, I need some rest. These pills are making me better, but while they kill off the cancer, they kick the hell out of me as well. Oh, one last thing. I have a list of names on a sheet of paper in my wallet. It's in the drawer there. Call the top three men on that list and tell them that I need to see them as soon as they can come down for a visit. I'd like that to be at 11:00 am this morning. They don't have much time, so tell them I said to come now and to lock and load. They'll know what that means."

Chapter 44

September 3, 2037
The White House

The president was sitting on the couch in the Oval Office when Alec walked in. Alec was reading a stack of papers and almost tripped over the coffee table. "Hey, take it easy. I can't afford to lose my Chief of Staff so soon; we have a lot of work to do."

Alec picked up the spilled papers and then sat in one of the chairs across from Gutierrez. "You look happy today."

"I was just reading this article in the *Times* by Cela W." He smiled and stared at Alec. "Even I can figure out Alec and Cela. Do the guys at the *Times* know Cela is you?"

"They're pretty slow, but I had someone tip them off. They know, and I know, but we both pretend we don't. That way we all have plausible deniability."

The president picked up the newspaper and began reading aloud. "Government officials stopped numerous felons crossing the border into Mexico carrying stolen money and treasures that rightfully belong to the American people. The FBI has declared the theft to be a major crime committed against the nation and will ensure all parties are indicted and tried." Gutierrez smiled. "How many, really?"

"Three actually. It was a pharmacist and his family. They had over a hundred thousand dollars and all the wife's jewelry."

"You are incorrigible." The president was smiling broadly.

"And effective!"

"What are you studying so hard?"

"We have a situation in Detroit, and we need to react to it. I'm trying to get all the information I can before you go on TV later today."

"TV? What's up?"

"A petty heroin dealer got shot last night by a young rookie cop."

"Tell me the cop was white."

"It's not that good, but almost. He's Hispanic."

"Damn!" The president laid down the newspaper and gave Alec his full attention. "So now the drug dealer is a hero of the people. And the cop is the bad guy."

"Something like that."

"Has his family been on TV to decry the death already?"

"Just the mom. He has no dad." Alec smiled. "Well, he had a dad I suppose, but he cannot be found, or identified. You know how that works."

"Did you pull the old files from 2015? You know, Baltimore."

"Got'em. We've talked to the young woman who is the DA in Detroit. She's ready to play ball with us. Now I just need to decide which side we take."

"Obama came out against the cops didn't he?"

"Yeah, but it contributed to Hillary losing the election in 2016. They really pissed off a lot of the middle class. It might play well in a local election to go after the cops in Detroit or Baltimore, but nationwide, it's risky. When they tried that in 2016 in Seattle, all the cops resigned the day after their officers were convicted, and all hell broke loose. We don't want something like that happening again."

The president studied Alec's face. "Those must have been interesting times for politicians."

"Yes they were. Everyone thought the Republican party was doomed. What a shock they must have had. Hillary was running for president, and the Republicans kept reporting how Hillary didn't give a damn about the men lost in Bengahzi or all the secret messages on her server. The Democrats back then figured most Americans really didn't give a damn about either of those things, but they were wrong. Same with all the funds she received from abroad while Secretary of State—they thought no one would care. But when people who could barely pay their bills learned of the amounts involved, anger took over. That's when politicians also learned that outright lying to The American people was not acceptable to many voters—especially when you get caught."

"Surprise! Surprise!" The president opened his drink cabinet and evaluated the bottles there. This called for more than coffee. "Yes, but it was still close. The conservatives totally misread how easy it would be to convince the women that they were under siege. What was it they called it? The *War on Women?*" Both men laughed. "Obama was so good at exploiting every minority in the country. Divide the people, and then convince them they are under attack from other groups. Damn, he was smart." He tipped his glass toward Alec. "I see you've been studying history."

Alec nodded. "The war on women was really only one issue— abortion rights. But the fake pay differentials gave them a platform to work with." Alec stopped to make a few notes on the stack of paper in his lap. "Everybody's got rights."

"Except the babies." The president was no longer smiling.

Alec turned sharply. "Wait a minute. Are you really going to church for your wife, or are you really still secretly worshiping yourself?"

The president's smile returned. "Now Alec, you know you don't have to worry about me. We both know what it takes to get the power we've attained." When Alec did not respond, he continued. "And you know I'll do whatever is necessary to keep that power."

"You had me worried there for a moment. You know how the party feels about that. After Obama was out, we even turned on the Muslims as well. That is what our people want, and that is what we promised them. The conservatives chose Christianity, and we chose to win elections." Alec still was not smiling.

"You're right. We chose all the victims, and we promised them whatever it was they thought they deserved. Damn, I hate that word *deserve*." The president sat again on the couch and swirled his drink in the presidential crystal glass.

"And we won elections, until Trump pulled off the biggest upset in political history."

"But we were smart and we learned from all of that. Hillary was a flawed candidate and still won the popular vote. There was a message there, and we read it very clearly. We came back very quickly. We just changed the promises, and even when we could not fulfill all the promises, the "victim" message sounded good and we started winning again."

"No one said the victims were smart; but at least they are *our* victims!"

The president raised his glass. "You are right. They are our victims; we own them or at least their votes. And we also own the press, nothing will change that. As a general would say, it was a successful war, and we also won."

Alec raised his own glass as well. "Mr. President, you are so right. Nothing will change that. For decades we have owned the minority vote in America. Their unemployment rate continues to grow; food stamps are a standard means of existence; the economy continues to shrink along with their standard of living, but still they give us their support. Like the press, they are ours. Obama developed the strategy that has kept us in Washington all this time. But I do have one concern, and I think you know what it is. What do we do when the producers quit working, or perhaps just leave? They are no longer a political threat, but we do need their skills."

"Obama and Hillary never had to face this threat. There was still a Republican Party then; the producers actually thought they might be able to win some elections when things got bad enough. Their strategy worked in the past, but we have a different threat that neither of them ever envisioned. We need production to keep the people satisfied. And we are quickly running out of production. That is why I am so adamant about our new law stopping the flow of people out of the country. We've had a slight setback with the recent shootings on the border, but we must persist."

"I understand. I've been against violence on the border in the past, but I'm beginning to come around to your side. New reports indicate the flow of folks over both borders has decreased significantly since the deaths. I regret them, but I am beginning to recognize how important this

176

really is. Something is amiss in this country. There's just too many things going wrong these days. We really need more competent workers. Perhaps if we can stop the exodus for a few years we will be able to grow our own crop of capable people. Maybe we could make it a temporary move, maybe for three to five years." The president finished his drink. "You're right, those leaving are not a political threat, but they are an economic threat."

"And like the old saying goes, people vote with their pocketbooks."

"Then let's figure a way to make them think they are doing better."

"That is getting more and more difficult to do, but I'll find a way."

Alec put his empty glass on the coffee table in the center of the room. "Carlos called this morning. He wanted to know where to send his contribution." Alec grinned at his boss. "Did you start a foundation?"

"You bet I did. I learned that lesson from Hillary. What did they call it back then? *Pay-to-play?* Did he mention an amount? Certainly money is no issue for him."

"No, but he did want to make sure I let you know. Maybe he needs a favor."

"What more could we do for him. We made his drug cartel legit. Now he has franchises on every street corner and no police interference. He probably has more money than the national treasury."

"That's for sure. He's not in debt for $33 Trillion."

"Is it that bad?"

"I'm afraid so. But no worry. The public trusts us, and they are dumber than bricks about the debt. I doubt one in a thousand even knows how big it is."

"I guess that includes me." The president smiled. "But seriously, should we be concerned? That sounds like a very big number. How will we ever pay that off?"

"Just like they did twenty-five years ago—we simply deflate the dollar and pay it off with ten cent dollars. It worked before; it will work again."

"Right, but it almost toppled our entire economy in the process."

"Don't worry, I have a better plan than they did." Alec turned to leave; he did not want to have to explain a plan he had not developed yet.

Chapter 45

December 10, 2037
Washington, D.C.

Mackenzie stroked Sam's cheek and looked into his sad brown eyes. He was dying, and they both knew it. She was in pain, but he was peaceful. His job was done. He wanted to tell her how he loved her, how he had watched her grow into a beautiful and intelligent woman. The time he had spent with her was the most wonderful of his life and, also, the most important. He knew the end was near. He could see it in her eyes, on her tear-stained face. If only he could help her now, as he had done so many times before.

She tried to control her tears as she brushed at her eyes. She didn't want Sam to leave in sadness but in joy. His was a life well-spent; he deserved to leave it in peace—even joy. But it was hard. She had loved him as long as she could remember. He had always been there for her, and she had always been able to depend on him when others had failed her. He knew her quirks and her quick temper. He also knew how she loved his gentle soul.

Somewhere in the distance a horn blew. People were going about their lives, while she sat silently, watching Sam struggle to breathe. It had all happened so suddenly. Or had she simply been unwilling to see the subtle signs of age creeping into Sam's steps along the path they walked together so many times. It really didn't matter; he was leaving her and she would be without her best friend the rest of her life. She had not let herself think about the future. It was just too hard. How does one change her life so drastically in such a short period of time? Yesterday she had told him all of her life's plans and goals while he sat attentively listening. And now he was leaving. How would she achieve any of those dreams without Sam there to urge her on in his own special way?

Sam felt the darkness closing slowly around him. He had to let her know it was going to be okay. She would do well without him, and he would always be there watching and loving her. With great effort he moved his head and looked into her eyes. She was crying, harder now. That was hard for him to see. He looked one last time into her eyes and tried to convey a lifetime of love. It pained him to see her so sad; he had to let her know. His reserves were mostly gone, but with all the strength he had left, he wagged his tail one last time and licked her hand. Then he closed his eyes for the last time.

Mackenzie cried out, then pulled the large Golden Lab into her lap and hugged him tightly. He had been her dog, and they had loved each other for so many years. Now she was alone in the quiet apartment. If only Mark were there.

Chapter 46

February 11, 2038
Washington, D.C.

The young man stepped from the crowded subway, surveyed the crowd carefully, and climbed quickly up the stairs. He looked at his watch; it was 7:30 am, and the train was late as usual. Mostly he was just glad it was working at all and that no strikes had closed the only mode of public transportation in this particular part of the city. At street level he looked carefully in both directions then turned left. It was cold, and the wind was gusting from the east. A half block down he stopped abruptly and turned back toward the subway entrance. As he walked his eyes checked all of the people walking toward him. A block later he did the same maneuver and again checked the people on the street. It was difficult to survey the people as they all leaned into the wind and covered their faces for protection from the gusts. Finally, he stopped, hailed a cab, and rode away, looking behind to ensure he was not being followed. The cab was old and worn. The seats were torn and the foul smell in the car was almost overwhelming. The driver only grunted when the young man gave him the address. Fifteen minutes later he arrived at a corner of a small crowded street. He climbed from the cab and walked up the street, turned and retraced his steps, carefully checking the faces he met. When he arrived at the entrance of a small restaurant in the working-class neighborhood, he ducked in quickly.

He had seen several police officers patrolling the neighborhood, but that was normal. Along with crime, the number of police officers was still climbing. The three he had noted nearby were chatting and smoking.

They appeared to have little interest with the activities on the street. The small restaurant looked dark and deserted from the outside, but inside the room was warm and inviting. The walls adjacent to the door were lined with booths, and eight small tables were arranged in the center of the room. A small plastic flower was floating in a small bowl in the center of each table. There were no tablecloths, but colorful paper napkins brightened each tabletop. The young man smiled at the bartender at the back and received a nod in return. Glancing quickly around the room, he walked to the back and took a seat at the last booth nearest the door to the kitchen. Mark Sagan stepped through the kitchen door and took the seat across from the nervous young man. Mark spoke quietly as he surveyed the room. "Great restaurant; hungry?"

"Yeah, sorry I was late. I thought I was being followed."

"Were you?"

"No, I'm just being careful."

"That's probably smart." Mark looked into the young man's eyes. "Did you get the information?"

"Yeah, but I don't think it will help. Whoever bailed you out knew what he was doing. He used a fake name and a fake driver's license. There is nothing to track him. All I got was a vague description."

"Well, we know he was a pro. He had a well-thought-out plan in advance, and that's something." Mark thumbed quickly through the file. "Ahh, you got a copy of the driver's license. That's something. The picture might be fake, but at least the general features have to be correct. Maybe." He looked away for a moment. "Maybe Jeff can do something with that copy. Very few people can make a fake driver's license that good. Perhaps it might give us a lead." He closed the file and folded it into the breast pocket of his coat. "Let's eat. I'm hungry."

The men were in the midst of ordering when Mark's cell phone began to buzz in his pocket. He listened for a moment then rose immediately. "Quick, follow me." They rushed into the kitchen. Mark put the phone to his ear. "We're leaving out back; is that clear? Okay. Let's go." He grabbed the young man by the arm and ushered him expertly through the kitchen and out the back door. As they rushed down the alley two inert figures lay beside three overflowing garbage cans.

181

"Keep moving." At the end of the alley a car pulled up and the two men climbed quickly inside. "Good work!"

The driver was a balding man in his mid-forties. In the right seat was a woman of the same age. They were married, and both were ex-CIA agents who had been fired when the current administration cut most of the funding to their organization. She turned. "Here are their wallets. They're clean. Nothing." She continued as she turned to watch the scene they were fleeing. "They'll be out for an hour or so. After that they'll be okay."

"Pros!"

"Looks like it, but we got pictures. We'll run them through the database."

"Did you get a picture of the guy in the Mercedes out front?"

"Ah, you saw him too. A little obvious, I'd say. Not too many nice cars like that around here. Yes, we got a good shot of him too." The woman in the front seat turned to look forward but kept speaking. "What's up? Do you think this has anything to do with Terry's death?"

"I'm not sure. If they were government folks, they'd simply come to my apartment and arrest me. These guys don't act like government agents. Why would there be no IDs or badges on those two out back if they were from the government? I think someone else is in this, but I'm not sure who. We're certain our people are not involved in any of this, including the death of that border agent; what was his name, Dawson?"

"We've got a few who would have killed him in a heartbeat for what he did to Terry, but someone beat them to it. We're convinced the guard was murdered, but we didn't do it."

"Do you think he was killed by government agents?"

"No. It was done far too carefully to be government folks. No, this was, as you keep saying, the work of pros."

"Wait!" The woman swung an old 35mm camera around and began snapping pictures as the car accelerated down the road. "I think I just got a good shot of the rest of the team that was following you. I think the man who was in the car out front is the one standing to the left in the group."

Mark turned to look but the car was turning into an alley and he missed the view. "I'd like to take a look at those photos as soon as you get them."

"I'll have them tonight."

* * *

The large man stood over the two groggy colleagues and shook his head. The younger man beside him spoke in quick, but quiet, heavily accented sentences. "We found them both in the alley. The target was gone. He must have escaped out back and overpowered them."

"One man takes down two of our best armed men? I think not. He had to have help.

I told you to watch him, not alert him. Now he knows we have him under surveillance."

"But he doesn't know who *we* are. He probably thinks we are government agents."

"Let us hope you're right."

The young man rolled one of the semi-conscious men over and checked his pockets. "Their wallets are missing!" He checked further. "As are their weapons."

"Well, well. We are dealing with a very skillful man. He obviously wanted their IDs."

"They were clean."

"At least you did that right. But if you had been smart, you would have had them carry government IDs."

The younger man looked back quickly. He was openly irritated by his superior's comments. "I didn't plan on having two of my best men taken down by a bunch of amateurs!"

"Perhaps we are not dealing with amateurs at all." The older man spoke quietly, almost to himself. After a moment of thought he turned to the younger agent. "Get them out of here, and search them carefully. I don't see any injuries or blood. They must have been drugged—probably a dart. Let me know when they recover. I'll need to talk with them." He turned and walked slowly down the alley, looking carefully for any evidence that might have been left. He dialed his phone as he walked. "It's me. We need to talk!"

*   *   *

Mark looked carefully at the pictures the woman had taken. They were sharp and clear. The old Canon had done a great job. He focused on the large man in the dark suit. He appeared to be in his fifties and had graying curly hair. "So, it's you. And where is your tan car?"

Ken Wilson and several others studied the pictures as well. "Anyone recognize any of these men? They were following me at the restaurant today." There were three in the picture, but the older man was obviously the leader. All of the younger men were paying him a lot of deference, looking at him with rapt attention.

Mark pointed to one of the pictures. "I suspect the older man may be the one who followed us after Terry was shot. I'm not certain, but I think it was him. I'll ask Mackenzie if she recognizes him from the sheriff's office. If we can discover who he is and what his intentions are, it may answer a lot of our questions."

"In the meantime, we'll send these pictures to Dalton's team. Perhaps they can help us identify who they are." Ken put the pictures in an envelope and handed them to one of his men. "And keep a copy for us here as well."

Chapter 47

March 23, 2038
The White House

Alec walked into his office and poured a stiff scotch. He stood for several minutes watching the sun slowly setting, then he took a long drink of the amber liquid. President Gutierrez walked in and sat down behind him on the worn leather couch against the right wall. "Alec, you look tired. Has the job driven you to drink already?" There was humor in the president's voice. Without asking, Alec walked back to his credenza and poured another. He put several cubes of ice in the glass and handed it to the President.

"I've just come from a meeting with the Veterans Administration folks. The contractor on the new hospital in Cleveland has stopped work—just stopped work. Seems the government hasn't paid its bills, or so he says." Gutierrez sipped his drink and watched Alec with interest. After a moment Alec continued. "It seems when the VA set up the contract they failed to establish any control mechanism for managing costs." He walked back to his desk and poured more liquor into his glass. He took another sip and resumed pacing around the room. "How could any professional project manager make such a mistake? How? The contractor complains there have been over three thousand changes to the requirements since the project was initiated."

"Anybody we know?"

"Herbert Ayers."

"Oh, yes, William's son."

"How did such an idiot get selected to manage a $600 million facility?"

"His dad has been a big Democrat for a long time now. That family has contributed millions over the years to help folks like me get elected."

Alec suddenly looked like a deflated balloon. He sat across from the president and drank the last of his scotch. "I guess I'd better start working on the spin for the press. Seems a lot of folks are beginning to notice the lack of management expertise on government projects."

"How do the corporations do it?" The frown on the President's face deepened as he asked the rhetorical question.

"What do you mean?"

"Corporations don't seem to make mistakes on the order of $1.9 billion. They seldom double the cost of a project, unless the government is paying for it. Why do you think that is?"

"They'd be bankrupt in a hurry if they did. They can't afford such mistakes."

"And we can?" Gutierrez looked directly into Alec's eyes.

"And, I guess if someone in the private sector managed so poorly he would be fired or demoted promptly. That would send a message to the others in the organization that incompetence would not be tolerated."

"Do we ever fire incompetent people?" Gutierrez was smiling as he watched his chief-of-staff.

"Maybe we should give that a try. Wouldn't that be a surprise to the government employees' union whose rules make it almost impossible to fire anyone."

The two men joked awhile, then finally the president got serious. "Well, we need to take care of Herbert, so don't go out and get him fired. His old man is too important to the party. Besides, I'll be needing him in the next election. Firing his son might not help that very much." The president was smiling again.

"I doubt we could get Herbert fired if we wanted to. We'd end up in arbitration with the union, and that would last for years. He'd die of old age before we could actually fire him. Besides, under the new contract I'm not sure incompetence was listed as a justifiable cause for dismissal."

186

"Well, one good thing to remember is that the VA hospital takes care of veterans, and vets don't normally vote Democrat anyway. All that discipline tends to make them suspicious of our base. Seems like all we can count on in the military are the generals, because we control them. They get on board, or they get canned. Funny, we can fire a general, but we can't fire an incompetent civil-service manager. Well, at least it ensures a lot of construction people have jobs in Cleveland. Heaven knows we could use some good news on the job front."

Alec held up a stack of papers on the corner of his desk. "I'm afraid we don't have anything to celebrate on the job front. Another bad month."

"How are you handling that, Alec?"

"I've got every spokesman we have out there blaming industry for the lack of jobs. You know, the old greed thing. It's old, but it still works." Alec dropped the stack of paper in a waste can. "Well, let me lighten your day with one item, Mr. President."

"That's a switch I would enjoy."

"I hear Senator Longfield is talking with Thomas Hudson as a potential running mate in an effort to unseat you in the next election." Alec was smiling broadly.

"Hudson? The actor? Are they crazy? I've been in office less than two years and already they are talking about the next election? They want to run against a seated president in their own party? Don't they understand the rules? We don't have primaries in this party when we have a one-term president."

"Well, Hudson would guarantee most of the women's vote!"

"You realize that this is not funny!" The president was frowning again. "That might work!"

"Are you kidding? He's slept with most of the women in California, and he knows nothing at all about politics. We'll have enough dirt on him to raise a garden."

"Philandering will not keep a man out of the White House; that's already been proven. Do you really think the voters care about that?"

Suddenly Alec got serious. "Hmmm, perhaps you are right. As a VP candidate he would get little scrutiny from the press. I guess if competency is not important on government contracts, then why would it matter in the White House?" Both men laughed at the last comment. "He's as nutty as most of the California politicians. But I thought you would get a laugh out of this."

"There is never a dull moment is there?"

Alec smiled at the president. "No, but I was thinking the other day that it would be nice if we didn't have to worry about elections. Then we would have time to really think about how to govern this place. When we finally killed off the Republican Party, we thought it would all be easier somehow."

"Well, I guess we could always ask Congress for some help."

"No, let's not get them involved. We have enough problems without that crowd."

The president rose and walked to the credenza and poured himself another drink. "Anything else I need to be abreast of other than idiot competitors in my own party?"

"The new regulations on housing just got distributed to the press. There are a lot of folks out there who will not be happy with these new rules."

"I understand, but most of those who will complain are conservatives, so I could care less. Our base doesn't own large homes. They will be the net beneficiaries of the new limits for square footage. The regulations restrict new construction; what are you doing about older homes and mansions?"

Alec didn't want to get into this topic, but he felt compelled. "Little by little we are taxing them into government deeds. Mostly it is being done on the local level by county officials. One new approach that seems to be working well is to allow the owners to remain in the homes with somewhat reduced taxes until they die; then the home becomes the property of the county."

"What does the county do with the homes after they take control of them? They obviously can't sell them; no one could afford to buy them at the rate they are being taxed."

"Some are being converted to low-income housing; others are being used for government offices; and I hear that some are standing vacant."

"Are they being maintained by the counties?"

"Not well. Most are starting to show wear fairly quickly. Government housing always seems to be in a bad state of repair. The counties, like all other levels of government, are in deep debt and struggling just to keep up payroll and pension checks." Alec stood for a moment and looked directly at the president. "Why this sudden interest in personal homes?"

"It seems that a few of our well-heeled Democrat friends are also being caught up in the broom of equality. Some of them are also on the list of large, expensive homes. Suddenly they are not so sure that this is a very good idea at all."

Alec smiled. "So that's the issue. Well, that is easily solved. All you have to do is to get me a list of names and locations. The party controls the county apparatus and those who assess the value of homes. Easily fixed!"

"Won't people complain at the unfair treatment?"

"Who will know? We own the political system that handles all of this. We can do whatever we want."

"Is that legal?"

"We control that too. If we say it is legal, it is legal. If we say it is illegal, it is illegal. Remember how Obama did it? No indictments for our folks! Period! And who appoints the Attorney General? You do!" Alec was smiling. "Obama really screwed up the Iranian deal, but he certainly understood how to use the Justice Department to serve his needs. And Mr. President, so can you!"

"Alec, every time we talk I realize just how valuable you are to my administration."

Alec held up his drink. "I'll salute that."

Chapter 48

April 16, 2038
Washington, D.C.

Mackenzie and Alec walked into the reception for the evening concert, and all heads turned to look at the striking woman on the arm of the President's Chief of Staff. Her auburn hair was up, and she was stunning in the long burgundy dress that only accentuated the beauty of the woman wearing it. They were immediately surrounded by political hacks who wanted to talk to Alec, and others who simply wanted a closer look at his date for the evening. Alec noted that several bars had been set up at either end of the intimate room. He guided Mackenzie toward the nearest as people moved aside to allow them to pass. "Two cabernets please. *14 Hands* if you have it."

"I'm sorry Mr. Woodward; we only have California wines tonight."

"Do you have *Dreaming Tree?*"

"Yes I do."

"That will be fine."

Several senators surrounded Alec, and he was soon involved in politics, his favorite topic. When one of the older men stepped between Mackenzie and Alec, she stepped back, then turned and walked away to survey the room. They were attending the Washington Symphony this evening, and she was excited about the music. She had no idea what they would be hearing, so she crossed the room to find a program. A familiar voice behind her spoke softly. "Program?" She turned to see Mark smiling as he took her arm. He spoke as they walked toward a quiet corner in the room. "Tonight you will be hearing William Cohen playing

Korngold's Violin Concerto in D major and Mahler's Symphony No. 7 in E minor, "Song of the Night." Cohen's solo will be a real gift. No one plays Korngold better since Vadim Gluzman. That will be followed by Shostakovich's Symphony No. 5 in D minor. Be sure to listen for the oboe to portray the cry of mankind and the famous three notes that represent the three knocks of Stalin's henchmen. You will also hear the slow tempo at the end as the composer meant it to be played as opposed to the faster presentation of a Bernstein or Previn." Mark smiled at the beautiful woman before him. "If Shostakovich could fool Stalin and his communist sadists in 1937, I'm sure our maestro can put one past our socialist president and the politically correct lackeys who surround him." He paused and looked at her a long while. "I just wish I could be seated beside you when you hear such beautiful music tonight."

She returned his smile and stepped back to get a better look at the tall man in his tux. "You are an amazing man, Mr. Sagan. Your understanding and explanation of music is surpassed only by how handsome you look in your tux tonight."

"Occasionally I have to remind myself that I am a gentleman." He looked her over carefully. "And you look beautiful tonight. Nice dress." He reached for his own lapel and removed a single rose bud. "I think this matches your dress better than my colorless attire." He carefully pinned it on the left side of her dress. "There." He leaned back and admired his handiwork. "What a match..." Before Mark could continue he was interrupted by a tone that echoed through the room. "Time to be seated."

He held her hand a long time. It was evident he did not want to let her go. Mark placed his right hand under Mackenzie's chin and lifted her face to his. He gazed into her eyes for a long time without saying a word. She simply stood looking up into his. Suddenly her eyes widened. He was looking into her mind, into her heart. She could feel it. It was unmistakable. They stood transfixed for several minutes. The people around them were lost in some kind of haze that shut out everything but each other. Mackenzie felt a small shudder of excitement run through her body. She felt strangely naked in a crowd. Mark was looking into her very soul. She wanted to speak her feelings, but she could not. She simply stared back into the eyes of the man she suddenly knew she loved.

191

Finally, he spoke. "Enjoy the concert." He leaned forward and kissed her, then turned and left.

Mackenzie felt the same old longing as she watched him walk away. How did he do it? It couldn't be just his intellect; no, it was his heart, and somehow it had connected with hers so long ago, and then more deeply again tonight. She tried to push the warmth away, but it was always there, that small little light that burst into flame anytime he entered her world. And that small flame grew and danced and carried her to heights of dizziness she had never experienced before. She tried to walk away from that intoxicating flight of her spirit, but she had never quite determined how to do it. She was the moth, and his was the flame that drew her to its brightness. But she feared that flame as much as she desired it. She knew the beautiful flame beckoned the moth to its death; perhaps she feared love might destroy her as well. Or perhaps surrendering her heart might just bring her the total happiness she was seeking.

The brief moments with Mark when she finally let go were filled with such wonder, but Mackenzie Selms liked control in her life. And she knew she could not control her heart if she ever fully surrendered it to the man who beckoned her toward the flame of love. Her smile changed into a slight frown as she walked back toward the politicians huddled around Alec. After standing behind him for several minutes, unnoticed, she turned and walked into the concert hall. She studied the program that Mark had handed her and scanned the room as she walked down the aisle to see if she could spot him. She could not. Finally, as the lights dimmed, Alec entered with the assistance of an usher. He quickly slid into the seat next to her. They were seated near the front of the concert hall in prime seats, so everyone saw his entrance. He waved the usher away and handed her a large tip. The uniformed woman smiled, bowed in appreciation, and left quickly as the music started. Mackenzie could feel Mark's eyes watching her; she could feel his presence. She wanted desperately to turn around and see his face, but she could not be so obvious so near the front row. But she knew. She knew.

He watched her from a box seat high above. As the music filled the room he saw her close her eyes. Very soon her spirit would take flight with the beauty of the melody as it drifted softly through the room and then more forcefully as it swept into her very heart. She would be oblivious to everything now, everything except the music. Mark watched her and closed his own eyes. She was lost in the beauty of the music, but he was lost in the beauty of the woman with whom he had fallen in love.

*   *   *

Alec walked into the meeting and put his coffee cup beside his note pad. Most of the high level government workers had electronic tablets, but Alec preferred hand-written notes that his secretary would later transcribe for him. Mostly he preferred his coffee. That was the fuel that kept him going. A young woman from the finance department studied him carefully. He was a bit short, but he was not an unpleasant man to look at. She smiled. "Who was that good looking man who kissed your date last night?"

Alec's face shot up immediately. He almost spilled his coffee. "What?"

"At the concert last night. I saw you there."

"Someone kissed my date last night?"

"Sure, while you guys were talking politics this tall good looking man had a nice chat with your date. He even kissed her before he left." She watched him for a reaction. It was not what she expected. His face grew very red. "Sorry, didn't mean to speak out of turn."

"No problem." Alec was clearly upset. "He's an old friend. Was he tall with sandy blond hair?"

"Yeah, that's him."

"Just a common friend. We all went to school together."

"Well, I'm glad to see that you like concerts. I love them too." She smiled seductively at him, but he did not notice. He was busily scribbling a note to make a call to the FBI as soon as possible.

Chapter 49

April 19, 2038
Washington, D.C.

The two agents walked into the office and sat without being invited. It was a small office, cluttered with the paraphernalia of government. A new Chinese laptop sat in the center of the walnut desk, closed and obscured by the cluttered stacks of paper and reports from countless government minions working among the endless rows of government desks in the endless gray government buildings. Alec rose and poured three coffees without asking if they wanted the strong dark drink. "Here gentlemen, the finest coffee to be found in America these days." They settled into the dark leather chairs and sipped their cups, nodding in agreement.

"The reason I called you here is I would like to prevent a small disaster regarding the death of one of our border guards recently. As you may recall, a Border Patrol agent was found shot to death near his home in Texas. There have been some rumors that perhaps the government was disappointed in the uproar he caused and may have actually had something to do with his death. Now we all know that is absurd. So I would like you to do a little digging to see if it is possible that the so-called Patriots had anything to do with this. That guard arrested one of their group the day before he was found dead—Mark Sagan to be specific. It is highly possible that the so called *Patriots* may have had something to do with that murder.

"Anyway, the President is concerned, and it would be considered a big favor if you could expedite this investigation for him. If this man

Sagan was involved in any way, we need to know that as soon as possible. More importantly, we need something we could use to prosecute him. I really don't care what it is or how you get it. I just want this man behind bars, so get something. Follow him and get as *creative* as you must; just get it done. I'm sure the President will want to thank you both personally as soon as this is resolved. I know we can count on your support in this sensitive situation. Here is my private number. I will be the President's personal contact for this. Please keep me advised as you proceed. And also, this is to be kept quiet. We would not like this to be discussed with anyone. Any questions?"

"None, Mr. Woodward. We'll take care of this for you."

"Thank you." And with that he ushered them past the Oval Office for emphasis of the importance of the people requesting their help. They were suitably impressed, and just after they left the White House, Alec picked up the phone. "Are you sure they will get this right? Good. Just make sure they do it quickly." He smiled. No one dare kiss Mackenzie Selms when she was out with him.

Alec reached into the third drawer on the left side of his credenza and withdrew a picture. It showed three very young students, two young men on either side of a smiling young woman. Both young men were staring raptly at her. But she was looking at the camera, not at either of her admirers. Alec stared at her face. She was the most beautiful woman he had ever seen, and he had been in love with her for a very long time. He knew Mark also had a crush on her back in school but would never admit it. But that had been so long ago. Alec was shorter than Mackenzie by about an inch, but he had worked hard and succeeded beyond even his own expectations. He thought his position would impress her, but Mackenzie was still the woman in charge. She had not yet fallen for any man he thought, but when she did, he wanted to ensure it was he. He was Chief of Staff to the President of the United States. What the hell did it take to impress that woman?

The three of them had been such good friends for those wonderful college years. They were always together. Then once, only once, just before graduation, he had seen her discussing something with Mark, and suddenly it was there—the look on her face. It was some mixture of admiration, amazement, and perhaps, just perhaps, affection. He still remembered the sinking feeling as he watched the two of them together. He had despised Mark ever since. Mark had gone into medicine while he had chosen politics, and it had been a choice that changed everything for Alec. It took years, but Mark was still in residency, while Alec was already advising top politicians in both state and national elections. Then he met Gutierrez, the candidate he had been seeking for so long. He knew more about the game of politics than Gutierrez would ever learn. He became indispensable, and he led this new client all the way to the White House.

Alec considered the situation. It was almost like a storybook tale. He just needed to insure that the ending was happily ever after—at least for him. Mark be damned.

Chapter 50

May 12, 2038, 10:00 am
The White House

Alec Woodward stuck his head out the door of his office. His secretary was talking on the phone; no one else was in the office. He returned to his desk, drank a third of his tumbler of scotch, and quickly put his glass in his bottom right hand drawer. He sat for a moment and savored the fine scotch, then walked to his coffee pot. The coffee was lukewarm, but he needed it to cover his breath so he drank two cups quickly. Alec nodded to his secretary as he started down the hall. "Marvin, I'm headed to the Agriculture meeting. It should last about an hour, maybe longer."

The room was filled with men and women in business attire. Each looked somewhat uncomfortable. Were their imported shoes too tight, or did they realize the gravity of the meeting they had been called to attend? When the President walked in, everyone rose. Gutierrez motioned with his hand and all sat down, except for the Secretary of Agriculture, who was standing behind the podium beside the large screen that hung from the ceiling. He stood opposite the President who sat at the other end of the long table. The President spent a couple of minutes studying his schedule then looked up. "Okay, Charlie, what do you have for us?"

Charlie Bennet came from a long line of Bennets who had served the Democrat party for decades. None had particularly stood out with his performance, but all kept their political offices and their government incomes. "I'm afraid the news regarding our agricultural sector is not too good, Mr. President. I am concerned about the production of both grains and beef going into the next winter." Bennet flipped the small controller in his hand and illuminated the first slide. It showed the production of corn, wheat, soybeans, and various other products on one graph. All were continuing the trend of the past five years—downward. The future projections were illustrated in blue and all showed moderate growth in the next three years, followed by rapid growth for the remainder of years on the chart.

The President studied the chart for several moments and then spoke. "Well, if we can just get through the next three years, everything looks good." Several others in the room nodded in agreement.

Bennet studied the chart briefly then turned back to face the president. "Yes, Mr. President, but it is the next three years that I am worried about."

Alec spoke before the president could answer. "Cut the statistics, Charlie, how bad is it—really?"

The Secretary grasped both sides of the small podium with his hands. He leaned forward and paused for several seconds. "It's bad. I've ordered the export of all grains to stop immediately. Furthermore, I am getting ready to do the same with beef next week." He leaned back slightly and waited.

Alec looked at the Secretary with amazement. "Stop all exports?"

"If we want a fighting chance of feeding our own people."

"Damn, we need those exports to allow us to buy fuel and manufactured goods."

The Secretary of Agriculture looked at the podium while Alec spoke. Finally, he raised his head. "I am well aware of the gravity of this situation; that is why I asked for this meeting. I consider it my job to keep you advised of such things, however unpleasant."

A female voice rose from the other side of the table. "How bad is it for the American people? Will there be enough food for them? What price levels are you expecting?"

"With the President's authority we can impose price controls, and since there are not too many private farms or ranches left, price controls should not negatively impact future production."

Gutierrez joined the fray. "Well, something damn sure has changed production levels. What caused these sharp drops? We haven't had any floods to speak of."

Alec raised his hand to stop the debate, but before he could speak, Bennet began answering the President's question. "Well, we've seen significant production losses in every major area except fruits and garden vegetables. All grains, silage, and meat production are down sharply."

The woman spoke up again. "Well, let's see. If I am right, all of the areas where production is down are in our government farm programs. The private farms seem to be okay. How are goats? The government didn't take that sector yet." Bennet flipped through several charts and found goats—they were up significantly. "Maybe our bureaucrats are not good farmers—or managers." The sound of her voice reverberated through the room's silence.

Alec was glaring at the upstart employee who seemed to have missed the team meeting at the department. She glanced at him, smiled, and continued. "Well, maybe someone else has a suggestion about why this happened. The government farms had their allocation of fuel, and another 15% for spring planting. They got their requested allocation of fertilizer, while the small private farms got none to grow their garden vegetables. Yet the private farms outpaced the government farms." She paused waiting for someone to answer. Then she resumed. "Seems the old Soviet Union had a similar problem with their food supply. Maybe there is a lesson to be learned there."

Bennet was staring straight at the young woman. Looking up at him and nodding, she didn't seem concerned in the least. No one in the room was aware that she already had her schedule to leave the country in two weeks.

Gutierrez looked up at his appointed Secretary of Agriculture. "Alright, enough talk of what happened. We can discuss that later. Right now I want to know what we need to do to get this straightened out. What do you need Charlie?" He used the secretary's first name to indicate he still had confidence in his appointee.

"I'm going to need about a billion and a half more in budget this year. That should be enough to avoid a disaster."

199

Alec slammed his pen on the table. "A billion and a half? We don't have that kind of money sitting around to fix mistakes!"

Gutierrez held his hand up toward Alec while continuing to look at Bennet. "Will that fix the problem or just get us through this winter?"

"Get us through the winter. If we don't do this, Mr. President, we will have widespread deprivation across the nation."

"I see. I'll find the money."

Bennet nodded and began gathering his papers. His staff rose and departed together. Only the young woman who had spoken remained. Alec studied her for a few moments. "And who are you? Are you with the Department of Agriculture?"

"I'm Jessica Meriwether. I work in the government Accounting Department."

"Who invited you to this meeting? What do you know about agriculture?"

"I invited me to this meeting, and it is obvious to me that I know more about agriculture than anyone else in the meeting. For example, why did the Department of Agriculture run through their fuel reserves before the spring planting even started? How did they consume all that fuel in the winter? Who was watching that data? And what happened to the seed that was never ordered until a week before planting time? And why was it stored in a place that was damp and incurred fungus with a loss of half of our seed for the year?" She stopped, but only momentarily.

"I could go on, but I think I've made my point. And oh, by the way, the private farms all ordered their seed in the early fall and stored them in their own bins. And their meager supply of tractor fuel was more than enough to increase production 12% over last year. The Soviets couldn't make socialized farming work, and it seems we can't either. Maybe we should give the farms back to the farmers instead of the bureaucrats. The farmers seem to be paying attention to what they are doing." Before either could say a word, she rose and left the room.

"Damn, Alec, she may just have a good point there. Maybe farms are different."

"Stay the course, Mr. President. We'll make this work if I have to fire the whole damn Department of Agriculture. Surely we can find someone to manage that job."

"Maybe we should put that young woman in charge. She damn sure has spunk."

"Well, she has bigger balls than Bennet; that's for sure." Alec scribbled a quick note to himself to have the young woman fired and slid it into his notebook.

Gutierrez watched Alec and guessed what was on the note. "Alec, I don't want you to do anything about that young woman. Leave her alone. Maybe we need more like her and fewer political hacks like Bennet. He certainly has the political resume, but he damn sure can't manage the Department of Agriculture. Leave her alone, and I'll take care of Charlie. And one last thing, get in touch with the press and let them know the Department of Agriculture is predicting significant increases in future projections of food production on our government farms. Make some point about how they are covering the low production of the private sector, especially in areas like wheat and beef. You know what to say."

"Got it." Alec paused to think a moment. "Any chance they could get conflicting information from other sources, like our Miss Meriwether?"

"The press will print whatever you tell them. That is all that counts."

"You know, if they ever turned against us, we'd be in real trouble."

"That is why we take such good care of them. We make sure their family members are given great government jobs, and we work hard to keep their favor. I have someone on my staff with direct ties to every major news outlet in this country. Trust me; it works." The President smiled and left. His Chief of Staff watched him go, but Alec was not smiling, he had another meeting to attend, and he knew it would not be pleasant.

Chapter 51

May 12, 2038, 3:00 pm
The White House

Alec was sitting in his office looking at the wall. He had all of his data ready for the call he knew would soon be coming. It was one he did not want to answer. He looked at the list on the pad in the center of his desk. It enumerated all of the things that were going well and those that were not. The second list was far longer than the first, and he knew the first was mostly lies, things spun to look good when in reality they were not. He focused on the top item and studied it for a long time—foreign debt. It was underlined, and there were circles drawn around it in several colors. Under it were a list of solutions—mostly crossed off, one failure after another. At the bottom, with a check beside it, was his only remaining option — one he feared most of all. He focused again on the circled item. It had lines drawn to several other items on the sheet. The first was unemployment. That was one of the largest lies of all. He knew it was bad; no, terrible. The American people were suffering the worst unemployment since the Great Depression. He wondered if the last ten years might not appropriately be dubbed The Slow Depression. It was like a cancer on American soil. People were destitute; factories were shut; and most all items on store shelves were from China or some other country in the Far East. He knew that it was even worse in Europe, but then the Europeans had made decisions that had led them to the precipice of economic disaster.

Alec looked up, his face turning suddenly very white. Were their decisions any different from those he and his predecessors had been making in America for years? He thought back to the early Democrats. What would they have done? Harry Truman? Probably he would be a Republican today. Alec smiled for the first time that day. Harry was a tough old codger. He would probably have chased all the current liberal progressives out of the country with a big stick. Big Stick? Teddy would have helped him for sure. What had happened to the ideals? What had happened to the plan? Why was it failing so badly? Why could America no longer compete? It had happened to Rome, to England, now to America? What was the common denominator that led them all from superpower to ruin? Had the people become too soft? How had that happened? How could this be reversed? He had only wanted the best for everyone, but it was not working. Why? The ringing phone shook him from his thoughts. He reached and pressed the intercom key.

"The president asked if you would join him in the oval office. He has the Secretary of Defense and the Secretary of the Navy with him."

"Tell them I'll be right there." Alec reflected on the attendance at the meeting. So, it was three against one, was it? Well, perhaps that would be a fair fight. He knew both political appointees. Their combined IQ would almost match his, but not quite. He rose, stretched, smiled, and gathered his papers. Time for Round One.

*   *   *

The Secretary of Defense looked across the table at Alec in total shock. "The Presidio? You are selling the Presidio? Surely you must be kidding!" As he spoke, the Secretary of the Navy rose and began pacing. "Tell me this is all a bad joke!"

Alec sorted through his papers and handed each of the other attendees a large document nicely printed and bound with a dark blue cover. The seal of the President of the United States was affixed to the document. The Secretary of Defense took the booklet and placed it on the coffee table without opening it. "Mr. Secretary, you will note in the first few pages of this document I have outlined the reasons behind the release of this property. It is not something we have done lightly. It represents the only solution we have to a very large problem. Surely you are aware of the current economic situation in this country. We are drowning in debt. Borrowing more to simply pay off the old debt is untenable. We simply are out of options. We have a trillion-dollar payment due in three months. We simply do not have that money, and defaulting on the debt is not something any of us would like to see happen. We have a bid on the Presidio that would allow us to pay that debt and perhaps give us some breathing room to find a better solution for future payments."

"Is there no other way? You are selling off America! The Presidio has been an American landmark forever. How can we ever tell the American people that we are selling our bases to pay our debt?"

"Look, the American people don't really give a damn about military bases right now. They are far more interested in their government checks that come at the beginning of each month. If we have to sell off the Presidio and other installations, I suspect they will not mind at all."

"I suspect the folks in San Francisco will mind."

"San Francisco? Are you kidding?" Alec broke out into a small laugh. "They'd be happy if we closed all military bases across the country."

"We've damned near done that already." The Secretary of the Navy spoke from across the room where he was watching the meeting with great interest.

"Why do we need such a large military anyway?" Alec watched the faces in the room. "Those days are over. We now have a UN committee that takes care of peace in the world. Why do we need a large military? Let's use the money for other things."

"Like welfare payments and government pensions." As the Secretary of the Navy spoke, the other men in the room looked at him with displeasure.

Alec tented his fingers as he spoke. "Is welfare of the people such a bad thing?" The standing Secretary turned to look out the window and said nothing in return. Alec continued. "Look, none of us likes this. Not me; not the President; but like I said, we have just run out of options. Unfortunately, we don't have a trillion in the accounts right now. We are still running in the red, and we need a solution. If you have a better one, I'm all ears."

The Secretary of Defense looked at Alec and the President for several minutes in complete silence. Finally, he spoke. "Mr. President, the Defense Department had nothing to do with the situation we are currently struggling with. There is little else we can do to reduce costs and help save money. We have cut back our weapons, our personnel, everything. I doubt we could adequately defend this nation today if we had to. So, the reason for our economic trouble lies elsewhere. I strongly suggest you look carefully and long at where the money is being spent and how those areas might be reduced, much like how we have reduced our expenses in the military. As for selling the Presidio, I find that abhorrent. I find that embarrassing for this nation and for those of us in this room. Finally, I have one last question, then I'm through. Just who do you think has the money to buy such a property? It is worth a fortune. Who are you dealing with?" He looked directly at Alec.

Alec did not look up but spoke very quietly. This was the question he dreaded most. He also knew it was a secret that could not be concealed any longer. "The Chinese."

The Secretary of Defense rose and looked straight into the eyes of the President. "Mr. President, are you in agreement with this plan?" There was incredulity in his voice. "What would the Chinese do with the property? It's a military base!"

"Now George, you know we are in a corner. We simply have no other alternatives...."

"I'll have my resignation on your desk tomorrow."

"And mine as well." The Secretary of the Navy joined his colleague and the two men walked out of the room together.

The President walked to his credenza and took a bottle of scotch from the bottom drawer. "Drink?"

"I need one."

"That didn't go very well, did it?"

"Actually it went much as I expected." Alec took the glass of scotch and took a long drink. "I just didn't think they'd quit."

"We need team players in this game." Gutierrez sat down across from Alec. "Do you think we'll have difficulty selling this to the public, or do they really not care, as you said."

"The American public could care less. It might make a minor ripple on the lake, but not a big one. Most people really won't care, certainly not the ones who vote for us. We'll tell them we are selling *some* of the Presidio property. We won't bother to mention that it is being used to pay interest on our debt. We'll make it look like we are raising money for a big public works project. That should be sufficient. I'll work it with our news folks. We'll get the right story out. Leave it to me."

*   *   *

The two men walked in silence toward the waiting staff car. A young ensign stood by the door of the car and opened it as the two older men climbed inside. In disgust the Secretary of Defense muttered. "I can't believe how far we have sunk. What has happened to this nation?"

"We haven't had good leadership in a very long time, and now it's time to leave."

"Bill, you didn't need to resign just because I did. That was not necessary."

The Secretary of the Navy loosened his tie and turned to his friend. "Yes it was. We've been friends for a very long time, and I knew you were right. Besides, if you had not done so, I would have done it alone. I simply cannot work for those socialist idiots any longer. They're ruining this nation, and I have made up my mind. I will not be a part of it any longer. I thought I could make a difference, but they won't listen. I fought for this country, and I watched a lot of friends die for it; now I don't even recognize it. It's time to leave."

"Bill, are you working with the Patriots?"

"Yes, I am."

"Will you introduce me to them as well."

"I'd be proud to, George. Maybe in some small way we can make a difference. They want to save America. I'd like to help in that effort."

"Then count me in, too."

Chapter 52

June 10, 2038
Downtown, Atlanta, Georgia

The five men and three women leading the Patriot movement sat around the long table and listened to the stark report being given on the economy. The day was cloudy and dark, much like the mood in the meeting. The dark storm clouds moved in rapidly from the southeast and threatened rain. The man presenting was middle-aged and already graying. Thomas Varies was a renowned economist and a government advisor until his reality came into conflict with the views of the Democratic hierarchy. It had cost him his job, but it had cemented his reputation among the people who understood truth. Today he was not smiling. "And that's about it. Our economy is in shambles. It is far worse than most know." He paused a moment. "Or care, for that matter."

The youngest woman in the group spoke first. "So real unemployment is actually around 22%."

"That's right. But don't forget, many of those working are only in part-time jobs. They'd like full time work if they could get it. If we factor them into the equation, unemployment is much higher."

"And what is Europe right now?"

"Roughly the same. Perhaps a bit worse."

"And Asia?"

"They are doing better. Unemployment is approximately eight percent." The presenter turned and flipped back through the set of slides. After a short search he found what he was looking for. "Remember, Asia is manufacturing like crazy. Those are good paying jobs. We are stuck in a society of service sectors. They usually pay much less. Waiters, for example, make less than factory workers." He paused a moment and studied his audience. "We're not doing well at all. Neither will our children, our grandchildren, our great-grandchildren, etc."

"They'll essentially be working for the Chinese. Right?"

"Yes. Unfortunately, that is the case."

"Prognosis?"

"We will continue to have intermediate sized crashes until the entire train goes off the track in a giant wreck. It will be like none the world has seen before."

"That bad?"

"That bad. Fifty to sixty percent unemployment; inflation over 1000 percent; chaos in the cities; looting, riots. It will be bad." The frown on his face accentuated the facts he was presenting. There were groans throughout the room.

Jake Dalton stood at the opposite end of the long table from the presenter. Everyone turned, giving him their attention. "One question, Earl. Is there any chance of saving the economy?"

"In this political environment, I would say no. First, the politicians probably don't have a clue how to do that. Second, even if they did know, they wouldn't be willing to dish up a medicine that strong to the public for fear of losing their jobs. After all, they were the cause of the problem in the first place. Finally, even if the politicians were willing to do the right things and prescribe the medicine we need for saving the economy, the people wouldn't let them. Remember, the people elected those idiots. Everyone wants his or hers, and everyone wants it to be easy and simple. It is neither."

Varies checked his notes and continued. "This would require a really tough president who was also smart. We haven't seen one of those in a long time. No, I suspect it would take that total collapse I mentioned earlier to set the stage for such a major change in all we do. It would require a move back to a free market economy; no more handouts except in very special circumstances; no more farm supports, a major reduction in social programs except for those who are legitimately handicapped.

Socialism would be abandoned, and capitalism would be reinstated. We would reward the productive people in society instead of punishing them. Government would be pared down to a reasonable level. Education would be for learning instead of a politically correct petri dish. I could go on, but you get the idea. An economist wrote about this long ago, a man named Wiedemer. He was a prophet, but typically, the people didn't heed his words."

"What if most of the productive component in this nation left, say within six months. How would that affect all this?"

"How much of the productive component?"

"Say 60 maybe 70%."

"The crash would come in about five months I'm guessing."

"What if all that productive component came back within six months, well, most of it anyway, then how long would it take to rebuild the nation?"

"First the people in the country would have to realize what they have done to themselves and what has really happened. That won't be easy. There are a lot of uneducated people out there, especially when it comes to economics. But just for sake of argument, say it takes three to five years for the nation to come to grips with reality and realize the actual condition of the nation, then I think it might be turned around in ten or fifteen years, maybe sooner if you have some good communicators available. But you would still have the debt to contend with."

"We'll worry about that later. For now, we have to figure how to get the train back on the track." Dalton looked around the room. "Any more questions?" He frowned. "I know there are many, but we must adjourn for now. We'll reassemble again next week. I'll let you know where and when by the usual means. Remember, no one is to mention anything discussed here. Not to anyone! Thanks Earl, I appreciate your analysis. Though it differs greatly from what we all see on TV each evening, I think we trust your work more." He walked to the door and opened it slightly. "Bart, are we okay?"

"It's clear Mr. Dalton. The parking lot is also clear. You may go when you wish."

209

Dalton turned to the assembled group. We're clear. Thanks for coming. For those traveling with me to Havana, I'll be in touch with the details early next week."

Ken Wilson and Mark joined the others as the group filed out of the room. When they were alone, Ken turned to his son. "Well, that was an uplifting report." He was frowning.

"But most likely true. Earl knows his stuff. He was once a great professor of economics at Chicago. That is, until his reality ran against the political propaganda of the day. What a loss."

"I'm glad he's on our side."

"Me, too. Just think what he will be able to do for the Cubans. He'll build their economy while ours sinks into the abyss."

"When is he leaving?"

"Next week, I think. It all depends on how closely the government monitors his activities. They really don't like him and would love to catch him leaving without a permit."

"Can't we set him up with fake documents?"

"No, he is on the special *no exit* list with pictures and everything— like you and me." Sagan laughed. "No, we'll have to get him out the hard way. Probably through Destin."

"They seem to watch the east coast of Florida more closely, don't they?"

"They do. But we'll take either way if it is clear. The Gulf Coast is easy to penetrate, as is the Mexican border. Just think how much easier this would be if Trump had not won back in 2016. The wall has made this more difficult."

"Wouldn't Trump laugh if he could see Gutierrez negotiating a deal with the Mexicans to help stop the flow of departures going south instead of north."

"True, but the Mexican government is as corrupt as it always was. A little grease will smooth those skids. I have contacts there. It won't be a problem. They'll tell Gutierrez whatever he wants to hear and pay for. Then they'll take his money and our bribes as well and help us along. What a deal."

The older man ran his fingers through his white hair. He looked very tired. "Not a pretty picture tonight."

"Well, in one respect it's not really all that bad, either. We need the country to finally fail, to completely crash around the idiots who are running things. Then maybe, maybe, we can convince the lazy and entitled that the gravy train is over and that America must rise on its own again. It will be the new American dawn."

"We've got a lot of selfish folks out there who are not used to working for their bread."

Mark frowned. "Well, when things get really bad, there won't be any bread left to hand out anyway."

"Did you notice how long Earl said it will take to turn this around?"

"Most of that time will be spent educating a very dumb, but by then motivated, population, unless, of course, something big happens to change all the rules."

"You mean like a war?"

"Hell no. America couldn't win a war today if our lives depended on it. Gutierrez disarmed our nuclear forces and reduced our conventional army to one of the smallest in the civilized world. We would be helpless in time of war." There was anger in Mark's voice.

"The fact is we have our work cut out for us, don't we?"

"This is going to be a long process, and it isn't going to be an easy one." Mark looked at his dad. "And you look very tired. Why don't you get some sleep?"

"You're right. But I've lots of work remaining tonight."

"I'll take care of that. You go to bed."

"First, I want a cup of tea."

"Good idea, Pastor. I'll join you, but I want a beer." Mark stepped outside and looked carefully in all directions. "It's clear; let's go home."

Chapter 53

June 2, 2038
Havana, Cuba

Jake Dalton, Mark Sagan, and two other Americans walked along Prado Street toward the Capitolio Nacional where they would meet with the new Cuban President. The city was busy; people filled the streets as they went about their daily lives. Jake found the walk to be both invigorating and educational. Mostly he watched the people. They were smiling and friendly to the Americans who were visiting their country. Cuba had escaped the tyranny of Castro's regime after many years of deprivation. Socialism had failed in Cuba. It was a fact that everyone understood and accepted. There was no debate; the people had witnessed their own history. They didn't need some professor to paint the picture for them. The grand socialist experiment had not gone as planned. It had brought a failed economy and totalitarianism, much as it had done in Soviet Russia, Nazi Germany, and Mao's Red China. But things were changing. The last dying gasps of communism were followed by a resounding shout of freedom from the Cuban people. Things were getting better. Jobs returned; prosperity was on the resurgence; and the population rose to grasp new opportunities. And as the economy began to revive and freedom returned, the people began to smile again. It was a new day, a new era in the history of this small country, and the people danced in the streets and sang on the beaches of their beautiful island.

*   *   *

The four Americans sipped their coffees and laid out their plan for the Cuban President. Hernando Anaya had earned his presidency the hard way—he had been elected in a very close election. Cuba had learned the lessons of socialism and totalitarianism well, and Hernando was determined that his country would not make that same mistake again. The Castro brothers had devastated a great people and had left them destitute. Hernando understood very well the difference between production and distribution. If there were no production, distribution was irrelevant. He had grown up in a very poor family in a very poor country. He intended to change all that. He wanted what America had once possessed—a vibrant, booming economy, and these were the men who could make that happen. "Gentlemen, I like your plans. You are most welcome in Cuba. We consider ourselves lucky to have you here."

Dalton spoke for the Americans. "And we are grateful for your hospitality. Our plan is to make Cuba one of the most productive nations in the world. You have a beautiful country and people hungry for success. We have resources, technology, and, surprisingly, a lot of technical equipment stashed around the world that we can recover immediately. But we are going to need more infrastructure: buildings, roads, airports, electricity generation, etc."

"Let's institute your plan. We can build roads, sewers, airports, whatever is needed. If you have the resources, we have plenty of people who would welcome the opportunity to join your organizations. Cuba has needed this chance for a long time."

"And we need your help as well. I propose we build a new vision for Cuba, one with prosperity for all of us." They raised their tea cups together.

"But I do have a question." President Anaya looked at the four men carefully. "Do we need to fear reprisals from America? President Gutierrez is under a lot of pressure now. Your economy, and perhaps even your social fabric, is unwinding. Might he try to use this as an excuse to attack Cuba?"

Dalton answered immediately. "It's possible, but I really don't think so. The U.S. military is crumbling, and most of the good military leaders have already joined us. They have already left." He did not

213

mention that several top officers still remained in the U.S. military to supply information to the designated *rebels*. "We can certainly expect a bit of saber rattling, but I doubt much more than that. The liberals don't like the military, and the military is keenly aware of that fact. Besides, I doubt they have enough fuel to sustain a prolonged sea campaign."

Anaya pressed the point. "In an extreme situation, what about nuclear weapons that could be delivered by missiles or planes."

Dalton answered slowly. "The U.S. disarmed ten years ago, along with the Russians and everyone else, or so we hope." He frowned slightly. "We were never really sure about the Russians."

The Cuban spoke up quickly. "The Russians insisted they disarmed as well, but we all know their words mean little to them or us."

"Right." The disdain was evident in Dalton's voice. "I don't trust them as far as I could throw them. That crowd is not known for its veracity."

Anaya changed the subject and moved on into the details of the new marriage between Cuba and the most productive segment of the American country. He was smiling—he should have been. It was the largest international coup in generations. Within four years, Cuba would be transformed from a Third World nation to one of the most prosperous on the globe. Anaya loved his country, and he would go down in its history as the man who turned it all around.

Dalton began unrolling large scrolls of plans onto the table in the Cuban President's office. Suddenly he stopped and looked up at the group. "How strange that the socialist system that destroyed your nation is the one that America has decided to adopt. And while they falter, we are here bringing our old system to you—the one that gave America the highest standard of living in the world for so many years."

The Cuban President nodded. "So true. We finally had the chance to escape socialism; we know its failures, we lived them; we welcome your free market capitalism. Socialism has never succeeded, anywhere. I doubt it will work in America as well."

Dalton nodded. "I agree; that is why we are here, Mr. President, to unleash the productive capabilities of this country and allow those of us who come here to share in that freedom."

214

"This will finally bring my people the prosperity they have not had for so many years. Show me your plans; we will work together to make this a reality for Cuba and the Cuban people. We welcome you as new citizens of this country." He turned to face the others in the room. "You may stay as long as you wish, or if you ever want to return to your homeland, we will assist you any way we can. You have my word on that."

"Thank you, President Anaya. You are wise to acknowledge our ties to our homeland. And we freely admit we may one day desire to return to save America. But even if that occurs, Cuba will always be a brother to us, a country that helped us in our time of need. We will never forget that."

Anaya raised his tea cup. "Here's to a future of success for both nations. In the meantime, let us all proceed with great care." All of the men in the room raised their cups in salute.

Dalton downed his tea and looked into the eyes of the Cuban President. He liked him; Anaya was a practical man who wanted more for his people. It was not just about him, though he would go down in Cuban history as the man who saved his country. But Jake knew that was not the motivation that had prompted this man to contact him. No, Hernando Anaya saw an opportunity to move his country forward many years. Perhaps he could make up for some of the lost years under Castro's communism. Was it possible that he could give his people hope, real hope, not the false promise of so many leftist politicians? Cuba had clamored to adopt socialism when Castro first came to power, but now they were seeking the proven success of capitalism.

Anaya had never understood how American politicians could have been so misinformed or perhaps, just plain stupid. The reason he did not understand was basic in the fabric of his being. He wanted more for his country, for his people. The liberal politicians in America were simply using the people for their own agenda. They would not have understood his system of patriotism any more than he could have understood their system of political exploitation. The leftists in America were perpetuating an electorate that depended on the government; that dependency was not to be found in the Cuban President's model.

215

Anaya held up his hand and got everyone's attention. "One last thing. Your administration hired a member of my inner circle to spy on all of us. They made him quite an offer, which he has accepted. He immediately confided in me, of course. Now, what shall we relate back to your president through this *informer*?"

Dalton looked up with disgust on his face. "I expected something like this. May I ask who was the contact?"

"The Chief of Staff, Woodward."

"I'm not surprised. Send a message back that the negotiations did not go well but are ongoing. That will sound encouraging to them, and realistic as well."

"Very well. And gentlemen, this must never be mentioned outside this room."

"Understood." Dalton thought a moment and added. "Actually this is an opportunity that is valuable. Now we have a way to influence their plans. This could be valuable." He turned to the President. "President Anaya, I'd like Mark to be your personal contact in such matters. He'll keep me advised of everything going on."

"Of course."

Dalton was mentally measuring President Anaya as they shook hands. *The Cuban President is sharp and shares our vision for his country. Good for him. No, good for us. Good for all of us.*

216

Chapter 54

July 8, 2038
Washington, D.C.

"Hey fat boy, what you doin' in this neighborhood?" The tall, overweight young man with sloped shoulders shrugged indifferently as he walked toward them with a slight limp. The limp was from an old war injury, like the scar that ran across the left side of his face, reminders of his time in Afghanistan. His clothes were obviously poor, but the case in his hand was just as obviously expensive. "Get yo' ass outta here. This here is Three Country. We own this side of town." The gang leader called after him. "And what you got in that case? Huh, boy?" The young man turned and started to move away, but the taunts continued. "Say, man, how'd you get so fat?" The second gang member joined the tirade. "And so ugly!"

Before the young man reached the corner, two more members of the gang blocked his path. Each had a large number 3 tattooed on his neck. The two behind the prey took advantage of his focus on the two before him. He stood shaking before his tormentors, but it was not they whom he feared, it was the screaming voices from his past that once again invaded his mind. As he grabbed his head to stop them, he never noticed that the men around him all had chains in their hands.

*　　*　　*

Donnie opened his eyes to stare at the ceiling above him. The pain was almost unbearable, but he grimaced and forced himself to maintain his focus. The room around him was filled with medical equipment, and the window opposite his bed was dark. He had no idea how long he had been unconscious, but he reasoned it must have been for several hours. A low moan escaped his lips as he tried to move. There was a bandage on his head and it partially covered his right eye. His mind traveled back to the incident on the street. He had been beaten savagely; he remembered that. Then it dawned upon his consciousness. He had been carrying his cello. His cello! Where was his cello? With great effort he began calling for help. He had to find his cello. The pain throughout his battered body was forgotten in that moment. He had lost the one thing that gave his life meaning. It was also the one thing in his life that could stop the screams from his past.

The police came the next day to question him and assured Donnie that they would watch for his instrument. He knew they were placating him. He also knew there was little chance they would investigate the gang that had nearly killed him. He lay in his bed and weighed his alternatives. If there was any possibility of retrieving his cello, it would depend entirely upon him. Donnie flexed his right hand; it worked fine. He squinted with his right eye. It was functioning, though not very well. He squinted and looked across the small room, then out the window at a building across the street. At a distance, his eyesight was not clear; everything seemed fuzzy. That was not good, but perhaps time would help heal that issue as well as the pain in his right side. Much of his body still looked like raw hamburger, but he had what he needed, if the eye continued to heal and his vision cleared. Until that happened he simply had to complete his plan. Donnie was patient. He would plan carefully, and he would be ready as soon as he healed.

He looked over at his wall. There was a large 3 penciled beside his door. It was a reminder that was not needed. He would not forget this task—not for a long time. They had beaten him to within an inch of his life. But more importantly, they had taken his cello, his most prized possession. The beating was bad, but loss of his cello was unthinkable. It was the only thing that maintained any semblance of balance in his tortured mind. When they took that, they crossed a line. But the score would be settled; of that he was sure.

* * *

The lock on the old door had been easy to compromise. Donnie slipped inside the deserted warehouse and switched on a small flashlight. He glanced at his watch. It was 2:47 in the morning. Almost a month had passed since his beating, and he had been surveilling the gang that was responsible for almost a week. He knew that the gang stored things in this particular building, away from the prying eyes of other thieves in the neighborhood; perhaps, just perhaps, his cello might be inside. This had once been part of a large manufacturing concern that supported the automotive industry in the United States. Like so many others, it had become a casualty of the declining economy. Inside the building was a large open area where parts were made and people worked with the infrastructure of manufacturing tools. Now it was simply a large tomb that served no purpose at all. Along the sides of the building, however, were small offices or storage areas that once supported the workers and their tasks. These drew his attention.

Donnie began a quick survey of those rooms. He quickly walked across the building, opening the doors as he went. Then he found what he had been looking for, a locked door, and the lock was relatively new. He had no key, but he came prepared and with considerable effort cut the lock with a small hacksaw that he had purchased earlier in the day. As the lock fell to the floor, the young man opened the door and looked inside. He was surprised at what he found. It looked like a small armory. There were several handguns spread across a small table in the center of the room. Around the guns were boxes of ammunition. There were also a number of large knives and two hammers and a hatchet. Those he ignored. He was looking for a cello, and that would be large and difficult to hide. He quickly opened several storage cabinets, but the cello was not there. Instead he found a fairly large stash of drugs and booze. Donnie cursed quietly and started for the door. Perhaps they had already sold the instrument, or worse, they might simply have destroyed it. What would a

219

bunch of ignorant gang members know about something as beautiful as his cello?

The young man was filled with both sadness and rage at the loss of his prized possession. He wiped his eyes and cursed them all as he crossed the room. That is when he noticed something leaning against the wall in the opposite corner. He stopped and aimed his flashlight in that direction. It was another tool he knew well, a bolt action .308 rifle. He walked over and picked it up carefully. It was the same rifle he had trained with as an Army sniper. He checked it carefully; it had been well maintained. It was most likely stolen, but it was certainly stolen from someone who knew how to appreciate the weapon. As he handled it, a smile formed on his face.

It wasn't his cello, but he knew the rifle might help in that pursuit. Quickly he began studying the ammunition boxes on the table, but they were all pistol ammo. He guided the small beam of light around the room and began opening the drawers under the shelf beside the cabinets. He found what he was looking for in the second drawer, four boxes of 165-grain bullets, and next to that a Unertil scope, one of the finest ever made. With this equipment and a bit of practice he could easily hit a target the size of a man's head a mile away. That all depended, of course, on the state of his right eye. It was still not completely healed, but it was improving daily. The smile grew larger as he shoved the bullets into his pockets and gathered the rifle and the scope in his arms.

Donnie pulled a large lock from his pocket and placed it on the door. He smiled thinking how the gang would find it a real challenge. It was a special security lock that would not be easily removed. That done, he hugged the rifle lovingly and walked out into the night, wrapping the rifle with his coat to avoid attention. That would mean avoiding the metro, but it would be worth the effort. Besides, the walk would give him time to start developing a new plan now that the odds against him had changed. The bastards still had his cello, but now he had the means to make it a theft they would come to regret.

Chapter 55

August 13, 2038
Washington, D.C.

It was the middle of a busy Friday afternoon, and the activity on the corner was increasing in tempo. Several young women walked up and down the sidewalk before the macho crowd sitting at the small tables around the bodega. Six tattooed men eyed the young women and called to them with laughter. They all knew the real party would start later, when the drugs arrived with Carlos, the leader of Red Three, a local gang. In the meantime, the cheap beer would have to do while they drank, smoked, and watched the girls.

Two hundred and seventy-three yards away, a heavy young man crawled slowly across the top of a two-story building. He was dressed completely in camouflage and dragged a large musical case behind him. It was old and scratched, unlike the one he had lost to the gang. When he reached the edge of the building, he stopped, opened the case, and withdrew the parts of a rifle and a large scope. He stopped for a moment and admired the weapon as he assembled it. Like his cello, it was a tool he knew well. Donnie Williams might appear to be a bit slow, but his mind and intellect were actually quite remarkable. Anything he set out to do, he did well. He had been the best sniper in his army unit, a skill he had used well in Afghanistan, but even that didn't keep him from being riffed from a military that was being disbanded. The once-proud American fighting force was a mere skeleton of itself. That money had better use in the current scheme of politics. It would be put into programs that would ensure votes from the poor and destitute, so Donnie had been reduced to making a living on handouts from playing his cello on the street corners of Washington, D.C. That was before the gang had taken his prized instrument. He watched them laughing as he loaded his rifle. There was a slight smile on his face.

Donnie had planned his escape route carefully. Few used the alley behind the building, and he had little concern for the Washington police. They were kept mostly for political purposes—controlling friendly and unfriendly crowds. The science of fighting crime had died many years ago. Even though the Second Amendment had been abolished by the Democrats and guns were now illegal, they were still plentiful, and most criminals owned several. And while the police would take reports of criminal activities and serious crimes, they seldom solved them. Competence was not a requirement for the desirable job of being a policeman in the nation's capital. All one needed was the right political contacts to secure the pay and the pension; pay and pensions were rare these days, and though desirable, they were certainly not enough to risk one's life in the sections of town where the gangs ruled.

One of the men on the street corner grabbed one of the laughing girls and pulled her to his lap. She squirmed for a short while then gave in to the attention of the waiting group. Their wait was short. Carlos strolled up with a confident look on his face. All of the others nodded and spoke. It was evident who was boss.

Donnie peered through the large scope and studied the man with a black ribbon tied into a tight pony tail at the back of his neck. Donnie blinked several times to clear his right eye. Luckily, the day was bright and the visibility was excellent. The eye was improving; the drops he had been taking were helping. The man he was studying was one of the four who had beaten him so badly. He would be first. He had laughed at Donnie as they beat him, and he was the one who had taken the cello. The second was the large man leaning against the store front. The order didn't matter after that. There were six in all. If he were lucky, he'd get three or four. Either way, he would return. After all, he was a very patient man. He rubbed the scar on his face gently and loaded his rifle.

Carlos held the bag of drugs high for the gang to see. They all smiled and urged him to open the stash. He waved the drugs in front of the young woman in Divot's lap. She reached for them, but he pulled them away quickly. Carlos laughed, then suddenly stared wide eyed as the back of his head exploded. The group stood in shock as Carlos sank to the pavement in a pool of blood. As he crashed face first into the concrete, the large man leaning against the graffiti painted wall jerked forward, a large blood splatter on the wall behind him.

Donnie carefully picked his targets and fired quickly as the gang began to realize what was happening. One ran into the small store; Divot struggled with the young woman sitting on his legs, while two others started to run across the street. None knew the direction of the fire; they were simply too shocked and too terrified. One of those fleeing fell in the middle of the street. The other was wounded but dragged himself behind a parked delivery van. When the firing stopped four of the gang were dead; one was wounded, and one had escaped.

Donnie smiled a grim smile, rubbed his right eye momentarily then folded his weapon and scope into the cello case. As he crawled back to the opposite edge of the roof, he picked up his shell casings and painted a large 8 on the roof with a can of black spray paint. He then climbed carefully down the fire-escape; fifteen minutes later he was playing an old borrowed cello on the corner near one of the large government buildings. The nation might be in a state of economic distress, but the government officials still lived well, and some even enjoyed beautiful music. He played more beautifully than he had since the beating three weeks earlier. The borrowed cello sang beautifully, and the pain in Donnie's side disappeared along with the voices that intruded his reality at will. When he played he smiled; there was no room for pain in the joy of his music.

Chapter 56

August 14, 2038
A Washington D.C. precinct office

The night shift sergeant rubbed his eyes and peered into his half-empty coffee cup. The coffee was cold, and something indistinguishable was floating in it. He started packing his papers as the new shift came on duty. An old detective strolled into the room, looking as if he had not been home that night. He looked tired and was disheveled and needed a shower and a shave. "Hey, Dick, you look like shit! Out all night?"

"Right!"

"Old lady throw you out?" There was laughter in the sergeant's voice.

"She did that six months ago. Last night I was catching up."

"Anyone I know?"

"No, and if it was, I'd never tell you. You got a mouth bigger than Texas." He straightened his tie and looked at the stack of paper on the desk. "Anything important happen last night?"

"Same old shit. 'Cept the gang war between the 3s and the 8s got hot yesterday afternoon. We just lost another four gang-bangers on the south side. Good riddance I say."

"Thanks for the tip. I'll make damn sure I don't get into that territory this week."

"One thing strange about all those hits. It appears they were all from over two hundred yards away. Usually those idiots do it up close holding their guns sideways." The Sergeant smiled and demonstrated with his hand. "Hell, how do they aim like that?"

224

"They don't. That's why they do it up close. Most of those gang bangers can't shoot worth a damn." He squinted his eyes in thought. "So how does one of them hit a target from two hundred yards away?"

"Beats me, and I could care less. As I was saying, good riddance to the whole bunch of scum. Just think, the average IQ in America increased ten points yesterday. We should give them more ammo and maybe even some practice shots on our range." They both laughed as the sergeant rose to leave.

"Thanks Bernie, I'll make sure we all stay out of that district for a while. If they've found a good shooter, I damn sure don't want any cops around there."

Chapter 57

August 14, 2038, 7:00 pm
An old abandoned warehouse, Washington, D.C.

The last member of the 8s slipped into the old deserted building just after 9:00 pm. He looked carefully out the door to insure he had not been followed then turned to the assembled group of young males. "Hey man, is everyone here?"

"We all here 'cept the Beast. Dunno where he is. We checked everywhere; he ain't round."

A tall and handsome young man walked slowly to the middle of the old building and got everyone's attention. "Everybody know 'bout the hit on the 3s right?" All heads nodded. "Anybody have anythin' to do wid 'dat?" All heads moved sideways. "Cops found an 8 on the top of a building nearby and think we done it." He smiled at the group with even, white teeth. "Wish we had! It was a good hit!" One serious voice spoke from the back of the room. "It had to be a rifle, and a damned good shot. That ain't us. We don't do rifles." Everyone agreed, then the man continued. "I think we better make it clear to the cops and everybody else that we didn't do dis."

Several others in the room began to shout the man down as a coward. "We ain't scared of no 3s or no cops!" There was general agreement from the others in the room. "Now we'll get some respect!"

"Or a bullet."

"Fuck the 3s. Most of 'em is dead now anyway." There was laughter in the room. One of the older members pulled a bottle of whiskey from his pocket and began to pass it around. Several others did the same, and soon the room was filled with laughter and shouting. It lasted for over two hours before the first of them started to leave. Two swaggered into the darkness outside the old building and were immediately cut down by bullets that were not seen nor heard. Two more stepped out the same door before they realized what had happened. In mere minutes four of the 8s were dead or dying outside the crumbling building. Inside, the remaining gang members huddled in panic. They crouched by two small windows and peered into the darkness outside. The leader finally took control. "Jay and Willie, go out d' back way and find dat bastard. I want his head on a stick."

The two chosen members looked at each other carefully then addressed the leader. "Why don't we just wait 'em out. They probably have the back way covered, too."

Another of the young men spoke in support of his friends. "Yeah, they got us cornered. But we in no hurry." Two seconds later the first of two Molotov cocktails crashed through the side window, igniting the dry wood floor. When the fire department and cops arrived twenty-minutes later, six of the 8s were dead. Two others were wounded, and four were missing. Later the survivors would tell stories of heroic fighting that they all knew were lies. They reported being ambushed by a large team of at least twenty shooters.

When the symbol of yet another gang was found nearby, all were surprised. It was not the 3s, after all, but another gang from several blocks away. And so the gang war began.

A week later Donnie trudged down the street with his cello case slung over his back. A wry smile crossed his lips as he read the newspaper report of a city-wide gang war that had cost many lives, one that he, alone, had instigated.

Chapter 58

September 2, 2038
National Airlines headquarters, Washington, D.C.

The short pilot walked into the VP of Operation's office and dropped his hat on the cluttered desk. "Mackenzie, we need to talk!"

She looked into the steely eyes of the pilots' union representative leaning on her desk and smiled secretly. She decided to stay seated. She liked Paul Robinson. He was short in stature but huge in spirit, and, more importantly, a man of integrity. There was no reason to stand and look down at him; that would not benefit either. She smiled. "Hi, Paul, what's up?"

"Not our stock." He grimaced then glanced around the room. "Any coffee?"

"I'll order some. The carafe is cold, I'm sure." She reached for her phone and placed the order.

"We've got a problem."

"We've got lots of problems." She watched as the look on his face grew serious. "Which one is keeping you up at night?"

"This recent group of new pilots!"

"I was afraid of that! How bad is it?"

"It's bad."

"What should we do?"

"Fire them—all but two. Two are pretty good." He paused. "Well, they're good enough to train. But not the other six. Have you seen their resumes?"

"I did." Mackenzie looked down briefly and closed her eyes.

Robinson caught it. He might be a technical man, but he was also an expert at reading other people, and he knew Mackenzie Selms very well. He respected this attractive woman who played hardball as well as any man he knew. Robinson gambled. "I know you objected to this batch, but I guess the brass overruled you, or was it HR?"

She smiled, recognizing the tactic, but decided to go along with it. If your IQ is off the chart, might as well use it, she figured. "Both!"

"Can you get it reversed?"

"It will be very difficult." She stood and walked to the window as Paul sat on the end of the white leather couch that was opposite the west-facing windows. She looked out the window until he was comfortably seated then sat on the end opposite him. "Will the union fight us if we dismiss them?"

"For show, of course, but I can get the union to fold when it counts."

"These ladies could crash a plane and kill people?"

"If they are allowed in the left seat, I can assure you that will happen."

"Training?"

"Won't work. Trust me, I know pilots; this group might be able to wait tables—well, except for one—not sure what she could do."

"How long before they could bid down to a small plane and get in the left seat?"

"With retirements coming up, it could happen in two to three years."

"Well, at least we have some time."

"Not really. In six months their probation time is over, and they'll be damned hard to fire."

"Any chance to talk some sense into them? Could you just spell it out?"

"No way! They figure this job is easy and a real plum; one told me she *deserved* this opportunity."

A knock at the door prompted Mackenzie to open it, take the coffee tray, and return to the couch. She placed the tray on a small table and poured two cups. She added two creams and two sugars to Paul's coffee and handed it to him. She took hers black. Paul drank his coffee as he lived his life, with relish. Mackenzie quickly refilled his cup but let him add the cream and sugar.

"Paul, this one won't be easy, but I'll talk to Goram. He's stubborn, but he's also practical. Okay if I use your name?"

"No way. If this gets out, I'm done in the union, and who knows who might get this job then. We have some real firebrands out there who'd love to face off with the company."

"Makes sense; I'll keep this on the sly, but you might start planting some seeds in ALPA's board."

"Good idea." Robinson finished his coffee and retrieved his hat. As he walked to the door, Mackenzie rose and walked back to her desk. Robinson paused at the door and looked back at the woman seated behind the desk. How could one woman be so smart and so attractive at the same time? If only he were fifteen years younger—and six inches taller.

The VP looked at the door for 30 seconds then reached for her phone. "Wanda, get Mr. Goram. If he's not available now, get me an appointment as soon as possible."

Chapter 59

Same day, September 2, 2038
National Airlines Headquarters, Washington, D.C.

Mackenzie Selms, Vice President of Airline Operations, walked into the airline president's office without an invitation. Continuing to focus on a large stack of reports on his desk, Frank Goram offered her a seat. She did not sit, but waited for his undivided attention. With a sigh he pushed the papers aside and looked up into the blue eyes of his colleague and trusted associate. "What's up, Mackenzie?"

"Did you see the list of new pilots we hired last month?"

"I don't typically get into that level of detail; that's why I have you here!" There was a smile on his face. It disarmed her immediately.

"Of course, you are right!" She smiled back. "Frank, I'm worried. We have some really inexperienced people on this list."

"Inexperienced?"

"Like less than 500 hours of flying time. One as low as 300 hours. Most of it in small props!"

"That doesn't sound right, does it?"

"No, it sounds downright dangerous!"

"Did you talk to Stokes about this? As VP of Flight Ops, this is his area of responsibility."

"Yes, it is!"

Goram looked up at his VP for a long while before speaking. "Mackenzie, this is not about a turf war is it? I thought we had already worked that out to everyone's satisfaction."

231

"Frank, this has nothing to do with our organization structure. I understand your decision to keep Flight Operations as a direct report to you. This has nothing to do with that. This is all about putting some unqualified pilots in our airplanes."

"Look, I'll agree this looks strange, but talk to Ed first. And if there is still a problem, then let's all three of us have a meeting and get it resolved."

Mackenzie stared at the president of National Airlines for a moment. "Sounds like a plan. I just wanted to give you a "heads up" before the fur starts to fly." She was halfway to the door when Goram leaned back in his chair and called her name.

"Mackenzie, one last thing. Where did you get that data?"

"ALPA, but that must not be repeated."

"ALPA?" He sat up straight in his chair. "The union gave that to you?"

"This even frightens them."

"Damn!" Goram rubbed his forehead for several seconds. He reached for a small leather notebook and scribbled notes with a large Montblanc fountain pen. Finally, he looked back at the young woman standing in his doorway. Even with her executive suit and her hair pulled severely back on her head, she was beautiful. "Thanks for letting me know, and keep me informed, please."

"Will do, and don't forget—no mention of ALPA." She turned on her heel and walked rapidly down the hall toward flight operations.

Goram watched her as she left; there was a small smile on his face. It would be an interesting meeting, and he felt sorry for Ed Stokes; Ed was no match for Mackenzie. He knew that eventually he'd be pulled into the fray between his two vice presidents; that was inevitable. He just hoped it would not be today; he had a meeting with his CEO tomorrow, and he needed to be prepared for anything. Business was falling monthly. Even with the government subsidies, the airline could not continue to lose so much money and survive. The economy was in the tank, and people without money don't take trips, especially on airplanes.

* * *

232

Ten minutes after Mackenzie walked into his office, Ed Stokes rose, walked to the door, and motioned to his secretary. "Maria, would you please bring coffee for me and Miss Selms. Make both black, please." He knew it was going to be a difficult meeting, and he needed a short break to clear his head. Stokes was a relatively young man for the position he held, and even at thirty-eight, appeared younger. He had few wrinkles, and his hair had not yet begun to grey from either stress or age. He had been in this position for less than four months, having come from a fairly high position in the government. He expected that in four more months he would easily look his age—and more. The adjustment to the private sector had been more stressful than he had imagined. The working hours and the responsibilities were greater, and the competition was palpable. He wondered what it had been like when the country had been primarily a capitalist country. It must have been horrendous then, he imagined. People were actually held accountable for their decisions in the private sector.

The meeting ended with much head nodding and "maybes," but decisions were not made, and Mackenzie was not happy. She knew when she was being patronized. "Okay Ed, let me summarize. (1). You recognize that there is a risk here. (2). You feel the socially responsible thing to do is to hire these people and give them a chance based on their ethnicity and their gender. (3). You agree you should monitor their performance and ensure that they sit in the right seat of our planes until they demonstrate an ability to take the left seat responsibly. (4). You agree that you are personally responsible to ensure that these things happen. Do I have this right?"

Ed looked up with a mixture of anger and exhaustion on his face. Just how did this woman feel she was entitled to treat him this way. He had come from the government with the express purpose of helping this struggling organization, and now he had to listen to this! "That's right!" And just where did she get all this energy? She was tall and beautiful. He had other ideas of what he would like to do to her rather than debate pilot capabilities. "It is my decision, and I'll take care of it."

"Right, and if one of these women crashes one of our planes, I'll personally save you a spot on the emergency table. Then you can make the calls to the families." She turned sharply and started for the door.

"Are you satisfied now?"

"No, I'm not." She turned back and glared at him. "And I'm going to fight you on this one. This is dangerous, and it is wrong. Quotas are a bad idea when we're talking about pilots!"

"Would it matter if they were white?"

"One is white. But it wouldn't matter if they were green. Only one thing matters when we hire pilots—their ability to fly. You know, the only one bringing ethnicity into this equation is you. You are hiring simply based on race and gender. I could care less about either. But really, fewer than 400 hours in a Cessna? Come now! There are lots of good pilots looking for work after being laid off at United and Delta. They have experience, and they don't need to be taught to fly!"

"You don't understand the big picture!"

"And you are making a bad judgment—about them and about me." As she left, he studied her butt in the tight pants suit, his anger giving way to fascination.

* * *

Mackenzie walked into her apartment and tossed a large stack of reports onto her couch. She stood there looking at the tidy, but lonely room. Somehow she knew she could not spend one more hour working on the airline's business today. She had been around countless people all day at the office, but she was lonely, and it was a deep need that could not be satisfied in her apartment. She picked up her phone and looked at it for several moments. Finally, she put it back on the table and walked to the small refrigerator in her kitchen. She poured a glass of wine and took one sip. She immediately put it down and retrieved the phone. "Mark, have you had dinner yet?" She listened for a moment then continued. "I'm really in the mood for Italian tonight and I know a great little place near the airport. Care to join me?"

The dinner was good and she was excited to tell him her about her day at work. He watched her intently as she talked and smiled her way through the desert. As she stopped to finish her dessert, he reached across the table and took her hand. "I'm glad you called tonight. I had just left the hospital and was facing a dark apartment and maybe a cold sandwich. Instead I have you, a wonderful meal, and even a decent wine."

"It's funny you say that. I had the same empty feeling when I got to my apartment tonight. I guess I still miss Sam more than I expected."

"He was a great dog. I miss him too."

Mackenzie looked at Mark in silence while he played with the last of his food. "It seems neither of us wants to go back home alone tonight, so why don't we just fix that." Mark's fork stopped in mid-plate as his head jerked up immediately. Before he could speak she continued. "Your place or mine?"

"Whichever is closer." He was smiling broadly as he grabbed some bills from his wallet and threw them onto the table. As he reached for his coat he saw that she was already half way to the restaurant door. He was still smiling as he followed her into the night.

Chapter 60

September 7, 2038
Linton Enterprises, southwest of Chicago, Illinois

The secretary walked into her boss's office and announced that two government officials were waiting outside. Harold Linton, president of Linton Enterprises, looked up, frowned, put down his pen and motioned for them to be admitted. Margaret looked at him and rolled her eyes. It almost made him laugh. They had worked together for more than 25 years. They understood each other quite well.

The two agents were dressed in suits that were not well-made, indicating that they were not very high in the government's pecking order. One was middle-aged, balding, and very heavy. The other was much younger and had an athletic build. As they walked into the office, Harold pointed to two chairs across from his desk. "Take a seat. What can I do for you?"

The two men sat down and the older pulled a long yellow pad from an old briefcase and began surveying the top three sheets. The younger of the two watched him with little interest. "Would either of you care for coffee?"

The balding man spoke immediately. "No, thank you. We have a train to catch so we will be brief."

"No need; the train is always late; it is a government operation." Linton smiled as he watched the two, carefully trying to perceive their position. He knew the meeting would not be pleasant. He just wondered what tack they might take. He knew they wanted his new chip process. He also knew they would never get it.

"We've found some discrepancies at your facility during our inspection. I'm afraid I will have to recommend fines for several of them."

"Really, what discrepancies did you find?"

"For one, your fuel storage is not in accordance with current regulations. All fuel is to be stored in the new plastic storage cans and placed in a separate building at least one hundred feet from other structures."

"And what did you find?" Linton looked straight into the balding man's eyes, which the man lowered to the pad quickly.

"We found two five-gallon gas cans inside the loading dock area. That is not allowed."

"Was there a truck there being loaded?"

"Yes there was, but that does not change the regulation."

"I see. And what else did you find?"

"We found two vehicles inside the manufacturing area with gasoline engines instead of the prescribed electric engines. You know that is not allowed. All new vehicles are to be electric now."

"Were those vehicles forklifts by any chance."

"Yes, they were."

"Are you aware that there are no electric forklifts in existence?"

The young agent looked startled, but the older man responded quickly. "That is of no concern to us. We don't write the laws; we only enforce them."

"Without thought or reason, I see."

"Now Mr. Linton, we are not here to be adversarial; we are simply doing our job."

"I see." He studied the two for several minutes and continued. "I have a question for the two of you. Just to help me understand the context of this meeting. Have either of you ever worked in the private sector before?"

"No, I have sixteen years with the government." The older agent said it with pride.

"So you wouldn't have a clue about what it takes to produce a product and run a business."

237

"Now Mr. Linton, as I said earlier, we are simply doing our jobs."

"Let's cut to the chase. How much?"

"How much what?"

"How much money do you two plan to take from Linton Enterprises?"

"Probably about one and a half million in fines I would expect." He looked up defiantly at Linton. "You can always file a petition if you feel the fines are excessive."

"Good luck with all of this." Linton glared at the two. "I suspect you both have a lot to learn about how business works. Well, this may be the start of that education. Now if you will excuse me, I have real work to do." With that Harold turned his attention to his laptop computer.

"Is that all you have to say?"

"That is all I have for you two." The two looked at each other briefly then rose to leave. "Please close the door as you leave."

The two agents walked out into the sunny afternoon. "Do you think he'll pay the fines?"

"Hell yes he'll pay. If he doesn't we'll bring the cops down here and drag his ass off to jail. That's where guys like him belong. They think because they're rich they can do anything they want."

"Yeah, it's all these rich folks that cause all the problems. You'd think they owned the world. He made a fortune off the backs of his workers, and now he thinks he's special."

"We don't need men like that in this country." They both nodded, not knowing how close to the truth they had come. They didn't want the Harold Linton's of the world, and soon they wouldn't have them. And 123,000 workers would be without jobs when Linton Enterprises closed.

Harold walked out of his office and leaned over his secretary's desk. "You okay Margaret?"

"I'm fine. A little sad maybe, but I understand." She looked into the gray eyes of her boss. "How about you, Harold?" It was the first time in over 20 years of working together that she had called him by his first name.

"I guess I'm sad, too." He looked at her and smiled a very thin smile.

When she looked up; there were tears in her eyes. "You know, this is the only job I ever had."

"And it will still be your job for a long time to come if you want it. We both are too stubborn to quit, so I guess we'll just have to keep working, but in a different place." He walked over to the wall and surveyed the pictures hanging there. "Which one would you like to take?"

Her eyes brightened. "That one. Of you and me and Tom at the company picnic."

He took it from the wall and handed it to her. "Here, in case I forget."

"We won't forget." There was fear in her voice.

"No, Margaret, the memories we built here will last a lifetime, for sure. And soon we'll just go make more memories in a very different place. The government is tired of our success, and frankly, I'm tired of the government's failures."

Chapter 61

September 13, 2038
Norfolk Naval Base, Virginia

Captain Nathan Jacobson walked down the pier and surveyed his carrier. It had substantial amounts of rust; the back-up turbines were questionable, and his crew was inexperienced. He was grateful he was not going to war. The two junior officers walking with him also were surveying the ship with displeasure. All noted the general lack of maintenance. He had never seen so much visible rust on a U.S. Navy ship in his entire career, and that spanned almost twenty-eight years. What had happened to the Navy Jacobson had entered all those years ago? Still, it was good to be going to sea. There had been damned little of that with the ongoing economic crisis and the fuel shortage.

The captain settled into his quarters aboard ship and sipped the hot coffee sent up from the galley several floors below. After two sips he pushed it aside and hoped it was not an example of the quality of the food he would endure for the next few weeks. A tall, thin man walked into his office and saluted. Jacobson returned it then stood and shook the hand of one of his best friends. "Hello, Mike. Looks like we get to take her out for a spin around Cuba."

"I'm looking forward to some salt air; it's been awhile."

"Yes, it has. Have you seen our orders?"

"Yes, Sir, I have. Any idea what this is all about?"

"Seems the President and some of his politician friends are getting worried about the brain drain."

"He should be worried. It's becoming more of a flush than a drain."

"Yeah, I've known a few of those who left. Good people."

"We've lost our share in the military, as well."

"Yes, we have."

Later the two men walked to the ship's bridge and stood silently watching the sea before them. It had been several years since either had left his boring job in the Pentagon, and both were grateful for the respite. For some men the sky calls their spirits to greater heights; for others it is the endless sea. These men loved the smell of salt water and the gentle swaying that even a large aircraft carrier experiences as it rides the ocean's bosom. Finally, the second in command broke the silence. "Will we be doing any flight operations?"

"Very little. I know the pilots want to practice a bit. Heaven knows they need it, but we are very short on fuel these days. I'm expecting further orders as we get underway, but I doubt it will involve flight operations. You'll also notice that we are sailing without the normal task force for a carrier. We will be sailing alone."

"I thought the government had received a shipment of oil from the Russians."

"We did, but the military got precious little of that."

"Still not among the favored few!"

Jacobson nodded then turned his attention back to the open ocean before him. After several minutes, he turned to the second in command and nodded. "Walk with me." The two men stepped out of the bridge and walked out into the fresh breeze blowing from the southeast.

When he was sure that the two men were alone, the captain turned abruptly to his friend. "I wanted to talk to you before we started this excursion, but I was told it was not a good idea, especially on the bridge. I'll have that swept for transmitters after we leave port."

"I was told the same, but I doubt the government has enough savvy to arrange sophisticated spyware out at sea."

"Then you're on board with our plan? I was not advised you were coming until this morning."

"100%. I met with the committee secretly two months ago, just in case this came up."

"You've been aware all that time?"

"I was one of the ones who planted this seed. Damn, politicians are dumb."

"Especially this crowd." The captain placed his hand on his friend's shoulder. "We're placing our careers on the line, you know."

"When I graduated from Annapolis, I swore my career for my country. That's what I'm doing now—trying to save my country."

"As we shall, my friend. As we shall!"

*   *   *

Alec and the President sat in the oval office and watched the TV coverage of the USS Obama sailing out to sea. He had wanted actual footage of the carrier underway, but technical difficulties had precluded the video from being used. He frowned. Somehow, several still shots on TV just didn't match the drama of a battle carrier actually steaming into the Atlantic on the evening news. But the boss seemed pleased; perhaps that was enough.

"Good job, Alec. Did you alert the Cuban Ambassador that we would be headed his way but that he should not be concerned?"

"Right." Alec lied. He had no intention of alerting the Cubans that the carrier was simply a ruse. He wanted them to think the tiger still had some teeth—and the will to use them.

"How long do you plan to have them off the coast of Cuba?"

"Not long. We don't have all that much fuel available now. Those carriers burn a ton of fuel."

"Maybe we should have rethought our ban on nuclear energy for ships." Gutierrez smiled as he watched Alec choke on his coffee.

"We've been through that before! You know what our environmental friends think of nuclear!"

"Yeah, but they are nuts—and we both know that!" The President was still smiling.

"What was it Lenin said about "useful idiots?"

"Careful!" Both men were smiling now.

"Hey, you don't have tapes going like Nixon do you?" Alec began gathering papers he had been working on. "Speaking of useful idiots, I've got a meeting with our friends in the press in five minutes. See you later."

Alec walked through the White House toward his office and thought about the challenges they faced. Since its inception America had been a nation of growth and expansion, first across the wilderness of the American West, then into space. Now it was declining. What had happened to the spirit of the strong men and women who had braved the Atlantic in small wooden ships to find freedom in a wild and dangerous world? America had captured the imagination of the best and brightest that Europe had to offer. The timid had not welcomed the challenge and risk of the new world. It was the strong and the brave who had dared leave their homes for a new land.

But now the strong were leaving America, seeking a different kind of freedom on foreign shores. He thought briefly about the ones who remained, the entitled people who took much and gave back little. If America lost its best and brightest, who was left? The thought made a cold chill run up his back. He realized his mind was beginning to go down strange paths, paths that frightened him and challenged everything he believed in. He quickly pushed those thoughts from his mind. They were not true; they could not be true. But somehow he knew they would surface again, and he also knew he would dismiss them again as needed. When you had lived a lie as long as he, how could you possibly admit the truth?

Chapter 62

September 23, 2038
Linton Enterprises, southwest of Chicago, Illinois

Harold Linton looked at the large building before him and could not decide whether to cry or to smile. He had spent most of his life building this business, and now he was going to burn it to the ground. He walked slowly back into the office area and confirmed that all of the engineering drawings and the patent applications were laid out in order over the long tables that were originally used to pack and ship his products. The early days of building the business had been difficult, but that was before he had discovered an entirely new process for producing computer chips, one that was quicker and so much cheaper. Now his business spanned four different states and employed 123,000 people. Tomorrow they would all be unemployed. There was a time when he would have felt compassion for the families that had shared his business, but that was before the unions stepped in and made him the enemy. His workers had disappointed him and, quite frankly, surprised him. They had voted for the union; they wanted more say in how he ran his company. He looked at the old table and wished he could take it with him, but he knew he could not. He walked over to it and ran his hands across the weathered wood. It was the most creative space in his life. He had used that old table to start a company that had succeeded beyond his wildest expectations. It was also the same table upon which his first son was conceived.

Harold closed his eyes and thought back to that night so long ago. He and Emily had been working through the day and into the night, sorting products for the growing list of customers who wanted the technology they had for sale. Late into the evening he had stopped his work to look over at his young wife. She was stacking boxes and leaned over the table to grab a few more. He had watched her figure with appreciation. That night they had both stopped working long enough to look at the other. The look became a laugh; the laugh a sigh; the sigh a kiss. From there they had initiated the old table and unknowingly started their family. Perhaps Barak Obama had been right when he said *you didn't build that company*. Harold had needed Emily. She had been his cheerleader and also his helper. Together they had built Linton Enterprises into a successful business.

Young Thomas had been born about nine months after that night together. Harold smiled as he remembered the times they had shared, his hand still rubbing the old wood gently. If there were any regrets, it was that he could not leave this company to his son. Tom had worked beside his dad and had learned about the business and about life. When the workers voted to join the union, Tom had wanted to fight. Only Harold kept him from pounding the fat union boss into the ground. Like his dad, the company also bore Tom's name.

Harold walked through the work area and stopped to examine an old box of tools, the ones he had used to get the machinery to work when the company was still struggling. He picked up a pair of pliers and studied them carefully. They had once belonged to his own father. As the cold metal weighed in his hand, memories flooded over him and startled him somewhat. He looked up at the picture of his first crew and walked slowly toward it. He studied each face. They were his work family. They would never have deserted him for the union promises and lies. Most were retired, but two were still on the payroll. There was no question in his mind how they had voted in the union certification. As Harold looked at the faded picture, he suddenly noticed that the picture was not nearly so clear as usual. Then he wiped his eyes and the clarity returned. He was just turning to walk back into his office when a movement behind him caught his attention. He spun around immediately. "Tom! What are you doing here? I thought you were going ahead with your mom and sisters."

"They are already safe in our new home, dad. I figured I needed to be here with you tonight. I don't think this will be an easy task for you."

"No, it isn't, son. This place holds lots of memories."

"I know. I feel the same way."

Harold looked at his son. How he had grown. Tom was now six feet two inches tall and as strong as he was smart. He was also a very handsome man—must have taken that from his mom. Tom walked to the old table and started moving the patents and other paperwork to a newer one nearby. "What are you doing son?"

"We're taking this old table. I promised mom I'd bring it. For some crazy reason this is all she wanted from the business. She said it was where you did your best work."

"She said that did she?" Linton smiled broadly.

"Give me a hand, this thing is heavy. I have a truck outside. I just hope we have enough gas to get to the drop off point."

Harold grasped the end of the table and began moving it with his son. He was smiling, but a single tear ran down his cheek and fell to the floor. He could always count on Emily. He knew that nothing would be left when the ashes were cleared tomorrow. He had built it, not the unions. He had spent the hours of research over so many years to find a better way. He was the one who had risked everything and had even mortgaged his home to raise the money to start a dream. Then the new shop steward announced that he would tell Harold how to run his company. That and the ever increasing taxes and regulations had finally made it impossible to compete in the global economy. The government even had regulations about how he could downsize to become more competitive. Their rules condemned Linton Enterprises to failure. Finally, it just became too much. Emily and the girls were now in Cuba. In a few days he and Tom would join them and start over. The U.S. government would not get his plant and especially his new process for building the best computer chips in the world. He had made sure no one else understood how it worked—no one. They might know some of the details, but they did not know the secret that had taken him six years to perfect. That would be enough to get them started in Cuba.

Harold Linton stopped and looked at his hands. They were older than when he had started out on this trek. He knew he did not have the stamina of his youth, but he also knew he had so much more wisdom now,

246

and now he also had Tom. It would be hard, but it would also be exciting. He would begin his life again and rebuild what he was now going to burn. Harold walked back into the maintenance area and located the last remnants of fuel from his allocation from the government. It was sparse, but it was enough. How appropriate, he thought, that he would use their very own fuel to destroy one more company that would not become a part of the public domain. No, damn them, he had built it, and he would destroy it. They had not worked the long hours or taken the risks. They had not spent the sleepless nights worried about making payroll at the end of the month. No, damn them, they would not get his dream. "Tom, take this and put it in your pocket. It is the key to the new computer chips I developed. The patents are wrong; I didn't share this with them, with no one." He handed his son the flash drive.

"I don't need this dad. You'll be building chips yourself in another week or so."

"I know son. This is just in case. You know—risk avoidance."

When Harold struck the match, his hands were shaking. He stood for several moments looking at the flame. Finally, he tossed it into the gasoline soaked designs; after that he never looked back. He could hear the roar of the fire as it moved quickly through the building, but he could not bear to watch. He stepped into the truck, and Tom drove quickly into the night. Another company was gone, but he was also aware that another would spring anew. He was an entrepreneur. He had done it before; he could do it again. In a month or so Cuba would be the largest exporter of computer chips in the world, and 123,000 union workers would be unemployed in Illinois. Now he just had to get to Jacksonville, Florida. A boat would be waiting to take him and Tom to their new home. Linton Enterprises was not dead; it was simply moving. And his creative table was moving as well. He looked at his son and smiled.

Chapter 63

November 16, 2038
The White House

Alec walked into the meeting and promptly spilled most of his coffee on the cluttered table. Around it several young government officials sat quietly watching him motion for help from the staff. "Damn, can't afford to waste good coffee."

After the table was cleaned a young woman stood and began a quick tour through a series of PowerPoint slides. After about ten minutes the electricity failed, and the group found itself seated in a very dark room. Eventually one of the young men managed to open the door and let in some ambient light. Alec began cursing quietly and fumbled through his briefcase for a flashlight that lived there perpetually. "There was a time when American industry could supply electric power properly. Obviously that time has passed. I guess there just isn't enough profit in that now." Several of the young people murmured agreement as the assembled group filed out into the hall.

"Shall I find another room with windows?"

Alec looked at his watch and calculated quickly. "No, these blackouts generally last about ten minutes. We only have a couple of minutes left." Almost on cue, the lights came on and everyone re-entered the small room. As the young woman sorted through the slides to find her place, Alec spoke. "Look, we've already lost 15 minutes and my schedule is quite busy today, so let's just get to the bottom line. What is the status on company closures?"

The young woman studied her notes and began speaking quickly as if the speed would help resolve Alec's schedule problem. "New company filings are still practically zero. Companies filing applications to go out of business continue to rise. If they have valuable resources or patents, they are approved immediately. We have taken over three million square feet of office space and almost an equal amount of warehouse space in the past month."

"Patents?"

"Over 38,000 class C patents were passed to the government last month, along with 20,000 class B patents, and approximately 3,000 class A patents."

"Was George able to put a price on those?"

"He has not completed his analysis, but he says we are looking at over two hundred million dollars easily."

"Not a bad month."

"No sir, not bad at all."

Alec rose to leave. "Tell George that I said he was doing a great job. I'd also like to know if he has any other good targets on the radar."

"He said to tell you Linton Industries appears to be failing. Their profitability has decreased significantly in the past six months."

"They're the ones making the new computer chips, aren't they?"

"Yes sir. Supposedly it will put them ahead in the global chip business. We might even get back into global exports again. This could be big."

"Thanks, please keep me advised on this one. And tell George to start checking those patents. If the new chips really work, the patents could be worth billions."

As Alec walked down the hall, one of the young interns muttered to another. "What good are patents if you can't build anything? We'll just sell them to the Chinese and then buy more of their products—on credit, of course."

"Be quiet. You know what will happen if someone hears you? Don't you like having a job? Most folks would give anything for this job."

"Most folks are too dumb to do this job. It must take at least a sixth grade education." He laughed quietly. "You know the smart people are leaving in droves."

"Yeah, I heard."

"Are you smart? Or are you as dumb as the folks who elected these bastards?"

"Quiet John. Don't get us fired—not yet."

"Not yet, but I assure you I don't intend to remain in this house of cards very long."

Chapter 64

January 6, 2039
The White House

The President walked into Alec's office before the sun had even risen. "What are you doing up so early? Want a cup of coffee?"

"There's a pot on my credenza. Help yourself, but remember, I make it strong."

"So you do. I'll just add extra cream." The President watched Alec as he poured the coffee. "What is that"

"The first draft of your State of the Union speech."

Gutierrez frowned. "I'm not looking forward to that."

Alec finally raised his head and looked at the President. "Why? It will be great. You're going to love this speech and so will the nation."

Gutierrez walked to Alec's desk and picked up the stack of paper. He studied it for several minutes. "Are you kidding? Do you really think this will sell?"

"Of course it will." Alec was tired, but he still exuded enthusiasm. "They will buy it all!"

"Nine percent unemployment and improving?" Gutierrez was reading from the paper. "Significant job creation in the past six months? Ten percent reduction in the Federal deficit for the past two years?" The President tossed the papers back onto the desk. "They'll laugh me off the podium."

"You didn't even get to the part about international affairs." Alec was actually smiling as he leaned back in his chair. "That's the best part of all."

"Seriously, Alec. How could I say that to Congress and the American people?"

"Just say it like you mean it, and remember to smile. You simply have to look positive while you speak."

"Right." Gutierrez was not enjoying the conversation. "And when the tomatoes are tossed?"

"Look, politicians have been lying to the public for years. *I didn't have sex with that woman. There were no classified messages on that server. No new taxes.* The public bought it all. You just lie with a smile, and if they ask you about it later you simply tell them: *What difference does it make now?*" Look, they all got away with it. You've got to remember that most Americans really don't listen to the news—which we spin like crazy. And if they do, they don't care what it says." Alec stood and walked around his desk. "Look at history. We've had plenty of liars living in this house. Just remember, as long as the issue doesn't directly affect most Americans, they could care less. Don't impart some mystical intelligence to the electorate that is not deserved."

"Maybe I could tell them we are pulling out of Afghanistan and taking all that money for roads and bridges."

"That's the idea."

"And we could raise the minimum wage again."

"Perfect, just don't mention what that might do to unemployment."

The President smiled at his Chief of Staff. "You know, I'm beginning to like this speech after all."

"Just say it with conviction and you'll be fine."

"When do you think I can look at the complete draft?"

"Hopefully by tomorrow. First I need to find some props we can use."

"Props?"

"Yeah, you know, like old Aunt Millie who lost her husband and is living on nothing but public assistance. We're going to give her a raise, but first I have to find a few like her so we can screen them. They'll be in the front row when you give your speech; we'll have reference to them by name in the speech. The press is going to love this."

"Maybe a few wounded vets from Afghanistan as well."

"We have to be careful about that. Most of them don't care for our policies, but it is a large sample, so I'm sure we can find a few we can recruit. After all, a trip to D.C. and a chance to be on TV......" Both men were smiling by this point.

"Well, I feel better already. I can see my speech is in good hands."

"Just be sure to get a haircut next week. I'll ensure there's warm lemon water to drink prior to the speech. You're going to be great."

"Now if only it were all true."

"Don't go getting religious on me."

"Get back to work. I need a speech to wow the nation!"

"It's on the way."

Chapter 65

February 12, 2039
Denver, Colorado

Janice Montgomery nodded to the young man at the computer. He looked back at her for another confirmation. For several minutes she just looked at him. Finally, she spoke. "Go ahead, Jimmy, send the note."

"You're sure, Ms. Montgomery?"

"Yes, I'm sure." She nodded again, and he turned to his computer.

Two hundred fifty miles away, Jason Miles watched the message being relayed to his computer. Slowly he walked out to the newest well in the Utah basin. High above it was posted the company logo. Northwestern Energy was a very large company and supplied natural gas to the majority of customers in the western United States. Jason wished it were summer; people not only would be unable to cook their food tomorrow but also they would be cold. The site was deserted due to new government regulations prohibiting overtime in the entire industry. He was glad to be alone, but he also knew most of the men would agree with what he was about to do. They had watched the government move quickly into their industry with more restrictions and more regulations. The liberal politicians played to their environmental fringes, the price for political support. Then came the increases in taxes and regulated prices. The once-proud company was slowly going bankrupt. That would be the signal for the government to take it over completely, as they had already done for so many of the smaller companies.

Miles was a large and disciplined man. He had worked in the field for many years and understood the work and the men and women who

254

did it. He was a great admirer of Janice Montgomery. She was more man than most of the men he knew. As he had told one of his colleagues, she is a beautiful woman with brass balls. He knew she would soon be leaving for Cuba. So would he. Perhaps they might just be on the same boat. He hoped so. She was younger than he, but not by that much. She trusted him; he wondered if she knew how infatuated he was with her. Probably she knew; women had a way of knowing such things. She had never encouraged him; but neither had she discouraged him. It was certainly worth a try now that she was no longer his boss.

Jason Miles was not a man without courage. His time in the Army had proven that. He and a tall young sergeant had pulled several Rangers out of a big firefight in Afghanistan and earned them both a reputation for bravery. It was a war that would last forever he conjectured, and it might never be won, but on a bright sunny morning three years earlier, he, Sagan, and three Army snipers had won a very decisive battle for their small part in the larger morass. He reached into the pocket of his overalls and extracted several sticks of dynamite. He examined them carefully and continued his trek. Yes, these would be enough to start the process.

Chapter 66

February 13, 2039
The White House

The two secretaries were fixated on a small TV. Alec walked over to see what held their attention. He was immediately drawn into the news alert that had most of the East Coast watching. Two hundred fifteen natural gas wells in Utah and a large refinery in Houston were in flames, spewing smoke and ash into the evening air. Fire trucks stood motionless as their crews watched the devastation. A pretty young announcer finally appeared on the screen, explaining the slim details that had been reported regarding the Northwestern Energy disaster. Finally, she mentioned that the company had recently been fined $250 million dollars by the EPA, the first of several lawsuits that had been finalized.

Alec knew there was one person he could depend upon for good information of a technical nature, Kim Flannigan, an ABC reporter who covered the science desk in New York. He dialed the number in his speed dial and waited for the familiar voice.

"Hello, Alec. Are you watching the same thing on TV that I am?"

"Kim, how bad is this? How much of our energy supply did they control?"

"A lot; I'm guessing about 25-40%. However, most of it is on the West Coast."

"California?"

"That's most of it."

"Damn, if we have a challenge within the party, this could be bad. We need them in this coming election." There was a long silence before Alec continued. "Was this an accident?"

"Hard to say this early. Do you think someone in the party did this to hurt Gutierrez?"

Another long silence. "I had not thought about that. What an interesting proposition."

"Who knows, it could have been an accident, or the Patriots, or anything. I'll let you know as soon as I get any information that might be helpful."

Alec Woodward walked quickly into the President's office. "Did you see the news alert?"

"What's up?"

"About a third of our natural gas lines in the western half of the country just exploded in a giant fireball. We also lost most of the wells and infrastructure as well."

The President sat at his desk and slowly drummed his pen on an empty glass. "What's the bottom line, Alec?"

"We have about 80 million citizens without heat, cooking fuel, and electricity. We also have thousands of companies and factories without power as well. Half of the gas lines west of the Mississippi are burning."

"Damn!" The President looked his Chief of Staff in the eye. "This is serious."

"Oh yes. It's serious all right! Longfield was already on the news calling for a congressional investigation. He wants to know who was responsible and why the government inspectors were not doing their jobs to prevent this. I think it's obvious he's getting ready for a run at your office."

"Damn him." Guterriez studied the coffee cup for a while then continued. "Perhaps you need to start leaking some of the information you have on Longfield."

"The FBI already has confiscated all records at the home office of Northwestern Energy. The president of the company has called for her own investigation as well. We can control what the FBI collects, but we have no control over the company investigation. So I'll try to make sure our guys get there first! What we cannot find we can always manufacture and leak to the press later."

"I guess I'll need to make a speech about this."

"The speech writers are already on it. I'll make sure the slant is right."

"Have them put something in about this not being the time to second-guess and make accusations based on conjecture. Something about this being a time to pull together to help those involved." The President stopped short. "By the way, was anyone hurt or killed?"

"No, our new union rules about overtime prevented anyone from being on site. We were lucky there."

"Be sure we get credit for that. Should I do a photo op and fly down to shake some hands and offer assistance to the locals?"

"I'm checking the schedule. I think that might be a great idea. Let me check into it; I'll get back to you."

The Chief of Staff had just walked out of the President's office when his cell phone buzzed. It was Kim. "I have some information that might be useful. It is preliminary, but it appears that the disaster in Houston was not an accident, and the Patriots are as busy as we are trying to discover what happened."

"So they were not involved?"

"Doesn't look like it, but of course, this is all quite preliminary."

"This opens some very disturbing possibilities."

"Got to run. I'll keep in touch, Alec." Kim placed the phone into its cradle.

Three hours later the President looked up to see Alec walk into his office and pour two glasses of scotch. "That bad, Alec?"

"I'm afraid so. Seems the Northwestern Energy investigation found four pictures of incorrectly installed valves on one of the main lines through western Illinois."

"What is so bad about that. It just gives us the opportunity to step in and help our union friends again. That will be a good thing; we've had strained relations recently."

"The pictures are three months old, and they were found in the government inspector's files." Alec took a long drink of the liquor.

The President's face suddenly turned very pale. "Oh shit! The government had the evidence for three months, and no action was taken at all?" The two men looked at each other for several long minutes. Finally, the President continued. "Where did you get this information?"

"TV."

"In the news already? How did that happen? Didn't they check with us first?"

"Longfield reported it on the evening news. He said it was just another example of government incompetence."

"That son-of-a-bitch. Call the press and give them all you have on him tonight."

"Can't do that. It will look too much like we're striking back to cover something. But I'll give him a call tonight. Perhaps I can convince him to stop this absurd approach. He has far too much to lose in this game."

"Is what you have on him real? Will he realize how much you know?"

"Most of it is. He'll know we have his number. I think that will be enough."

"I'd like to kick his ass."

"Just be calm and let me do the dirty work. You try to stay above it all. You won't even know what it is all about. Act as if he were your best friend. In fact, agree with him that an investigation is needed. We can always fire a couple of inspectors if necessary. Unlike most of our predecessors, we will practice accountability. Nothing soothes the public more than a few government officials fired for poor performance. Then we quietly put them to work on a campaign somewhere." Woodward smiled. He always had a plan. Always.

"Thanks, Alec; keep me advised."

"I'll kick Longfield's ass for you." Alec smiled. "I'll let you know the details. I suspect he will squirm a bit."

The President sipped his scotch and took a different tack. "Isn't Northwestern Energy a privately owned company? Weren't we trying to take it over? As I recall a rather attractive woman ran Northwestern

259

Energy. Give her a call; I'm thinking she'd be willing to turn over control now."

"She's missing. Someone bombed her house within an hour of the announcement of the pictures. There's speculation the union may be involved. Either way it doesn't matter. Northwestern Energy is worthless now."

"How big was it?"

"80,000 employees. Hundreds of millions in infrastructure. All gone!"

"Is there any good news anymore?"

"Doesn't seem like it." The phone on the side of the President's desk began to ring loudly. Both men looked at it until it finally ceased its raucous noise then downed their drinks in silence.

Chapter 67

March 22, 2039
The White House

Alec Woodward looked up from the editorial pages of *The New York Times* and rose to meet the distinguished looking man who walked into his office. He smiled as he reached to shake the familiar hand. "Good evening, Senator."

"Hello Alec, you look busy this late hour of the day, but I guess that's to be expected from the Chief of Staff."

"It's been this way for two years. The President is a demanding man."

"And so is your job." The Senator sat in the new leather chair across from the cluttered desk as Alec returned to his seat.

"Would you like coffee or scotch, Senator?"

"Scotch. Seems you can't find a decent cup of coffee in this country anymore. The quality has gone to hell, but you can always count on scotch."

Alec rose and filled two glasses, handed one to Senator McGregor, then returned to his seat. "How can I help you, Sir?"

The Senator took a sip and peered into the glass as he savored the strong drink. Finally he spoke. "I'm worried, Alec. I don't like the things that are happening in this country."

"What do you mean, Sir?"

"I think we are losing control."

"Losing control? Are you kidding? We took 65% of the vote last year. The Republicans had less than 30%. Their old mantra of less government and lower taxes didn't sell at all." Alec smiled as he sipped his own drink.

"Not to those who don't pay taxes, that's for sure." McGregor took another large drink and played with it in his mouth as he considered his next words. "No, I'm afraid we are losing control from within."

"Within our own party?"

"Yes, the unions are demanding more, and frankly there's nothing left to give them."

"We gave them the governing share of employees in every industry in this country. What more do they want. Their leaders make a lot more than you or I make—and we are educated." Alec looked around as if checking to see that no one heard his remark.

"So we did, and so they do. And now they control every losing business in America."

"What do they want now?"

"More protection for their jobs, their benefits. They want guarantees. As corporations continue to fail, the unions are beginning to realize that they are losing the geese that laid their golden eggs. It's amazing it took them so long to figure that out."

"We passed the most severe protectionist measures ever seen to protect their inefficient corporations. We have all kinds of quotas and the tariffs. The World Trade Organization is screaming, and all of our trade partners are retaliating. We're already in crap up to our necks trying to meet their demands. And now they want more?" There was anger and frustration in Alec's voice.

"All that helped for a while, but eventually the failing economy is dragging everything into the toilet. They just feel they deserve more. They want their fair share of the wealth."

"How can we get people to buy cars when they can't afford the prices. Every time we raise union rates, the price of their cars go up. Did any of those guys ever take an economics course?"

"They only want a decent living for a hard day's work." The senator was smiling.

"Do they have any suggestions about how we can do that?" Alec frowned slightly. "And what do they know about a hard day's work?"

"As a matter of fact they do have a suggestion, and frankly it shows a lot of creativity for that crowd. They want us to buy more cars for the government—twenty million cars."

"Twenty million cars? Are they kidding?"

"You have to remember that we are dealing with unions—this is just a starting point for negotiations."

"Tell me, senator, could we just give the unions to the Republicans?"

"The Republicans are far too smart to take that headache!" The older man laughed, then suddenly his face became serious. "Unfortunately, we need the unions. Their own leadership has been responsible for much of the loss of their membership. I think they are down below 10% of the workforce, but they still contribute much of our campaign funds. Ever since we passed the Kennedy-Martinez act, they have managed to increase their numbers in the government sector and even a bit in the private sector." He finished the scotch and put the glass on the edge of Woodward's desk. "By the way, they also want us to increase our yearly subsidy to the union itself."

"With what? Our tax revenues keep dropping each year while our needs increase."

"Can't you raise taxes?"

"We are already at 83% on the marginal dollar for incomes over $180,000. When we increased that last year, the tax income actually fell."

"Frankly, I didn't know we had anyone in the private sector making that much. Maybe the Laffer Curve was right after all when it forecast a drop in total tax revenue when tax rates on citizens were raised beyond some reasonable level." The senator smiled.

Alec ignored the comment. "People tend to quit working when they reach the maximum rate." He paused, took a long drink, then added. "Many quit work in September or earlier, and a lot of those people have just left the country."

"So the people who are successful enough to earn that much money cut back on their work and the folks who don't work at all keep demanding more. That doesn't sound like much of an incentive to increase production. Quite a conundrum." The senator frowned. "I know you have been trying to stop the exodus from our country. How's that new law working?" The senator looked directly into the eyes of the younger man.

Woodward pushed his glass across the desk and stared back. "Not well. They are getting around it. They're organized better than we thought. A lot of people have left the country." He thought for a moment. "You know, we once wanted a porous border to bring in poor voters we could tap. We could count on a border then that was essentially a sieve. Now, when we really want it closed, we don't know how."

"Well, there is some good news, I suspect. At least our vote percentages will be better next year. I suspect most of those leaving are Republicans." There was a look of concern on the senator's face.

"We're losing a lot of people we need."

"And we're keeping a lot of people we don't need." The senator's eyes narrowed as he gazed at the Chief of Staff. "Maybe we're losing the brightest and best."

"I prefer to think of them as selfish and greedy."

"Right, we take 83% of everything they produce, and we call *them* greedy." McGregor finished his drink and swirled the ice in his glass. "Yes, selfish. Our union friends want more for producing less, and those leaving want more for producing more. I suppose that is also a form of selfishness. I'm just not sure which is worse for the country." The senator refilled his glass a second time. "Maybe I've been listening to our friendly senator from Wyoming too much recently."

Those words caught Alec by surprise. He did not expect such candor. "I see that our union friends have become tiring. You sound a bit pissed. Just remember that we need them every time an election comes up." He walked around his desk and refilled his glass as well. "And what do you mean by your comment about Senator Lovett. Is he getting sympathetic with the Patriots?"

"You know Lovett; he's a bit conservative like most of the cowboys out there in the West. But he really cares about this country, and I have to admire that." MacGregor swirled his drink without sipping it. "And you're right about the election. The unions may be a pain in the ass, but we do need their money." The senator paused, took his glass and downed half of it with one gulp. "I fear, Alec, that we are governing a nation in decay."

"Listen, Senator…"

"Call me Wayne." The older man sat again in the large chair. He looked very tired.

"Listen, senator, this is all going to work out okay. It just needs time. We damn sure don't need more greedy CEOs overpaying themselves like they used to."

"I agree, but we could sure use some entrepreneurs and new businesses springing up everywhere like we had years ago. And I'd sure like to see a few more American engineers and doctors. I went to a doctor here in DC last week who could hardly speak English. I didn't understand a word he said!" His voice trailed off as he spoke.

McGregor finished his drink and sat the glass back on Woodward's desk. "You know, Alec, we used to build airplanes and submarines. Now we can't even maintain the ones we have. We lost three of our best fighter aircraft last week, and we aren't even at war."

"The President took care of that."

"The crashes or war?" There was a touch of humor in the older man's voice.

"We're through with war. The President's new policies are working. We're talking to our prior enemies; we have peace in the world; we've disarmed our nuclear weapons. Why do we even need such a large military? We're wasting money on that." Woodward looked at the work waiting for him on his desk. "Look, Senator, I know you didn't come down here to philosophize with me today. There are far better philosophers than a tired government official, so what can I *really* do for you?"

Wayne McGregor looked down at the floor a moment and then spoke. "I need a contract for Colorado. I'm hearing noises. The people are impatient. I promised them a lot of things last fall, and I need to deliver something. Seems like all the new programs are going to California. There was a time when Colorado was Republican—all those independent ranchers and farmers. There are still a few around, and they are stirring up problems. All these years later they are still talking about

265

the EPA disaster that caused all that cancer in the southern portion of the state. They feel they deserve *something*."

Woodward leaned back in thought. Suddenly he leaned forward and smiled. "We're looking at some R&D work for global green issues. What about the old aerospace plant southwest of Denver. It's been closed for years; maybe we could convert that."

"That's a great idea."

"It's going to be tough. The budget is tight."

"It's always tight." McGregor played with his empty glass. "Make this happen for me. I need it." There was a quiet desperation in his voice.

"Wait, what about your crime rate. We have budget left for public safety, and gang activities are on the rise in every large city in the country."

"Our crime rates are high, but it is the same everywhere else. Nevertheless, we could always use some more cops. I realize that union hasn't supported Democrats since Obama left them hanging out to dry. Still, it would bring money to the state."

"I guess we could use some of the money we get from the drug taxes. After all, Colorado was one of the first states to legalize marijuana. Since then you've legalized most drugs, and the money is pouring in. Last year tax revenues were 20% more than we expected from that."

"That's good news." The senator stopped and considered his words. "I guess."

"I'll see what I can do, but I need something in return. We thought we had covered the citizen ID chip program fairly well, but we're beginning to get a lot of pushback. When it hits the Internet, there will be lots of questions about the new policy. I expect it may even get to the Senate. If it does, I need your support. We *have* to keep that policy in place for the foreseeable future. We need that to help stop the exodus. Besides, the company that makes the chips is using one of our confiscated patents. We'll make a fortune on this. Every citizen in the country will have a chip implanted in them—just think of how many chips that is." He watched as the senator nodded his consent.

"And you can use that to track people?"

"That's what the experts say. We'll know where everyone is and where they go. This will be especially useful tracking those who want to leave the country."

"Can't they simply remove them?"

"We're perfecting a way to make that very painful, so I expect most of them to remain in place for a very long time." Alec watched for an adverse reaction before continuing on another topic. "I also need some confidential information, and I know you have connections. This is something that might be of benefit to both of us."

"Just say the word."

"We know many conservatives are leaving. On the one hand we need their assets to help finance our programs. On the other we need key people to stay and help support the economy. If we could get someone inside their organization, we might have a much better chance of stopping them."

"And you think I might be of some help with that?"

"You are the one who needs more government money." Woodward looked the senator straight in the eyes. His message was clear. He needed the senator to find a spy for the government.

"I'll see what I can do."

Chapter 68

April, 2039
Suburbs west of Denver

The old pickup pulled off the main road and traveled about ten minutes southwest from Evergreen. It rounded a corner, and there it was, The Brookcreek Inn. It was old and in much need of repair, but the large quartz rocks that composed the walls were still bright and glistening from the early afternoon rain. Wilson looked over at Mark with a look of surprise on his face. "I know this place. I used to take Marion here when we were first married." He peered through the rain-streaked windshield and continued. "That was such a long time ago. Damn, she's been gone eight years, and I still miss her so much."

"Of course you do. You two were inseparable." Mark watched the old man's face and saw the sadness in his eyes. "You know she will be with us tonight."

Ken smiled. "Yes, she will. I suspect she watches over us a lot these days."

Mark opened the door of the truck and tested the rain. "Let me help you; this mud is treacherous."

The meal was almost over when the young chef walked over to the two men. "Reverend Wilson, it is an honor to have you in our restaurant tonight. My father recognized you when you entered. I wanted to shake your hand. I have heard much about you, sir."

Wilson smiled and stood to address the young man in the apron. "Thank you, young man. Your dinner was remarkable tonight. It has been a long time since I had a dinner that delicious. I was afraid we had lost that art."

"Thank you, sir. This is my last dinner at this old family restaurant, and I wanted it to be my best."

Wilson was surprised. "Your last dinner here? I am sorry to hear that."

Mark smiled broadly. "Very soon he will be cooking in a new restaurant near Havana. I cannot wait to see what he can do with black beans and rice."

The young man smiled. "I'm already practicing with Cuban recipes. I think we will have a great fusion of tastes to play with. It should be exciting."

"Then I promise to try your new restaurant soon." Wilson hesitated a moment before continuing. "If God permits."

When the two men sat back down Mark studied Ken's face carefully. "How bad is it? Really?"

"I'm fine, son. Really, I'm fine."

"Bull shit! We've been too close for too long for you to lie to me now. And you know that. Besides, I'm a doctor." Mark reached over and put his hand on the old one on the table. "I've called you Dad most of my life. I've loved you as dearly as any son could love his father. What we have has always been based on truth—how many times have you told me that over my life."

The old pastor looked up into the reddened eyes of the man he had called his son for so many years. "You're right Mark. You're right." He reached and drained the last of his water and then continued, very slowly and very deliberately. "Kim did all he could; but miracles are not of men. I have cancer, and it has progressed pretty far. The government hospitals would not allow me access to the better drugs. They say it is because of my age. Kim managed to sneak a supply of them, and we've been trying them for several months. It doesn't look like it is making much difference. I also tried the ones you gave me. They seemed to help for a while, but Kim says I may have started too late."

Mark bowed his head and tried to register what the old man was saying; his racing mind had stumbled and stalled at the news. Cancer—

it should have been eradicated by now, but medicine had taken a major step backward twenty-five years earlier when it became a political tool rather than a scientific world of knowledge and exploration to alleviate mankind's pain. "Dr. Kim is a great doctor, and he says your new medicine is working wonders for several of his other patients, but I guess I'm too old, or maybe God just needs me now. Either way, it has progressed too far, I fear."

Wilson watched the pain on his son's face. "Mark, enough about me. I'm a tough old guy. I still have my faith. If God needs me here, He will provide. I keep telling Dr. Kim that he is a tool of God right now. I'm not positive that is reassuring to him. But I keep reminding him." He looked straight into Mark's eyes. "I'm not worried about me; I'm worried about you. I've never seen you so tense and angry." He waited; when Mark remained silent, Wilson continued. "Alec was once your friend. Now you are filled with hatred for him. That's not good, son. It will eat you up inside."

"I can't believe how much he changed since we were in school together. He was my friend. He was Terry's friend. Now Terry is rotting in some grave somewhere, and Alec is strutting around in expensive suits condemning the very people who built this nation. How does one change like that?"

"Remember, Mark, Christ prayed for the men who crucified him. You've got to release the anger and the hatred. If you don't, they win."

"I'm not sure I'll ever be able to do that. Some would call that compassion. Right now I would call it surrender. But I don't want to talk about Alec. I want to talk about you and your condition."

"Look, I've spent my entire life living for the day I leave this earth and go to meet Jesus. I don't fear death. He died a horrible death on a cross. Mine will just take a bit longer." When he looked up, his eyes were red. "I just wish it had not been cancer."

"I know. I've thought about that too."

"But don't worry, I'm full of tricks. I've got too many things to do before I go, so it may take a bit longer than the doctors think."

270

"Yeah, most likely you're right." Mark placed several bills on the table, and the two men walked out into the evening. Both were quiet on the way home.

Chapter 69

May, 2039
The White House

As the group rose to leave, Alec watched them carefully. He had worked for months to assemble such a group. It was perfectly balanced with each minority and all four sexual orientations; they even had a fairly good sample of handicapped citizens. What he was most proud of was that most of them were actually capable of handling the jobs they had been given. They might not have been the most capable of the candidates, but they were the most representative, and that was what counted when elections rolled around. But soon that would not be a problem. Soon, elections would simply be perfunctory. His attention returned as the President rose and walked to the door of the oval office. "June, send in Walt Brown."

The man who entered was short, his head mostly bald except for a small ring of white hair that circled his head. He was smiling, but Alec knew the smile was painted there. It did not reflect the sharp and calloused mind hiding inside the ex-president of the largest union in the nation—the government workers' union. He was the "ex" union president because he had just lost the job in a highly contested election. The fact that he was a charter member of the American Communist party had not been enough. He had lost to a young usurper, a man about whom little was known—yet. Now it was payback for years of political support. A large hand reached for that of the President. "Good to see you, Mr. President."

"Good to see you, Walt. Are you ready to meet the press?"

"I am, and I've been briefed." Alec smiled as the President nodded to him. It was Alec's job to insure that the union block of votes stayed with the President. Should Walt show anger at losing, it would not help the President's cause. The vote had been fixed, but still Brown had lost. Now he had to be a gracious—and well-rewarded—loser. His new appointment would not match the $1.5 million he made as the union boss, but money was not the issue for Walt Brown anymore. Prestige was far more important at this point. He already had more money than both Alec and the President combined. Now it was all about "face" and prestige.

"I'll offer you a drink after the interview." Gutierrez was not being gracious but rather was reminding Walt to follow the party line. There would be congratulations for the winner—a man Brown loathed. There would be thanks to a President who had always supported the union rank-and-file. Then, and only then, he, Walt, and Alec would share drinks in the White House and discuss Walt's new job with the administration, a job Alec had created just to fit a longtime supporter. And while it was all happening, another man, the new president of the union, was being handed an invitation to meet with the President the following Wednesday. Already the transition was being made, and the new union boss was probably noting how well ex-union presidents were taken care of—as long as they stayed in line.

Alec smirked. When you had all the resources of the presidency and a selfish constituency—it was all just so easy. Everyone marveled at his genius, but it really wasn't genius at all. America's first black President had shown the way. The strategy was simple—divide the nation into groups and then pit the groups against each other. Make it a nation of competing interests, the poor versus the wealthy, blacks against whites, illegal immigrants against the order of law. Threaten every group's perceived self-interest; convince women that others were trying to take away their rights; convince the uneducated that the wealthy class was depriving them of their rightful share of the fruits of the nation—even if they contributed little to the fruits that were produced. There was only one catch, and Alec understood it well. Self-serving politicians had perfected it since Obama's example proved so successful—just make sure the groups that back you are more numerous than the opposition. Then

273

all you have to do is turn them out to vote. Indifference was the only threat to the plan. And that could be controlled by simply introducing the threat of competing interests. What is good for America gave way to what is good for each competing group.

And it worked. Obama had been able to convince more than half the nation that essentially paid no taxes at all that the one percent who actually paid forty percent of the entire federal income tax bill were not paying their "fair share." It was easy because that was what the people wanted to believe. Obviously their failures were not their own. Certainly someone else must have cheated them of their rightful success. Then you simply take taxpayer dollars from those who produce things and buy votes from those who pay little or no taxes at all. But in the back of his mind a dark cloud was gathering; Alec was beginning to worry. All those resources were beginning to dwindle. It seemed each year the people wanted more, and each year he had a little less to distribute to the faithful. The nation's producers were not cooperating. It was their greed that was hampering his well-planned strategy. Their production levels were beginning to fall.

How could he get them back in line? How could he entice the entrepreneurs to go back to work? Someone had to produce the spoils he needed to distribute to the Democrat base. How can you distribute phones and housing and food and healthcare if you have none to hand out? Perhaps Schumpeter had been right. Perhaps when the entrepreneurs leave there is nothing left to save. Alec frowned. He needed some down time to think through this scenario. How could he change it? What could he offer the producers in society? It was their money he was using to buy the votes. The one thing he never counted on was happening. The smart folks were leaving, in increasingly large numbers. Perhaps if he would let them keep more of what they had earned; perhaps that might work. But he had already decimated their ranks and denigrated the group as selfish crooks who stole from the nation's poor; now, he realized, he really did need them, like he needed the doctors they had savaged, or the engineers they had criticized, or the others who worked to build the nation they were now selling so cheaply. He just had to find a way to keep the slaves working.

For the first time that day, his smile vanished and a deep furrow formed between his eyebrows. Five presidencies had survived on this plan. Each had seen a slowly diminishing standard of living; each had sold off America's resources and drowned the nation in debt to purchase the power they desired so desperately. Perhaps they were finally running out of rope. Now the smartest folks were leaving, and the inmates were, indeed, running the asylum. And here he was, participating in the sham of rewarding one of the men who had helped destroy the nation that they had sworn to uphold.

Alec watched the old union boss carefully. How dumb the union officials had been. They had missed the impact of technology and even the devastating results of the global economy. And all the while they had become wealthy leading poorer men into poverty as unemployment grew in all sectors of the economy; it had been so easy to convince the masses that the problem was always the same—wealthy men who only wanted more profits. They blamed management while they stood blindfolded before the "invisible hand" of economic reality. And the profits dwindled and disappeared along with the jobs. America's great manufacturing capacity became a joke. The products were too expensive and, finally, even the quality dwindled as more and more of the cost was devoured by wages, pensions, and healthcare programs that were unrealistic in the global marketplace. And the workers walked sullenly out of America's remaining plants while the last management personnel locked the gates behind them. Then they all were unemployed, and few understood what had happened. And the few who did were afraid to speak the truth as the politically correct press continued the drumbeat of the common myths of greed and profits. Finally, even the producers tired of the constant rhetoric of blame, and they, too, quit, and in time, left.

America plunged deeper into the morass of socialism and all of its promises that were never kept. The nation traded the finest standard of living in the world for a system that had never worked well anywhere or at any time. But ignorance prevailed, and the people demanded more and more from their government. Slowly they traded their freedom for goods they felt they needed or wanted. And the shouting, cheering masses made it all seem right. Alec watched the union leader smiling at the camera and wondered if he was really so dumb that he did not know that the very political machine the unions had supported with their money and votes had betrayed them. The liberals had welcomed the illegal masses that came into America and reduced worker wages for everyone. They had sided with the environmentalists who crippled the companies that provided the jobs. Finally, the influx of illegals began taking the jobs the union workers had once held in perpetuity. And all the while, the ignorant rank-and-file union members paid their dues and financed the campaigns for the very politicians who led them into poverty. Did the union officials realize what they were doing? Did the workers on the assembly lines realize what was happening? Obviously they were as oblivious as he had expected. How easily they had been betrayed.

Alec suddenly shook his head and walked quickly to his office, closed the door and poured a large scotch. He downed it quickly and then poured another. "It doesn't matter that they don't understand," he told himself. "They vote for us, and that is all that counts. We won; that is all that counts." He walked to the window and stood looking out for a long time. Finally, he turned and poured another drink. He drank it quickly, with no pleasure in the excellent liquor.

Chapter 70

June 6, 2039
Reagan National Airport, Washington, D.C.

The union workers at National Airlines watched with interest as the Vice President of Operations walked briskly through the door into their ready room. It was evident from her stride and the frown on her face that she was not pleased. She turned sharply and entered the office that served the shift managers. The short man seated behind the desk quickly threw the magazine he had been perusing into the top drawer and stood to greet the frustrated woman standing before him. She spoke first. "Who the hell is running this operation?"

He stood speechless a few moments then stammered. "Is something wrong?"

"Is something wrong? I've been sitting on the flight to Boston for twenty-five minutes, waiting for bags to be loaded. I can see the bags from my window in first class. I can see lots of ramp workers standing around all over the airport. What I don't see is someone managing this operation. I assume that is your job?"

"Ah, yes ma'am. I was not aware that there was a problem." The fear in his eyes was apparent.

"And how could you know that there was a problem if you're in here looking at girlie magazines instead of being out on the ramp doing your job?" When he said nothing she continued. "How long have you worked for this airline?"

"Eight years, ma'am."

"Would you like to work here another eight years?"

"Yes ma'am."

"Then I recommend that you get your butt out there where the work is being done—or not—and manage it. Am I clear enough?"

"Yes ma'am."

"Good. That flight turns in Boston for a flight to San Francisco. It had better make that turn on time. And I'll know. I'm on it. And one other thing, this is not a government job, and you are not a union worker. You are management, and you can be fired." She turned on her heel and walked out.

Several ramp men walked by the office and made smiling gestures at the embarrassed manager as he grabbed his hat and followed her out the door. Sometimes he wondered why he had ever chosen to move up from the union ranks into management. He was perpetually caught between a management that did not understand and a union that did not care. He could please neither. At first he had cared; he wanted the operation to be smooth and successful. Then he realized how little control he really had over the union workers. They could do pretty much as they wished, and they could not be fired. Working hard got them nothing but condemnation from the shop stewards; doing little more than the minimum had no consequences at all. In time, most all of them gravitated to minimum effort. He had thought he could change that. He could not. But management always wanted more. They wanted the planes out on time; they wanted the bags loaded on the right aircraft. They even wanted the work areas to be relatively clean.

He looked across the taxiways to the tall National Airlines building. From the 12th floor of the Admin Building it was hard to see the reality of the operations on the ramp. And now he was being chastised by this woman for doing a sloppy job. He knew she was right, and that was what hurt the most. He watched her figure as she climbed the Jetway stairs to the open door of the plane. He could only dream of a woman like that. Then, for the first time that day he smiled. She had already screwed him, and it really wasn't all that good.

Chapter 71

July 6, 2043
Galveston Bay, Texas

It was well past midnight when the three men slid the boat off its trailer into Galveston Bay. From Smith Point it was only about 12 miles to open water in the Gulf of Mexico. The night was quiet, and the moon was hidden behind the thick rain clouds that threatened the Gulf Coast. The leader of the group gave hand signals and spoke quietly when necessary. They hid the boat near a small cove and covered it with camouflage. They placed three large cans of gasoline onto the floor of the boat then drove away.

Less than a hundred yards across the bay on an old deserted barge two border guards watched the proceedings. Between them they had one pair of night goggles, but the quality was bad and the image was poor. "Can you make out who they are?"

"No, dammit, and keep your voice down. Sound carries across the water like a fart in church."

"What are they doing?"

"Looks like they're hiding a boat."

"Ahh, the Patriots."

"Looks like they're planning on leaving the country." Both young deputies peered into the darkness. "Yep, they are driving off toward Anahuac. My guess is they are headed to Baytown."

"Hot damn, if we drive back down the road a piece and get a trailer, we can nab that boat before they return."

"Damn, Frank, you're dumb as shit. We don't want the boat. We want them—the folks who are planning to ride it out into the Gulf and meet up with a big old Cuban ship to take them away from here. You know, those rich folks who think they're better than anyone else. You know, like the program on TV said the other night."

"My TV is broke, and I can't afford another right yet."

"Shit man, after we pass this information up the line, we'll be heroes. I'll bet you can afford a new TV then." Randy folded the night goggles into a small denim bag he carried around his shoulder. "We just got to be careful that Rollins don't steal our discovery. He has a tendency to do that you know."

"Yeah, I know what you mean. He's got a way of stealing the credit when someone else done somethin' good. Ever since the chief started talking about retirin' Rollins been trying to get his job. He thinks he's better than the rest of us."

"We'll just have to think this over real careful like."

"Yeah, real careful."

* * *

"Do you think they saw us?"

"Oh yeah. It was Frank Jordan and Randy Middleton. What a pair!"

"Now if they just don't try to confiscate the boat, we're in business."

"Yeah, if they are just smart enough to leave it and wait for us. But if that is the key to this mission, I'm worried." The two men laughed as they drove on through the night. It was beginning to rain, but that was how they had planned it. Rain is just another cover.

* * *

The three men walked into the warm room and took the tea extended to them. "How did it go?" Mark Sagan shook hands with the leader. "Did they see you?"

"Looks good. Two border guards watched the whole thing from the old barge parked out in the bay. They got an eyeful. We left Richard to

280

watch from a distance to see if they take the boat or wait for us to come back."

"Which benefits them most? A boat or a group of us *and* the boat?"

"Last we heard from Richard, they drove over and checked the boat but left it alone. They also saw the other ropes for more boats and the extra fuel as well." He paused for a moment. "Damn, I hated to give them that much gasoline!"

"If this works, it was worth it, and if it doesn't work, we'll just steal it back."

"This damn well better work. My wife and kids are in this group."

Mark patted his friend on the shoulder. "Don't worry, Jon. This is going to work."

Chapter 72

July 11, 2039
The American Mid-West

As was the case throughout socialism's history, the American experiment in socialism started to unravel when reality collided with lies and a broken philosophy. As the disaster became more widespread, the prophets of capitalism crawled from beneath the rubble and began to preach a new way. One of the most effective was old Jesse Holbrook who had taken up the cause and drove his Harley across America telling the working people to give it up, to quit. He had been the least-expected Republican in the world. He certainly didn't look like a wealthy business man. He was old, fat, and he had a snow white beard. He rode an old beat-up Harley, and his torn jeans, leather jacket, and red bandana were unmistakable. He looked like anything but a conservative. Maybe that is why he was so successful. For a while even the liberal press gave him air time. They were laughing at him, but he had the last laugh.

Jesse's message was simple—why should we work so hard to support the government and all of its minions? It was time for those carrying the load of the nation to revolt. He preached that fairness was more than just equal distribution of goods; it was also fairness in doing the work of producing those goods. And revolt they did. Little by little, they simply began walking off their jobs. Alec thought back to that cold morning in November when Jesse pulled his bike to the front door of a Whirlpool plant in Benton Harbor, Michigan, and walked to the front door shouting. "Quit, go home! Are you all fools? Don't you know the rest of the nation is sitting on its collective ass while you try to support them.

282

The guys down in the pool hall are living off of your work, and they make almost as much as you do when the taxes are figured in. Go home. Let the socialists starve! Show them you know better! You'd need to damn near double your salaries to make more than those living off your taxes. We will not be their slaves! We won the war about slavery once; it's time to do that again."

Like those from the press, Alec had laughed as the old man strutted around, shouting at the building. But soon Jesse was surrounded by workers flowing from the factory to hear what he had to say. They listened and talked to the angry old white-headed man. Then they all went inside to the cafeteria and had lunch together. The next day only half the workers showed up for work. Just three of the management staff reported for their shifts. Within two weeks production was a mere fraction of its usual level. Within a month, the entire factory closed. His message had been simple: you are too smart to be their slaves. Why should you work hard for a government that will take everything you produce and give it to those who contribute nothing? By the time the press realized what he had actually done, he was on his way to another company, and six Whirlpool workers were off on their own bikes, spreading the word. Jesse had developed a following; he called them his disciples.

What had surprised Alec most was how the message resonated with those in management. When Jesse proclaimed that America was buying Chinese *products* while they bought our *assets*, the engineers, doctors, executives, and professionals of all types were the first to grasp what old Jesse was saying. He had called it the return of the Tea Party, and he was Paul Revere. He rode from town to town proclaiming, "The Socialists are coming! The Socialists are coming!"

That was when Alec saw the crack in the dike. What happens when the nation's businesses start shutting down? For years they had been denigrated and condemned as the greedy capitalists. But even Karl Marx had admitted that the capitalists were the ones who were productive. They were the ones who built capital and created production beyond everyone's imagination. The masses who gave the liberals political power were really uneducated fools. Secretly Alec held them in contempt, as did most Democrat politicians. But they were his "useful

283

idiots." They were the basis of political power, but they were also the greatest threat to the nation's survival, and deep inside Alec recognized that. But he had a plan. He would save them with an all-powerful government that would make their decisions and control their lives. A small cadre of experts would run the nation; certainly he did not trust *the people* to actually run things. They simply were not smart enough to do that. It was a big challenge, but he knew he could make it work. All he had to do now was keep the President in line and find some way to harness the great productive potential of the nation.

But Jesse had stumped him. Jesse was able to make working people understand his message—and they joined his revolution. It was the rabble that followed Alec and the other statists; Jesse had the smart ones, those with IQs greater than their age. Alec wondered about his base. Most just wanted what the government could give them. The others were just folks who had been raised in the liberal ideology, and they would never admit that they were wrong, even in the face of apparent failure. But the first black President had shown the way so clearly. The divisiveness he perpetrated ensured the voter turnout that gave him victory. How smart Obama's controllers had been. They had ruined the economy, made a joke of America internationally, and destroyed the nation's health care system. But they were experts at spinning disasters, and when the Middle East went up in smoke, they had the perfect excuse for their failures. No one noticed that the nation's slide had already commenced when the sky filled with Israeli missiles and the entire Arab world was destroyed in a matter of minutes.

Alec stopped for a moment to reflect what it must have been like when the first missiles struck Iran, Syria, Lebanon, and all the other nations that had rejoiced at the destruction of Israel. Their victory had been short-lived, indeed. Now they would all rot in Hell. No virgins there! There were still many who did not understand the American President's declaration of three days of mourning after that fateful day. A few Americans actually observed that period of mourning; many others did their own share of dancing in the streets.

*   *   *

Alec watched the White House disappear in his rear view mirror as he struggled to drive and study a Washington city map at the same time. After many wrong turns he finally spotted the small bar he was trying to find. He parked a block away and pulled his fedora close over his face as he walked toward the small establishment. He stepped inside and waited for his eyes to adjust. After a few minutes he surveyed the room and noticed the man he was meeting sitting at the far end of the bar. He joined him and placed his coat and hat on the adjacent stool to give them more privacy. The man facing Alec was roughly his own age, well-dressed, and alert, even with a half-empty drink in his hand. Alec slipped into his seat and glanced quickly at the floor. A large wet spot showed on the soiled wooden floor. He guessed his colleague had not been drinking at all. Nice cover. "I'm glad you came, Darin."

"I'm here to serve."

"Good. I have a very special job I need you to take care of. It should be quite simple for a man of your talents." Darin nodded and waited for Alec to continue.

Alec reached inside his coat pocket and withdrew a picture. Looking around carefully to ensure they were not being overheard, he slid it down the bar toward Darin. "Do you know this man?"

"That's Jesse Holbrook, the old idiot who is stirring up trouble around the country."

"That's right; he's a real threat to our nation; I suspect he's also guilty of several crimes."

"Like maybe treason."

"Right."

"Treason is a serious crime—punishable by death."

"So it is."

"I'll take care of it, Mr. Woodward."

"Thank you, Darin. I knew I could count on you. And I'm sure the President will also appreciate your dedication to our country." The FBI agent nodded and turned and left without further discussion. Alec finished Darin's drink and grinned as he dropped several bills on the bar and left.

Chapter 73

July 19, 2039
The White House

Alec looked quickly at the President who returned the surprised look. The new union president who had just walked into the Oval Office was not at all what they had expected. First of all, he was very young. Alec guessed him to be in his early 30s. He was well-spoken, clean-shaven, and his suit more expensive than either of theirs. He placed his leather-bound notepad on the table, opened it, and laid his Mont Blanc fountain pen beside it. Alec noted the University of Chicago class ring. It was five years old. The new union boss raised his head and looked the President squarely in the eye for several seconds, then did the same with Alec. "Good morning, gentlemen. Thank you for your invitation."

"Thank you for coming, Mr. Fontero." The President smiled and gestured at the coffee that had been poured. "Coffee?"

"Yes, thank you. And please call me Don." He reached for the first cup and placed it in front of the President. He then placed the second in front of Alec. Lastly he placed a cup beside his notepad. "Alec, I'm glad to meet you as well."

"Likewise." Alec reached for the coffee and doctored his carefully. He was already impressed with this man; he certainly knew how to handle people.

Gutierrez sipped his coffee and took command of the conversation. "We congratulate you on your success in the election. That was an impressive show. I'm glad you are not a politician aiming for the presidency." Both men smiled. "I suspect you could teach all of us a few things about politics, however. To what do you ascribe your success?"

"Your failure, and the failure of a number of liberal Presidents before you." Fontero leaned back and let his words sink in. The President was clearly startled, and Alec actually slid forward in his chair. "At least that's what some of my constituents told me. But what do they know?" Alec slid back into his seat.

The President carefully placed his cup on the table before him and sat back, watching the young man. "And what failure is it your members are referring to, Mr. Fontero?"

"Now Mr. President, we both know the workers of America support you and the Democrat Party. The relationship between the unions and the Democrat Party is a fact that has existed for decades. We are all committed Democrats, and you can certainly depend on the members of our union—and me." He paused long enough to sip his coffee again, carefully studying the two politicians before him. "The truth is, most of the union membership don't have a clue about our economy or how it really works. They worry about two things: their jobs and their paychecks. And right now most all of them are worried sick about both. But a few are beginning to delve into the things that have threatened their livelihood, and they are concerned that perhaps we are doing things that are not in their best interest—like continually raising taxes and supporting those pantywaist kids who run around shouting the sky is falling all the time, or the interminable influx of illegal aliens who take our jobs.

"The membership has watched its old enemies—the corporations— get beaten into submission and then into their graves, and you know, a few of the folks are beginning to believe that maybe, just maybe, those corporations were good for them and maybe for the nation as well. And while we don't want them to run roughshod over our members, we don't want them to die either. We have actually discovered that we really need them. They paid our salaries for a very long time. Keep them in line, but don't kill them off. The Asians are killing us in manufacturing. Currently we don't stand a chance in that game. It's like we used to do with our military—we asked them to fight wars, then tied their hands behind their backs to insure they didn't win. We are doing the same thing with our corporations, and it isn't working."

Alec finished his coffee and poured another. "So that was your platform?"

"It really wasn't too hard at all. I simply asked if they were getting what they really wanted and if they were happy with what they were getting. Then I reminded them about the definition of insanity—keep doing the same thing and expect different results. So they decided they really had nothing to lose and voted for a change. It's a bit like Trump tried to do with African Americans when he ran for president. He pointed out that they had been wasting their votes on administrations that basically ignored their real needs. Fortunately, there were enough black leaders in that community making a good living off conflict, so they were able to get most people to march in step and vote Democrat, even though their poverty levels were rising and jobs were disappearing. I just want to make sure my constituency gets enough change to fulfill my promise."

Gutierrez finally reached for his coffee and took a sip before continuing. "And how strong is the union's displeasure with the environmentalist groups?"

"Very strong. My members are workers. As I said, they want jobs, and they want paychecks. They see these young idealists as a threat to both. There has been talk about a demonstration at the next "Green" meeting."

"That cannot happen." The President spoke forcefully. "Especially leading up to the next election. You've got to keep everyone in line until after the election. Then we can find a solution. I know some of these kids can get carried away, but overall they mean well. We just need to control them a bit better."

Gutierrez tented his fingers and thought for a few moments. "Alec, I'd like you to meet with the environmentalist leadership and see if you can't get them to back off on their demands a bit. Don is right; we need to give our corporations a fighting chance in the global marketplace. Damn, he's also right about our losing in that arena." Gutierrez watched Fontero's face as he nodded in agreement. "And Don, you work your magic with the angry members in your organization. Look, I understand their frustration. The entire nation has been struggling these past few years, but we have some plans that should turn this economy around soon. Just keep things calm, and give us a chance. Can I count on you in this?"

"Of course, Mr. President, but we all need to find some solutions fairly quickly. There are a lot of American workers out there mad as hell. My people want to work. They don't like sitting at home watching TV all day."

"I understand; we hear your message and will give it a lot of thought." The President rose. "I have another meeting in five minutes. Let's all do some work on this and get back together later. Alec, you set that up on our schedules?"

"Yes sir."

The two politicians watched the union boss walk out of the office. Alec closed the door. "Wow, there for a moment I felt we were going to have a real serious problem with our new union chief."

"I'm not sure we don't. He's smart, and he also has a good point."

"And if the rank and file start feeling that our policies are hurting them, we are in deep trouble next election." Alec walked across the room and poured his third cup of coffee. "We've got to keep an eye on this guy. An idealist in the AFL/CIO. That hasn't happened in a very long time."

"My thoughts exactly." Gutierrez walked to the window and looked out for several minutes then turned back to face Alec. "Whose idea do you think it was that we are killing the corporations? His or the rank-and-file?"

"I was wondering about that as soon as he made the comment. It could well be either or both, and he rode that wave to victory, you can bet. Smart young man."

"Frankly, he's lucky to be alive."

"My thoughts as well. Union politics can get pretty rough. I'm surprised he was able to surprise Walt Brown. I hear it was a close race."

The president looked straight at Alec. "You are right; union politics can get damned rough. Like I was saying; he's damned lucky to be alive now." He turned back to the window. "Check into Fontero's background. See if we have anything on him. How can we use leverage against him if we need to? Is he really an idealist, or is he as cunning as I suspect he is?"

"I'll make some discreet calls. I'm sure he must have something in his background we need to know." Alec stood to leave. "All that rank-and-file crap is just that, crap. I haven't seen a union chief who really gave a damn about the rank-and-file in my lifetime. It's all about power and money. I suspect deep down inside Fontero is no different than the rest."

"If you don't find anything in his background, get creative. He may think he understands politics, but he's playing in the big leagues now."

"I'll take care of it."

Chapter 74

July 26, 2039
Moscow, Russia

Yuri Rashinko walked into the large office of the President of the Russian Republic. The room was resplendent. With walls sixteen feet tall and red velvet curtains fringed with gold braid framing each of the eight floor-to-ceiling windows, it was very different than the average Russian worker's apartment in one of the government housing units. Yuri stood erect in spite of his age and the arthritis pain in his joints. "Greetings, Michael Anatoly Gornavich. I came as soon as I got your message."

The younger man stood and walked across the room to shake the hand of the man he had known most of his life. "Hello, Yuri. How are you, old friend?"

"I'm ready to climb into a fighter and challenge any man alive who threatens Mother Russia."

"And any man who would accept that challenge would be a fool." Both men smiled and hugged each other.

"What do you need of this old soldier, my President?"

Both men took seats across from the President's desk. A young orderly brought tea while they chatted about mundane things. As soon as he left, the sharp-faced head-of-state spoke. "What is happening with the Americans? I reviewed your reports about the shooting of the brain surgeon at the border. Our press is reporting every aspect of the event."

"Much to the embarrassment of the American government."

"Do you think it might slow the exodus?"

"I don't think so. These people are committed. Most of them sent their families earlier. They have little reason to stay. It seems there are still some remaining who cannot abide the changes of socialism. In time I feel they, too, will leave. Socialism has been a part of their history and their culture for more than 20 years, but still many do not accept it."

The President attentively watched his old friend as he spoke. "And these are the ones we need to assist in their efforts to leave. When they do, those remaining will soon discover that entitlements left the country with those they drove out. They have been spoiled for far too long."

"That is true, my President. They have become a weak people."

"We need to insure that the government doesn't find a way to stop the elite from leaving. We need them out. It will weaken America even further and is a major part of our plan."

"The entire country deteriorates by the day; they cannot compete in the international arena, and the entire economy is sinking like a foundering ship."

"More importantly, their military is a paper tiger. What was once a great world power is little more than a broken nation of misfits." Gornavich sipped his tea. "Isn't it strange that thirty years ago we learned from their successes, while they copied our failures. And now we are the preeminent nation in the world, where we should be. Mother Russia is taking her rightful place as leader of the world, but, as you know, our real problem is our neighbor to the east. The Chinese have proven their capability at organization and production, but they still lack two major inputs—oil and food."

"That is true my President, but they have been very busy buying both all over the world. They already own most of the resources in Africa, and now they are buying most of the resources of the Americans. It is very worrisome. They basically own the Americans, and both nations know it."

The Russian President sipped his drink and thought carefully. "That is why we must move quickly to gain control of America before the Chinese can make their move. Whoever controls America will control the world. If Russia had America's resources and food production, the

Chinese would be kept in their place for many years to come. With insufficient oil, China is a toothless dragon."

"How much oil do the Americans really have? We have all heard the stories of their potential, but just how real is it?"

"My experts tell me it is amazing; the reserves they are sitting on rival what the Middle East had before they destroyed themselves. It seems their government is saving it for someone else—us!" President Gornavich smiled broadly at his own joke.

"Energy is the key to the future, yet the Americans have allowed a small group to halt energy production and bottle up all their potential while their economy shrivels as rotten fruit—another example of how the changes in America are leading to disaster. They allow the environmental fanatics to control the entire nation simply because they are the loudest group around. Simply amazing!"

"You see, my old friend, oil, once again, will determine the winners in this global contest."

"Yes, and the Israelis did us all a favor when they single handedly removed most of the oil from human reach. Who would have guessed?" The older man smiled. "Now we are rid of all the problems in the Middle East. The idiots finally killed themselves off. Twelve nuclear bombs were all it took to end that fruitless war."

"And remove the tool of Islam used by ambitious men to lead other ignorant men to their deaths—all in the name of a god that we know does not exist."

"It ended it for good; that is for sure. And it left little room for doubting the power of nuclear weapons."

Gornavich knew that event had changed much in the world. It had also left Russia with most of the world's available oil. As America had sunk deeper into socialism, the entrepreneurs disappeared—just as the economist Schumpeter had predicted. And with the loss of the entrepreneurs, so went the prospect of finding a real solution to the energy problems. The Americans were sitting on the largest reserves of oil in the world, and their own government would not allow them access to most of it. All the government labs in America had accomplished little in the search for a "greener" solution. Gornavich wondered what a couple of good companies could have done with the prospect of enormous profits for the solution. If only they had listened.

Russia had listened. An enlightened leader had led Russia into the realm of capitalism ten years ago. It was still in its infancy, but it was working, and the oil provided the capital to make it happen. Now things were changing. People were working hard; they were creative; they were leading the global economy in growth. They had found the way, and they had the discipline to make it work like the Americans never understood. They had studied the demise of their old enemies, and they had learned. A decision was made to keep education at the highest levels. People would work; there would be no welfare families on the public dole for generations. Drug dealers would be dealt with; Singapore had taught them that lesson. New businesses would be encouraged. Energy would be available, and the infrastructure of the nation would be the best in the world.

The President was pleased. Yes, they were the best; now they simply had to demonstrate that to the rest of the world while keeping their old enemy, the Chinese, at bay. When Russia conquered America it would be obvious. Then the rest of the world would understand and surrender to the superior nation, and Russia would transform the world with the order it deserved and needed—and Russia would have the American heartland—the breadbasket of the world and all the energy stored underground, waiting to be exploited. "Yuri, what is your plan?"

"I am developing that, my President. We have to be very careful. There are two immediate problems. The Chinese are increasingly buying major companies and resources in America, and the exodus of the brightest needs to be expedited. It is working, but it needs to proceed faster, before the American government can totally stop the departure of their most productive citizens. Both of these are a challenge to our plans. I have a strategy for dealing with the Chinese; I also have a plan to help those Americans leaving to do so more easily. And of course, both of these will be done with great secrecy. I have twenty men with me; that is enough for both tasks."

"You must be especially careful with the Chinese. They must never suspect our involvement."

294

"That is why I have such a small team of experts. The Chinese are vulnerable in America; there are still a lot of guns on the streets. I do not worry about our Chinese adversaries. Those Americans leaving, however, are smart. They are the brightest of the population. If they discover our help, it could backfire. So we are staying out of the light; my agents are working from the shadows. We are slowing the government's efforts to stop those trying to leave. We are also working to incite anger about the shooting that happened. The government tried to keep it quiet, but we had it online immediately."

"Good, you are using their own tools against them."

"Their government owns the media, but the Internet is still difficult to control."

"Can they trace the reports back to our people?"

"Those leaving probably could. But we are careful. Thus far no one is checking. It appears to be simply local people who are angry."

"Who is leading the effort to stop the exodus?"

"Primarily the President and his Chief of Staff. I suspect Woodward is the key. It was he who proposed the law to make it illegal to leave without permission."

"Can we stop him?"

"He is highly placed in the government, but we may find a way to discredit him. If not, I have another option. As the process unfolds, the right approach will become apparent."

The President leaned toward his friend. "Be careful, Yuri. This must never be discovered until we reach Phase Three."

"I know."

"If it is, I will be forced to disavow all knowledge of what you are doing."

"At the rate that America is failing, I suspect we will be able to achieve our goals within two years."

"That soon?" There was surprise in the President's voice.

"That soon! Ignorance and mediocrity are easily managed by a disciplined and intelligent force. Years ago the American people bought into the liberal philosophy of having someone else do their work—then it changed to allow someone else to do their thinking. Today they are lazy and easily manipulated. We need fear only those we are trying to help escape."

"But once they are out, America will fall like the pathetic mess it has become. History will chronicle the fall of another of the world's crumbling societies—doomed by the excesses within." Gornavich almost gloated, one President changed the course of history for a nation of complacent and willing losers—to use their own term. While he turned to a failed socialism, we turned to a successful capitalism that had built the highest standard of living in the world. He promised change—and change they got! Wait until they see the changes we have planned for them!"

Chapter 75

August 3, 2039
Galveston Bay, Texas

As darkness fell upon the South, dark rain clouds moved slowly across the marshes and densely wooded bayous and threatened the small town of Anahuac, Texas. It was here that the first shots of the Texas Revolution were fired, and that same spirit was still alive among the inhabitants of the town. A small convoy of covered trucks and one old school bus sat idle in the parking lot of a small church as people loaded their belongings into the vehicles. There were several babies in the crowd, and one was beginning to cry. An older woman walked to the young mother and promptly pulled down the top of her dress. She pressed the baby to the mother's breast; immediately, the child began nursing and was quiet. "Always works!"

"Thanks, Mrs. Thompson."

"I'll grab your suitcase; you go along and get on the bus. I'll be right behind you."

There was an air of nervousness among the group. They were families, not spies. Their lives had been forged in kitchens and workplaces across the nation. They were not used to clandestine activities like these. After about an hour, the trucks and the bus were loaded. The old pastor stood beside the tall pine that guarded the driveway and said a quick prayer. Then he forced a smile and waved as the convoy drove off into the night.

Fifty miles away in Houston another meeting was being held, but it was in a government building. The Washington agents stood out in their suits while the locals wore blue jeans and cowboy boots. "Rollins seemed damned sure that this is the night the next group is planning to leave. Do you agree, Thompson?" William Thompson had been an outstanding deputy sheriff for eight years. But tonight he stood in the misty rain and worried about his family. They were among the Patriots leaving in the current group. It was a secret he wanted to keep to himself. Thompson knew his wife would be strong, but he worried about the children and especially the small ones. At that moment every government agent in Texas and half from Louisiana were sitting in the dark watching a lone boat tied up on a small river bank, eighty miles west of the actual exit point.

"We finally broke the code on the note we found, so this must be it. They sure picked a rainy night if you ask me."

"Are your men down at the river where the deserters planted the boat?"

"We have fifty men there right now, waiting for the group to show up."

"Fifty?"

"Yes ma'am, there were ropes and fuel for at least four other boats. We figure this to be a large exodus."

The FBI agent-in-charge was young and pretty. "Must be their families. It's hard to stop a man who wants to leave on his own. Damned hard. But families, that is another thing altogether. They will need bigger boats and more equipment."

While the Washington crowd quizzed the local agents, several local police walked back to the coffee room in the rear of the building. The new sheriff waited for his deputy to pour him a cup. "Why do you think they are leaving, Thompson?"

"Mostly I guess it's the taxes and regulations. Those who are leaving are paying a hell of a lot of taxes to keep this country going. People came to America looking for freedom from such things. I guess they just feel they paid enough." Thompson looked carefully to see what reaction he had stirred. When the sheriff said nothing, the deputy took his coffee and walked out into the evening. He breathed a sigh of relief that the government had actually decoded the simple message that Mark

Sagan had composed and had deposited in the bottom of the old boat. Many in the Patriot camp had said the government agents might not decode the message in time, but Mark had made it simple and they had finally broken the code. If they had not, Thompson was ready to step in and help.

A sound behind him caused him to turn quickly. "Hello Thompson, you guys did a fine job down here. I'm sure the boys in Washington will be very happy to hear about this endeavor. Good work."

"Well, I keep my men sharp. I figured this was coming soon. I'm guessing they don't want to be doing a lot of this later in the winter. Damn, this rain is a mess for the guys out there in the weeds."

The lead agent resumed her analysis. "How many roads lead to the escape point? Have you put any observers along those routes?"

"Only two roads make sense. I have three men stationed along them with radios."

"Great work. Now we just wait."

As they were talking a radio crackled on Thompson's belt. "Thompson!" He listened carefully for a couple of minutes then responded. "Good work, keep me advised." He turned to the young woman in the dark suit. "One of my men just intercepted a call from the Patriots. We found one of their radios in the boat. Seems they have been delayed a bit. I guess the weather is a problem for them as well as us."

"Well, alert the men that it may be a long night. And tell them to keep quiet. We don't want to alert the rebels that we are around." As Thompson and the agent were talking he felt the small vibration in his left pocket from the phone that connected him with his family and the others who had made the decision to leave. The vibration was short, then it stopped. After a couple of minutes it repeated. That meant the boats were loaded and underway. Ten miles to the ship and his family would be safe. It would be a rough ride in this weather, but he knew the boats and the men who were piloting them. He smiled and walked back into the building in search of a tolerable cup of coffee.

*   *   *

The normally placid Gulf was thrusting and thrashing as the storm grew in intensity. The women and children had it the worst. Several were seasick and hung their heads over the edge of the small boats to discharge their last meal. Some of the children loved the ride and squealed with excitement; others cried and clung to their mothers. The ride should have taken about an hour, but it was almost two hours when they finally pulled up beside the freighter. Men crawled over the side of the ship and jumped into the smaller boats to help the women and children climb the rope ladders. An older man fell into the water, but two young men jumped from the sides of the freighter and pulled him to safety. When all were aboard, one old man tied all of the small boats together and started the return trip to the shore. The boats were too valuable to sink or abandon. They would be needed for the next group. With a wave he gunned his motor and disappeared into the darkness, headed north.

*   *   *

Thompson walked into the small control room and looked at the men seated around a group of maps. Several were discussing Cajun food; two others were almost asleep. "Any news yet?"

"No sir! The boys at the river say the only thing that showed up thus far are mosquitos—lots of them."

"Well, daylight is coming. What's your plan, Rollins? You were the one who alerted the world to this opportunity."

"I'm guessing the weather caused the problem. I'll have my men wait until nine, then leave a couple and send the others home. I really doubt they would try to leave in daylight."

"I agree, that would be far too risky. I think your plan is a good one. I'm heading back into town for breakfast. Want to join me?"

The sound of breakfast was enough to win Rollins. He nodded and rose to leave with Thompson. "Why not? I've got a radio if they need us." The bright morning sun was quickly climbing into the eastern sky; it would be a warm day in Texas—but then, most were. But it wasn't the heat that put the smile on Thompson's face. He had received the second and third sets of vibrations during the night and had then walked out to

300

the small backwater pond where he threw the small phone into the brackish water. Its job was done; his family was safe. Now he could relax and plan the next exodus—his own.

Chapter 76

August 5, 2039
The White House

The old white-haired man walked slowly into the Chief of Staff's office. There were deep furrows on his obese face, and he moved with difficulty. Alec immediately recognized the Senator from Georgia. He had been in the U.S. Senate for a very long time, and while he was a Democrat, he was still a very practical man. He did not appear happy. "Hello Senator, what can I do for you?"

"You can knock off all this foolishness about closing our Army Base in Columbus for starters."

"Senator, I believe you have been misinformed. We have no intention of closing Fort Benning. We just want to close *part* of the base."

"And send about half of the soldiers there packing. That will wreck that part of the state. They depend on all that government money to keep the economy going. They've depended on that base for a very long time; I don't intend to see it cut in half on my watch. I have constituents down there, and they are worried."

Alec walked quickly around the desk to move the chairs around to assist the portly man. "You're right, the government has spent a lot of money at that base for a very long time. The problem is that we no longer have that money to spend."

"And why don't we have the money now?"

"The conservatives spent too much in the past and left us with all this debt we keep trying to pay off."

"That's bullshit! Most of this debt came from our side of the aisle, and you know it. Obama doubled the debt all by himself in only eight years. We just spent the money on the wrong things. You just keep giving it to every voting bloc in town and forget the security of our country. Hell, we once were the strongest nation in the world. Now we're

302

just damn broke." The senator's voice was climbing in volume, and Alec was desperate to calm the old man down lest he have a heart attack there in his office. "You know where the money went. It bought us lots of votes—and what do we have to show for it? Even more people with their hands out for government assistance. Damn, Alec, you know that government money is like fertilizer; whatever it gets poured on just grows and grows. We just pour the money on the wrong things. And right now we need to pour some money on that base in Columbus, not cut it in half. I have people there depending on me."

Alec folded his hands and studied the Senator. He wondered what he would say when he opened his own mouth. "You know that even the generals have okayed that reduction in force."

"Those boneheads are politicians just like me. They'd say anything Gutierrez asks them to say. We've had damned few real generals in this nation since World War II; a few, but not many. They're all just politicians. So most of their opinions aren't worth a damn. The President will make this decision, not some ass-kissing general." The senator paused for a moment and watched Alec closely. "He'll make that decision after you brief him and tell him which way to go."

"Don't underestimate the President. Gutierrez is a very strong man."

"Right, and I'm Atlas. He couldn't make a decision if his life depended on it. I've been around here long enough to know how it works. That's why I'm coming to you. Find a way, Alec. Take the money from some other group; hell, take the money from the unions. They've had a soft go for a long time. Maybe it's time for them to do some real work for a change. Look, I backed that dumb idea about reducing our nuclear arsenal along with the Ruskies and the Chinese. I even helped push through the total drawdown of all nuclear weapons when you asked for my support, and that was not an easy sell either. So now it's your turn. Now I need *your* support."

Alec secretly pressed a small button below his desk drawer. Seconds later his secretary stuck his head into the room and reminded him of his meeting. He rose, looked at his watch in alarm and started for the door. "Damn, I'm late. Look, George, I'll see what I can do about the base. I can't promise anything, but I'll try." In a flash he exited the room and rushed down the hall for the fictitious meeting. Three minutes later his phone rang once and he returned to his office. "Thanks, Marvin, that was becoming very difficult. Everybody wants money from the government; they all want freebies—how did it ever get that way?"

Alec frowned. He wondered how many senators he would face when it was announced that both the Air Force Academy and Annapolis were being closed next year. All three services were being cut and West Point would easily handle the remaining cadets from all three branches. The savings could be directed to other more pertinent things like the increased medical benefits for welfare recipients. That could be handled easily in the press. The real money, however, would be gained by selling both of the closed academies to a large Chinese corporation that had already expressed interest in the facilities. The money from such a sale would be essential if the government had any chance to avoid default on some of its larger loans with the Chinese.

He would need a well-coordinated PR campaign to get this through, but he knew the press would support him. Still, he was uncomfortable. How does one dispose of something like the Naval Academy or the Air Force Academy without a huge public outcry? The tradition was long, and the defiance would be great. He jotted that on his list for the following week. He would worry about that later. He had other issues to deal with now.

Chapter 77

August 16, 2039
Cedar Rapids, Iowa

The Harley was old, but it was well-maintained. When Jesse Holbrook mounted the worn saddle and started out of the factory driveway, it seemed that most of Cedar Rapids was lining Highway 27 heading south toward Interstate 80. The people cheered, and many held cans of gas for Jesse's bike. He was just passing the Wright Brothers Boulevard when a young man ran out of the crowd and placed a three-gallon fuel can on the back of the bike. Very quickly he strapped it onto the worn saddle bags then saluted the old man as he rode south.

Jesse Holbrook's life had been one of adventure. He had always taken the path less-traveled. The only thing he had loved more than his life of adventure was his wife, Margaret. When she died three years earlier, he spent three months riding around the country, searching for himself. When he returned he was a changed man. He now had a purpose – his two granddaughters. Jesse was not a learned man, but it required little education to see what was happening to his country. His concern became anger, and the anger turned into resolve. Early one morning he walked out to his bike with a big smile on his face. The world was not ready for Jesse Holbrook, but it would have to move over to let him pass.

By the time Jesse was passing the Hawkeye Wildlife Management Area, the crowds were gone, and he was able to increase his speed. He loved the air blowing through his thinning hair. He and the bike were a pair; they had traveled the country for years together. It had given him great joy in his life. He rode on, singing to himself. There was little traffic; fuel was far too sparse for most people to drive. It was a beautiful day, and he was happy. He was making a difference, and he knew it.

Three miles farther up the road a thin young man crouched atop a small hill. Darin's view of the highway was clear; his orders were also clear. The FBI agent watched for the old man on the motorcycle. It would have a red plastic fuel container strapped on the back. That was his target; one shot and the explosion would appear accidental. As planned two cars were travelling together ahead of Jesse; they would slow the target at the right moment to facilitate a relatively easy shot. Darin rechecked his rifle and the small stand he would use to steady his shot. He estimated the distance to be no more than 100 yards and there was no wind to consider. The Chinese radio beside him crackled and a voice reported "two out." He lay down and adjusted the scope. There was a small bush beside the road that served as a sighting for him. Then he saw the two cars driving slowly, side by side down the highway. Behind them was the Harley. He was just focusing on his target when the heavily accented voice behind him spoke. "You move; you're dead."

The shooter rolled to his back and stared at the man behind him. He barely recognized the make of the pistol when it fired. The first bullet struck him in the neck. The second was a head shot. It was over in seconds. The Russian picked up the rifle, admired it briefly then fired three shots into one of the two cars leading the Harley. The car swerved sharply and crashed into the ditch beside the road. The second car sped off to the south as the Harley reversed course and headed back toward Cedar Rapids. It was an hour later when Jesse opened the red fuel can to fill his bike. He knew immediately that it was not gasoline. Jesse had not always been an old man. He had once been a demolitions expert in the Army. He understood that the red can on his bike was most likely a target for his demise. One well-placed shot would have been enough. For the first time that afternoon, the ambush of the white car on Highway 27 started to make sense. Had they been firing at the car, or him? Jesse found a small bar on the outskirts of town and quickly made a call. "Wilson? We need to talk. Can you get Mark?"

*　　*　　*

The men in the second car returned to the shooting scene 30 minutes later. They carefully scoured the area and found the dead driver of the crashed car in the vehicle. Two of them climbed the hill and found their other colleague lying in a pool of blood. His rifle was gone as was his ammunition. "What will we do with Darin?"

"Well, we can't leave him here." The two turned at the same time as an explosion ripped their car apart and left a large plume of smoke and fire in the air. "Oh shit!" They were on their bellies immediately, looking in all directions for an attack that did not happen. After several minutes they rose and started toward the road. It would be a long walk back to town.

*   *   *

Mark walked into the small restaurant south of Denver and waited for his eyes to adjust to the dim interior. When they did, he spotted Ken sitting alone in the corner. Mark walked over and ordered a coffee and a piece of apple pie. "I appreciate your coming home on such short notice, son. What did you guys learn?"

"It looks like there may have been a plot to kill Jesse, after all. Our investigators found a lot of blood on a small hill right where he said the shots were fired toward the car. Someone died on that hill. He may have fired at that car, or the person who killed him did. It's possible the original shooter may well have been there waiting for Jesse, but someone else was waiting for him, or perhaps they just didn't agree on who to shoot. Either way, we'll soon know who died on that hill. I have some of our people working on it now. Whoever drug the body off was not professional at all. They didn't cover anything, tracks, blood, even some brains." Mark grimaced. "I have a couple of good men looking into what happened. Luckily we have a contact in the sheriff's office. With that and the blood, we'll probably know something in a couple of days."

"This is strange, indeed. But we had better tell Jesse to keep a low profile for a few days. Where is he anyway?"

307

"Somewhere outside Cedar Rapids. He'll be heading south to Texas tomorrow. And good luck trying to get Jesse to keep a low profile! Jesse is no stranger to danger. I suspect he relishes it." Mark was silent as the coffee and pie were served. When the waiter left he continued. "Can we get him a gun?"

"We'll do that, but we have to be very careful. Getting caught with a gun is as bad as using it."

"Well, Jesse damn sure knows how to use one."

"That's right, you two saw action together didn't you!"

"Back then his hair was the same color as mine! Every new Sergeant needs a seasoned old troop to teach him the ropes. He taught me how to be a soldier." Mark smiled.

"Did he still have that damned Harley-Davidson back then?"

"When I knew him back then he was driving a Humvee with a fifty-caliber machine gun mounted on top."

"That's what we need, a fifty-caliber machine gun strapped on his handle bars!" Both men laughed at the idea. Suddenly the lights in the room died completely; the owner and several patrons cursed loudly. Within a minute they were back on again, but the two men in the corner were gone.

The two government men waited for their eyes to adjust before checking the room. When they didn't find what they were looking for, they turned and left.

Chapter 78

September 8, 2039
Denver, Colorado

Mark's heart began beating faster as he pounded on the door, cursing quietly that he had left his keys in his luggage, which was somewhere between Washington and Denver. He knew his dad was home, yet no one came to the door when he knocked. Reaching under a large empty pot on the porch, he quickly found the key and unlocked the door. He rushed inside without even looking to see who or what might be waiting for him. Then he heard the retching sounds coming from the tiny bathroom in the rear of the house. There he found Ken, leaning over the toilet, vomiting repeatedly. Mark rushed to his adopted father and quickly ran warm water over a bath cloth he found hanging near the sink. "Here, Dad, try this." The older man reached for the wet cloth and wiped his face. He took a deep breath and stood up, still watching the toilet. Within seconds he leaned over and began vomiting again. Mark put his hand on Wilson's shoulder and stood with him until the spasms stopped. The pastor stood by the toilet for several minutes, unsure if there was anything left in his body to expel. Finally, he turned and walked slowly back into the kitchen and sat at the table. He looked very weak and tired. "What did you eat today, dad?"

"Mark, you and I both know this is not about what I ate today." Wilson forced a weak smile. "After all, you are a doctor."

"Can I get you something to drink?"

"I think a cup of hot green tea might be good."

309

Mark placed a teapot on the stove and lit the gas under it. "How long has this been happening?"

"Throwing up? About a week or so. It happens now and then, not every day." Wilson took two tea cups from the cupboard and handed them to Mark. "But I think it's getting worse."

The younger man looked at the floor for a long time before he finally spoke. "Tell me the truth dad, how bad is it? Really? I know you saw one of our oncologists last week. What did he tell you?"

"It's not good, son. He thinks I may have about six months."

Mark closed his eyes and rubbed his forehead with his right hand. Finally, he looked up into his father's eyes. "Damn! That's not much time." Mark rose and walked to the stove where the water was boiling. He turned his face away from Ken for several minutes. Then he squared his shoulders and turned to face the sick man before him. Wilson spoke before Mark could.

"We'll just have to share a lot of life in a short time."

"This isn't going to be easy, dad. Cancer is a tough opponent."

"I know, Mark; as a pastor I have walked that road with many people. I'm well aware of the reality of what this means."

"I'm not ready to let you go, dad. I'm just not ready for that now." There were tears in Mark's eyes, but he was fighting to hold his emotions intact.

"And I'm not happy about this either. But I guess The Boss has plans I just don't understand yet. Right now I just need His strength."

"Well, I'd like a few words with *The Boss*. You don't deserve this. You've spent your life tending to others." Mark's voice trailed off as he struggled with words.

Wilson sipped his tea and looked at his son for several minutes. When he spoke, his voice clear and resonant. "Mark, I don't understand all of God's plans, but I do trust Him, and that trust is what will get me through however many days I may have left. Think about it this way, son. I'm seventy-seven years old, and most of those years were a blessing no man could ever deserve. I had Marion for thirty-three years, and God also gave us you. She was my present and you became our vision for the future. I was blessed with both of you and a lot of fine people who needed

310

me now and then." He paused and sipped his tea while he watched his son. "I know it's hard to understand at thirty-four, but at seventy-seven, one has a much different perspective."

Wilson looked around the small house. "This place isn't much, I suppose, but do you have any idea how much love and gratitude have existed in this little house? I wouldn't trade those wonderful moments in my life for all the castles in the world. Marion and I moved into this house the month after we learned we would never have a child together. That was a tough period for both of us, especially her. But I kept telling her that God would find a way to bless us; we just had to keep believing. Sure enough, not too many years later I got a call from a parishioner who was a policeman. He had a little boy who needed me that night. As soon as I set eyes on you, I knew our prayers were answered. It took a while to make it official, but from the moment I first saw you sitting on that park bench, I just knew you would be a part of our family and our lives."

He watched Mark leaning against the kitchen counter and after a few moments of silence continued. "I have been truly blessed, son. I have known and shared great love. I have climbed the mountains in spring and counted a million small wildflowers put there just to please me and anyone else who was willing to take the time to find them. I've watched the sun rise over the Rockies, and I've seen it set in glorious shades of red and orange. Do you remember the first time we ever climbed a fourteener? You were about fifteen as I recall."

"It was Grays."

"Do you remember what I told you we were doing?"

"You said we were climbing to get closer to God. And when we got to the top, you had me turn in three hundred sixty degrees so I could see God's handiwork."

"That's right."

"And where is his handiwork now?"

"Remember what I said about trust?"

"I'm sorry, I'm having a little problem with that right now." Mark's voice was tinged with emotion. "I'm not as strong as you are, dad." Mark turned and put his cup in the sink. When he turned back, a single tear escaped his right eye and raced down his cheek. He rubbed it away immediately.

"You're a lot stronger than you think, son. You have strength you haven't even called upon yet. When you need it, it will be there."

"I'll help you through these next six months. You know that."

"Of course I do. And who knows, I may have a bit longer. I'm a stubborn old man, or at least your mom thought so." That caused Mark to smile. "And I still have a few things I need to do. My work here is not yet complete." He winked at Mark knowingly.

"If you think you're going to get me to forgive Alec, then you're going to need to live a very long time." Mark walked over and took Wilson's cup and placed it in the sink with the other. "He doesn't deserve it, and he'll never change."

"Forgiving him may not change him; but it will certainly change you. You'll find a way. And when you do, the rage will be gone, and you'll be free."

"Like I said, dad. If that is the last task you need to accomplish, you'll live a very long life."

"The Boss moves in very strange ways sometimes." And then he did something Mark had seen him do so many times in his life. With a wry smile, he nodded and winked at his son. It was his way of saying he knew something no one else understood. The wink and that smile had been there for most of Mark's life. He loved his dad, and this was his dad at his best. It broke the tension in the conversation immediately.

"Well, the world has been in need of a good miracle for a long time. Perhaps this will be it, but don't bet on it anytime soon."

"That is a bet I will take, and one I will win. You just wait; I'll remind you." Wilson's eyes grew suddenly large as he rose from the chair. Placing a towel over his mouth, he started quickly down the hall toward the toilet.

312

Chapter 79

October 6, 2039
Interstate 10, halfway between San Antonio and Houston, Texas

Jesse pulled off Interstate 10 onto State Highway 90 and searched the signs for Waelder, Texas. Ten minutes later he parked his bike in the front yard of the old Texas farm house. He looked carefully around and slowly started up the stairs of the worn porch. He felt the handle of the pistol that he had stuck in his belt in the back of his pants. It was cold and hard. The feeling brought back so many memories from his early life in the military and then as the sheriff of Guymon, Oklahoma. The warm evening air enveloped him; he felt at home. Jesse approached the door with caution. A voice within called his name, and the front door swung open. Raymond Johnson ran forward to greet his old friend. He noticed Jesse relax and stepped back. "What's wrong, Jesse, you in trouble?"

"Hell, I'm always in trouble. Can't remember a time I wasn't in trouble."

Raymond laughed and slapped his friend on the back. "You carrying?"

Jesse suddenly became very serious. "Yes. Some idiot tried to kill me last week."

"Really? Well, if them idiots come around here, I suspect they will find more than they can handle."

"You're damned right. That's why I headed your way for a few days. Still got your sniper rifle? We might need it."

"Right by my bed." Raymond got very serious as he looked into Jesse's eyes. "I got a call from Mark. He said you were coming and to be careful. I sent Martha and the girls up to her sister's house. Then I made a few phone calls."

"You got some place I can hide my Harley. Don't want anything happening to my baby. There aren't many of these left. They built the last one in 2017. This baby is priceless."

"Was it Mark that told you to come by here?" Raymond was suddenly serious.

Jesse stopped and looked carefully at his friend. "I was ridin' down this way and both of us thought it might be a safe place for a day or two."

"Mark's a good man, and I think he's on to something, so leave your bike out front. We'll turn on some lights and the TV, then we're going to stay in the shed by the barn tonight. This could be interesting."

About 12:30 am the two men sat upright in the shed and listened as two vehicles pulled off the main road onto Raymond's driveway. The trees that lined the drive made it difficult to see them, but they stopped just off the main road. Both men grabbed their weapons and crouched behind the hay bales stacked beside the barn. As the figures crept closer, Jesse's eyes got larger. "Damn, there's a bunch of them."

"Three for you and three for me." Raymond looked through his night scope and counted the crouched figures again. "Damn, I see three more coming from up by the main road." No sooner had he spoken than gunfire erupted along the drive. Raymond swung his scope back and forth, surveying the situation. It was over in less than a minute. Shortly thereafter a vehicle started up on the main road and raced back toward the Interstate. The two friends waited for half an hour before returning to the house. Raymond called the sheriff while Jesse watched the yard. Ten minutes later a pickup with lights flashing arrived, and three deputies followed the sheriff along the drive. Jesse and Raymond walked slowly toward the activity and watched as bodies were being stacked along the dirt road. The sheriff waved and walked over to Raymond. "For Heaven Sakes, what the hell is going on out here?" His face was contorted in the light of two flashlights.

"Damned if I know. I heard two vehicles pull off the road and saw some men dressed in black with weapons. I guessed they were here to speak to Jesse."

314

The sheriff turned to Raymond's friend. "Are you Jesse Holbrook?"

"That's me."

"Damn, I'd like to shake your hand. I've heard a lot of good things about you."

Raymond turned toward the bodies. "Well, someone else has heard about him, too, it appears. Shortly after this group starts down the drive, another sneaks up behind them, and this is the result." Raymond nodded toward the stack of bodies bleeding into the soft Texas soil.

"You boys know any of these guys? Damned if they aren't dressed like a bunch of Ninja warriors."

Ray and Jesse walked over and looked at the bodies. "Nope, never seen this bunch before."

The sheriff pulled a worn pad from his pocket and made a few notes. "Well, nobody needs to worry about them anymore. But I wonder who took them out. They were all shot from behind. These guys all have .45s. None of them were even fired. Someone caught them completely by surprise. Shell casings look to be 9mm. It was pros who done this."

"But who?"

"Don't know, but damn sure glad they were here. You boys want anyone sticking around in case anyone else shows up?"

"No, we're fine."

The sheriff noted Raymond's rifle. "I'm sure you are. Just one question. Do you have any coffee in the house? It has been a short night and I could use a cup."

"I was just going to make a pot, soon as I check my bike. If one of those goons hit my Harley, I'm going to really be pissed."

* * *

Mark took notes as he talked to Jesse. Wilson was there with him in Denver, listening to the conversation. "What did the Sheriff discover about the assailants?"

"Seems they were a bunch of hired punks. Totally non-traceable, especially since they are all dead now. One had Raymond's address on a piece of paper, and they were obviously paid well. Each of them had about $3000 in his pocket."

"What about the shooters who took them out?"

"Not much to go on. We didn't get much info from the site. Appears they stole a truck from town and followed the punks to Raymond's place. My guess is that they got there no more than two or three minutes after the bad guys arrived. They damned sure knew what they were doing. The killing all took place in less than a couple of minutes. They just snuck up behind them and shot them in the back. We found ten 9mm shell casings."

"Sounds like pros."

"I'll say."

"You okay?"

"Hell yes. I'm pulling out tomorrow on old Betsy. I've got work to do. And Raymond is going to follow in his pickup for a few days. We served together in the Army after you went back to school. He's pretty damned good with a rifle."

"I know Raymond. He's a good man to have on your side. You two try to stay out of trouble, okay?" Mark spoke slowly to his friend who was listening attentively. "I'm worried about you two, but it seems someone else wants to make sure you're safe as well. I just wonder who it is. Any ideas?"

"No, but it would be wise for us to find out."

"I agree. First, I want to thank them. Then I want to know who the hell they are and what they are up to. I don't think any of this is our people. I just can't figure it out."

"Well, whoever it is doesn't seem to be following our plan of peaceful resistance." There was mirth in Jesse's voice.

"That's for sure." Mark paused for a moment. "We'd better find out just who these guys are. We need to know what this is all about."

Wilson leaned closer to the phone to join the conversation. "In the meantime, the government will probably think we had something to do with all this."

Mark answered with the idea they all were considering. "And that could be very problematic."

316

Jesse's voice suddenly seemed very far away. "Well, my guess is that someone in the government sponsored the first group of assassins, so they may not want to make too much of all this. It could easily get to be embarrassing for them if we could connect the bodies with the Feds."

"Why do you think the Feds had anything to do with this?" Mark was puzzled.

Wilson answered. "Who else would want Jesse dead?"

"Good point."

Chapter 80

October 11, 2039
Denver, Colorado

Yang walked into his hotel room in the Marriott west of Denver and threw his briefcase onto the bed. It had been a difficult day dealing with dumb Americans who were not making his job easy. He had offered them a price that should have concluded the deal immediately, but they continued to stall. He was after a small mining company in Idaho Springs, Colorado, or rather, he was after a process they had discovered that made gold extraction much cheaper and cut the processing time in half. He knew he could not simply buy the process—that would raise far too many flags. But while buying a process was out of the question, buying the entire company, including the process, was achievable. Now he had to convince Norbert Smith, the owner of the company, that his offer was real. Both he and the small man who started the company knew that the federal government was quickly taking control of similar companies and confiscating their assets—including their patents. Taxes were a formidable tool in the hands of unscrupulous government agents. The negotiations had been progressing slowly; then suddenly the entire business had been lost in a fire. Nothing was left, including the small leather faced man with whom he had been dealing.

Yang had immediately checked the patents, only to find that they were incomplete. There was enough data to fool incompetent government appointees, but the real details of how the process worked were gone. He stood looking out the fourth floor window at the mountains in the distance. Smith had disappeared, and the process was lost forever. He guessed that this process was a critical link in some plan that was important to Beijing, and now he had failed. Perhaps he could find Smith and convince him to sell the real plans. Most likely Smith was leaving in the exodus that was underway. If he had, all Yang had to do was find him. Then he could extract the information any way he wanted. No one would question the disappearance of one more executive. Like most entrepreneurs in America, Smith was unwelcomed in his own country.

How strange that a government would cause their most productive citizens to flee. Was the long-term fate of the nation worth such a short term political victory? The Americans were fools. They had once been the preeminent culture on earth; now they were watching their nation and their standard of living slowly declining into chaos—and they didn't have a clue how it happened. In China they would do the opposite. They would reward the most productive and send those who contributed little to the nation to the rice farms. It all made such sense. Yang turned quickly from the window, fumbling in his pocket for Smith's home address. The two beers he had consumed in the hotel lobby were beginning to cause him some discomfort, so Yang turned into the small bathroom to pee. As he opened the door, he was vaguely aware of a swift movement from his right. That was the last thought of his life.

*   *   *

The bright orange rays of the morning sun were climbing over the Colorado plains and illuminating the dark mountains to the west as the tired firemen watched the final flames from a pile of litter that had been stacked in the alley behind the Marriott hotel fade into gray trails of smoke that wound into the cold morning air.

"Chief, you need to take a look at this. We have a body beneath all this crap." The short red-headed fireman ducked inside the yellow tape that blocked the alley and walked quickly to the soaked pile of rubbish. There, on the ground was the body of a small man, lying face down in the refuse.

319

"Call the cops. This looks like something they'll need to check out. And make sure no one touches that body until they arrive. We have enough trouble without the police giving us static."

"Got it, chief."

Twenty minutes later Detective Wanda Brown joined the fire chief and stood silently surveying the body. She finally reached over and shoved the body to its back. It was partially burned. "Appears to be Chinese."

"By the looks of the quality of his shoes and clothes, I'd say you were right. He obviously had money." The chief smiled. "Therefore, not American."

Brown stared at the fireman for several minutes before nodding. "Looks that way." She knelt over the body and studied it for a few minutes. Then she rifled through all of the victim's pockets and placed the items in an old yellow envelope. "A black eye and a slit throat. Probably a mugging." She searched the man's wallet. "Yep, money's gone. Muggers." She studied the wallet a few more minutes and then exhaled loudly. "Damn, Chinese diplomat! There will be hell to pay for this. Looks like overtime tonight."

Wanda Brown was smiling as she slid into her patrol car. The ring she had slid into her pocket would be worth a considerable amount of money. Certainly the diplomat didn't need it any longer. But how did the muggers miss a prize like that. Thieves must truly be getting dumber—just like so many other folks in the country. She reached for her keys, then stopped and looked up at the building beside the alley. It was one of the few nice hotels left in the city. Slowly she pulled the identification card from the soiled envelope. "Diplomat," she breathed.

With a disgusted grunt she climbed out of the car and started walking toward the front of the hotel. Five minutes later she stood behind the hotel manager as he fumbled with a set of keys. Finally, he found the right one and opened the door. Brown walked in following her drawn pistol. Finding the room empty, she holstered her gun and began surveying the room. She nodded to the manager, and he left promptly. There was blood on the bathroom floor and the bedspread was missing. She noted the expensive laptop sitting in plain sight on the coffee table and a large bottle

320

of imported scotch. Obviously this was not a mugging. Someone had planned this carefully and had executed the plan with skill. She grabbed the scotch and the laptop and walked back to the elevator.

In the lobby Detective Brown called her division chief. "We've got a bit of a problem here. Someone mugged and murdered a Chinese diplomat. I'm on my way in and will give you a full report later." She could sell a mugging. A few days of poking around the neighborhood, and it would be over. But a deliberate homicide of a Chinese diplomat; that was another can of worms—one she did not want to crawl into.

Chapter 81

October 21, 2039
Washington, D.C.

The young woman stood before the wreckage and smiled into the camera. "An Amtrak train derailed today forty-seven miles outside Washington, D.C., killing thirteen people and injuring thirty-three. Officials on the site are investigating the accident to determine what caused this disaster. It is the third such crash in a little over a month." She smiled prettily into the camera then turned to an older, overweight woman standing beside her. "I have beside me Lillian Maybeth who lives nearby and was passing this area just after the accident. Miss Maybeth, please describe what you witnessed…"

Mark Sagan sat in a small office with several of his friends in the Patriots group, watching the newscast. He stood quickly and shook his head. "What the hell is going on? What are the odds of another train crash?" He grabbed the newspaper lying on a small table near the TV and scanned it quickly. "Here is a bridge that collapsed, and here is a plane that skidded off the runway; and here is a phone system that has been down for days. What the hell is going on?"

One of his colleagues frowned and replied. "They left the idiots in charge of the asylum—as you so often say!"

"No, this is something else. The nation is in decline, but not this fast!"

"Look, most of the people in charge got there by political fiat. They don't know their jobs, and many of them really don't care all that much either. What you predicted is happening. The government-run economy is failing. Competence is the last requirement to get or hold a job these days, especially in the government. The real question is how much political smack you have. Besides, many of the best government workers have already joined us and left."

"This just doesn't look right. This country shouldn't be failing so fast. And every one of these is suspicious, if you ask me."

"Well, what do you want us to do?"

"Check one—just one—carefully, and see if something is amiss. Humor me on this."

"Okay, what about the rail crash."

"That's fine. The rail crash should do just fine."

The other men in the room nodded as an older man with gray hair rose and started for the door. He looked back at Mark. "I'll take Jack and Will. We'll need a few days, but we'll get back to you as soon as possible."

*   *   *

The young secretary stuck his head into the Chief of Staff's office. "Mr. Woodward, you have a call on line two. He says it is urgent."

"Listen, Marvin, I really don't have time right now. I've got to get this report to the President before three o'clock. Just how urgent is this?"

"I don't know; Mr. Sagan wouldn't give me any details. He said you would understand."

"Sagan?" Alec shoved the papers aside and reached for the phone. "Hello, Woodward here."

"Alec, something funny is going on. The rail crash outside Washington was not an accident."

There was a long pause before Woodward spoke. "Were you bastards responsible for that?"

"Of course not! You know me better than that. I have no idea who did it, but I'm checking. If I find anything, I'll let you know. But I'm sure it was no accident. You may also want to check some of the other mishaps that are occurring across the country, like that phone outage in California, or the bridge that collapsed in Ohio."

"Listen, Mark. If you guys are sabotaging this nation, I'll personally see you all hanged. Do I make myself clear?"

"Dammit, Alec, get your arrogant head out of your ass. If we did these things, would I be calling you right now? I'm actually trying to help. Something weird is going on, and neither of us knows what it is. Park your ego for a while and get busy figuring this out. People are dying while you guys are contemplating your navels." Mark slammed the phone down with anger. "Stupid ass!"

Alec slowly placed the phone in its cradle and turned to look out the window. He knew Mark was not the one behind the sabotage; he didn't have it in him. Mark still believed in the old principles of honor; he still had integrity. Alec's mind wandered to an argument between two close friends in college. He could still hear the words from Mark as he outlined his old fashioned set of values. Alec still admired his friend, but Mark had so much to learn, so much, and he had made so little progress along the way. One didn't get ahead with old-fashioned values anymore. The world had changed. A man had to be smart and succeed with wiliness today. Alec shook his head and turned his thoughts back to the present; he called his secretary. "Marvin, get me Dave Jenkins over in the FBI. Ask him to come over as soon as he can."

*   *   *

When Mackenzie opened the door, her hair was disheveled; her robe was barely around her shoulders, and she had no makeup on. He thought she looked more beautiful than he had ever seen her before. She looked at him for several moments as she tried to bring her mind from sleep to reality. "Mark, what in heaven's name are you doing here?"

He stepped around her and closed the door as he spoke. "Sorry, but I've been followed for the past few days."

"What? Who is following you, and what the devil for?"

"I think it is some of Alec's goons, but I'm not sure."

She frowned as she stumbled toward the small kitchen in her townhouse. As she put a water kettle on the stove, she turned back to the

324

man who was admiring her legs. "Do you always have to bring Alec into your issues?"

"Only when appropriate." He was smiling as she caught him looking at her. She pulled the robe tighter around her shoulders and lit the gas stove. She noticed that Mark had turned his attention to the floor—he was deep in thought. How often had she seen him do that; what was going on in that marvelous mind of his? He could be looking at her one moment and then lost in a web of thought that no one else could even comprehend. Someday this would probably drive her up the proverbial wall, but not now. Now she just marveled at the man standing before her—staring at the floor, lost in some conscious, or perhaps even unconscious, thought pattern that only he could decipher. Finally, he looked up, his eyes wide, full of surprise. "It is not Alec! Then who?" He looked back at the floor for just a moment then raised his head again. "And why?"

Mackenzie would never know in a million years why she did what she did next, but she just walked across the room and kissed the man she had been watching. And there it was again, the look she had seen only a few times but had memorized. It was a look of delightful surprise, and joy, a joy that she could not completely fathom. Mackenzie was not a small woman at five feet ten inches, but she had to rise on tip toes to kiss the tall man before her. When she finished, she stepped back a step. Mark reached out and took her face in his two large hands. Very gently he kissed her back, for a very long time. And for the moment, they escaped the cares of the world as they were lost in the beauty of love and passion. Mackenzie looked into his eyes and knew she and Mark had crossed the danger line yet again. She smiled inside; damn the line; damn convention. She loosed the robe, and it fell to the floor.

Chapter 82

October 23, 2039, 9:00 am
The White House

Alec listened to the final words of the Chinese ambassador and silently replaced the phone on his desk. Something was happening to a number of Chinese diplomats and businessmen, and he had no idea who was behind the murders. He made a quick note on his private journal to find some connection with the Patriots, or just invent one. He knew there were a lot of Americans who blamed China for their misfortune. It was a lie the government had cultivated. It provided a small amount of cover for the failing economy and the continuing loss of jobs. When the Chinese orchestrated the ouster of the American dollar as the international currency for trade and oil supplies, America's standard of living dropped precipitously, roughly 25% in a matter of months. It was the first time most Americans even realized the significance of such a previously unimaginable move. Most were easily misled to believe it was an international political decision, when in reality it was the precarious American debt and the uncontrolled federal spending that destroyed the dollar. It was simply sound economics and risk management on the part of the Chinese.

Originally Alec had hoped the American workers would find a way to compete and get back into the global economy. What he had completely missed was that the working class had bought into the liberal tenet that they were owed a good living and the government should orchestrate that for them. When Jesse Holbrook and his followers began spreading a different message, the reality of their gospel became apparent, and anger began to grow among those who were trying to carry the nation's struggling economy. That anger eventually led many to walk off their jobs. Others simply began working slower, and overtime disappeared as workers refused to do more for those who did nothing. Demand continued its sharp increase while supply was drying up.

There were times Alec actually envied the leaders of the exodus. Their members would be successful wherever they finally settled. Secretly, he knew his own constituency could not succeed anywhere on its own. He simply had to find a way to keep the producers producing in order to provide for the entitled masses. But now he had another immediate problem. The Chinese Ambassador was demanding a meeting with the President, and the Ambassador was angry. Six Chinese VIPs had been found dead in the past two weeks. Furthermore, America was months behind on the interest due on its debt to China, and there was no way the country could pay that bill. He had sold every major asset the country possessed that would not incite a national riot. He simply would have to find something else with which to barter. This would not be a very amicable meeting, not amicable at all. He frowned as he punched the President's number into his phone.

*　*　*

Alec walked quickly out of the Oval Office and started for his office when the President's voice caught him. He turned and reluctantly walked back as the Chinese Ambassador gathered his notebook, bowed politely, and left. Gutierrez was frowning. "That did not go well."

"I've got the FBI and every police department in the country alerted to this situation. I'm sure we'll discover who's behind this."

"Why is it taking so long. This has been going on for weeks now."

"I know. I talked to the FBI director yesterday, and all he said was that they are doing everything they can to break this case."

The President stood and walked around his desk to sit on the couch adjacent to Alec. "Know what the ambassador said?" Alec nodded in the negative. "He said if we cannot solve it, they will."

"He said that, *to you*?"

327

"In no uncertain terms. He was actually working very hard to control his temper at the time."

"What the hell does that mean? They'll take care of it?" Alec looked directly into the eyes of his boss.

"Not sure, but I don't think it would play well with the American public if they hear that the Chinese are now investigating crimes in America, so I suggest we get the law enforcement folks on overtime."

"Speaking of overtime, we have another ambassador scheduled in ten minutes—Cuba."

"That should be interesting."

"I suspect it will." Alec rose to leave. "Do you have my notes that I gave you yesterday morning. It might be a good idea to review those again before the meeting."

"I have them memorized."

Chapter 83

October 23, 2039, 4:00 pm
The White House

The President of the United States stood formally as the Cuban Ambassador entered his office. Gutierrez walked around his desk and shook hands, motioning his visitor to the sofa in the middle of the room. Alec entered a few minutes later. After they were seated, the President turned to the Ambassador and spoke gravely with a condescending smile on his face. "Now, Jorge, I just wanted to spend a few minutes discussing the embarrassing situation that we all find ourselves in today." Jorge Famosa watched the President's face without displaying any emotion at the words. He knew what to expect in this meeting, and he was well prepared to defend his country and the course it had chosen. If this arrogant man thought he could frighten either him or Cuba, he was wrong. It was well-known that the tiger had no teeth. The America that had won several world wars existed only in history, a history that no longer was even taught to the descendants of the patriots who had fought for their country and for the world. The old patriots were dead—or they had left.

Gutierrez continued without even probing the Cuban's thoughts or his expressionless face. "As you know, we have passed some new laws that restrict Americans traveling abroad, much as your own country did back in the '60s and '70s. We have good reason to believe that many of our citizens who violate these new laws are traveling to Cuba and Argentina. Naturally, we would like to stop such actions." He paused for some reaction from the Cuban diplomat. When there was none, he continued. "We do intend to enforce our laws, and we intend to punish any who would support such illegal activities on the part of American citizens." The President rose and walked to the window, speaking quietly, forcing the other two men to strain to hear his words. "We would very much appreciate Cuba's support in this endeavor." He paused and turned dramatically to face the two men who were leaning in his direction.

The Cuban Ambassador leaned back in his seat and spoke equally softly. He smiled to see the American President walking quickly back to the center of the room to hear his words. "I understand your predicament, Mr. President. It must be very embarrassing to have your citizens trying to escape their own country. I suspect the same must have been said about the people of East Berlin, or even my own country many years ago." He looked up at the standing President with a wry grin. "As I recall, that ended poorly for the Soviets. Socialism failed in Cuba as well—as you know. Now we are on a more productive track." Then he was quiet.

Alec squirmed slightly in his seat. This was not going well, and he knew he needed to step in and save his boss. "Mr. Ambassador, as you well understand, this is a very serious situation and one that needs your help in resolution."

The Cuban smiled to himself. *Yes, he thought, now you need a small country like Cuba to support a failed system in the U.S. How the tables have turned; how far you have fallen.* As he watched the mouth of the Chief of Staff move, he thought how embarrassing it must be to have been reduced to begging for help from such a small and insignificant country as Cuba. What goes around, comes around, he thought. *Now you are getting yours.* The President's face was getting redder by the minute as he considered the arrogance of the Cuban to treat the President of the United States in such a manner. Did he not know to whom he was speaking? "What is it you wish Cuba to do, Mr. President?"

"We would like you to send our citizens home and stop any more from arriving."

"And why should we do that?" Famosa was playing hardball now. He knew he was moving onto very shaky ground, but he had his orders, and he had no fear of the two men with whom he was negotiating. He could stall them as long as he wanted so long as the dialog continued. The Iranians had used this ruse well to get their nuclear bomb; just keep

330

the politicians talking. That was all that was needed. Just as the Mullahs had outmaneuvered Obama, so he could certainly keep Gutierrez at bay. This current President, like his predecessors, has a very large ego and a very small grasp of the reality in the world around him. Such men are easily controlled. You simply feed their ego and continue to talk. And, Famosa reminded himself, it is okay to lie to a liar. They understand that truth is a scarce attribute among politicians.

"For one thing, relations between our two countries would be severely damaged if we felt no cooperation in enforcing our laws."

"What if we felt your laws were illegal? What if the World Court agreed? Shall we address this issue there? You have become big supporters of the international courts and tribunals. Perhaps that is the answer." Both Americans looked at each other. This Ambassador had the two top American politicians on the ropes, and everyone in the room knew it. There was little chance the international community would support fencing in an entire population. Hadn't the U.S. fought that idea long and hard for many years? It would be easy enough to resurrect those old speeches. Also, the embarrassment would be significant. And how would this play in future elections? That was something both the President and Woodward feared.

"I don't understand your wanting to stop the exodus of the few conservatives remaining in your country. Why would you socialists want them to stay? They certainly don't support your views for America." Famosa smiled inwardly; he knew the liberal groups were beginning to split. Everyone wanted more, and increasingly there was less to share. It had happened in the same fashion in Cuba under Castro. As the taxpayer base eroded and the economy continued its downward spiral, the cry for more benefits and more assistance grew. 'Let them eat cake' had not worked in France, nor would it work in America. Already there was talk of a challenge to Gutierrez's second term from several who were crossing the nation demanding increased spending on everything from free housing to improved healthcare. Didn't these radicals understand that such things cost money, and the money was leaving for Cuba.

Alec realized it was time to shift this conversation. He didn't like the way it was going at all. "Mr. Ambassador, we have reason to believe that some of these deserters might be planning retaliation against the United States, and we intend to ensure that doesn't happen. You will note that we have sent the USS Obama to the waters off your coast to protect our vital interests."

Gutierrez noted a change in the impassive face of the Cuban diplomat. He studied it carefully but could not be sure what the expression denoted. Was that anger, or fear? No, it was neither of those. Then it became obvious. It was surprise—mixed with humor.

"You have sent a carrier to Cuban waters?"

"That is correct." There was false pride in the President's tone.

"When will it arrive?"

"It is there now. It sailed early last week."

"That is strange, indeed.

"What do you mean?"

"We have not seen your carrier anywhere near Cuba, and it would be hard to hide a carrier group."

Both Americans looked at each other for a long time. Finally, the President spoke. "I hope you will convey my concerns to your government. I would appreciate your cooperation in this matter and would like an answer as soon as possible."

As Gutierrez finished, the Ambassador rose to leave. "Thank you Mr. President. I shall convey your request and will let Mr. Woodward know when we have a response." *Like next decade*, he thought to himself. "In the meantime we will keep an eye focused on the waters around Cuba in case your carrier shows up."

*   *   *

It was nearly dark when Woodward walked into the President's office and poured two glasses of scotch. He handed one to Gutierrez and sat down. He looked very tired. "He was right!"

"He?"

"The Cuban ambassador, Famosa. The carrier is missing."

"Missing? How the hell does a carrier go missing?"

"We don't know. It's just missing." Woodward drank deeply from his glass. "The Navy lost contact with the Obama three days ago. They assumed it was just communication failure—they've had a lot of that recently—so they sent a plane out to check. They found nothing. It wasn't where it was supposed to be."

"There's only three carriers left in the world, and ours is missing? And we can't find it?" The President leaned on his desk, head down. "Is there any chance the Cubans could have sunk it?"

"With what? A fishing boat? We're talking about a carrier."

"Has any of this leaked to the press?"

"No, but why is that an issue? We own the press."

"I don't know. I've seen some questionable articles recently. I think the party is beginning to splinter."

"Yeah, I know. I've been worried about that too."

Gutierrez walked to the sofa and picked up the other scotch. He took a long drink then sat down. "Hell, maybe it would be smart to just let the idiots try this job for one term. That would be a real lesson."

"Right, and they'd undo everything we've put into place."

"You're right. I guess the nation needs me!" The President smiled and saluted with his glass. "Back to the issue at hand. What are you doing about the carrier now?"

"I've got everyone I can trust on this. The Navy is out trying to find the carrier. We are checking every port it might try to enter. If it is floating, we'll find it." He took another drink. "Sure wish we still had a satellite system."

"We used that money for homeless shelters, remember? With the economy in the tank, there are more and more homeless people to take care of, and sometimes they even vote. Carriers don't."

"And now the public is crying for even more and better shelters." Alec rose and poured more scotch into both glasses. He knew it would be a long night.

Chapter 84

December 7, 2039
Washington, D.C.

Mark Sagan watched Mackenzie's concentration across the table as she worked. He watched her eyes, her nose, her lips. It was so easy for him; he loved the woman he was watching. Finally, she looked up and caught him staring at her. "What?"

"You were cursing." He smiled.

"I swear this job will make me an old woman."

"I'll still love you—even with wrinkles." He smiled broadly. "What's wrong?"

"Well, for one thing, we almost lost a plane yesterday due to a fuel line that ruptured."

"How did that happen?"

"It was installed incorrectly."

"Aren't there designs to prevent that from happening?"

"We put one in the specs, but it wasn't in the final design engineering."

"Why not?"

"Language problem. "

"If we had more American kids going into engineering it would be very useful, indeed." He studied her face as he spoke. "At least we could communicate with each other."

"It wasn't the engineer's fault. The engineering was in French, and the design was by a Chinese national. The problem was with us. The Chinese engineer handled the French better than our American team."

"Can't you find any of the old engineers who used to work for Boeing?"

"They all retired or died, and, besides, the Europeans wouldn't touch one of them. It took a long time for the Europeans to shut down Boeing, and a lot of those old wounds have still not healed."

"Well, the truth is they didn't shut Boeing down; our own government did that."

"You're right, but I doubt many would admit that today."

*   *   *

The President walked into his Chief of Staff's cluttered office and watched Alec's back as he cursed into the phone. "Dammit, I'm really tired of all the excuses. I just want the connection to work! This is my third call, and I *need* my email!" He listened briefly then shouted into the phone in exasperation, "That's what you told me yesterday, then again this morning—just get it fixed!" Woodward held his head in his hands and rubbed his brows vigorously. Then he turned and recognized the man behind him.

"Sounds like a rough day, Alec." The President was frowning.

"We have a nation to run, and these bozos can't even get the internet to work in the White House for heaven's sake!"

"Is that still down? Did you talk to the facility folks?"

"Who sent me to the communication folks, who sent me to the electronics folks, who sent me to the Internet idiot!" I've been on the phone the better part of the afternoon!" Alec stood behind his desk until Gutierrez sat down.

"What about the campaign committee? Are they online?" There was grave concern in the President's voice.

"At ten o'clock this morning they were okay."

Gutierrez rose and walked to the cupboard to the right of Woodward's desk. He selected a 12-year-old scotch and poured two strong drinks. "Here, try this. It will relax you."

"Mr. President, if I drank every time something like this happened, I'd be an alcoholic in less than a week. What's with these guys. Can't

335

anyone do their jobs right anymore? I don't think America was always so incompetent. Somewhere back there we lost the handle."

"Maybe we need a Competence Czar!" The President smiled and took a sip of his drink. "Were you looking for anything specific online?"

"Burrows from the AFL/CIO was arranging a photo op in some factory. We're trying to arrange the venue."

"Damn, we need those guys. They contribute a large share of our campaign funds." He looked at his drink closely without drinking. "The venue can't be too hard. We don't have that many factories anymore." When he finished he took another long drink.

Woodward smiled for the first time that day. You mean, he thought, *they invest in our campaign. Then we pay them back with interest later— in the form of union friendly laws — but those laws make it more difficult to compete in the global economy, which means more jobs lost. So you invest more money in our party to protect your workers, and it all starts over again. Such is the price of politics.*

"Why don't you just give him a call?"

"Have you ever tried to call the union headquarters? Besides, these Chinese phones may well be transmitting everything we say to people we don't want listening."

"Maybe we should manufacture phones here?"

"We did 15 years ago; some company near Chicago. They closed a long time ago."

"Too bad." The President finished his drink and poured another. "What if we subsidized production of phones. I'll bet we could find enough people to produce them."

"Remember what happened when we got into the auto industry?"

"Yeah, that didn't work out well, did it? Kinda like our foray into solar panels." Gutierrez quickly tired of the conversation and changed the topic. After all, he had come for an entirely different reason. "Have you talked to Parker about the progress on the campaign funding effort?"

Alec frowned. "Mr. President, are you sure Donald Parker is the right man for this job?"

"You don't think he is?"

"Frankly sir, no, I don't."

336

"Other than the fact that he's a wimp and not too bright, what else is there you don't like about him?"

Both men laughed with Woodward spitting scotch across his desk. Finally, he composed himself. "That's about it, Mr. President."

"Alec, you know why he's there. He's connected to the big bucks, and we need that money in this coming election. I still think this could be a tough primary."

"Another useful idiot! I guess we are just lucky he didn't kill himself in that accident last spring."

"He was hurt quite badly wasn't he. How long was he in the hospital?"

"His government allocation was only three days, but we pulled some strings. I think he actually spent 15-20 days."

"Twenty days for a broken leg?"

"They set it wrong and had to re-break it to get it right. He's still limping terribly; I suspect they still didn't get it right."

"What hospital was he in?"

"Walter Reed. I pulled those strings as well."

"Damn, that's *my* hospital. Now that's a comforting thought."

Alec downed the last of his drink and placed the empty glass on his desk. Without looking up he spoke. "I don't think you came over to discuss our failing technology or the miserable state of our health care."

"You're right. I've been thinking about the campaign. This one may be more difficult than we expect. I want to be ready for a challenge within the party."

"Do you think anyone could actually mount a real challenge?"

"Things aren't going very well now. Unemployment is at an all-time high, even with our doctored figures; the debt is still out of control; and now we have a mass exodus underway, and the ones who are leaving are the ones we depend on to pay the bills." Gutierrez studied Alec's face. "Yes, yes, I do think a challenge is possible, and even realistic. Longfield just might have the funds to get in the race."

"I'll do a little checking. As I said before, we've got enough on Longfield to take him down quickly. When the time is right, I'll talk to him."

"It's amazing that he could be so blatantly stupid!" Gutierrez frowned. "He shouldn't have the funding to wage a real campaign; we need to find out if anyone important is backing him."

"He's an absolute embarrassment, but his constituency would keep him in Congress if they had all personally witnessed him raping a child."

"I know. I can even remember a few seated Presidents who would fit that bill. Competence was not a key requirement for them either." Gutierrez shook his head while watching the ice float lazily in his drink. "But maybe the rest of the nation has a couple of brain cells and might find your evidence interesting. Of course, it can't come from us."

"Don't worry, I've got contacts in the press who'd give their first-born for this information, and they will be discreet. But first I want to know if he has any large donations. If he does have any substantial backers, we need to know who they are."

"Alec, we also need a gimmick. That is how elections are won— slogans and gimmicks—*A New Beginning for America*, or *Changes We Need and Deserve*. You know, something like that. *Hope and Change* fooled enough people in the past. The people bought it all back then. They never understood what it really meant, but by then it was all a done deal. I think we can do the same today."

"Did you try the campaign chairman? Did he have any ideas?"

The President frowned. "He suggested *Hope for the Future*, but I don't like that. It makes it seem like we've led the nation astray and are now trying to get back on track."

Alec shook his head slowly. "I'll work on that and get back to you."

Gutierrez rose and turned for the door. "Thanks Alec, I know I can count on you. I always do."

Woodward saluted with two fingers. When he was alone he poured another drink. He knew they were on the wrong track, but it was their direction, and the people could easily be fooled into believing whatever they wanted. Well, enough people could be fooled—or bought. He paused to stare into nothingness as reality crawled into the dark recesses of his mind and screamed obscenities at the lie he was living. He grimaced; his plan had to be true because the people believed it was true. All it took was a slogan to demonize the rich and successful, a reference to the handful of greedy CEOs who were grossly overpaid, any excuse for the losers to believe in. It really was that easy. The bright people could certainly see through it all. But they were leaving in droves now. They had been denigrated by their own government and robbed of their earnings, and freedoms were slowly being eroded. Their dream had died, so they were leaving in search of it elsewhere. And that was what Alex feared most. Who would drive the train to keep the economy on track? The government? Hell, they couldn't even keep the internet working in the White House.

Alec swirled his drink and stared at it a long time. Could it be possible, just maybe, that he was wrong, his ideas failing? He quickly pushed the thought from his mind. He would address this later when he had not consumed two large drinks. That was it; the alcohol had weakened his resolve. Lenin was afraid of music because it weakened him. What was he afraid of? What led to his weak moments? The truth? Alec shook his head and placed the drink on his desk. Perhaps he should stop drinking so much. He looked at it for a moment then poured the remainder of the scotch into the sink. Alec was not smiling. Reality was loose in the back of his mind, and the message it was shouting threatened the very foundation of all he believed in.

Chapter 85

January 9, 2040
Washington National Airport

Mark settled into the worn seat and began searching for the seatbelt. Somehow it seemed to be missing. He was still searching when the pilot's voice came over the intercom. "Welcome to National flight 433 from Washington to Denver." She continued to read her announcement as the customers moved slowly down the narrow isle.

"Mark, get up. Follow me." Mark looked up into the eyes of the Vice President of Operations for the airline. Mackenzie was not smiling.

"What?"

"Get your things and follow me. I'll explain everything later, just get your things."

Mark had never seen the look he saw on her face. It was a strange mixture of fear and embarrassment. He didn't understand it, so he just did as she asked.

"What about my luggage."

"I'll have it sent back later today. Don't worry about that."

*   *   *

Mackenzie Selms leaned back in the small car and rolled the window down to allow the air to blow across her face. It was obvious that she did not want to talk, so Mark remained silent as they drove away from the airport. Twenty minutes later she turned into a small restaurant and climbed out of the car. "I'm hungry. Let's get something to eat."

After several barbecue ribs each, Mark looked across the table and broke the silence. "What's up? Why did you want me off that plane? I wasn't going to get into trouble in Denver. I was simply going to check on Ken."

"And talk about what?"

"Come on Mackenzie, we both know the purpose of my trip was not something you would pull me off a flight about. What's going on?"

For a long time she said nothing. She looked at the center of her plate, thinking. Mark knew she was struggling with something, so he just waited for her to speak. "I can't tell you. You'll just have to trust me."

"Okay."

"Thank you."

$$* \quad * \quad *$$

At 7:00 pm Mark knocked at the apartment and waited for Mackenzie to answer. When she opened the door, it was obvious she had been drinking. He stepped in and guided her to the couch. There was an empty wine bottle sitting on the small coffee table and a glass half full beside it. "I saw the news."

"Eighty-seven people killed in a crash that never should have happened." Her eyes were red.

"Pilot error?"

"Pilot error with bad weather as a factor." Suddenly there were tears streaming down her face. "Dammit! Dammit! Dammit!"

Mark looked at her a long time. "Is that why you pulled me off the flight?"

Mackenzie put her face into both hands and tried to speak, but no words would come. Mark put his arms around her and pulled her to him. He held her tightly as she sobbed uncontrollably. Finally, she pushed him away and began walking back and forth across the tiny room. "I tried; I really tried. I argued and fought, but I lost. I knew she couldn't fly, but everyone wanted a minority woman in the left seat. Damn Ed Stokes; damn his politically correct hiring policies. I told him she couldn't fly the damn plane." She began sobbing again. "And she couldn't."

341

Mark rose, but she motioned him away. "The weather in Denver was crap; I even went to Paul." She paced across the room for several minutes in deep thought. "But I lost. They wouldn't hear me. The damn politics were more important than logic, more important than risking 87 lives." She stopped pacing and stared at the man who was watching her. "I wonder what they will tell the families. Do you think Stokes will explain it to them? Will he tell them how badly he screwed up?"

She stopped in the middle of the room and stood very still a long time. "I knew I couldn't let you get on that plane. I couldn't take that chance. I love you too much. I had no control over anything else, but I did have control over that." She began sobbing again as she spoke. "But I couldn't save the others. The system, damn the system, it wouldn't let me."

Mark put his arms around Mackenzie. Though she tried to push him away, he wouldn't be constrained. He held her forcibly until she finally put her arms around him and hugged him with what little strength she had left. When she was finally calm he put her on the couch and placed a pillow under her head. By the time he returned with a blanket, she was asleep. He looked at her a long time then went back for another blanket and another pillow. He drank the last of her glass of wine and settled onto the floor beside the couch. It would be a long night, but that was okay; he had much to consider and decide.

Chapter 86

February 16, 2040
Washington, D.C.

The middle-aged Russian sat alone in the corner of the small Italian restaurant. The food was mediocre, and the service was even worse, but the wine was excellent. He tore the last piece of bread and wiped the last of the sauce from his plate. Fortunately for him, quantity was equally as important as quality. That was easily verified by his girth. Thank goodness for the expandable-waist trousers he had specially made in Hong Kong. He frowned at the bill, drank the last of the wine, and pulled a few bills from his pocket. He left a small tip and walked out into the hot summer evening. Twenty minutes later Yuri walked slowly toward the cellist seated on a small box on the sidewalk. He listened attentively for several minutes until the crowd thinned considerably as people rushed to the bus that lumbered to a stop by the corner. Then Yuri bent down and placed a sizable bill into the musician's hat. Donnie never looked up, but he recognized the shoes. As Yuri walked away, Donnie reached for the bill and placed it inside his breast pocket. He looked up briefly, surveyed the street, then continued playing.

Yuri Rashinko walked down the litter-strewn street with purpose. When he was sure he was alone on the street, he reached into his pocket and withdrew the small phone. It was the latest from Russia and surpassed anything the Americans had produced in years. The Americans demeaned success and it had disappeared. Russia was rewarding success, and it was growing at an amazing pace. He knew the phone was safe; he just had to ensure that he was in a place where he could not be overheard.

He slowed his pace as he strolled down the street, watching carefully as he dialed. Two men across the street had been watching him with interest. They stood in the shadows, partially hidden by their hoodies and heavy jackets that blended well with the layers of graffiti that covered most of the walls in Washington. His clothes were expensive and well-tailored; that made him a target. As he continued down the street both rose and started walking in opposite directions. Yuri quickly determined that they were muggers who intended to block both of his escape directions should he run. He did not, but put the phone back into his pocket and patted the large bulge under his coat. Before him on the street was a bench where people waited for the busses that ran through this section of town — when the busses had fuel. He sat and patiently waited.

The men approached from opposite directions at the same time. Both were heavily tattooed on their faces and necks, and both were very large. Yuri smiled at the first as they approached. "Hey man, gimme yo wallet and all yo money! Now!"

"Of course, of course. Just don't hurt me." The first man held a large knife in his hand and made threatening motions toward the seated man. Yuri looked quickly at both men as he pretended to fumble with his wallet. The one on his left had the knife. He could not see what the man on the right held, so he had to assume it was a gun. This was not a time for hand to hand combat or anything fancy. There were risks in that, and he preferred not to take risks. "Here, it's all I have." He tossed his wallet onto the sidewalk between the two. As they both turned to the prize, he pulled his pistol from his shoulder holster and fired two shots into the man on the right. As the thief collapsed, Yuri turned the gun to the man on the left. "So, now do you feel like a big man with that puny knife?"

"Hey, man, stay cool. No problems; I'll just leave slowly. No problems; okay?"

"No, it's not okay." He fired two shots into the second man. As lights began to illuminate the houses along the block, Yuri reached for his wallet and turned quickly into an alley nearby. Ten minutes later he was strolling along another street several blocks away, dialing the phone again. He smiled; now the locals would have another reason to protest and destroy yet another part of the city.

"Yes?"

"It's me."

"I'm glad you called. I have an operation that needs your special touch."

"Good; I'm getting bored here."

"Excellent. Listen carefully. Check your coded emails tonight and you will find the particulars. You are to blow up a nuclear plant; but, of course, it has to look like an accident."

"Their security will be easy, but making it look like an accident will be the difficult part. I'll need some supplies, and the planning will take some time."

"Everything will be explained in your coded orders. Our experts have provided information that you may find useful. Check the details carefully, then call me tomorrow evening at the same time. And if you need some technical assistance, I can send the proper support."

"Of course, and by the way, I am developing the plan to remove the obstacle we discussed. If all goes well, I should have it completed quite soon and he will be taken care of. That will make it much easier for the Patriots to leave." Yuri heard the click on the other end of the line and closed his phone. He carefully set the self-destruct button in case he was compromised or taken. How amazing, he thought. I am standing in the middle of an American city discussing how to blow up a nuclear plant on a simple phone—and the Americans can't intercept my messages. They have fallen so far behind us. He smiled. And that is why they will soon surrender to us.

Yuri stepped into the shadows and reloaded his gun. That done, he started to stroll down the street slowly; perhaps he could find a few more muggers before the night ended. He found it interesting that America was finally experiencing an onslaught of crime like other socialist countries. Crime of all types was on the increase in America, but the leaders seemed too preoccupied with politics to even notice what their countrymen were experiencing. Crime and socialism had been synergistic partners for many years. Socialism breeds poverty, and poverty breeds crime. It was all quite simple if one only looked at the facts, but America seemed too mired in political correctness to notice. Russia knew how to deal with petty criminals—and not-so-petty ones as well. The Americans were so soft; they didn't even have the stomach to execute mass murderers. But that was okay. The Americans would get a new set of rules very soon. They would learn quickly how things *should* be run.

*   *   *

Yuri found that his answer for the nuclear plant was far easier than he had imagined. The reactor fuel rods were to be changed the following month. These controlled the nuclear fuel in the reactor, and were a special grade of 316 stainless steel. All he had to do was substitute a similar rod with less strength, one that would melt in the reactor. It would take an accomplished worker to recognize the difference between common steel and 316 grade stainless steel; few skilled technical people worked for the American government any longer he guessed. He had the specs within a week, and the "replacement" rods even before the real ones were started. A small rail accident during shipment of the new rods would be sufficient to allow the replacement rods to be substituted for the real ones. It would not be difficult, but still it would require careful planning. Yuri did not like leaving important events to chance.

Chapter 87

March 6, 2040
A nuclear power plant near Tunkhannock, Pennsylvania

Willie Jackson looked at the myriad gauges on the console before him. He was the new Manager of Operations for the three-year-old Susquehenna River nuclear plant, but he had no clue what any of the dials meant. He was leaning over a newly hired employee who should know the significance of the red danger light that flashed in cadence with the loud horn that blared throughout the facility. "Jimmy, what did they tell you about this during your training program?"

"I ain't had no training."

"None?" Willie was incredulous.

"No, I missed the training sessions, but they put me on the schedule anyway."

"Dammit, Jimmy, you're not supposed to even be in this building without training."

"Ain't nobody never told me nothing about that. What about you? Do you know what we should do?" It was evident that Jimmy was getting more nervous as the warning signals continued.

"I'm the manager, you idiot. I'm not supposed to do *your* job. I *manage!*"

Three other men rushed to the console and joined the two staring at the various indicators. Finally, one spoke. There was panic in his voice. "We better get some help!"

Before anyone reached the door, it swung open and an older man rushed into the room. He was breathing heavily and his eyes were wide

347

with fear. "Damn, get out of my way!" He shoved Jimmy aside and began emergency fuel retraction. Sweat was streaking his face when the red light and the horn finally ceased. He sat there for several minutes before rising to face the assembled men. He looked at each a long time. "Didn't anyone recognize that we had an overheated reactor? Anyone?"

"We knew something was wrong; we just didn't know what it was!" Jimmy spoke with some conviction.

"You damn near killed us all and probably half of the people in this state! Who in hell is in charge down here?"

Willie spoke hesitantly. "Me."

"Have you any *idea* what nearly happened here?"

"Yes." Willie looked at the floor.

"Who was sitting in that chair?" He turned to Jimmy. "Was that your job?"

The young man nodded. "You're fired." The man said it calmly.

"Fired? But I didn't do nothing."

"You're right, you didn't do anything, and your lack of action nearly cost all of us our lives." He turned to Willie. "You're fired, too. Now get out of here, both of you." The two men looked at each other in disbelief. "Now! Out!"

Willie stammered slightly. "Don't we get a second chance?"

"If I had not walked in when I did, none of us would have a second chance. This isn't some insignificant community development project, dammit; this is serious business."

A flicker of anger flashed in Willie's eyes. "Wait, I recognize you. You just got replaced by my friend James Lewis. You're out of here."

"Tomorrow is my final day, but I still have the authority to fire you both today. Now get out before I call the guards."

Willie turned to the younger man. "Don't worry Jimmy, I'll call James and get this all straightened out. He can't fire us, he's leaving. They done fired his ass." Willie smiled at the angry man before him.

"You may well win this one. But when you get home tonight and lay awake in your bed, just think what would have happened if I had not been here today. If you had any brains at all, you'd both be very embarrassed right now and frightened as well." The white haired man turned and left.

*   *   *

Eight TV crews busied themselves around their vans as Willie Jackson readied himself for the interview. Three of the crews were having difficulty with their equipment, so the interview had been delayed. He was thankful for that. It would give him time to rehearse his story. It had to sound professional. James had briefed him on everything he was to say, but he just kept repeating that it was important that Willie sound professional. No emotion, no bravado—professional. Fifteen minutes later he sat before six cameras, sweating and smiling. One of the reporters stepped forward with questions. "Mr. Jackson, can you tell us exactly what happened at this nuclear facility?"

Willie's face became suddenly serious as he spoke. "At 2:10 this afternoon while making my rounds of the plant, I stopped into the facility control center to observe some of my new employees. At that time the plant experienced an overheat situation in the main reactor, and the team immediately took charge to prevent a nuclear incident. Their quick work and professionalism prevented a major disaster and significant loss of life." He smiled; it seemed plausible to him, and James said so himself.

President Gutierrez, Colin Thompson, the President's Technology Czar, and Alec Woodward stood before the large screen TV in the West Wing office and watched the proceedings.

Colin spoke first. "We were damn lucky today. That could have been a *major* disaster."

"Sounds like they handled it okay." Thompson rolled his eyes as Alec spoke. "Are you saying that was not the case?"

"Well, let's just say the actual facts have been changed a bit to protect the guilty." Colin smiled a disarming smile. "I think the word they used to use was "spin!" He looked at the President and continued. "If I may, I'd like to suggest that we put the remaining nuclear plants on standby until we can check them all carefully."

349

"But that is a large amount of this nation's electricity since we abandoned coal."

Colin looked at the floor as he responded. "Yes sir, but we have not maintained them very well, and a major disaster would be difficult to overcome next election." He knew how to get the President's attention.

"Well, I guess it would please a segment of our friends on the far left. They've been after me to get rid of nuclear power for years."

Suddenly the three stopped their discussions as a man on the TV began shouting something about a nuclear leak. Then the screen went blank. Without a word, Colin Thompson turned and sprinted from the room. He had one of the few remaining government smart phones in the Washington area, and he was punching numbers into it as he ran from the room.

Chapter 88

March 7, 2040
Washington, D.C.

Yuri sat at a corner table at a breakfast cafe and read the reports of the nuclear disaster in Pennsylvania. *The Washington Post* had little else on its pages except reports and pictures of the catastrophe. It was warm for early March, and the humidity was miserable, but Yuri didn't notice. He was engrossed in the article on the front page. The Susquehanna River plant warning system failed to operate, and the surrounding communities had no warning at all. What had started as a relatively minor incident had suddenly escalated into a full nuclear meltdown at the facility. Local fire departments rushed to the scene and were all lost due to lack of training in nuclear emergencies. The first three pages were filled with reports of the dangers of nuclear energy and the drastic loss of life that was still being analyzed in Pennsylvania. He knew that within days the media would whip the public into a fevered mob demanding the end of nuclear power in America. And America would take one more step in the direction of total economic collapse. He marveled that it was so easy...so easy.

As he drained the last of his weak coffee and rose to leave, Yuri considered that perhaps he should send a check to the media in America. They certainly had made his job much easier. They might not know it, but they were definitely on his side, at least until the nation failed. Then he would see to it that they were all jailed or shot. Media stooges of the American government would not be favored in the new Russian empire. He didn't trust them, and he certainly did not respect them. Yuri was a

351

military man; he did not like weak, unprincipled men. He looked at the people sitting in the small restaurant. Many were clearly upset; others seemed oblivious. Perhaps they had no TVs; perhaps they didn't know what had happened. Or maybe they were too numb to even speak. They simply munched their bagels in silence. Finally, one man walked up and banged on the old TV set attached to the wall. When he could not get a picture or audible sound, he just unplugged the set and left.

*   *   *

President Gutierrez sat in his office and studied the typed report about the nuclear disaster. He was visibly shaken. He didn't look up as Alec walked in with a large stack of papers and news reports. Alec looked at his boss and stood silently staring at the floor in front of him. Finally, he raised his head and spoke. "How the hell does something like this happen? I thought we had safeguards in place to protect against nuclear accidents."

The President put his report on his desk and began rubbing his eyes. "I know. It's hard to conceive isn't it?"

Alec dropped his papers on the coffee table and sat on the couch behind it. "I just don't understand...."

Gutierrez had never seen his Chief of Staff inert in the face of a disaster before. But he also recognized this was no normal incident to be resolved. They both sat in silence staring at the floor. Finally, Gutierrez rose and began pacing. After a few minutes he stopped before the window and began speaking. "Well, Alec, we've got to shake off this inertia. We're still in charge, and we need to take control of the situation. We've never faced anything of this magnitude before, but we need to organize all of the government's resources and do what we can for our people."

"You're right. I'll call some of our key people and get a plan in process for how to deal with this mess."

When Alec walked back into the Oval Office several hours later, his mood had changed from gloom to anger. "Can you believe it? Senator Longfield is trying to use this disaster for furthering his political purposes."

"What's he up to now?"

"He says incompetence is the reason for this disaster and he is pointing all the way to the top of the ladder." Now it was Alec who was pacing. "The nerve of him to use this situation."

"Did you just say *use* this situation?"

"It's like one of our predecessors said about 25 years ago: never let a good disaster go to waste. Longfield is going to use this to start his campaign, I'll bet." Alec walked over to the coffee pot on the credenza and poured two cups. He put lots of sugar and cream in one and handed it to his boss. He took the other and sat beside the presidential desk. "For three hours I've been working with all of our agencies to get help to Pennsylvania, and ten minutes ago I realized I also need to build a plan to protect you from those who would use this day to their advantage. I've never seen politicians stoop so low in my entire career."

"You're right. We need to circle the wagons on all this."

"Longfield will be planning to blame you for this situation. We just need to get out in front and make you look very presidential. Instead of a detriment, we need to make it an asset to fend off him or anyone else thinking about a challenge from within the Democrat Party. There are folks out there who covet this office. Our job right now is to make sure they don't get it." The President nodded and rubbed his forehead with both hands. "I understand, Alec. I know you are doing what is best. It is just such a shock to see the scope of the disaster that has occurred. How can we insure this sort of thing does not happen again?"

"Well, we have two options. We could fire a bunch of incompetent people who did not manage our nuclear energy plants as professionals. Somebody obviously failed in his or her job." He frowned. "But that might create a large number of vacancies in the Nuclear Energy Department."

He looked up for a response from the President; getting none, he continued. "Or, we could simply point out that nuclear energy is inherently dangerous and therefore banned for the future in this nation. That would certainly make a lot of our constituents happy. We could even tie it into environmentalism and demonstrate how it hurts the environment even when it operates relatively safely. That should solidify a large sector of your base right there."

"And the first option leaves open the possibility that some of my competition might point out that the very folks we fired were most likely hand-picked by me—at least by my staff."

"We avoid that argument all together and play to your base."

"Great idea, Alec. Great idea!"

"I thought you would like it. I'll review the final plans for this with you by 2:00 pm. We've got to move on this very quickly. I'll notify the press that you will be speaking to the nation later this afternoon. That okay?"

"Sounds good. Get the speechwriters on it right away. Tell them I'd like to see a draft in two hours."

"I've already done that. It will be ready for review in an hour."

"There are times I wonder why I ever got into politics."

"And today is certainly one of those, to be sure, but we'll get through this. We'll do what we can to help the people in Pennsylvania. We'll also protect this office at the same time."

Chapter 89

March 8, 2040
The White House

Alec strolled into the Oval Office and saluted the President. "That was a great speech. I suspect that even some of the conservatives will applaud your closure of all nuclear plants."

"Thanks, Alec, but I'm worried. How will we handle that loss of power on a grid already stretched thin? We have several large states that depended on these plants to heat their homes. We might have a lot of angry citizens come next winter."

"I've got some engineers working on that. We'll figure something. We may have to ease up on some of the regulations on natural gas, but we'll come up with something. In the meantime, a dark house seems a lot better than being vaporized—your speech today emphasized that very well. We lost over 200,000 people yesterday. The country won't forget that very soon."

"Did you see the email note that Colin got from the departing manager of the site? He indicated that there was a training problem or a personnel problem of some kind. Is that what really happened?"

"I saw that and had Colin erase it immediately. As far as anyone knows, it was just old equipment that had outlived its useful life. Who knows, there are a million reasons that plant might have failed. The important thing is that we just solidified your base on the left for the next election."

"And we did it with minimum complaint on the right! Perfect! Now we just have to find someone to figure how to get power to three states as soon as possible."

"I assigned that to James Lewis, the newly assigned district manager for National Power. He's to get back to me at the end of the week."

"Is he up to that job?"

"He's as good as we've got. And he's your new campaign chairman for Ohio." The conversation stopped abruptly when the President's press secretary ran into the office. Her face was one of shock.

"Quick, turn on the TV."

Alec turned the TV on and stepped back to watch. A frantic reporter was standing before what was obviously a crash site. "The National Airlines jetliner crashed just outside Charlotte, North Carolina, this afternoon at 3:43 pm Eastern Standard Time. All 72 people on board are presumed dead. I take you now to the Vice President of Operations for National Airlines, Mackenzie Selms." She handed the microphone to the tired woman to her left. Mackenzie looked at the ground for several seconds before looking up into the camera. As she began speaking static splashed across the screen and her words became unintelligible. Alec cursed and tried to adjust the TV set.

"Damn Chinese electronics—they are cheap, and they are crap!" He hit the television lightly. "Why can't we produce a television in America? Why can't we do that?" Mackenzie came back into focus for a moment, then disappeared again. Alec grabbed his cell phone and punched in a number. After a moment he cursed again. Damn! No coverage in North Carolina."

"Or the White House." The President grimaced.

The static on the screen slowly faded and a union shop steward was now holding the microphone. He sounded well-trained. "Our people cannot be held accountable for this accident. The allegation that the plane was serviced incorrectly is only a management theory; it is not provable. The inventory at the base could well be wrong. Our union workers are abused and overworked as it is. If the airline had more ramp service people handling the workload they have been assigned, things like this might not happen. Management is responsible for this disaster. If they had enough workers, the workforce would have sufficient time to recheck their work. People can only do so much. I call for a thorough investigation to look into the workload of our people. It is just too easy for management to blame everything on the unions. This is a matter of fairness."

The President stood silent for only a moment. "How do we stop these constant accidents? What is going wrong in this country?"

Alec spoke as he stared at the floor. "I don't know, but I'll find out."

*   *   *

Mackenzie walked into her apartment and threw her purse on the small table beside the door. She walked straight to the kitchen and opened a bottle of wine, a Cabernet from Chile. She drank the first glass quickly and poured another. As she placed the bottle on the cabinet, she burst into tears. That's when he spoke.

"I wanted to be with you tonight. I figured you might need the company." She turned quickly to see Mark sitting in her living room, watching her carefully. "You okay?"

"How do these things happen? This is our third crash in five months. Three crashes; one hundred eighty-two people dead! How do these things happen? Last week we nearly had a crash due to a fuel filter that was changed in routine maintenance. Luckily that engine wouldn't even start and we caught the problem. How can a mechanic install the wrong fuel filter and not even notice that it doesn't fit? How can someone be that dumb? He was probably high on drugs at the time. But since they are mostly all legal now, we can't even demand a drug test. It's like the entire nation suddenly quit caring. Can't anyone do their jobs right anymore?"

"Just the Vice President of Operations."

"Did you see that union shop steward on TV? Seventy-two people dead, and he's spouting union crap for the world. No, they couldn't be held responsible. If there were more people working on the ramp they would try harder to kill fewer passengers." She was mocking his voice. "What an ass!" Her tears resumed; she put the wine glass on the cabinet and sat beside Mark. She was holding her head in both hands as he put

357

his arms around her. He smoothed her hair gently as he pulled her closer to him.

"It's not your fault. This entire nation has slipped into the abyss of incompetence. All the smart people are leaving. I wish you'd join us."

Her head snapped up suddenly. Her eyes were red, and anger was on her face. "Quit? And run? No way! I'm going to get this airline back on track if it kills me. I will not quit and run!"

"And if you don't quit, it just might kill you." He looked into her eyes as she pulled away. "They don't deserve you, Mackenzie. They don't care. I do; I love you."

"Well, I'm not looking for a way out—not if it means just quitting and running. I'm for finding a way to fix this mess." She raised her head, her eyes filled with tears. "All of you just want to leave. What happened to your patriotism? What happened to your desire to make things better?" She turned and looked straight into his eyes. "You're all just quitters!"

"We tried Mackenzie, we really tried, but they outnumbered us, and they outvoted us. In this case, democracy failed." He looked at Mackenzie a long time then rose and walked slowly toward the door. "I hope you will reconsider and join us. The only way to fix this nation is to fight or leave." He turned and waited for a response. When he got none, he continued. "The last civil war was far too bloody. We cannot do that again, so we are leaving. In time the failure will get even worse. Then, when everything seems lost, we will return and save this great nation."

He opened the door then stopped and turned to her again. "I love you, Mackenzie; you know that. I always have, and I always will. If it were not for you, I would have been in the first group that crossed the border. But I stayed because I need you." Mark looked at the floor for a moment then continued. "I'll stay here and work with you until you need me that much as well." He turned quickly and left without looking back.

Chapter 90

March 22, 2040
Washington, D.C.

Mackenzie brushed the last remains of a piece of toast into her half-filled coffee cup and looked at the newspaper spread before her. She was reading about another train derailment, this one somewhere in Idaho, killing 48 and injuring over two hundred. The automatic warning system that was supposed to alert a speeding train of a problem ahead had failed—again. Already there were management and union officials arguing about who was at fault. Mackenzie frowned and downed the last of her barely warm coffee. It was terrible. She looked carefully into the bottom of her cup, fully expecting to see mud. *What had happened to America?* It was as if all the intelligence in the nation was slowly draining away. Incompetence was everywhere. No one seemed to do a good job; everyone had an excuse for why he or she failed. It was always someone else's fault.

She looked at the paper again and grimaced. There were two misspelled words in the first paragraph. Maybe it was drugs. Perhaps that was one of the major contributors to America's demise. But then, who fought for legalizing all the drugs—the same ones who now demanded that someone else pay all their bills. When she could stand the story no longer, she skipped to a different one. Another robbery; another shooting in the middle of town, but no one saw anything! She folded the paper slowly then threw it into the trash can beside the sink.

In the back of her mind, one of Mark's old sayings was gaining strength. "What you reward, you get more of; what you punish, you get less of!" What was being rewarded in America? Competence? No, that only brought more taxes and regulation. Entitlement? Yes, that was what America had perfected. The search for new products and new services had given way to the Art of Entitlement. How do you get more of what someone else has produced? That was the question. And to add insult to injury, they now called those who actually produced things greedy. There was no moral requirement to help others by producing things they needed or wanted. There was only the moral requirement to give the products to those who contributed the least. And it seemed as if Mark must be right, for the nation produced less and less each year. But everywhere, groups wanted more.

Mackenzie frowned, groups? No, *constituencies*. They had perfected the division of America into constituencies. Everyone belonged to one or another—and they all demanded their "fair" share. She poured more coffee into her cup, thought about it a moment and poured it down the drain. It was barely passable when hot; it was intolerable when barely warm. She would have liked to get more details on the train crash, but her TV was no longer working, and the local TV station would only carry the "approved" reporting anyway. Somewhere in the process, truth had become victim to political correctness. She was far too smart to believe the slanted media reports.

Mackenzie felt sorry for the people who had lost their lives or loved ones, but somewhere deep inside she also was glad it was not a plane crash. At least she didn't have to deal with the guilt of managing incompetent and, in some cases even uncaring, workers. She knew the airline had its share of slackers. Accountability was nowhere to be found in America any longer, certainly not in the workplace. But still, today the failure was not one she had to explain or witness. She had seen the results of ignorance far too often in her career. But not today; today some rail manager would be standing before a camera trying to explain how a stupid mistake had cost so many lives while blaming the entire event on someone else.

Chapter 91

April 18, 2040
Washington, D.C.

President Gutierrez raised his hand and the presentation stopped. "Mr. Lewis, I appreciate your presentation today, but I have a few questions before we continue. Just what is your educational background?"

"I have a law degree, Mr. President." James stood proudly and adjusted his tie. He had a law degree from one of the most prestigious Ivy League schools in America. He had not graduated near the top of his class, but he had graduated, and that was all that counted. His political connections were far more important than his grade-point average.

"Then you are not an engineer?"

"No sir, not at all. I am a lawyer."

"I see. So how did you come up with this plan you are presenting? It seems to have a rather large amount of technical data in it."

"Well, sir, I got a group of experts together and asked them to make a recommendation as to just how we might solve this energy problem. This is what they recommended."

"And where did you find this group of experts?"

"The Department of Energy—right here in Washington. I figured they would be our best experts. They work for the government."

Alec sat with his head in his hands with his elbows propped on the table top before him. After a pause he looked up. "Thank you Mr. Lewis. I fear we are out of time today. We'll call you when we can find the opportunity to finish this meeting." He looked at the President as Lewis and five of his committee packed their things to leave. After they had gone, the President smiled, then laughed.

"That was amazing. That young man was actually serious. He actually felt that plan was going to work. I, too, am a lawyer, but I am not a fool. That was the dumbest plan I've ever heard."

Alec did not laugh or even smile. "We have a serious problem. We have to find a way to generate more electricity before winter sets in. And cold weather will be upon us before we know it. This kind of work does not happen overnight. Now I may not be an engineer or a lawyer, but I know that much."

Gutierrez's smile slowly faded. "I think we need to find someone competent to solve this. Any suggestions?"

"Not from the Department of Energy—obviously."

"What about Northwestern Energy? They used to do things like this."

"Gone!"

"Gone?"

"Out of business three years ago. All that is left are their patents— that we now own."

"Who has those, maybe they......"

"Department of Energy!"

"Damn!" The President's brow furrowed in the center. "What do we do?" There was a hint of panic in his voice.

"Give me a day or two. I'll think of something."

"Thanks, Alec, I have a feeling this is going to be tough."

Alec flashed a thin smile. He knew he would have to come up with something, but he was quickly running out of sources. "Don't worry; I'll take care of it."

* * *

Alec stood up and leaned with both hands on his desk. His head was down as he considered the options he was being presented. "Now let me see, you have three alternatives and you freely admit that the first two have less than 10% chance of success. Do I understand that right?" He still did not look up.

"Yes sir, that is correct." Roberta Gonzalez had a degree in physics from the one engineering school that remained in America. She had been promoted over many men with far more experience, but this political move had not been without some success. Roberta was not only Hispanic and female; she was also very smart.

"And number three is to subcontract this work to some foreign company. Is that correct?"

"Yes sir." She watched him silently for a long time, waiting for some reaction.

"And just how much will this foreign company cost?"

"I'm guessing about $250 million plus infrastructure upgrades, but that is only a guess until we get a proposal in hand."

"Is there no company here in the U.S. that can handle this kind of work?"

"I'm afraid not. All of our technical talent is gone. Their companies were put out of business by the EPA and the IRS long ago, so they left." She knew the truth would not be palatable, but this was not the time for political lies. The nation was facing a winter without heat if this problem was not resolved—quickly.

"And where would this company come from?"

"Russia could do it, but Cuba has the best in the business right now, and they are probably the only ones who have a chance to get the work done before the first snow flies."

Alec suddenly raised his right hand and pounded on the desk. After a moment he looked up, his face very red. "Thank you, Miss Gonzalez, I'll get back to you later today. Right now I need some time to prepare for a meeting with the President."

Roberta smiled to herself as she walked out. She was always amazed at politicians. They lived and worked in a fairyland that admitted nothing resembling reality. Somehow they would simply demand that something be done, and the engineers and technicians would make it happen. Only now there were few engineers left to carry out their orders. Suddenly political correctness became a large liability when the nation would be without heat in the coming winter. Woodward recognized the problem and was visibly upset. At least he understood the issue at hand. He did not, however, recognize that Roberta's background was Cuban, not Mexican.

Chapter 92
May 25, 2040
Washington, D.C.

Donnie smiled as he played on his favorite corner. It was a warm May afternoon and the locals were more generous than usual. As he played a familiar hand reached down and dropped a small piece of paper into his hat. It soon was lost beneath a handful of small coins dropped by appreciative music-lovers. The cellist played with his eyes closed, lost in the music, but he recognized the footsteps and nodded as the man turned and left.

When Donnie completed Bach's unaccompanied Cello Suite No.5 in C Minor, he paused and retrieved the small paper. It was a note; he studied it briefly. How strange; normally the large man with the expensive shoes left a few bills in appreciation for his music. He placed the message in his shirt pocket without reading it; there would be time for that later. The crowds passed, and several of the government staff stopped to place coins into Donnie's hat and watch him momentarily as they waited for the buses to arrive. But then a car backfired nearby, and the young musician abruptly shouted and dropped to the ground. Those around him stepped back quickly as the young musician eyed them fearfully. For them the music had stopped; for him it had been replaced with screams in the distance and the sounds of war.

Most of the startled onlookers backed away and left, but a few in the crowd watched as he crawled to his cello and frantically began scraping the bow across the strings. The sound mimicked the screams he was hearing in his mind, the horrors of battles from his past. He was breathing heavily, and his wide eyes stared into emptiness. Slowly the scraping sounds began to soften, then they changed to fast, sharp notes, and finally to the softer sounds of a melody. The battle in his mind raged, but Vivaldi was coming to rescue the ex-soldier. The transition was watched with both fascination and perhaps a bit of fear as the cello player frantically sought the voice of his instrument, a voice that could calm his mind and allow him to resume his music. An older man walked over and placed a bill in the hat. As he left he put his hand on the musician's shoulder and said simply, "Thank you for your service."

Fifty yards away the man in the expensive suit watched with interest as the young man struggled back onto his small chair and resumed playing. The man pulled a small pad from his jacket pocket, made a quick note, and walked away quickly.

*   *   *

Donnie unfolded the small piece of paper and studied it carefully. The big man wanted to meet him about something personal. But he wasn't willing to specify what it was about. The note mentioned that Donnie could make a lot of money helping him. He felt compelled to go; the man was a regular customer, and Donnie certainly needed the money. A new cello was expensive.

Three days later he was playing the borrowed cello at his usual spot as the evening rush began, government workers passing on their way to the dirty busses that would take them to their apartments. The music stopped abruptly as a large man leaned down and placed a new cello case beside the musician. "The case is new; the cello inside, however, is quite old, and valuable." He patted the young man's shoulder. "I heard what happened and managed to get this back for you. The idiots had destroyed the case, but the cello is fine. It just needs your touch."

The young man quickly opened the case, removed his old friend, and examined the cello carefully. He held it to his breast as tears welled into his eyes. He found his bow inside and began tuning immediately. He looked up from the Italian shoes into the face of the man who had saved his cello. No words passed, but the message was clear as Donnie closed

366

his eyes and played. The man smiled and stepped back to listen as the sounds from the old cello echoed into the evening air. When Donnie finally opened his eyes, the tears flowed down his cheeks. The large man was gone, but he saw a small folded paper in his hat. He reached for it and slipped it into his pocket. He closed his eyes again and began playing for the unseen audience that passed quickly by.

It was almost dark when Donnie entered his small apartment, locked the door behind him, and unfolded the paper. On it was an address and a time. So, the big man wanted a meeting. He had saved Donnie's beloved cello, and Donnie knew he would be forever indebted to the stranger who loved his music. He pinned the note on the wall beside his door; it was a meeting he would not miss.

Chapter 93

May 26, 2040
Washington, D.C.

Donnie walked into the dark cafe and looked around carefully. He was early, as he intended. Spotting a small table in the back of the room, he ordered a coffee and moved to the corner where he could watch everyone enter. His wait was short. The imposing man with the expensive suit walked into the room, stood for a moment as his eyes adjusted, then moved quickly back to the corner where Donnie sat. The man was not only large but also obviously fit. He looked like the right tackle on any major football team, except he was quite a bit older. Donnie guessed him to be in his mid to late 50s. "Greetings, my friend." It was the second time the man had spoken to him, and Donnie had considered the accent. He guessed it to be Russian.

"Thanks for getting Martha back. I missed her."

"Glad to be of service."

"Any trouble with the gangbangers?"

"None whatsoever. There were only two; I killed them both." The Russian said it matter-of-factly. "I'm guessing between the two of us, and a little help from a couple of other gangs, they're a much smaller group now." He laughed quietly.

Donnie smiled and waited for the man to continue. A barista brought a cup of steaming coffee to the Russian, took his money, and left. Yuri watched him leave, sipped the hot coffee, then spoke quietly. "I have an important assignment, and I wanted to meet to make sure you were willing to do this. If not, I will have to find another way. You were considered the best sniper in the American Army several years back, and I know from your handling of the gang members that you are still a very good shot. I need you to take care of someone for me. He slipped a piece of paper across the stained table. Donnie took it, read it twice and exhaled. "Is this who I think it is?"

"Most likely it is." Yuri slid a picture across the table to the startled young man.

"I'm not an assassin for hire. The gangbangers just pissed me off. The world is better off without those scum."

"I agree. This man is also scum. He represents a huge threat to someone you owe a great deal to, a man who saved your life twice in Afghanistan."

"Sergeant Sagan?"

"That's right. Woodward has sent a couple of FBI agents to take care of Sagan, and I have proof." The Russian pulled a large envelope from the breast pocket of his coat and spread its contents on the table. There were pictures of two agents tailing Sagan and others of them sitting in a car across from his house. "I even have a recording of one of their conversations where they talk about Woodward's orders to *get* Sagan."

"What's Woodward got against Sergeant Sagan?"

"Two things. The woman they both love is having an affair with Sagan. And secondly, Sagan is very active in the Patriot movement. He was there when they killed the surgeon on the border down in Texas. That murder has been all over the news, and Sagan knows Woodward ordered it. Sagan knows too much, but I'm guessing the woman is the driving reason."

"What's your interest in all this?"

"I'm working with Sagan in the Patriot movement. But it's all very secret. Sagan doesn't know I'm here talking to you. He's not even supposed to recognize me; I'm obviously Russian. He doesn't want it out that we are helping them, so you must not mention this to anyone, not even Sagan. Do you understand? It would endanger him." Yuri watched the young man's face to see if the lie had worked.

Donnie squirmed uneasily in his seat. "You want me to kill Woodward?"

"Yes. I'd do it myself, but it must be done right and at a distance. I am no good beyond 25 feet; you are good up to a thousand yards." Donnie was obviously uneasy with the request. As the tension grew in his head, he could hear the faint sound of voices in the distance. He grimaced and narrowed his eyes lest he lose control before the strange man he was meeting. Before he could speak, the Russian continued. "I respect Sagan more than any other man I have known. He would gladly risk his life for us. I am willing to do the same for him, but sadly, I cannot. My pistol has a very short barrel, and there is no way I could get that close to Woodward. Your rifle, on the other hand, has a very long reach. I recognize the risk; I also know it will take time and planning, so I have some money to help in that effort." He slid a dark brown envelope across the table and into Donnie's lap.

Finally, Donnie spoke. "I am indebted to only two men in my life. Sagan for saving my life and you for getting my cello back for me. But I'm not sure about this."

"I understand; take the envelope with you; study the contents. Listen to the tape, then decide. If I had your skill, I would not be making this request. I would do it myself."

Donnie squinted his eyes and tried to concentrate on the man's voice before him, but instead he heard explosions and screams intensifying in the back of his mind. He knew he had to leave quickly, so he nodded and slid from the booth, stopping only long enough to pick up the envelop. "I'll think about it."

"I'll be here tomorrow at the same time. You can tell me your decision then."

When the young man walked out into the evening he could feel the pressure building in his mind. The screams were getting louder. He had to get to his cello quickly. Only that could blot out the voices calling to him from so far back in his past.

*   *   *

370

Donnie arrived early as usual, but his Russian friend was already seated. Yuri was drinking vodka at a secluded table near the rear of the restaurant. "When does this need to be done?"

"As soon as possible. You pick the time and place, but make it soon."

"How am I supposed to do this? How will I find the opportunity? Woodward will not be easy to track; I'll never know his schedule. I can do the job, but I have to have the opportunity. I'll never know when or where to find him." There was a tone of desperation in Donnie's voice.

"You are right." Yuri sipped his drink a moment. "I have a contact who can help us. All we need is his schedule. I think I can get that with little difficulty, but it may take several weeks."

Donnie noticed a second glass of vodka on his side of the table. He stood and drained it with one gulp. "Good, I'll need that schedule." He turned to leave, coughing softly under his breath. "Let me know when you get it. I can't plan anything until I have that. You know where to find me. In the meantime, I've got work to do. I haven't fired this weapon before, but a couple of weeks will suffice for that."

"Yes, you do. If you need anything, put a note in your hat when I stop by in the afternoons."

"Got it." He paused and looked back at Yuri. "I'll give you an estimate on the time after I've done some planning. I'll probably need a week or so after I get his schedule."

"I understand." Yuri watched as Donnie left. He signaled the barista for a cup of coffee as he studied everyone in the small shop. Fifteen minutes later he walked out into the afternoon rush and keyed his phone. "It's done. It was even easier than I thought. We have some preparation and a schedule to integrate with our plans. I'm looking at a little over a month."

"Do it quicker if you can; when it's finished, be sure to take care of the shooter. He must never implicate us."

"Don't worry. I'll take care of him."

"Good; I've studied the situation, and you are right. Woodward is the biggest threat to the Patriots."

"Not for long."

371

Chapter 94

May 28, 2040
Washington, D.C.

Six men listened as the small recorder played the voice of a confident Russian agent and his contact in the Kremlin. Jake Dalton was shaking his head as he concentrated on the heavily accented voice. Finally, one of his men stopped the recording and looked at the assembled group. "That's as much as we have on this recording. We have more recent ones that should be decoded within a week. We've been tracking this guy since we were able to identify him from the pictures Wilson's team supplied. At first it was trivial talk, but recently it has turned serious. We thought you'd better hear this yourselves. You all have the English translation in printed form. Anyone want to hear it again?"

Dalton never took his eyes off the machine as he spoke. "I'd like to have the voices analyzed. I'd like to know for sure who that is on the other end of that call. It sounded a lot like President Gornavich."

"Good idea. We'll check that as we go through the rest of the recordings. Mickey Scalero is doing the analysis; he's the best we have."

Jake slid the electronic device toward one of the analysts and nodded. "Good plan, and thanks for having the conversations translated. I want to study them in more detail. These recordings may answer a lot of questions some of us have been asking for weeks." All of the regional commanders of the Patriot movement concurred. Only Ken Wilson was absent; Mark attended in his ill father's place.

Dalton raised his head and spoke to the entire group. "Well, you were right, Mark. The Russians are definitely up to no good here." He scanned the entire group. "Any ideas? Should we alert the government?"

One of the older men raised his hand like a small school boy. "We might be best-served by keeping this quiet for a while. Gutierrez and his clowns might contact the Russians and spill everything before we even begin to understand their end-game."

Mark nodded his head. "I agree; I think we should keep this quiet for the time being. We'll know when the time is right to disclose all we have. Besides, I suspect Gutierrez and his folks might not believe us anyway. They really don't trust us; just like we don't trust them."

Dalton nodded. "I know. Besides, the government couldn't really do anything about it anyway. We're still the best hope for America."

Dalton nodded to the two technicians running the electronic equipment. "Great job!" He then turned to Mark. "Why don't you get a team together after this meeting. I think you should take the lead on this effort. We need all the information we can get on what these men are planning. Review the remaining messages as soon as possible and let me know what they are up to." Dalton raised his arms to get everyone's attention. "I need not remind you. This is top secret. No one is to mention this—no one! Understood?"

The group nodded together and slowly filed out of the room. Dalton looked at Mark for a long time. "It's hard to believe isn't it?"

"Like you said, this answers a lot of questions."

"But it raises many more."

"Yes it does."

*   *   *

"Jesse, I understand you did a lot of the surveillance work on this Russian. How did you get so close without being detected?" Mark talked as the two men walked out into the cold evening.

"Dalton asked me to tail him for two weeks, and I finally got a chance to try out my homeless clothes."

"You dressed as a bum?"

"Hey, it's easy for me to look like a drunk." Both men chuckled as Jesse continued. "And I even smelled like one. It's a trick I learned from an old Clancy novel I once read."

"I wonder why he had no bodyguards along?"

"He has a team, but he tends to work alone most of the time. He just calls them each morning and gives them orders. Then he spends the day on his own, checking on things. And he also participates in the work. He's a "hands-on" kind of guy, and those he puts his hands on seldom live to talk about it. I have a strong feeling he is the one behind the sudden loss of several Chinese diplomats and businessmen."

"The Chinese and Russians have never had cordial relationships; you may be right. I'm glad you were tailing him."

"It paid off, and Scalero's folks did the rest."

Mark stood thinking before responding. "Now that we know who the joker is in this deck, I propose we increase our surveillance of their communications. It would be really nice to know just what they are up to."

"The Russians have some very sophisticated equipment these days; they had no idea we have some folks who could break into their network. We put some of our best engineers on it as soon as you alerted us."

"Great work, Jesse. Between you and Scalero, I believe we just broke the code. Nice job."

"Mark, how is Ken doing? Is he okay?"

Mark turned to his old friend and spoke as directly as he could. "Jesse, Ken's not doing well at all. He has some good days but more bad ones; the cancer is slowly winning."

"Damn, I'm sorry to hear that. Ken never told me he had cancer."

"No, he's been rather private about his illness, in fact it might be best to keep this between us. He's a proud man."

"He's a good man. And there are damn few left like him."

"You are so right about that." Mark patted Jesse's shoulder and walked away.

*   *   *

Two days later Jesse walked into Mark's small living room with several sandwiches and two cups of coffee. "I assume this will be another all-nighter."

Mark was seated on the floor. He looked up momentarily then stood with several stacks of paper in his hands. His face was one of shock. "I've been through all of the new conversations with Gornavich, and I think I just figured out what the Russians are up to." He walked across the room and took one of the cups of coffee without taking his eyes off the papers he was reading. He laid them carefully on the table then sat down on the floor again, in the middle of the stacks of reports. "They plan to strike the U.S. with a nuclear device." He said it in barely a whisper.

"What? Are you sure?" The older man placed the food on the table and started to read the files Mark had placed on the table. "Why?"

"Let's work our way through this. Look at this most recent file. Just yesterday the Russian agent was told to return to Moscow before July 16th. He was also told if for any reason he could not, he was not to be anywhere near the Washington area. That seemed to take precedence over being in Russia—stay *out* of the Washington area. Note the direction was also to stay *far away* from D.C." Mark rummaged through the stacks of transcriptions of the various conversations between the Russian agent and presumably the Russian President. "Here it is. Far away! That rules out something like a demonstration or terrorist attack. He also says something about the weapon being ready." Mark checked the calendar on his phone. "July 16th is on a Monday. That is one week after the July 4th holiday recess ends for Congress. The entire government will be in Washington on that day."

"Sounds like a nuke attack."

"Russia and China both want America. They both know how weak the nation has become. It is a piece of fruit waiting to be picked."

Jesse nodded his head. "And whichever gets America will control the world."

"Right. And how would you do that if you were the Russians?"

"Remove the head of the snake. Nuke D.C." Jesse rose and began pacing. "We'd better notify Dalton immediately. We also better start

375

contacting all of the best engineers we have on our team. We're going to need them ASAP."

"You're right, we need a plan, and we need it fast."

Chapter 95

June 1, 2040
Denver Colorado

The men and women seated around the table looked like engineers. There were no suits, no fancy pens, nothing to denote their education or capability. They could have been any group of blue-collar workers in the country. But Mark knew each of them; he knew their education, their experience, and mostly, he knew their politics. Dalton had asked him to lead this effort, so he had read and re-read all of their dossiers. These were the best of the best, and they were all Patriots. They understood the socialist track to destruction their countrymen had chosen, and they were smart enough to reject it outright. Most were already located in Cuba, but when called, they immediately made their way back to Denver.

Ken walked into the room with coffee and donuts. The old pastor knew how to work with engineers. "I'd like to thank all of you for coming on such short notice. We have a critical issue facing all of us, and we desperately need your help. We may be asking you to perform the most important task you've ever undertaken. A great deal of lives may depend on those of you in this room today."

With that said, he introduced Mark and then began pouring weak coffee as Mark walked to the end of the table. The tall doctor spent several minutes briefly describing what had transpired in the past few days and the conclusion that had been drawn. When he finished, he poured a cup of coffee for himself and sipped on it as he studied each of the faces in the room. When the silence in the room became oppressive, Mark continued. "Ladies, gentlemen, this is our chance to save this

377

country. It has not always been good to us, but it is worth saving, and in doing so it gives us the chance to redeem America and make it a great nation once again. So I'm asking you for your best work on this project, a project to save our country. America is still the last great hope for mankind. Certainly that is worthy of our efforts." There were nods around the room. "Any questions?"

"What, exactly, do you need us to do?"

Mark smiled inside. He had passed the first and largest hurdle with this group. He never had a question about their capabilities or their support for the Patriot cause, but he worried about convincing them of the reality of this political problem. Once they were on-board with the threat, the rest would be easy. "We think there is a very real possibility that the Russian President is planning a nuclear strike on Washington, D.C., roughly in mid-July." It was very quiet for a brief period of time, then the questions started to surface. What kind of nuke? How would it be delivered? How confident was everyone regarding the date? Finally, Mark raised his hand to silence the group. "You have heard the tapes. You have transcripts to peruse if you wish; by the way, none of those will leave this room. We are fairly confident in the date, but we don't know how it would be delivered. We assume either a missile or perhaps a suitcase bomb. We tend to think the missile would be more appropriate for the size weapon we anticipate they would use."

"Then you need us to provide an anti-ballistic missile." It was said with finality.

"That's right, a missile, a laser, something to stop a missile attack if that is what they decide to do, and we need it rather quickly."

"You need an ABM by July 16th?" There was incredulity in his voice.

"Actually a couple of weeks prior; we're going to have to get it out to a carrier in the Atlantic. That's not much time, I know." Mark watched the group carefully. Already several were beginning to confer.

Suddenly the oldest man in the room stood and held up his hands to get everyone's attention. When the side conversations stopped he smiled. "We can do it."

"How? In a month? You've got to be kidding." Several of the younger engineers were now standing.

"We can do it!" The white headed engineer continued to smile. "It seems the Russians were crafty enough to put aside a few nukes when the world disarmed. Well, some American engineers I know were also smart enough to put aside a few ABMs, just in case. We never really trusted the Russian government or even our own politicians, so we put some insurance in an old bunker by the Titan test stands near Waterton Canyon."

"They've been in there a long time; they will need a lot of work."

"You are right, but a month is enough time to refurbish them if we work around the clock."

"How did you keep them secure for such a long time. No one discovered them?"

"We simply told the public that the entire area was contaminated from the rocket fuel that had spilled there years before. It was easy to get the liberals to buy into that. Hydrazine proved to be a believable deterrent."

Ken rose and faced the speaker. "It is a chance. That is all we need, a chance." He paused briefly. "Do you think you can make it work?"

"We'll make it work, pastor. You have my word on it. If anyone can do it, the engineers in this room can make it happen."

"Thank God!"

The old engineer turned to the assembled group and spoke with authority. "I think most of you know me. I'm Jack Krinsky. We start work tomorrow morning. Meet at Heritage Square at eight o'clock, and we'll give you directions regarding how and where we'll be working. Tell your families you'll be away about a month, but no one is to discuss anything about our mission. You tell no one, not even your spouses."

Ken nodded. "He's right. We can't let anyone know our plans, especially our own government. We simply cannot risk their reaction."

As Ken and Mark gathered the remnants of the donuts, they watched the engineers file out of the room. Ken spoke to his son. "I told you God would find a way."

"So you did."

Chapter 96

June 10, 2040
Two miles off the Cuban Coast

Admiral Jacobson saluted the sailor who stood at attention in the door of his office. "Sir, I have a classified message for the Admiral."

"Thank you, Jackson." The senior officer reached for the envelope and dismissed the sailor. He opened it, read the message, then called his second-in-command into his office. "Mike, take a look at this. They plan to complete the missiles by June 27th and fly them to us in an old C-130 while we are underway to our launch site. I hope their pilot has carrier experience!" The commander read the classified message twice then handed it back to Admiral Jacobson. "That's good news. We have to sail a long way and get as far north as possible to be in range. If they launch missiles from Russia the trajectory will be coming from the north. But what about the launch racks and other support material?"

The commander nodded as he spoke. "They plan to deliver all that before we leave Cuban waters. It should be here in a week. It will take us that long to get ready to leave."

"They've been working on the missiles for about a week now, and they say the preliminary testing is going well. The schedule will be tight, but they think they can make it." The admiral rose and leaned over a large table covered with maps. "They're right about the schedule being tight, Mike. Let's make damn sure we have everything completed on our part. Double check everything. We've got to get in place in the North Atlantic by July 10th. It's a long trip; we'll need extra stores and fuel."

"I've had the crew inspect and check everything three times. We've made minor repairs to the engines. We're ready to sail."

"Good work. We don't want anything to slow us on our voyage."

"Will we need all the fighters on board?"

The admiral thought for several moments before answering. "Better keep them just in case this cloaking mechanism were to fail. It's also possible the Russians might have a few ships in the area."

"Can you imagine what that cloaking would have meant in the Pacific in World War II?"

"It would have been an asset all right. But those old guys did okay with what they had."

"Well, I'm glad we have it now. The element of surprise is always a good choice in battle."

"In our case, it should prevent a battle. If they can't see us, they can't shoot at us."

The commander studied his boss for several minutes. It was obvious he had further questions. The captain was a military man who understood other men very well. It was an asset he had cultivated over a long career. "Mike, you seem worried. The cloaking mechanism?"

"No sir, that obviously works. When they turned on the light wave phasing system last week those two planes searching for us flew within a couple miles of the ship and never saw us. It's amazing." He paused a brief moment. "No, I'm worried about the missiles we are waiting for. How do we know they will work? They haven't been tested operationally at all. And what about a C-130 landing on our deck?"

"I know. Those are concerns to me as well. All I can say is that the smartest engineers in the world built the missiles, and they say the system will work. It damn well better work if we have to use them. And as for the C-130, I've known many pilots who could handle that task if they just add a tail hook to that old aircraft."

"A failure of any part of this system would be unthinkable."

"Yes, you're right." Jacobson stood up from the map table and stretched his back. "So, let's check everything again about how the missiles will be stored, where the launch racks will be installed, everything that is within our responsibility. It has to be perfect. I just hope we don't need them."

"So do I, Sir. So do I."

Chapter 97

July 11, 2040
Washington, D.C.

Donnie walked slowly up the crowded street, avoiding the beggars seated against the buildings to his left. He could feel the warmth of summer radiating from the buildings as he walked along, and the sun was quite high on the horizon, casting short shadows. Yuri had delivered Woodward's schedule and Donnie had found the best chance of success on July 16th. He would have liked a few more days to plan, but the 16th was okay if the weather stayed clear. He made a mental note of the temperature and reminded himself to check the winds as well; both would be important to his calculations later that evening. As he turned the corner, the White House came into view in the distance. He stopped and looked at it briefly, awed as he always had been by the majesty of that old building and all it stood for. A passerby bumped into him and cursed quietly as he hurried along.

Later that evening Donnie sat with his diagrams and studied them carefully. The distances were marked clearly on the sheets. Sun angle was figured for various times of the day. Risks were analyzed and noted. There was even a note about normal wind currents in the area. It had all been memorized. He had found the right place. It was high, secluded, and it offered an easy escape route that was good for approximately 12 minutes. After that it might be a bit dicey. Two days later he would climb the stairs, cello case in hand, assemble his rifle, then record the time to disassemble it and climb back down the stairs and escape along the alley behind the building. He knew he could have the rifle disassembled and packed and the shell casings secured in three minutes. That left nine minutes to climb down four flights of stairs and make his escape. It would be tight.

Donnie knew he would need one more risk assessment to ensure he had not forgotten anything. Then the only question that remained was the accuracy of the schedule he had been given for the target. The Russian Ambassador was to meet the President at the White House on the afternoon of the sixteenth, and Woodward was scheduled to be there to welcome him. It had been arranged that the Ambassador would be in the third car of a four car entourage. That would force Woodward to walk down the curving drive to greet him and allow better visibility and tracking.

Donnie didn't like the assignment, but it was a debt he needed to repay to the two men in his life who had felt he was important. One had saved his life; the other had saved his cello. It was a debt he intended to repay. When the voices in his head were silent, he had great misgivings and questioned his decision, but when the screams returned, he played his cello and found the courage he needed. Recently the voices returned more often and were more persistent.

Chapter 98

July 14, 2040
Washington, D.C.

The Russian walked confidently into the cool evening air. His contacts had served him well, and Donnie had all the information he needed to complete his planning. A moderate amount of money was all that had been required to get a copy of Woodward's schedule for a *news agency*. A pretty face and five hundred dollars could work wonders in Washington. The schedule confirmed that Woodward would, indeed, meet the Russian Ambassador as requested. Yuri now had only one task left, to arrange for Donnie's death as soon as he had finished the assassination. He had already decided who would complete that task and would brief that agent the following morning. He regretted that Donnie must be killed, but it was necessary. That was how international espionage worked; all loose ends must be taken care of.

Yuri was still marveling at the tequila he had just sampled. It was Mexico's finest, and it surprised him with its smooth character. He had not been aware such Tequila existed. It was far closer to sipping whiskey than the Tequila he had tasted in shots or margaritas. As he walked, the cold air sobered him somewhat. Yuri had been a soldier most of his life, then an intelligence officer. In both he preferred his action out of doors. He loved cold nights; they reminded him of home.

As Yuri turned north at the first intersection, he noticed two young men running from an old woman. The first punk had the woman's purse in his hands; he was laughing. As they passed, Yuri reached out and struck the robber in the neck. He went down like a sack of potatoes dropped from a shopping cart. The second stopped abruptly. "Hey, what do you think you are doing?" He pulled a long switchblade knife from his pocket.

Yuri looked at the skinny figure menacing him. "I think I am kicking your ass tonight." He paused. "No, I don't think I am; I know I am." The young man lunged with the knife, but Yuri dodged quickly and tripped the assailant, throwing him to the ground. Before the thug could recover, Yuri kicked him twice in the side; he rolled, moaning, to his back on the cracked pavement. The first mugger jumped to his feet and looked at Yuri briefly. Quickly he decided his friend would have to fend for himself, and turned to run away. He had taken only two steps when the switchblade caught him in the middle of the back. He went down immediately with only a small grunt as he hit the sidewalk.

Yuri walked over, picked up the purse and took it to the old lady. He smiled, but said nothing. The old woman thanked him and walked quickly away. Yuri turned to ensure that the second mugger was still down in the street. He had not moved. The Russian smiled and continued his evening walk. He was becoming the super-hero of Metropolis, or rather Washington, D.C. Although the streets were quiet and mostly deserted at such a late hour, he still found the occasional mugger to keep his skills honed. Americans did not go out much after dark. It was both too expensive and too dangerous. The Democrats deserted the police, and the police deserted their cities.

The sharp tone of his phone interrupted his thoughts. He fumbled with it briefly and then answered. "Yuri."

"Hello, my old friend."

"Greetings, my President. How can I be of service?"

"Are you secure?

"Yes, I am alone."

"Things are moving fast, my old friend. There are political issues here, and I am moving forward with our original scheduled. Monday will be the day. You need to leave immediately."

"I'll book my flight tonight and leave tomorrow."

"See me as soon as you arrive. I have encountered some resistance to our plan here; after it is complete, I may need your help getting everyone on board. I know how persuasive you can be." There was mirth in Gornavich's voice.

"Excellent. I will see you soon."

Yuri was trying to switch off his special phone and process what he had just been told when he noticed the short man stumbling down the sidewalk toward him. The man was obviously drunk, his legs unsteady. He was barely five feet away when, suddenly, he stood straight, threw back his coat and pulled a semi-automatic pistol from his belt. He began firing before Yuri could even reach his own weapon. As he fired, he threw off his hat that had covered most of his face. He was Chinese. As Yuri fell to his knees, he looked into the man's face. The Chinese agent spoke two words. "For Yang." Then he walked up to the wounded Russian, pointed the gun at his forehead and completed his job.

Yuri pitched backwards, then fell to his right side. He was already dead when his head hit the concrete. The Chinese agent took a small camera out of his pocket and took several pictures of the dead Russian, then he turned and left.

The dead Russian's face was one of surprise and shock. The Chinese were settling scores. Four other Russians were murdered that night, one in Atlanta, two in Los Angeles, and one in Philadelphia.

The battle was drawn. It had become apparent to both sides that the conflict had escalated. Lines had been crossed, and unlike some American politicians, crossing lines meant something in both China and Russia.

Chapter 99

July 15, 2040
Washington, D.C.

Mark held up one finger to get Ken's attention, then put the phone he had been listening to on speaker to allow his father to hear the conversation. Senator Jenkins was frantically talking when the speaker came on. "Something is up with the Russians. Based on our recent discoveries, I suspect this may be urgent. Gornavich has demanded a teleconference tomorrow morning at ten o'clock. He insisted the entire cadre of American leaders be present. I just got the call myself. It looks like your assessment might be right, Mark."

"How high up the leadership structure did he go?"

"To the top. Gutierrez. But he also included key Senators and Congressmen as well."

Ken looked at his son then spoke quietly. "This could well be the call we've been preparing for."

Mark stared at the floor for several minutes then looked up, determined. "You've got to get us into that meeting, Senator. Our entire plan may depend on that."

"I've already taken actions to get you both a pass into the meeting as my guests. I still have *some* influence around this town."

"Thank goodness for that."

"Is Dalton in D.C.?"

"No, he's in California. Ken and I will have to do. I'll give him a call to let him know what's happening."

"I'll send a car around to pick you up tomorrow morning at eight thirty. It may well be FBI, but they're on our side."

"Thanks for the call, Senator; we'll see you then. In the meantime, say a prayer."

Chapter 100

July 16, 2040
The White House

The President walked briskly into the crowded room. It was not the gait of a man in charge, but rather of a man upset. The Russian's tone had been direct — "Just be there!" Gutierrez was not used to having his presence demanded by other men, certainly not in the past three years. Most of the leaders of the nation were standing silently, looking at the screen mounted on the far wall. The Speaker of the House, the Majority and Minority Leaders of the Senate—all were in attendance. Few looked at the President as he entered. Alec turned to his boss with a mixture of confusion and concern on his face. He knew this was not going to go well. But he had no idea just how bad it would be.

The picture on the old screen was not as clear as desired, but it was adequate. A series of gray and black dots moved slowly from left to right, and the sound crackled now and then as proof it still worked. After several minutes, the dots disappeared and a face slowly materialized on the screen. It was the Russian President.

"Good morning, gentlemen, ladies; I'm glad you all could be here on such short notice. I see my message got everyone's attention. I won't waste your time but will get straight to the issue at hand. Russia is not satisfied with the American payment of its debt to us or the way you are managing your resources, so we will be taking control of your government. You will surrender immediately, and all government officials will submit their letters of resignation through proper channels. An international committee, led by Russian officials, will land in

Washington within the week to take control and establish the new government."

"Like hell you will!" Gutierrez spoke forcefully; the anger in his voice evident in each word. "You can go straight to hell! This is America, and I am the President of this nation." He paused a moment to catch his breath. "And it will stay that way until another American is elected to take my place."

"Perhaps you would all like a few moments to discuss your current President's position."

"Screw you!" It was the leader of the minority who spoke quietly, but forcefully. "How dare you dictate to us." Several others in the room began to murmur in concurrence.

"I felt you might take that stance; how unfortunate." The Russian President turned and signaled someone in the background then resumed speaking. "Our position is not negotiable. And since you refuse to obey our demands, we will be forced to take appropriate actions. Please observe the screen closely." The old screen crackled loudly as the picture changed. The screen dissolved into a dark gray cloud that slowly focused on a bright line streaking from the top right toward the center of the gray mass. "What you are seeing is a mid-sized nuclear weapon targeted for Washington, D.C. Your capital will be destroyed in approximately seven minutes. Afterwards, I'm quite sure your remaining countrymen will be more accommodating to our demands."

The men in the room watched the line moving across the screen in silence for several seconds, then the room broke into bedlam. Finally, Gutierrez spoke. His voice was edged with anger. "We all agreed to disarm our nuclear weapons. You gave us your word."

"So we did. Fortunately, we kept a few around for situations just like this."

"You lied to us!" The President was shouting at the screen.

"You were fools." The Russian President was smiling broadly.

Suddenly the room became very quiet as everyone watched the missile streaking across the Atlantic toward the United States.

In the back of the room, Mark Sagan pulled his phone from his pocket. It was a Patriot device that he depended upon. Unlike the general public's phones, his operated from a satellite high above, not the deteriorating national cellular infrastructure. He checked his text file and sent a quick note. "Status?" Almost immediately a note appeared on his small screen. "Tracking Russian missile. Three missiles launch in 2.7 minutes." Mark put the phone back into his pocket, took a deep breath, and said a short prayer. He knew the ABMs had not been adequately tested. There simply had not been time. He also knew the men who built them were the best in the world. At least, he hoped so; the nation's future depended on it. He broke the silence in the room and drew everyone's attention. He was nervous, but his voice was strong and confident. Mark stepped forward along with Senator Jenkins. "President Gornavich, you have exactly three minutes to destroy those missiles and surrender yourself."

Alec looked at Mark in utter amazement. "What the hell are you doing here?"

The Russian laughed. "And why would I do that? You'll all be dead in three minutes. The world will be singing a much different song then, one with a Russian beat."

"No, I don't think so. Are you also tracking that missile?"

"Of course." There was a smirk in the Russian's voice.

"Where is it now?" Mark was composed; his confidence might be a bit questionable, but his demeanor was solid and shocked everyone in the room. Suddenly the line on the screen was gone. It simply disappeared. Mark worked hard to keep from cheering in front of everyone; the team of engineers had done their job.

The Russian's voice suddenly changed to one of disbelief. "What happened?"

"Train your trackers to the same bearing as your own missile but look about 10 degrees higher." The old TV crackled and the gray lines slowly focused on two bright lines headed back toward Moscow.

"What is that?" The Russian's voice was tinged with shock and panic.

"Now it is you who has a little less than three minutes."

"How did you do that?" The Russian was incredulous.

"We have a carrier in the mid-Atlantic these days, and some bright Americans recently developed some extraordinary missiles. Perhaps it is you who is the fool. If you listen carefully, the only music that you will be hearing right now are the drums of Berlioz's Tuba Mirum. His Requiem!" Mark walked toward the screen. "These are not nukes, but they will be sufficient to destroy Red Square—little else—and by the way, this entire episode is being broadcast real time to the entire world. Your own people are watching as you admitted your crimes. They will also watch as you receive the same fate you offered us."

"No, you can't!" The screen abruptly went blank.

For the second time the room in the White House was suddenly quiet. For several minutes no one spoke; they simply stared at Mark. Finally, the President walked toward Mark, his hand outstretched. Mark looked at the hand but did not take it. "I expect the resignation of the entire Administration by noon tomorrow. We will hold another election within three months."

The President was shocked. "And why would I do that?"

"Because the American people also witnessed this debacle in real time. Even now they are realizing how you failed in your first order of business for a President—to keep your nation safe. You have bought and sold votes to ensure your failed policies stayed in effect. That time is past. Total disaster was too close today. The American people have seen your true colors; I suspect your own party would impeach you promptly if you don't resign. So I guess how you go is up to you, but you *will* leave the office of the President of the United States. The American people deserve better."

Mark paused a moment then turned to Alec. "The same holds for you." He turned to Senator Jenkins and shook his hand. "Senator, thank you for inviting me today. I do hope you'll consider my comments about a new election. This nation needs a man or woman of integrity at the helm. We have been far too long without one." Then he turned and walked out into the Washington morning.

Chapter 101

July 16, 2040
The White House

It was cold and wet; a heavy fog filled the air and clouded the sky. Mark breathed a sigh and said a very quick prayer as he walked toward the gate. "Mark, stop!" He turned to see Alec running to catch him. "Don't be so smug. It isn't over yet. I have enough evidence to have you hanged for Flight 433."

"What the hell are you talking about?"

"The bomb that took down that flight was in your luggage. And you got off the flight at the last minute. I have two FBI agents who will support me on this."

"Are you crazy, you know I didn't put a bomb on that flight. It was pilot error and you know it."

"It doesn't matter what I know. All that counts is the evidence I have to prove what you did."

"Evidence you fabricated."

"Evidence that will ruin your…" The bullet smashed through Alec's right shoulder and knocked him to the ground. Four hundred and eighty-seven yards away, Donnie squinted through his scope. The fog was making his job extremely difficult, and his right eye was still not seeing clearly. It is hard to hit something you can barely see, even if you were once the best sniper in the Army. Several senators and congressmen who were following the two dashed back inside the door of the White House and shouted to Mark, who had jumped behind a limousine parked in the driveway. Another round ricocheted off the pavement beside Alec's trembling body. The wounded man slowly turned his head; his eyes met Mark's; they were filled with fear. "Help me."

Ken Wilson ran out and stood behind a large column for protection while shouting at his son. "Mark, stay down."

"Can't do that; you taught me differently. Hang on, Alec. I'm coming." A second shot ricocheted beside the downed politician's head." Mark ran to the side of the wounded man and began dragging him to safety. When he did the old pastor also ran forward and stood between the shooter and the two exposed men in the driveway. He looked in the direction of the shots and muttered to himself— "Today I am the example of Your love." The next shot struck Wilson in the chest and threw him several feet backward. For a moment he struggled to get back to his feet, then he fell face forward onto the pavement. His right hand was clutching his lapel.

Mark turned to the pastor lying in a pool of blood on the pavement. He rolled him over and stared into the face of the man he had admired and loved throughout his life. "Dad!"

"I'm proud of you, son." The old man's eyes opened wide for a moment then closed. His hand slipped from his lapel and fell to his side.

Mark knelt for only a second then turned back to Alec. He quickly gripped the wounded man under his arms and began dragging him out of the line of fire. As he did, he looked up in the direction of the rifle fire. Four hundred yards away Donnie peered through his scope and focused on the desperate man trying to pull his target to safety. He was beginning to squeeze the trigger when his mind raced back to a hot day in Afghanistan. He stopped suddenly as he recognized the man struggling to help Woodward. Donnie relaxed his finger on the trigger and studied the face of the man looking toward him. In shock he lowered the rifle and sat back against the worn plastered wall. He looked at his hands; they were shaking. He had almost killed Sargent Sagan, the man who had twice saved his own life. He raised the scope to look once more. For sure, it was him.

Donnie leaned back against the wall as the pounding in his head intensified. He closed his eyes but he could not remove the screams of men lying along a dusty road somewhere in Afghanistan. He could hear the rattle of machine guns and feel the concussion of mortar shells as they fell around him. He reached for his old wounds but they were gone. Perhaps he was already dead. His body tensed and his eyes opened wide with fear. He could feel his right leg trembling and the sweat flowing into his eyebrows. He forced his eyes closed and screamed out loud. Then it was quiet except for the sounds of sirens below.

Donnie's head jerked back into consciousness and he looked quickly at his watch. How long had he been there? How many minutes had passed? Then the screams returned. The sounds of wounded and dying men are horrendous. They were sounds he had lived with for so many years. Donnie forced his mind to concentrate as best he could. His hand touched something beside him; it must be his cello, but it was hot and burned his hand. If only he could play it the voices would leave, but he could not find his bow. He grasped the cello and hugged it to his chest; It felt strangely small, but he had to save it, and he had to escape. He rubbed at his right eye and started down the stairs. Outside he could hear voices. It must be the men screaming in his head. He would find them. He would play his cello for them and the screaming would stop.

Six uniformed policemen were moving toward the back stairwell when Donnie ran out into the sunlight. They saw his rifle and began firing.

*　　*　　*

In the distance the ambulance raced toward the White House with several police cars trying to clear the roads ahead. Mark was kneeling over Alec, a doctor doing what many men and women of medicine had done for so many years before him. He was trying to save the patient. The wounded man looked up and watched his old roommate in silence. Finally, he spoke very quietly to Mark. "Why, after all I did to you?"

Mark paused from his work for only a moment to look into Alec's eyes. The voice that responded was that of a man, but the message came from the heart of a small boy of eleven who had struggled to save his mother. "I have to live with myself tomorrow, and a better man than either of us kept telling me that forgiveness was important."

Alec closed his eyes and a small tear escaped, racing across his pale cheek. The last thought he had before slipping into unconsciousness was to question the alternative path his own life had taken.

Chapter 102

July 18, 2040
Washington, D.C.

They lay together in each other's arms in the darkened room where a single candle glowed faintly in the darkness. Only a half hour before they had needed each other in the greatest act of self-giving love that would always ensure the world would go on and life would be renewed. Now their peace was streaked with sadness as the reality of the world returned to invade their joy. Mark cradled her face in his hands and stared into her eyes for a long time before speaking.

"The road back is going to be a tough one for this nation. We're going to need all the help we can get to make this work, because what America was and what it is today are very different, but I don't mind the difficulties as long as I can face them with you beside me."

"But won't the Constitution guide us as we seek the way forward? With time and strong leadership can't we once again find the vision that made this nation a beacon for the world?"

"I think we can, Mackenzie. This day can mark the beginning of a new dawn in America. The exodus is over, and now we can begin to recover what was lost."

*   *   *

The tired Cuban president turned off the TV, got up from his desk, and walked out on the balcony of the Presidential Palace. His white linen suit was crumpled, evidence of the tense situation the world had faced just hours before. The shifting balance of power had again changed the world. A smile began to cross his tanned face as he looked out over the palace grounds to the city he loved. People were beginning their day. Shop owners swept their sidewalks and opened their doors to the morning breeze. Small cafes served dark Cuban coffee in small cups as smiling customers enjoyed their sidewalk tables. Excited children were playing ball in the street as children, rich or poor, would always do. Tobacco warehouses on the edge of the city were packing cigars for shipments around the world again.

He felt a renewed energy in Cuba these days. Almost imperceptibly over the last few months, more and more foreigners from all over the world visited this beautiful island, and things began to change. It wasn't only the freedom-loving Americans among them who shared ideas and led the way to establishing new businesses.

Now his eyes could see the rise of tall buildings on the horizon as new tourist hotels were appearing, built by international corporations from all parts of the globe. Marcos's eyes were misty and his heart was full. He considered his American friends as he smiled and spoke to an old dog sitting quietly by his desk. "They came and lived among us here in Cuba, but their hearts were always in America. I knew the day would come when they would want to go back. They were our countrymen for such a short time, but now they will be our friends and brothers forever."

Now both Cuba and America together would advance the cause of liberty in a world of pain and doubt. It was not a challenge he feared; it was one that excited him.

He continued to stare out over his city and listened to the cacophony of sound coming from the street below. Havana had changed. It was now a city filled with hopeful people. The change had been even more exciting than he had anticipated. Cuba had found its rhythm again, and it was a beautiful melody indeed. As he stood there smiling into the sun a small boy on the grass below shouted up to him. "Good morning El Presidente." As he waved back, Marcos thought once more. This small boy is Cuba's future, for it is in the people where the desire for freedom lives.

"Good morning to you, too."

Author's Note

November 15, 2016

I wrote the note below prior to the recent election that saw the conservatives win the White House and also the Congress. Congratulations to President Trump and all of the others who will lead this nation in the future. My prayers will be with you; you certainly have a formidable task to perform. I still feel, however, that the warning of this novel is pertinent. The nation remains divided and the acrimony is evident in the rioting mobs. Let us hope that the direction the nation follows is one that leads us forward into even greater decades of progress for all.

October 15, 2016

On a beautiful Colorado morning, I was sitting with a group of friends discussing the changes that are occurring in our nation. Many of these changes are disturbing. Values and institutions once respected are being challenged and changed dramatically. A divided Congress incapable of passing effective legislation reflects a divided nation. We have many societal problems that seem insurmountable, yet politicians who should be servant-leaders are in politics for personal gain, as are so many in their constituencies, groups who put their personal agenda before what is best for the nation. An unsustainable federal debt increases every year to fund programs which are proven ineffective. Political correctness is driving the nation into a place of silence where ideas and thoughts are not even spoken or expressed. Our once-sacred system of justice and the greatest investigative force in the world, the FBI, have been converted into political tools that favor the political elite. Some corporations, banks, and CEOs have adopted a culture of greed that weakens the nation's economy and its ethical business foundations as well. America's manufacturing base has been overly regulated, and poorly conceived

400

international trade deals are negotiated, both of which reduce American jobs. Religious values are derided in a nation in great need of an ethical compass. The United States military preparedness has been reduced to dangerous levels in a volatile world. American education, among the costliest in the world, has fallen to 29th place in a very competitive global economy, failing our children and limiting their futures. Some young men playing sports are not even willing to stand and honor their nation's flag and the men and women who did stand to defend those athletes' freedom and the opportunity they have to earn millions of dollars each year. We have a government that is even selective in which laws are enforced. Some are quite openly ignored as millions of illegal aliens cross our borders and move into sanctuary cities.

We are becoming a weak, divided nation devoid of strong leadership, a fact observed by our allies and enemies alike. Thoughtful people who have worked, and in many cases fought, for this nation do not like what we are witnessing. Saddened by the travesty, there is concern for the future of our children and grandchildren.

Yet, I am still optimistic that America can once again become the great hope for the world. Those who grew up after WWII did so in a time of great expectations. We were excited about economic growth and the freedoms and opportunities we shared. It was a time of great hope and possibility. Today our children live in a world of global communication and technological innovation that astounds us all. Their world can also be one of great opportunities and possibility, one of unlimited potential for all people to soar in the achievement of personal goals, or it can lead to the loss of everything precious in life. The values and beliefs our children hold will have much to do with the direction they take, and those values must form the foundation of a national consensus. Critical thinking must be encouraged in our universities and in our homes to guide all Americans to reach their full potential rather than rely on government for the answers in their lives. Individual excellence, personal responsibility, and free enterprise must once again become the foundation of American success. What we reward we get more of in society; what we penalize we get less of. Let's stop penalizing success and encouraging dependency on government. People have always risen to overcome challenges if they believe in their own strength and reject the role of victim.

One of my friends asked that morning, "What can we do?" As a novelist, I decided to write this book. I hope the reader enjoys the plot and the characters. I also hope the reader perceives the deeper purpose behind this novel. Ebenezer Scrooge asked the Ghost of *Christmas Yet to Come* if the visions he was shown portend what *will* happen or what *might* happen. We face that same question about our future today. The choice is ours to shape.

Douglas Fain

Douglas Fain is a graduate of the Air Force Academy and holds graduate degrees from Georgetown University and the University of Southern California. He flew more than 200 combat missions over Southeast Asia and was awarded a Distinguished Flying Cross for Heroism, a Distinguished Flying Cross for Achievement, fourteen Air Medals, and an Air Force Commendation Medal. He is the president of CEBG, Inc., an international consulting company, and has worked in more than 30 different countries in that capacity. He has taught for four universities in both undergraduate and graduate programs as an affiliate faculty member and was a candidate for the U.S. Senate in 1992. Doug has served on several boards and is the author of *The Phantom's Song*, an award winning novel about the Vietnam Air War.

Made in the USA
San Bernardino, CA
28 September 2017